Project Hermes was like ~~~~~~~~~~~~ ~~~~~ ~~~~~gh the heart of the Earth. Or maybe more like a sword. A sword of Damocles…

Think of it as looking through a funhouse mirror, the physicists told them. "Main Event Power is at 62%. 'The Tube' is forming."

—Welcome to the Funhouse—

The time we are granted marks the bounds of a journey—through love and loss, incomprehensible mysteries and unimaginable discoveries.

One man is about to begin the ride of a lifetime.

Join him.

Within a Sheltering Darkness

Published by HadaBase Systems, Inc.
Operations@HadaBase.com

Revision 2
2007

Within a Sheltering Darkness

Alan Havorka

Table of Contents

Alan Havorka

Foreword (Recommended Reading)

This work is divided into three sections: Books I, II and III. Book I, covering the start of Alex Boten's journey, also contains sections of letters, journal entries, ship's log pages, newspaper clippings and so on. Where ship's log entries appear in Book I, not all entries are shown, and those that are shown are not always shown in their entirety. Only those portions relevant to the story are included.

If the reader approaches those sections with the mindset of a researcher (or even a detective) searching for those tidbits of information which frame an understanding of the more important matters transpiring in the background, that reader should enjoy the author's intended effect.

The said items originate from—and the rest of the novel is primarily set in—a world called Mirrus, which has many aspects disorientingly different from Earth. These aspects will be made manifest during the course of the story. However, understanding a few basics will be useful to get one started.

The culture from which these items are taken has never seen daylight. They have fire (including oil-fired lanterns) by which to see, but they are in perpetual night. A more detailed discussion of the ramifications of this perpetual night will be found in Appendix B, labeled "Assumptions". However, the briefest and most salient points are these:

- Throughout their year (a period of some 238 Earth days) approximately 40 Earth days are spent in starless darkness.
- During the balance of their year, they have, to varying degrees, a fantastic star display. Stronger than Earth's full moonlight, this star display arcs slowly across the Mirran sky.
- When this star display has fully set, the period of deepest darkness resumes for the balance of the Mirran year.

Those wanting a fuller background to understand references to time and distance, and to understand how the Mirran language is handled, should see *Appendix A: Recommended Reading, Continued.* However, said references do not need to be understood to follow the story.

Alan Havorka

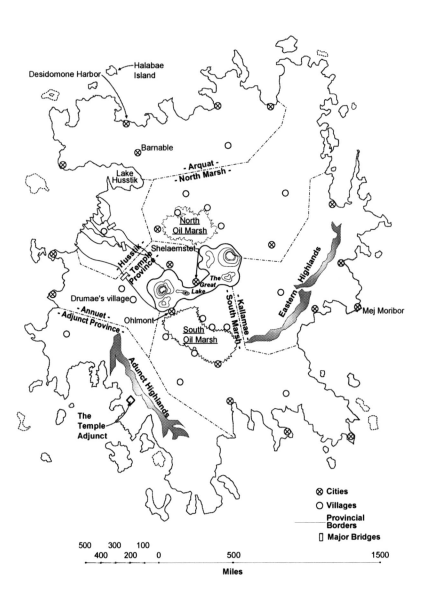

Mirran Character List and Definitions

MAIN CHARACTERS		
Anned Islak	ĂNN-ed ĬZZ- lak	Scientist
Abbik Dollapan	ĂBB-ik DOLL-a-pan	Captain, Ammanon Deloré
Igren Doel	ĬGG-ren DOH-el	Glassware fabricator
Andril Degg	ĂND-ril DEGG	Priesthood student, possible sailor, cousin of Opper Degg
Lannae	la-NĀY	Dollapan's daughter
MINOR CHARACTERS		(Some only by reference)
Opper Degg	ŎPP-er DĔGG	Sailor, cousin of Andril Degg
Arken Mennetek	ĂRE-ken MĔNN-e-tek	First Officer, Ammanon Deloré
Vinasa	vi-NĂSS-ah	Dollapan's wife
Drumae	drue-MĀY	Aunt to Opper and Mother to Andril
Ullamar Kloe	OO-la-MĂRR KLŌE	President, Seaman's Concord, Desidomone
Ilbe Rass	ĬLL-bee RĂSS	Officer, Ammanon Deloré
E. Finnean	FĬNN-ee-an	Purser
JUDGES		
E. Raddem	RĂDD-em	Senior Judge
Buelle	BYOO-el	
Poznanek	PŎZZ-na-nek	
Usettet	YOOSE-tet	
Lode	LŌDE	
Platius	PLĂTT-ee-us	Junior Judge
PLACES		
Desidomone	DĔZZ-e-dom-ŌHN	Harbor town
Halabae Island	HĂLL-a-bay	Island off of Desidomone
Arquat	ĂRE-quat	Province encompassing Desidomone
Barnable	BĂRR-na-bul	Landlocked town
Connovan Street	CŎNN-o-van	Docking for Ammanon Deloré
Ohlmont	ŌLE-mont	Refining town
Shelaemstet	Shell-ĀIM-stet	The Temple City

SHIPS		
Ammanon Deloré	am-MĂNN-non de-LŌRE-ay	
Estmae Denshaw	ĔST-may DĔNN-shaw	Galleon, lost in Eastern DevilsJaws
Innotek Assan	ĬNN-oh-tek ass-ĂHN	Vessel lost to the DevilsEye
CELESTIAL BODIES		
Hon	HŌNE	Yellow moon
Dessene	des-SEEN	Orange moon
Andilla Prime	an-DILL-ah	"First jewel of the Crown"; first major star to rise
MISCELLANEOUS		
Desidomone Beacon		Newspaper
Temple Bell		Newspaper
Pinoae	PĬNN-oh-ay	Fruit drink; may be mildly alcoholic
Lyderis Acid	LĬDD-er-iss	Poison; fast-acting
Sedres	SĔDD-ress	Type of wood
Tersa	TŬRR-sah	Type of wood
Orbid	ŌRR-bid	Black, glassy rock
Chelsit	CHĔLL-sit	White stone

Dedication

To missionaries everywhere, accidental and otherwise

Thanks to my wife, Carolyn, for persevering when it seemed rational to direct energies at something more tangible, or at least more probable.

Thanks to my sister Pam, whose editing skills, wisdom, and willingness to help were hugely important, and whose enthusiasm and praise came at a critical time.

Thanks to Bill, whose editor's eyes caught so many mistakes in the additions after Pam's pass.

And Gerry. What can I say.

Special thanks to Dr. Roberta M. Humphreys of the University of Minnesota, whose simple question at the end of Astronomy 101 began it all, decades ago.

And my final thanks for the best Ghostwriter in the business. I've given up trying to figure out what parts are Yours and what parts are mine; we are one.

BOOK I – Transition

Book I
Chapter 1: Alexander Boten

Seen from space, Earth seems like a delicate, floating ball. He had read it more times than he could count, heard it in person from nearly a dozen fellow astronauts. But Alex Boten could never see it, himself. To him, Earth seemed every bit as rock solid from orbit as it did when standing on the rocky scrabble of the high desert of New Mexico.

Maybe from the moon, he thought. Maybe at that distance, with Earth reduced in the field of view, maybe then it would seem to float. But not from here. He watched Earth slide by beneath him, slow, steady and firm, as the shuttle nudged into the docking port of the Hermes orbiter. Hermes 7. He liked the sound of it, the mythic connotations. But soon, and for the next nine hours, he would be in the Command Capsule, dubbed *Sirocco*. Who was the genius that came up with that name? If they were set on a wind theme, how about something quirky, like *Dust Devil*? Or at least with more character. Maybe *NorEaster*. Well, maybe *NorEaster* would be too ominous. There was certainly nothing ominous about a name like *Sirocco*. It was nice, safe, bland.

The docking clamps engaged. *Focus*, thought Boten. Perhaps it was his attention to irrelevant aesthetics, rather than core mission objectives, which contributed to keeping him off the mission crews. Maybe support personnel pondered naming conventions, while mission crews focused on, well, the mission.

The hiss of primary equalization began, and then faded. Through the shuttle window, he looked to the left and down, to the spiny framework of the Hermes guide tower—aimed squarely, even menacingly, down to Earth. He smiled. It had been an uncomfortable image for the public, ever since Hermes 6 became the first of the series to point like a gun at the earth. And there should be no mincing of words; a gun it appeared to be, and a gun, in point of fact, it was.

3

Within a Sheltering Darkness

It was a dangerous gun, in the minds of those who did not understand its concept, or who doubted the physics of it, or who simply figured that somehow, sometime, something would go wrong. The image was a frightening one. Maybe not a gun, thought Alex. Maybe a sword. A sword of Damocles, ever hanging over their heads.

He laughed out loud. *Damocles*, not *Hermes*. They should have named the project *Damocles*. Rub it right in the critics' faces.

The softer hiss of secondary equalization kicked in. Unbuckling himself, Boten pushed off and drifted weightlessly to the hatch, grabbing the handhold and hitting the com switch.

"Ready to open hatch, Hermes. Please advise."

After a brief pause, the reply came: "Read you. Hold for clearance."

Waiting for the final clearance, he had a few moments to dread what lay just ahead of him; the awkward handoff from the mission crew personnel—the real deal, the ones who had made the grade—to himself, the second-stringer. A fraction of a point in the Final Analysis Summary—a hair's breadth, a whisper—that was the margin by which he had missed the mark. There was always Hermes 8, and 9. But the margins would keep getting narrower, the competition more acute, as the final prize approached. Hermes 7 was "merely" attempting to pass through the Earth as if it were not there. Hermes 8 was slated to span interplanetary distances, though staying in the solar system. Hermes 9 would be the big one, launching the capsule with no receiving tower. If that could be done successfully, there would be no limits. No pesky fuel concerns. Not even nuisances like the speed of light to hinder sudden, limitless exploration. The dawn of the post-Euclidian era. The competition for that mission would be unimaginable. *I'm a fool to keep dreaming*, he thought.

"Commander Boten, you're clear. Hatch locks released." Sliding the portal aside, Alex peered into the Commons chamber. Then he slid through the narrow passage, his helmet held out ahead of him, and greeted the men preparing to depart. Hammond was fully disconnected, and the two techs were just beginning to swarm over Janus.

"No surprises, Alex," reported Hammond. "They pushed the

alternate shutdown test into your list. And they cancelled the speed test on the new chipset for the MainCom. But that's about it."
"*Cancelled* the speed test? Any word on why?"
"Nary a peep. You can be sure the ground unit tested way slow, and they don't want it on the books as a shipboard shortfall."
"God forbid there should be any hint," said Alex, "that anything is less than nominal."
"Nominal?" laughed Hammond. "It's budget time, Alex boy. Nominal is failure for the next few weeks."
Hammond was pleasant as ever, no hint of condescension. No lording it over the teammate who simply couldn't make the grade. Boten shook his head, as if to dislodge the thought itself. Would paranoia keep a man off the mission crew? Maybe. If he *were* paranoid. But none of his screenings showed it. It wasn't mental aberration that had set their positions here—Hammond and Janus as mission crew, and himself (like Harrod, Lange and Sartori) as glorified techs. All of them climbing in and out of the same Command Capsule. But only two climbing in when it really counted. It was that lousy quarter point.
As the technicians made the final adjustments to Janus' suit, Boten floated over to the window. The view here was better; you could see the entire length of the Hermes Launch Gantry. The launch rail's aspect drew its bead across miles and miles of empty ocean. When the time for actual launch came, both the launching and receiving towers would be above empty ocean. It was the Agency acquiescing to public outcry: "Entrance and exit points" both over uninhabited, low risk areas. But it was just one more example of the politicians being unable to grasp the concept. There was no "entrance" into Earth, and no "exit". The whole point of Hermes was that anything between the launch and receiving towers, be it Earth, or just thousands—even millions, or billions—of miles, was simply bypassed.
"You okay, Alex?" asked Hammond, drifting up beside him.
"Yeah," he said, not looking away from the window.
"Any change on your dad?"
Boten didn't reply at first. But after a moment, he turned to

Hammond.

"No," he said, offering a slight smile. "My sister's with him now. I'm shuttling right back down to Earth after this shift, so I can go out to join her. We'll both stay with him." *Death watch*, thought Boten. He thought of Abbey, sitting alone with their father, watching him fade. Alex had been offered an opt-out for this shift. He probably should have taken it. But this might be his last shot at being in the capsule before the launch. Boten's mind drifted, to the comfort of the bustling testing and checklist routines, and then back to the long, awkward silences he would share with his sister at their father's side. Waiting.

"Kathy going with you?" Hammond asked.

"No," said Boten, snapping back to the here and now. "No, she doesn't need any of that right now. She'll be staying home with the twins."

"Is she doing OK? I bet those girls can be a handful."

"She's a trooper," Boten chuckled. "She's gotten used to handling the chaos since I made the Hermes team. And… it's not going to be that long, until he goes. Not nearly."

Hammond looked away, cursing under his breath. He had wanted to be comforting, but he was just making it worse. He watched Janus slide out through the hatch to the shuttle. The techs were ready to prep Boten.

"It's not that bad," Alex said. "He hasn't even been conscious for two days now. It's not like he's suffering."

One of the techs called out: "Captain Boten?"

"In a minute," Hammond snapped, and then turned back to Alex. "If she wants some help, or just some company, she should have Suzanna come over. She's just going nuts around the house with the kids gone to college, anyway. Do them both some good."

"Thanks" Alex said, slipping past him to the fitting stand so the techs could begin coupling the connections to his suit. "I'll mention it to her."

Hammond slid out, into the shuttle, and the portal closed. During the connection prep procedure, the techs were fully absorbed in their work. There was no one for Alex to talk to. His mind drifted

6

back, to when he had last been with Abbey in the hospital.

"There's no point in your being here 'round the clock," he had told her.

"I don't have anywhere to be."

He stood at the foot of the bed, staring down at her as she sat at the bed's side.

"You're thinking... what?" he asked. "That he'll come out of it?"

"Maybe. Maybe for a moment. Just for one or two... lucid... moments."

"And if, by some miracle, it happened? If he woke up?"

She looked up to him, and sighed.

"There's a lot to say, Alex."

"But none of it's new. So what will you say, Ab? What will you ask him? Will you ask him why he was the way he was?"

She had no reply, and he pulled up a chair next to her.

"Maybe you were right all along," she conceded. "Maybe there are some questions... that you just... don't...."

Laying his hand on hers, he had felt a strange coldness to her skin. It was like she had been absorbing the death around her.

"But maybe," she insisted, softly, "maybe there are some questions that just *have* to be asked."

"And if you get your chance? If you ask him the kind of question you were always smart enough not to ask? What do you think he'll say? 'Gee, Abbey dear, I guess you're right. I shouldn't have been such a...' " Alex let the thought trail off, while Abbey fiddled absently with the lines that kept the old man hydrated, and breathing, and monitored.

The techs connected the last of Alex's lines, the lines that kept him cooled, and breathing, and monitored. Without speaking to them, Alex moved into the capsule.

Although the Hermes 7 mission called for a two-man crew, and most aspects of testing called either for the mission crew or a pair of stand-ins to be in the capsule, some procedures mandated only one crewman. So, for this round of testing, Alex Boten sat alone in the Captain's seat. The capsule was snug and utilitarian; the controls, simple. The complexities of the Hermes project were much more on the physics side, in the Main Event Generators of the Launch and Reception Gantries. There wasn't much piloting to do. Hammond had taken to referring to the command compartment as "the cargo bay".

In fits and bursts, various segments of the launch routine would be enacted, running various subsystems through their paces.

After four hours, the power to the main systems in the Launch Gantry was activated. "The Tube" was live, if only at one twentieth power. Looking forward through the main window, everything looked normal. Very Newtonian. Very Euclidian. Not like it would later in the day, when the power levels would be eased up. Then the frame-dragging would begin, and the entire length of the Gantry would seem to take a twist. The twisting would be imperceptible at first, but gradually would become alarming, as if the whole structure were approaching an inevitable stress collapse. And then, for the crew of the actual launch, running the system to even higher power, it would twist on. The Earth below would join in on the twisting, into absurdity and beyond. It would be then that the anti-nauseals in their systems would do their part. Hermes 2 through 4 had all been launches through open space, with nothing between the Launching and Receiving Gantries. Hermes 5 had been the first to aim at passing through an intervening barrier, and during the two thirds power-up run, her crew had been the first to feel the effect of staring into something substantial, something more than the starless black of near-Earth orbit. It's one thing to see a thin, wiry Gantry spin into a corkscrew point. It's quite another to have a broad, flat expanse of grid-painted metal seem to be swirling down a bathroom drain. It was a moment her crew wouldn't soon forget. Nor would the luckless techs that were honored with the job of cleaning out the inside of the mission crews' helmets.

"Sirocco, we have an upload for you."

"Houston, I copy that."

"Alex, we're going to go off-book for a bit here."

Boten grimaced. "Houston, if we're going off-book because of the software you're uploading, then I'll wager Mark Grossman's nearby."

"One moment, Sirocco."

Boten watched the progress meter on the upload. Sixty-five percent, seventy percent, eighty-five percent.

"Good morning Alex."

"Marky, what kind of bug-ridden crap are you sending me?"

"My, we are testy today. Absolutely no known flaws."

"Whoa. You'll need a chainsaw to trim that hedge. What's the story?"

"No big deal. We just brought in some new programming modules, a handful of functions, from a new contractor. The code looks clean, but I haven't had a chance to run it through all the test eventualities I'd like to."

"So you want me to do it, in orbit? What part of Double-Delphi Procedure calls for that little maneuver?"

"Gentlemen," announced Grossman to the Control Room, "I think we have a first here. An astronaut actually requesting *stricter* adherence to D-D Protocol."

"Yeah fine," Boten laughed. "Put this voice com on a disc so I can always have a remembrance of the moment. But you're saying we're going off-book during an *orbital* test? And Jiggs has OK'd this?"

Down on Earth, Bob Jiggs smiled from his place on "the Nest", a ten-foot diameter circle, raised one tall step above the main floor near the back of Hermes Mission Control. The Nest gave him a good view of the other eight work islands. Each of those islands was a semicircle of workstations, monitors clustered in the middle, each oriented so the specialists assigned to them had a more-or-less direct line of sight to the large Mission Status Board. The Mission Board was high on the wall, at the front of the room. The layout was a version, both scaled back and improved, of the early space launch control layout.

From his console at Launch Control Programming, Grossman waved and pointed to Jiggs. Reaching down, Jiggs switched the Com line from LCP to the Nest. "Yes, Alex. Roger on that off-book orbital test. Launch Control Programming is significantly behind schedule. A full live-system test will do a lot to close the gap."

"So in the interests of pulling the estimable Mr. Grossman's ample butt out of the fire..." and here Mark Grossman gestured a message via Jiggs, which Jiggs declined to translate verbally to Alex, "...we just plug in the code and run it. And we pretend we didn't, by declaring it off-book."

"Double-Delphi Protocol does allow a specified amount of testing activity, in non-event conditions, to be performed off the books."

"We pretend we didn't do it."

"Yes Alex, we pretend we didn't do it." Jiggs swiped his hand from his brow back across his bald head, deftly skimming over the headset, and bringing his hand to rest on his neck. "I don't recall you complaining when Physiology had you skip the third-order disorientation drill two weeks ago."

"Okay, Jiggsy. Lighten up. If I didn't have the chance to yank Mark's chain from time to time, what joy would I have left in life?"

"Did I get a confirmation of download completion?"

"Sorry. Revised program upload at one hundred percent."

"Load and run," Jiggs said. He stood, his tall wiry frame boosted by the raised Nest, dominating the hive of activity before him. "Let's roll."

Over the next several hours, Jiggs and Boten took the Hermes 7 complex—Command Capsule, Launch Gantry, and the Receiving Gantry orbiting opposite—through its paces. Among the milestones in that testing were power-ups to fifteen, twenty-five, and sixty percent power. Since visible distortion begins around forty-four percent, Boten engaged his helmet after the twenty-five percent phase. During the tests, the following irregularities were diagnosed:

- A significant drop in the Prime Backup Computer efficiency, later traced to a failing IC chip.
- A transient variation in main electrical bus power, which was never localized. The variations never approached threshold limits, however.
- A flaw in the procedures manual regarding the sequence of equipment shutdown in a non-emergency evacuation, which

allowed power to still be On to Communications when main power was cut, thus allowing unnecessary stress to the Comm systems.

• Five programming errors in the revised programming code, only one of which was later deemed likely to have escaped normal testing procedures, had those procedures been followed.

Among the problems not diagnosed at the time were:

• A material defect in the charge of one of the explosive bolts intended to detach the Sirocco from the launch sled, later deemed to have resulted in equal parts from the manufacturer's allotting insufficient cooling time after the pouring of the explosive, and a total absence of random line testing (an investigation of which continued for two and a half years after the lack of testing was discovered).

• Seventeen instances of programming code errors, five of which were ultimately ruled trivial, and ten of which were ruled non-fatal.

• A faulty diagnostic control module, which manifested itself during the firing up of "The Tube" to sixty percent power.

"Sirocco," said Jiggs, "sixty percent. We're showing back-up ventilation engaged."

"Roger, Control, I have that. Also engaged are backup for Com3 and... the controller for Electrical Bus 5. Checking into it now."

Jiggs switched off the line to the Hermes. "Talk to me people. I assume we are not looking at a simultaneous triple failure."

"Can't be," Head of Systems muttered, scrolling through his displays. "Got to be a monitoring error. Some single sensor system misreading all three."

"Or," said Jiggs emphatically. Slipping his hand into his shirt pocket, he grabbed the single hard-coated square of nicotine gum, and popped it into his mouth.

At the Systems island, Chuck Monroe turned to him, then nodded. "Or a catastrophic mechanical, in close enough proximity. What do the techs say?"

"Hermes Launch Tower, please report," Jiggs rattled off. "Do you feel any vibrations?"

"Negative."

"Any unexplained sounds."

"Negative, sir."

"Check the view. Any floating particulates or debris, expelled gasses, liquids."

"No indication here that anything happened. Or is happening. Will continue to monitor, Houston."

"Sirocco," Jiggs said calmly, "we're leaning towards thinking you've got a monitoring systems error. Anything on your end to contradict that so far?"

"No, Cappy. That's the only thing that makes sense to me. You want me to power down?"

Jiggs looked to Systems. At Systems, Jack Cromwell leaned over to Chuck and spoke, shaking his head. Chuck leaned back in his chair slowly. "We could, Bobby. But the more we start messing with the systems, the harder it'll be to backtrack later."

"Alex? Jiggs again." He hesitated. "How would you feel about doing a live orbital diagnostic?"

"That's fine, Bobby," Alex came back at once. "I don't want to be up here all day and all night trying to put the pieces back together. Let's put this puppy to rest. I'm starting with the Main Electrical Diagnostic."

"That's my boy," Jiggs said. Cutting the line to the Sirocco, Jiggs called over to LCP: "Marky, we sent up a pile of new code a little while ago. And we've got a pile of new problems now. You have anything to say to me?"

"Checking, Control. But I'm not seeing any commonality. This new programming code should only be touching one of the affected systems. But I'm still checking."

Then Jiggs noticed the new kid at Telemetry waving tentatively, but without looking up from his monitor. "Telemetry? If you have something for me, I'm ready to see it."

"Printing to screen, Control," the kid reported, then hustled over to the Nest and stood next to Jiggs. He began explaining the onscreen document that appeared there. "This is a list of what just went out.

And here's the list of systems monitored by Electrical Variance Mod 345-31. All the affected systems are routed through there."

"And lots of others," Jiggs said. "This module also tracks a lot of systems that we don't have any problem reports on."

"I know. I know. But the whole module wouldn't have to be bad. It could be a partial failure. Wait a minute. This is Re-Entry Nav. And this, this is Com6. Are those systems even active?"

Jiggs flipped on his line to the Sirocco; it was in use. "CapCom, I need Boten. Who's he on with?"

"Physiology, sir. Heart and respiration are up."

"Yeah. Ain't everybody's. Ask medical if it can wait. If he isn't hyperventilating, I want him."

Ten seconds later, Boten was on the line. "What's the word, Cap?"

"Alex, would you activate your RE-Nav for me?" There was no response. "Sirocco, do you copy on RE-Nav activation?"

"Copy that, Houston. Jiggs, is there something you want to tell me?"

Jiggs smiled. "Steady, Alex. I don't want you to use it. We're just looking for a status check."

"Roger that. Activating Re-Entry Navigation now… wait a minute… RE-Nav offline, backup engaged. Okay gentlemen, speak to me."

"Sirocco, we may have a possible commonality here. Fault reports may be bogus. Continue monitoring systems while we review." Jiggs switched the Sirocco back to CapCom. "You have a way of testing this? One that doesn't involve Alex Boten ripping out half of the Sirocco's guts?"

"I need to isolate this from the affected systems. But then it's just a matter of sending a 'Test' command. Half an hour?"

Jiggs winced. "We're sitting at sixty percent. Try to trim that time."

Boten stared out through the main window, to the corkscrew Gantry that defined "The Tube", and to the strangely twisted swirl of Earth beyond. *Just think of it as looking through a funhouse mirror*, the physicists had told them. Baker was the quantum geek who thought up that one, as best as Boten could recall. Well, welcome to the funhouse. His eyes flashed between the distorted swirl before him, and the banks of lights—most still green, but way, way too many red—on the panel before him. His eyes went back to the swirl. With the earth constantly sliding beneath him, the swirl seemed in constant flux. It seemed to be deepening. He looked to the Main Effect Power meter. Steady, at sixty-two. He looked back to the swirl. It still seemed to be deepening. He picked a point on the edge of the window, and sited it. Waiting, waiting. The distortion was unchanged.

MEP at 0%

MEP at 62%

"CapCom, this is Sirocco. If Bob Jiggs isn't on a coffee break or anything, you think I might talk to him?"

"Sorry to leave you hanging, Alex. We think we have it."

"Glad to hear it. You can make my day if the solution starts by stepping down the MEP."

"I think that's for the best. I want to get a replacement module installed before going any further."

Hardware, thought Boten. *That lets Marky off the hook.*

"Give us another fifteen minutes, to confirm we've got the

problem identified," Jiggs suggested.

Looking at the distortion down The Tube, Boten answered, "I'll be here."

Book I
Chapter 2: Departure

After twenty-five minutes, Jiggs confirmed to him: It was, indeed, a bad sensor module.

"We'll go ahead with a power-down. The only thing," said Jiggs, "is that with that bad module, we can't be sure of the status of the systems it's monitoring. We'll just need to have you run a few extra steps before effecting ME power down. Uploading procedures for you now."

"Download complete. OK, this looks pretty straightforward. But have somebody at Andrews draw me a bubble bath, OK? I'm gonna need to unwind after all this."

"Roger that bubble bath, Alex. You've earned your paycheck today."

"Extending Inhibitor Bars, One through Four, now. I suppose if none of this crap ever happened, all we ever would have needed would have been a Hermes 1."

"Boring, boring. Sirocco, I still show your Inhibitors retracted. Is there a problem?"

"Evidently, Control. Reinitiating extension."

The Inhibitor Bar status on Jiggs' screen showed no change. He flipped off his line to the Sirocco. "Systems? Quick summary: Launch Sled, Inhibitor System, Contingent Functions. My screen, in forty-five. Telemetry, confirm for me: That bad module doesn't have any connection to the Shutdown Inhibitor Rods." He flipped the line to the Sirocco back on. "Looks like we are No-Go on the Inhibitors. Do you concur, Sirocco?"

"Affirmative. They won't move due to a red light on coolant temperature."

"Sirocco, I am reading green, repeat, condition green, on Main Power Coolant."

"Affirmative, Mission Control, I am reading the same thing, on my Coolant Systems Display. The problem is, Main Computer is showing red on coolant."

Jiggs switched his screen to a slave display of Boten's. "Okay, Alex. I see what you're seeing." The list from Systems of possible systems problems that could interfere with Inhibitors came up on Jiggs' screen. Seventh item on the list was excessive Main Coolant temperature. He looked over to Telemetry; the kid shook his head 'No'. "Alex, I'd like to put all shutdown procedures on hold briefly. Do you copy?"

"Copy, Control. I would concur. Keep me posted as you work through this." He knew a final answer would likely not be coming soon; this was not a situation for which they had been drilled.

"Mark?" said Jiggs. I'm sending over the last thirty seconds of coolant telemetry. I'll meet you at your station." By the time the display came up on Mark's screen, Jiggs was at his side at Launch Control Programming.

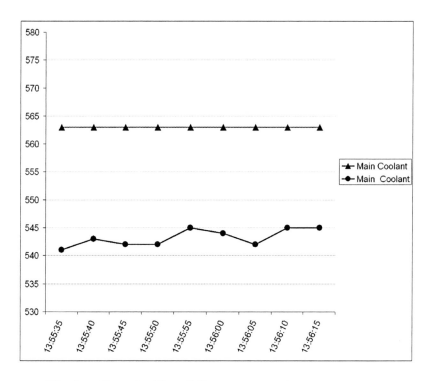

"Coolant Temp by Time," Jiggs announced.

Both lines on the graph, though significantly different, were identically labeled as "Main Coolant".

"Main Computer reading is triangles," ventured Grossman. "And circles are the direct coolant system readings?"

"You got it."

"Main Computer is showing no delta."

"None that I can see," said Jiggs.

Grossman touched the blue triangle furthest to the left, closest to the scale. "What is this? Five Sixty-What? What's the exact figure?"

"CapCom?" said Jiggs. "Give me Sirocco." A moment later, the static level in his earpiece jumped slightly. "Sirocco, how are your systems holding up?"

"Everything's steady, Control. Over."

"I'd like you to check your coolant temp. *Main Computer reading* of Main Coolant temp."

"Now that's very, very steady, Con. Thank you for noticing."

"What is the exact reading?"

"5-6-3, Control."

Grossman plopped down into his chair, cursed angrily, and began pawing through his documentation for the freshly uploaded programming code.

"Roger on 5-6-3, Alex. Looks like this one's Mark's baby. Extending Launch Inhibitors is assumed to 'up' the heat levels, so there's a lockout if the coolant is already too high. Mark's trying to figure out why your MCom is reading this spurious 5-6-3. Once we resolve that, we should be able to proceed with shutdown procedure as listed. Suggest you spend this time reviewing the balance of those procedures, over."

"Control, are you monitoring Coolant Temp? Actual Coolant Temp?"

"Sorry, Alex," Jiggs said, hustling back to the Nest. "I was AWOL for a bit there. OK, I see it now. You're up in the 550 / 555 range."

"Unless Marky can get his code straightened out in the next ten minutes… fifteen tops… then the real reading is going to top 560, and those rods are going to stay put."

"Understood, Alex. I will be back to you very, very quickly." Jiggs walked quickly by Grossman's station, tossing off: "I want a prelim, A-sap." Turning back, he added, "Don't make me wait." That brought him to the Head of Systems. "Chuck, I see only two options here, once we cross 560. Either we fire up to one hundred percent, so the coolant systems go to full and drop the temps—or else we squirrel in a procedural bypass to hyper-circulate that coolant."

"Those are both viable, *if* we convince the MainCom to ignore this phantom 5-6-3."

Jiggs looked back at Grossman, flipping through his sheets.

"Let's consider that a given. So, if Main Computer is reading true: We fire up, or we improvise. Am I missing an option?"

Chuck Monroe dropped his chin onto his chest, puffing out his jowls. "Nope. That's it, as I see it. Normally I'd say fire up."

"But not now," Jiggs finished, with a leading tone.

"Going up to one hundred makes me nervous, without knowing what's actually happened so far. Get an answer out of Grossman, and I'll give you a firmer recommendation," Chuck offered. Jiggs raised an eyebrow. Chuck shook his head: "Full power-up, versus tinkering with an unknown instability—live, at…" he looked to his monitor, "…sixty-one plus percent?" His eyes met Jiggs. "OK. I vote power up," Chuck said. Jiggs nodded and headed back to Grossman. "But that's prelim," Chuck called after him. "I want answers before we proceed."

Jiggs waved to him without looking back. As he came up beside Grossman, he announced: "Let's dance, Marky."

"Okay," Mark said, sweating now. "I think I've got it here. The contractor didn't have the new simulator for the coolant input, so I okayed a patch, for use only…."

Jiggs' hand went calmingly onto Mark's shoulder. "Condense, Mark," he said gently.

"Sirocco's MainCom is being directed to *assume* Main Coolant temp. Based on a *formula*—Main Power level, for how long. Once we stayed at sixty percent long enough, a 5-6-3 reading was automatic. Jiggs. How long have we been at sixty percent?"

"We're at sixty-one plus change. Maybe fifteen minutes."

"It's going to jump any time now. It's due to refresh its values."

"CapCom? Sirocco, now. Alex, watch your Main Coolant temp. *MainCom* Main Coolant. We're expecting a jump to…" he twirled his fingers over Mark's papers, and Mark punched some numbers into his keypad.

"5-7-5" Mark whispered.

"…575. Copy that?"

"I copy, 5-7-5. Mission Control?"

"Go, Sirocco."

"Might that be… 5-7-*4*?"

Mark sat down, and sped the numbers into his keypad again. Then he leaned back and looked up to Jiggs; he held up his left hand, with thumb folded in.

"Roger that, Alex. Correct target number is 57*4*." Jiggs returned to the Nest. "OK Sirocco, here's the scoop. Your MainCom readings on coolant temp are bogus, but the whole system's too hot to shut down now. With me so far? Over."

"Absolutely, Control."

"We haven't even started looking into a bypass to allow you to manually overcool the system, but I have to tell you I don't like the curve."

Boten watched his coolant temperature, the real coolant temperature, creeping higher.

"I'm with you, Control. I don't want to be looking over my shoulder while I'm trying to bottle-feed this thing. That leaves us with pulling up the coolant level within system parameters."

"That's the route I'm more comfortable with, Alex. You OK with going to one hundred percent?" Jiggs asked.

"Thought you'd never ask. Is that bogus reading going to stay at 574? Or is this problem going to be nipping at our heels the whole way?"

"Will advise on that before we proceed, Sirocco. Suggest you start reviewing final leg power-up procedures." Jiggs switched off his line. Pulling open his pencil drawer, he looked at the half dozen pieces of nicotine gum scattered there. He slid the drawer shut, and moved back down to Grossman's station.

"Checking it now, Cap," Mark said. "It definitely is an issue. The same formula applies to the whole curve. It only kicked in at sixty because we idled there for so long tracking down that bad module. It *will* kick in at one hundred also, if we stay there long enough. Looks like... excellent. Our coolant margin is the broadest at one hundred percent, and the formula reflects that. We can sit at..." and here he leaned back in his chair and smiled. "Cap, we can hang at one hundred percent for nearly an hour before those Inhibitors lock up again."

"Finally," said Jiggs on his way back to the Nest, "a margin we can live with. CapCom, put me on. Sirocco, how about some good news?"

"If that's all you've got, hit me with your best shot."

"Everybody's favorite Director of Software is just feeding through some numbers to me… OK. Fifty-three minutes. Think you can handle a ten minute shutdown over fifty-three minutes?"

"If I can, it'll be my first success of the day."

"Scuttle that attitude, Sirocco.   None of this is your fault. Multiple unrelated failures. This is the sort of thing you can't predict on paper. It only happens in use. This is why you're up there."

Wrong phrase, thought Jiggs.

Knew there was some reason I was up here, thought Boten. "Are we Go for one hundred percent power-up procedures?"

"Roger that, Sirocco. Begin your safety checks."

For the next seven minutes, Boten took the controls, step by step, through every procedure to prepare for the final phases of power-up. Then he eased the Hermes 7 station up through sixty-five, seventy and eighty percent power.

"Sirocco, your outer hull is developing static charge."

"Compensating, Control.   Charge dropping… dropping…. Nominal charge. Pushing up to eighty-five percent power." From time to time, Boten looked down to what he knew, intellectually, was Earth. But it no longer bore any resemblance to Earth. He had only been scheduled to go to sixty percent. Fortunately, procedures called for a full regimen of anti-nauseals on runs that involved any power-up of the Gantry. "Ninety percent."

"Software says your MainCom should read coolant temperature dropping to… 5-2-9. Any time now."

"Monitoring, Houston.   Ninety-five percent power-up."   The distortion began to change. No longer seeming flat, it seemed to stretch away from him—as if the center of his field of view were at the tip of a long cone, with him on the inside, near the base. "The Tube is forming, Control. No change in MCom. My actual Main Coolant temp is bobbling around 475. But MainCom reading of Main Cooling is not, repeat not, budging."

"Reading you, Sirocco," said Jiggs, with a perfectly level voice. "Showing Gantry power at one hundred percent." He began gesturing in tight measured motions to Grossman, and used his other hand to grab two nicotine gum squares from the pencil drawer, as he continued. "While we wait for those MainCom values to refresh, let's check environmental conditions down The Tube, beginning with particulates. CapCom, passing Sirocco over to Physics." Jiggs switched off his line. He popped the squares into his mouth. Out of the corner of his eye, he saw Mark Grossman starting to move toward him. He held up his hand, gesturing 'Stop'. Still not shifting his gaze, he whipped his hand into a pointing gesture, downward, roughly to Mark's station; he held the pose. Mark moved back to Launch Control Programming, and resumed reviewing the code documentation. Eventually Jiggs pulled his hand back down to the edge of his desk. He paused, and then moved down to Grossman.

"I don't know," Grossman said. "It should have reset by now. There's something else going on. Something I don't understand."

Jiggs' eyes locked on his. "Can you get me back in control of the Sirocco?"

"Not fast enough. Not fast enough for a normal shutdown."

Jiggs nodded, and continued to nod as he processed the idea. "There's no way to go back to the original programming." It was more statement than question.

"No way. Not with the program locked in an operation"

"Okay then," Jiggs said, moving toward the Nest. "Systems, I want options. System shutdown, without Inhibitor Rods."

"On your screen," said Chuck Monroe, coming up behind him. They climbed the riser together.

"Why, Chuck," said Jiggs in mock surprise, pulling up his own chair to the front of the work surface. "You don't trust Mark's abilities." He began scanning the onscreen document.

"He'll sort it out," said Chuck. "But not in time. I think he's just realizing he's got himself into a rat hole."

"At least…" Jiggs said distractedly, his finger sliding down along the screen, "…Operational Planning… won't bully him into outsourcing any more… programming code. Here," he said, tapping the screen. "This is the one. The closest thing to a good alternative."

"I can't see you going any other way," Chuck concurred.

"Hmm. But every plan has to have a backup. Get ready for the screaming to start. Thanks Chuck." Jiggs spat his wad of gum into his wastepaper basket, and flipped his main audio line to Global. "Listen up, people. I want Hermes Gantry personnel ready to scrub for possible EmEvac. I want Armed Forces alerted for possible tracking."

Alex Boten's mike crackled to life: "Jiggsy, no way am I gonna cut and run, and watch this whole tower melt."

"Captain Boten," said Jiggs with a smile, "You will do whatever Mission Control instructs you to do. Fortunately for both of us, Emergency Evac is *not* in our immediate futures. However: Enough of this project has flushed down the crapper in the last two hours that I'm not taking any more chances. EmEvac is now our official backup plan, and it will be activated at such time as the Mission Controller sees fit. Now if I could trouble you to clear the channel?"

"Sir, yes sir."

"Hermes Receiving, what is your Main Power Level?"

From the far side of the globe, on an orbiting tower much like Boten's, came the reply: "Mission Control, we are holding steady at twenty-two percent power, ready to accelerate as needed."

"Thank you, Receiving. Prepare for a dustup. We're going for one hundred percent. Power-up procedures to commence approximately five minutes, will advise. What is your angular deviation?"

"Sorry, Control, we've let her go to point zero one two. Will have her nominal before power-up commences."

"Roger and out, Receiving. Physiology, how's our boy?"

"Stressed, but not seriously."

"Sirocco, you ready to get your butt in gear?"

"Ready, Control. However, I do not have a ticket for this flight. So I assume we are going to do a launch and abort."

"That is the plan, Sirocco," said Jiggs.

"Unscheduled launch and abort isn't going to look too good on the scorecard," Boten reminded him.

Jiggs ignored him: "We'll go for nominal launch thrust. Program your bolts to blow at... T plus two point five seconds. Do you copy on two point five seconds?"

"Houston, I read you, but request we draw it out. The drive sled will only be crawling at two and a half seconds, over."

Jiggs bit his lip. He stared at the orbital map, tracing the Hermes 7 Launch Complex and Hermes Recovery in their separate courses across the Mercator map of the Earth.

"Control, I'm not asking to hot dog it. I'd just like to be clear of the launch bay before those generators discharge. Give me seven seconds, Houston."

"Copy your request for seven seconds, Sirocco. Just a moment." Jiggs punched up the launch sequence simulation, and watched the capsule traverse the length of the tower. "I just don't want you reaching the end of the Gantry, Alex," Jiggs said.

"And I just want to get out of the bay before discharge. Dumping the sled is preprogrammed; there's no human error there. The timing's automatic. Once the bolts are blown I have one, maybe two seconds of reaction time before I begin firing my thrusters. How badly can I mess up? Seven seconds is what the book says for a Launch-and-Abort, Jiggsy. We didn't just pull that number out of a hat. I was part of the team that ran the simulations. Over?"

"'Go', your request for seven second delay in dumping the drive sled, Sirocco. Alex, I want those thrusters firing on the 'one' side of 'one or two seconds'. You read me?"

"I read you, Con. Let's do this."

"Hermes Receiving?" asked Jiggs.

"Receiving is green for power-up. Angular deviation, point zero zero four."

Jiggs laughed. "Keep holding a zero zero four, and you'll find your standards revised to expect it."

"We'll take the chance. Thought you'd like something at better than nominal. Go for full power-up?"

"Roger, Receiving, on your request for one hundred percent power-up." The Hermes Receiving station began the gradual, and uneventful, slide up to one hundred percent power. "Hermes Tower, what is your deviation?"

"Houston, we are holding at point zero niner."

"Roger point zero niner, Tower. All right, people. Let's put this day behind us. Mission clock set to T minus two minutes. Light the

Board."

'Ready' messages began coming in from the various mission departments, switching yellow status lights to green on Jiggs' Go Board. In the end, only one yellow remained.

"LCP, report."

Mark Grossman spun in his chair, looking up to the Nest. He spoke into his headset.

"Cap, I don't like this."

"You want to get your code debugged before we go?" Jiggs asked.

"Not *debugged*," Mark said testily. "I would just like to *know* what the problems *are*. Fixing 'em can come later."

Jiggs motioned him up to the Nest. When Grossman joined him, Jiggs slid off his headset; Grossman followed suit.

"And how far have you gotten through the process of 'finding the problems'?" Jiggs asked pointedly. Grossman turned to the Go Board display, and didn't answer. "You know," Jiggs said in a lowered tone, "that by the time you finish going through the code, we're likely to have a coolant temp reading, either real or bogus, that's going to be so high it won't just lock out the Inhibitors. It'll scrub the launch." Jiggs' voice dropped to a whisper. "And that leaves EmEvac, with the Gantry at one hundred percent power. You want a nightmare scenario? Picture that Gantry tower glowing bright red and buckling. Picture the reactor blowing. Picture Hermes 7 as a meteor shower."

"Launch and abort was not on today's menu, Bob. You're asking me to green-light code… that I haven't even looked at."

"I'm asking you to put your ass on the line," said Jiggs. "You're either going to do it or you aren't."

"So I get to decide whether the tower gets blown to bits."

"No," said Jiggs, looking out across the Control Room, but maintaining the same hushed tone. "You don't decide that. That tower is not going to blow." He looked again to Grossman. "Because we're not going to have an EmEvac. We're going to have a launch. I either get a green light from you, or I get a red. And if I get a red, I log an override—to LCP condition green. So it's your ass on the line,

27

or it's mine. *That's* what *you* get to decide."

Grossman looked him in the eye. Neither man blinked. Neither man breathed. Grossman turned and stepped off the Nest, went to Launch Control Programming, and sat down, staring at his documentation pack.

Jiggs slipped his headset back on, and looked to his board. None of the greens had switched to yellow or red. Launch Control Programming remained the only yellow. He was about to speak into his headset, when he noticed Grossman's headset was still on Jiggs' workspace tabletop.

"LCP," Jiggs said, loud enough for his voice to carry. "I still read yellow. What is your status?"

Grossman didn't move. Jiggs waited. Grossman reached up and punched a key on his keyboard. The Go Board went all green.

"Sirocco, we are at all green. Preparing to start the mission clock."

"Roger, Houston," said Boten with relief. "Dinner's on me."

"Starting mission clock... mark." The digital display in the upper corner of the global tracking display began its methodical countdown from minus two minutes. The Control Room remained silent, except for the requisite pronouncements along the way:

- 1:45, Sled rockets primed.
- 1:30, Particulate and radiation check, nominal.
- 1:10, Main Power auto-sequence engaged.
- 0:45, Main Power at one hundred fifty percent.
- 0:40, Distortion field at 11,165 g.e.k
- 0:35, Particulate check, normal. Beta scintillation commenced.
- 0:30, Pre-launch coolant dump commenced.
- 0:15, Sled rockets ignited.
- And from twelve through zero, the traditional reading of the count.

Immediately after zero came the declaration "Sled restraints 'Off'," and the clock resumed counting upward, with no minus sign. Sirocco began accelerating down the Gantry. In the swirling field of distorted Earth, Alex Boten imagined he saw an image, as if he were taking a Rorschach test. It was a sonogram image; it was the twins.

"T plus four...."

Dreamlike, he imagined Kathy's voice: "Do you see them, Alex? Do you see them?" He shook the thought off, wondering if he would be honest enough to admit to it in the post-flight debriefing. "Remember them," Kathy said.

"T plus five...." He was amazed at how time seemed to crawl. *Full post flight debriefing*, he thought. *Sorry, Abbey. You're stuck with Dad. I won't be there tonight.*

When the mission clock reached T plus seven seconds, Sirocco automatically detonated the restraining bolts that affixed her to the accelerating sled.

What happened next was the focus of considerable speculation, study, and investigation for the next two years. In the end, it was concluded that of the three restraining bolts holding Sirocco to the sled, bolts one and three fired normally. Bolt two, although it fired, contained a defect in the explosive material itself. Due to improper cooling, a long, irregular finger of material within the explosive had been rendered inert. This both significantly reduced the explosive force, and resulted in the inert segment, now broken into two, being expelled as solid projectiles. The investigating panel concluded that the first portion cleared both the locking assembly and the Sirocco, lodging harmlessly in the Gantry framework. The panel went on to speculate that the second portion impacted into the locking assembly itself, affixing the Sirocco capsule to the accelerating rocket sled. Although no physical evidence would remain to verify this conclusion, the investigating panel was precisely correct.

Three ten-thousandths of a second after the firing of the explosive, the contact pins still showed no separation, and so a red light tripped in both the Sirocco capsule and on the mission boards in Houston. Reflexively Jiggs bit down, and cut into the edge of his tongue.

"Alex!"

"Read it... refiring charges... negative effect."

"Pitch and yaw!" came the report from Telemetry.

"Thrusters, Alex. Attitude is destabilizing."

Chuck called out: "Even if he's stable, his thrusters can't beat the sled rockets."

"Stabilizing," said Telemetry, "But he's two degrees off-beam!"

"Alex," said Jiggs, his calm returning, "don't fight the sled. Correct course and go on through. Get on beam and go through. Reception Tower is Go. We'll catch you on the other side." There was no response, but clearly Boten was making corrections.

"Pitching again. He's close to the Gantry...."

The Sirocco grazed the wiry metal frame of the Hermes Gantry, and began to spin. Instinctively, Boten ceased thruster fire until he could re-orient himself.

He heard the reports: "Five degrees deviation... approaching The Tube." Going with his gut instinct, he maneuvered the thruster controls, and Sirocco straightened out. He was looking backward, up the Gantry, the launch bay receding. *Seconds*, he thought, *only seconds*. His mind raced, working to reverse his instincts on thruster vectors. Or *did* it reverse when moving backward? *No ticket for this flight*. His body tingled, and the edges of the window began to curve. The Gantry curved up to the distant launch bay.

As if in a dream, he sat at his father's bedside. His sister looked up at him, and her lips moved silently: "Bye, Lex."

"Abbey...." Blackness.

*   *   *

For a moment, Jiggs stood speechless.

"Hermes Reception," he said at last. "Do you have him?" He spat the blood from his mouth, onto the floor beside him.

"Houston, we have nothing. We... we never even registered any Beta flux."

"Maintain particulate and radiation monitoring. Widen your angle." He spat out more blood. "Tracking, what have you got?"

"Negative contact."

"You're saying you've got nothing? No sled, no capsule, no escape pod? No debris?"

There was no response. Jiggs crashed down into his chair. "Tracking..." he pleaded.

"Confirmed, Mission Control. No debris. We are tracking Hermes 7, Gantry only."

Jiggs took out a handkerchief, wiped out the inside of his mouth, and held it against his tongue to stanch the blood. Control Room personnel began to gather at the Nest, but none came up except Chuck Monroe. Jiggs pulled the handkerchief from his mouth, and tossed it aside.

"Tracking... how small an item can you register? At Hermes' orbital range."

"Control, we've bumped up our resolution. We're reading down to about two centimeters. No contacts. Broadening our sweep. Will advise, over."

Jiggs slipped off his headset. "Over," he echoed.

"We made all the right decisions, Bobby," Chuck said. "You know that. You know it."

"Wherever he is," Jiggs whispered. "I pray to God he's dead." He swallowed a mouthful of blood. "'Cause we have no way of bringing him back."

31

Book I
Chapter 3: The Mirrans
(Earlier)

Treachery. Her lithe hand sped the pen across the paper, pausing only ever so briefly as she sought a word, a phrase. Her eyes never left the page. Except once. Once she looked up, across the bustle of the office, across to the conference room door. Beyond it, she knew, her mother still sat—fuming, betrayed.

She took in the smells of old paper, old wood, and the scent— faint, but ever-present—of burning oil from the lamps. Oh, to be away from all this, she thought. Her hand, her eyes, her attention all returned to the last word she had written. She continued with her betrayal. That was not what her mother had called it, but it was what her mother felt.

Initialing the document, she motioned to the page. He approached her, past the accountants and the adjusters and the clerks.

"To a rider, and with all haste," she said, sealing the letter with wax.

"Anything for you, Miss," he said, lifting it gingerly from her hand. His eyes lingered on the white ring she wore. "Anything you ask."

She masterfully combined a smile and a subtle shake of her head.

"Off with you," she said with a playful dismissiveness. She sat for a moment, allowing herself to wallow in thoughts of her present and future, of her prospects. Of fumbling young pages and clerks. Of the sea captains and sailors whose fates they directed. Of how her status, and the reaction of such men to her, were fated soon to change. Unconsciously, she spun the ring on her finger.

Then, steeling herself, she rose and crossed with purpose toward the conference room, to try and undo the damage she had caused. Pausing at the door, she turned to look out the office window, to watch the page disappearing into the darkness beyond the streetlamp, and to say a prayer that the letter he carried had been rightly written.

To Captain Abbik Dollapan, Ammanon Deloré, Late of Mej Moribor

From Shocktele Shipyards, Desidomone Harbor, Arquat / Comptroller, Shocktele

Issued on 5H/3R/Platius

Dearest Captain Dollapan:

The proposal for chartering of the Ammanon Deloré has been received and reviewed.

Our Shocktele directors' meeting has just been completed. Despite the absence of the founder of Shocktele, it is clear that he favors this charter, and his vote was thus noted.

Be advised that the cofounder of Shocktele is unalterably opposed to this voyage.

Sadly, this leaves it upon myself to cast a deciding vote. Clearly, all interested parties understand that the role of tiebreaker was one I never seriously entertained. I accepted the position of Comptroller to resolve legal requirements for the formation of Shocktele, as well as to eliminate problems connected with inheritance. Yet now I find myself compelled to choose between two courses of action—and in so doing, choose between the wills of two people that it breaks my heart to find at odds with each other.

Sadly, in understanding the motives behind these two options, I have reached three conclusions:

~ First, both are unalterable.

~ Second, both are right and true, in their own ways.

~ Third, both are (in their own ways) selfish.

However, a fourth conclusion has decided this issue. Despite the elements of selfishness in both positions, one position also exhibits an element of self*less*ness. Owing to that virtue, I feel compelled to cast my vote in favor of the charter.

I pray I shall be able to mend relations with her whom I have wronged in so deciding.

Feel free, then, to begin your preparations. Keep us advised as to your progress in securing your peculiar requirements for this journey.

Allow me to leave you with two warnings.

First, do all in your power to keep your preparations secret. News of this charter would spark a most undesirable controversy.

Second, knowing that news of your preparations must, despite your best efforts, eventually come to light, know with all certainty that the entire matter will land you before the Temple Court. In light of this I urge you to rely upon your friendship with Senior Justice Raddem. I suggest here no improper leveraging of influence; rather, Justice Raddem knows your character, and he therefore has insight into your motives.

May the God of land, sea and sky be with you as you sail from Mej Moribor to Desidomone. And all the more so, when your charter begins.

Regarding our conversation upon the hills south of town before your departure—know that, despite what you may think about yourself, only a man of sure underlying faith would entertain helming such a voyage as the one you have presented to us.

Upon that voyage may you come to hear the voice of him, whom we all seek to one day hear again.

L.D.

P.S. I recommend you contract with Highland Iceworks rather than Jellic Supply. Highland's prices will be higher, but I trust their discretion over Jellic's. Regarding your more standard trappings, I have no qualms over Desidomone Supply; that odd little man Raleus seems discreet enough.

Captain Dollapan held the letter as if still reading it, allowing his eyes to wander across the familiar handwriting. He said nothing. Beyond his cabin, voices above decks shouted orders. A gentle swell caused the Deloré to strain against her moorings.

"Well, man? What does she say?" The squat man across the table leaned forward.

Dollapan dropped the paper to the table. "Rest easy, my friend. We sail." Then, cocking his head, he called out: "Mr. Mennetek?"

"By the grace of God," said the little man, as much to himself as to the captain, "we are going to do this."

"By the grace of God," the captain corrected, "we are going to try."

Picking up another letter from the table, this one in his own hand, he read through the list it contained. First Officer Mennetek entered his quarters. Ignoring him, Dollapan held up the paper.

"Anything to add?" the captain asked.

"No," his friend said. "Nothing you can secure from your suppliers. My needs are more... specialized."

Dollapan handed the paper to his first officer. "To the purser, and with all haste. Have him add these to our order."

Mennetek read over the sheet. "Yes, sir..." he said absently. Then lifting his eyes, he looked to the short man. Then he looked to his captain. "Yes sir," he said firmly, and left.

"You trust his discretion?" Anned Islak asked.

Dollapan arched an eyebrow. "Trust his discretion?" He grunted contemptuously. "And do you trust the discretion of this glassmaker of yours, from Barnable?" Dollapan asked.

Islak shrugged, and smiled. "I do trust him. With my life, it would seem."

To Desidomone Supply, Desidomone Harbor, Arquat / Mr. Raleus Barnume

From Purser Finnean, Ammanon Deloré, Late of Desidomone Harbor

Issued on 6H/3R/Platius

Trusted Raleus,

Please advise pricing and delivery time for outfitting of perishables and accoutrements for a full complement of twenty-five officers and crew, assuming full supply in all matters save standard clothing and tools, sufficient for a journey of two shortmonths, with the following exceptions:

36

~ Full rain gear quantities increased to accommodate 38 men
~ 38 pairs heavy gloves, such as suited to barnacle scrubbing
~ 38 pairs heavy duty boots, divided roughly between medium and large sizes
~ 1 barrel narbig fruits, fully preserved
~ ¼ barrel narbigs, fresh
~ 5 barrels fresh water *beyond* the standard allotment.
~ 50 bales of hay

Time is likely to be pressing, thus kindly advise whatever costs would be associated with any optional expediting of delivery. Additionally, we will consider having our men take delivery at your doors, should any delays arise due to scheduling of your delivery crews.

Lastly, I understand some items on this list may draw attention and inquiry. Your discretion in guarding this list, and filling this order quietly, will be appreciated by Captain Dollapan as surely as by myself.

Remaining as always your friend, and confidant,

E. Finnean
Purser, A.D.

To Artisan Glassworks, Barnable, Arquat / Ig Doel, Manager
From A. Islak, Late of the Brigantine Ammanon Deloré, Late of Desidomone Harbor
Issued on 7H/3R/Platius
Kind Igren,

The lenses you delivered on 6 Hon have proven most excellent in both material and form; my compliments to your craftsmen, and my apologies for my brusqueness over the prototype. The calming intervention of time has bestowed upon me the benefits of a more objective review of the circumstances. I must confess to the lack of clarity of thought in my instructions.

Kindly produce for me two more sets identical to the set just delivered, assuming the same price may be had.

Also advise as to whether a third set could be produced using glass tinted, full spectrum, to an index of between 3.5 and 4.0. If such a set could be produced with the other two, with the charge for this third set being no more the half again more than a standard set, please take this letter as confirmation to so expand my order.

Sadly, time is of pressing import in this matter. If the order, or any part thereof, cannot be completed within two quarters, or at the latest by the coming Honset, please consider that portion of the order voided. By then, God willing, I shall have set sail—on a journey that may prove to be of some length.

I eagerly await a committing word from you.

Islak

Ig Doel smoothed out the order on his desk with thin, potash-smeared hands. As he re-read Islak's words, he cursed the heat radiating from the backroom kilns and wiped the sweat from his brow.

"Tinted to an index of... what *are* you trying for?" A quick check in his reference books confirmed his recollection: A tinting index of four was nearly opaque. For a third time, he read through the order.

"...'I shall have set sail...' " he muttered. "Desidomone Harbor." He tapped the page. "Essmin!" he called out, in no particular direction. A worker in a heavy apron appeared in the doorway leading to the ovens.

"Sir?"

"Doesn't someone here receive newspapers from Desidomone?"

"The Beacon. The Desidomone Beacon. Yes sir, one of the boys gets them."

"See if he has any recent issues about. And ask if he can pass any new ones to me when he's finished with them." Then he added, just to himself: "Get all mysterious with me, will you little man?"

38

7th Hon, in the 3rd Reversal of Platius

For Immediate Post in and around Desidomone Harbor, Province of Arquat

Departure Notice Brigantine Ammanon Deloré

The Captain of the brigantine Ammanon Deloré herewith announces fifteen positions open to men of character true, body strong, and skills harmonious to a voyage of some fair length, for the purpose of rounding out a well-seasoned and trusted crew.

Said voyage to commence no later than the coming Honset.

Pay to be one part in five free and clear above the Harbormaster's stated norm.

Inquire at once, shipside at Connovan Street dock.

Shipsmaster,
Ammanon Deloré

Dearest Aunt Drumae:

Hoping this letter finds you well, your household prosperous (so much as can be hoped in times such as these).

Fortune has treated me fairly; I still find odd tasks about the harbor such to maintain lodgings and board, though permanent positions aboard ship remain scarce. Shipping traffic is still down, and no doubt will be for some time. Although the drought hit farming first, its effects are now keenly felt in the harbors. I fear that, even when the rains return and your fortunes change, we shall be lagging in the benefits even as we lagged in the sorrows.

However, just now I have received, from a friend in a printer's shop, a draft of a new posting that may alter the fortunes both of myself and of your own household. In a few short quarters, a brigantine here at anchor will set sail. Curiously, fifteen of her twenty-five positions are vacant. This, with the fact that the destination was left conspicuously absent from the notice, leads me and other boys about the harbor to think the journey will be an arduous one. This suspicion is compounded by the fact that the wages offered for this voyage exceed the harbor standard, when for some two longmonths now the Harbormaster has approved waging at three-fourths standard without need for review. A corrected Notice of Departure will need to be posted soon, and all will be made clear at that point. But meanwhile, I view the opportunity for work and the generosity of wage as too strong of lures, no matter the details. I plan to apply immediately after sending this post.

And this brings me, at length, to the reason for this letter. If the drought has continued to idle the farm, and if Andril is not using this idle time to advance his studies, then send my cousin at once and with haste to apply for this same opportunity with me.

News of this notice, even in advance of its official posting, is spreading quickly. I cannot say a position will remain for Andril upon his arrival. (I cannot say one remains for me even yet.) With hands idling about Desidomone, I cannot imagine these fifteen slots lingering for long. Word has it that no less a man than Anned Islak is the backer for the trip. But even if the journey fails to secure Andril this position, the change of scene will do him well. And it has been too long since I have raised a glass with him.

I remain as always,
Your loving nephew,
Opper

The old man in the Harbor Patrol uniform walked along Connovan Street, the yellow moon setting ahead of him and the orange moon rising behind; nothing else disturbed the starless expanse above. At the Connovan Street dock's message board, his weathered hands rearranged messages and postings until he cleared enough open space to pin up another of the Departure Notices he had been given. He turned toward the next dock along Connovan Street, one more in a long series of stops. Too much walking, he thought, on legs that had already walked enough. Moving on, he allowed himself to slip into the dragging shuffle he had seen so many other former sailors adopt. He pretended not to notice.

Running footsteps came from behind, slowing as they approached.

"Kind officer?" said the breathless man. "Might I have... a copy... of that?"

The patrolman turned, laboriously.

"Son, I seek no trouble from the Seaman's Concord. Harbormaster said you might have a word. But I am simply told to post the notices. They are nothing to do with me."

"Not with the Concord. The Beacon. I'm with the Beacon." His breath was returning to him now. "Just one copy. If you please."

The patrolman handed over a copy, and the reporter turned away. Reading it as he walked toward his newspaper's office, a scowl came over him. His editor would tell him there was no story. And he would be right. At least, so far.

"Just a notice," the patrol spoke after him. "Don't see the need for any great fuss." He turned again to his course, stepping directly into a large and rather displeased looking gentleman.

"I, on the other hand," the new man said, "*am* with the Seaman's Concord. If you please?" He held out his hand, and the patrolman gave him a sheet.

"You get one. That's what the Harbormaster says. The rest get posted." He brushed past the agent of the Concord.

"Hold on," the agent said. "You cannot be posting this."

"Now son," the patrolman said without turning back. "You are too young a man for your ears to be giving out. I said: 'You get one. The rest get *posted*'."

The paper crumpled within the agent's hand. "We'll see if Ullamar Kloe agrees with you on that."

41

Within a Sheltering Darkness

To Harbormaster, Desidomone
From Ullamar Kloe, President, Seaman's Concord
Issued on 7H/3R/Platius

Sir: With all due haste, kindly explain yourself. A Departure Notice has been posted via your offices listing neither a destination nor an arrival date. I scarcely think it necessary for me to remind you that these facts are not optional in a Departure Notice, nor have they been optional since the Judgeship of Illaneg.

As President of the Seaman's Concord, I cannot stand by as sailors, in distress over the current conditions, find themselves compelled into uncertain service of ambiguous duration.

I hereby petition the retraction of this invalid document, and the enforcing of harbor rules retaining the brigantine Ammanon Deloré at dock pending the filing of a proper, and complete, Departure Notice.

U. Kloe, President, S.C.

The reporter approached his editor's desk, where the next edition's draft was laid out.

"'No story' still means 'No story', lad," the editor said, without looking up. "A surly tiff between the Concord and the Harbor authorities may be amusing gossip, but it is not a story." Silently the reporter held up a sheet of paper. The editor looked up. "What?" he said, taking the sheet.

"Public Postings says this is on page six, of the very edition you are reviewing."

Dropping the paper, the editor turned his draft to page six. He wiped his hand across the page, as if it were rumpled and needed smoothing to be read, or as if he were clearing away some obscuring debris. The words still read the same.

"How could they... set this type," he murmured. "Run it through print. And not understand what it means?"

The reporter turned up a corner of the draft.

"Shall I dispose of this, and tell the men to prepare to run another?"

"Too late," the editor said, swatting at his reporter's fingers. "Start composing text for the next edition. And get me a rider," he said, scooping the paper up off the floor. "This is going to Shelaemstet. To the Temple Bell."

The reporter waited, studying his editor's face, smiling.

"You think this amusing, then?" the editor asked, proffering the sheet.

"No. Only your reaction to it." He took the paper.

"Too young," the editor said sadly. He blew out one of the two oil lamps in his office. "You are too young to remember. The Innotek Assan was before your time."

"The Innotek Assan," the reporter echoed playfully. "Sea-wives tales."

The editor blew out the other lamp, but made no move toward his door. In the darkness, he moved to his old, hard chair. He sat.

"You never saw them. You never saw their eyes."

From 'The Desidomone Beacon', 7H/3R/Platius, 2ⁿᵈ Light Quarter, page 6:

> **Notice Amendment**
> The following amends the Departure Notice for the Ammanon Deloré, sailing Honset, 7H/3R/Platius:
> Destination: Northern   DevilsJaw Boundaries and beyond.
> Arrival Date: One shortmonth.

From 'The Temple Bell', 7H/3R/Platius, 3rd Light Quarter, at the bottom of page 1:

Into the Jaws

Word is out in the northern harbor town of Desidomone that an expedition is being mounted to enter the Boundary Waters. Aiming for the DevilsJaws to the North, the brig Ammanon Deloré hopes to navigate the peril with but a shortmonth's sail time. Among the questions being posed that stand as yet unanswered:

- *Who would sponsor such a voyage?* Rumor has it that a private charter is involved. The Deloré's Captain, however, is unavailable for comment.
- *What ship owners would dedicate their craft to it?* Shocktele Shipyards, based in Desidomone, is not responding to private or official inquiries.
- *From where will they gather a crew?* Fully sixty percent of her crew has been reported put off, with notices placed in a desperate effort to replace them.

It has been near unto 75 years since any vessel has ventured into a DevilsJaw, and that a mightier ship than a mere brig. The galleon Estmae Denshaw, manned by nearly 50 sailors of proven skill, disappeared without word or trace in its effort at the Eastern Jaws.

Nor has any craft braved any Boundary Waters at all since the voyage of the Innotek Assan some 21 years on. Would that it had been that no trace had been found of her. And now comes a voyage to the Northern Jaws, so near to the Innotek Assan horror.

From all appearances, Desidomone's Harbormaster intends no hindrance to the endeavor.

The leadership of the Seaman's Concord of Desidomone appears caught between his first duty, to the lives of the seamen of the harbor, and the pressure within the ranks for certain hands, too long idle, to find a position no matter how perilous it seems to more objective eyes.

Failing the courage of the local Concord, the officers and crew of the Ammanon Deloré have till Honset to assemble their affairs.

Petition to the Temple Judgeship
The 7th Hon, in the 3rd Reversal of His Most Honorable Judge Platius

Most Honorable Judges:
I beg your indulgence to intercede in a matter of gravest concern. It has no doubt come to your attention that an expedition is being mounted which promises to destroy the lives of more than twenty men. Circumstances preclude my intervention in any way that will have meaningful impact on this disastrous turn of events.

Your intervention will save the lives of many, at a time when financial need blinds men to their truest interests.

On these grounds, I plead you to order the Harbormaster of Desidomone to secure the ship Ammanon Deloré at port until such time as a new and safer charter can be secured for her.

In the hopes you will act upon this matter, and on the chance you may have need of inquiry, I am setting forth presently for the Temple, and will be available to you with all due haste.

I am most humbly yours,
Ullamar Kloe
President, Seaman's Concord, Desidomone Harbor, Arquat

To Anned Islak, c/o Ammanon Deloré, Desidomone Harbor
From Igren Doel, Owner, Artisan Glassworks, Barnable, Arquat
Issued on 7H/3R/Platius

Islak:
You disreputable charlatan. For months we have corresponded and worked together, and it falls to me to assemble meaning from the

tidbits scattered about me.

Even a backwater such as Barnable has access to news. Word of the Deloré's quest is out, and it now seems obvious to me what you intend. Or did you think I would make no connection between your colored lenses and the Northern Jaws? Perhaps you thought I was ignorant of geography? Or that I was too young when the Innotek Assan returned to port to avoid having those images indelibly planted in my mind? Burned into my mind, if you will?

But your intentions are clear to me now. So here, then, is my proposal:

~ As for the time to completion, my craftsmen have dropped all other projects—either placing them on hold or directing them to our competitors.

~ As for the quoted price, consider it voided. The pricing is hereby cut by one third.

~ The only condition for these two considerations is that you secure for me what is rumored to exist: A position as seaman aboard the Ammanon Deloré.

Failing word otherwise from you, I shall set forth for Desidomone within a quarter, your order in hand, equipped as best as I can be for the sea. If there is gear I need, I trust it can be secured in a port town.

Don't fail me in this, you lowlife conjurer. If you do not secure me a place in this voyage, then the lenses I bring to Desidomone will be the last you will see from me. See if you can find another smith able to meet your specifications. Or another who will bring a flask of Pinoae, to toast a departure to doom.

Irked, but willing to forgive,
Ig

Dearest Aunt Drumae:
Just a quick note to advise, Andril has arrived safely in

Desidomone, and is nicely settling in to shared quarters with me. The journey was not a vain one; we have both secured positions on the voyage soon commencing—though Andril's petition was most nearly rejected.

I was first to be interviewed by the Shipsmaster. My experience, coupled with the lack thus far of other applicants, made the master's acceptance of my petition almost guaranteed. After this I tarried to be at Andril's side—both to lend comfort to him, and to offer my testimony as to his character, and his eagerness and ability to learn. The Shipsmaster, however, seemed intent on excluding anyone so lacking in sailing history. The master was nonetheless sympathetic to Andril's earnest desire for a position, and with no other applicants waiting, he talked with us extensively about Andril's background and skills.

Through these discussions, we touched upon Andril's desire to join the Temple priesthood, and his occasional breaks from farming life to undergo training. It was this, apparently, that caught the ear of the man in the chamber adjoining ours. This man, somewhat slight of stature and portly of form, with the close-cropped hair of a landsman rather than a sailor, came in and spoke with the Shipsmaster. I was mystified as to his position, for he was not dressed as sailing men tend to dress, nor was he one of the several officers of the Ammanon Deloré with whom I was acquainted. Most of the conversation between this man and the Shipsmaster I was unable to divine, though what I did hear concerned Andril's priestly training. Their discussion finished, the man left. And the Shipsmaster pronounced Andril hired. And that, my dear Aunt, was that.

At the risk of pressing the matter, I inquired of the master as to why Andril's training for the Temple was of such concern (even though at that point I was in fact guessing that his training was the deciding issue). And his reply to me? I tell you truly, he answered me: "If the man booking the charter wants a given hand on board, then that hand is hired aboard."

And there, dearest Aunt Drumae, you have it as pretty as you please. Your son has been hired under the direct influence of Mr. Anned Islak himself.

Within a Sheltering Darkness

Now I know there has been some fair rumor and bustle and noise over the nature of this trip. Insofar as is possible, let me lay your worries to rest. The Captain is a fine man with years of experience. And with a man of Anned Islak's wisdom and knowledge behind us, I couldn't be more confident if he himself were to join us on board.

Be assured I'll be at Andril's side the whole trip. We'll look out for each other. And if you still bear worry over this affair, take heart in this: We might not even sail. The local S.C. has raised a petition to the Temple Judges. He and the Captain of the Deloré have been called before them yet within this very quarter. They are en route even as I write.

If we are stayed, Andril is as safe as in his own bed, and will return to you by-and-by, once he tires of the seaside life. If however we go, we go with the blessing of God himself.

What more comforting dilemma has ever beset two cousins?

Remaining always,
Your loving nephew,
Opper

Book I
Chapter 4: Sanctions

In an envelope addressed 'Captain, Ammanon Deloré, Connovan Dock, Desidomone'

Devoted Husband:

News has reached me that you are proceeding to make provisions for Islak's charter. More to the point, not only are you willing to sacrifice the Ammanon Deloré to this madness, but you yourself intend to captain her. And a fine thing it is, to have such a report come to me by the hand of strangers; it seems you have persuaded even my own flesh and blood to evade my questions. Clear now are the reasons for your failure to respond to my letters.

I knew the time spent with this man Islak would come to no good. I care not a whit about his popularity. Too much change in too little time clouds men's minds, as yours is now so plainly clouded.

Sail well. Take your time. Be in no hurry to return to us. Neither I nor your daughter is in pressing need of the influence of a man so obviously in the sway of suicide.

And if this charter ends the way it seemingly must, we shall be comfortably taken care of by the bounty of your estate.

I remain,
Your Wife

Transcription of Hearing
The 7th Hon, in the 3rd Reversal of His Most Honorable Judge
Platius
Case 9

Attending Consultants, recognized by the court:

Captain Abbik Dollapan, of the sailing ship Ammanon Deloré

Ullamar Kloe, of the Seaman's Concord of Desidomone Harbor, Arquat

Usettet: Mr. Kloe, I am forced to begin by questioning whether this hearing should be called at all. Desidomone has a Harbormaster, by all accounts a competent and reputable man. Why not raise this with him?

Kloe: Your Honor, that is the standard procedure, and I would have preferred to take that route. But, at the moment, such an approach is… impractical.

Platius: Impractical?

Kloe: Sirs, the current drought has brought shipping traffic to a crawl. The men of Desidomone are out of work. Many are approaching desperation.

Platius: So you want this voyage to occur, or not?

Kloe: Most emphatically not, Your Honor. My point is, popular opinion will sweep aside anyone who stands opposed to a prospect of pay, no matter how tenuous or ill advised.

Usettet: So you come before this court, that we might do your job for you? And spare you from being thrown out of office?

Kloe: Not at all, Your Honor. I have served as President of the Seaman's Concord for some fourteen longmonths. I have other prospects. Other options. But if I am removed from office so that some puppet can be installed, some lackey who will tolerate this disaster, then I would do as well to approve this business, and send those men to their doom, myself. And that is something, Your Honors, that I will not do.

Lode: It still seems to me that you want the members of this Temple Judgeship to function as leaders for a local concord. And that is something none of us were appointed to be.

Raddem: Are you saying, Mr. Kloe, that desperate times have, in this instance, fouled the normal workings in Desidomone?

Kloe: Yes, sir.

Raddem: And are you further saying that this breakdown of the normal order now puts at risk some twenty-five men's lives?

Kloe: Yes, Your Honor, I am. And that this risk of life is the matter I bring before Your Honors. Because the simple truth is that, in the end, these men will die.

Raddem: And it is your contention that matters of life and death *do* fall within our purview?

Kloe: *No response recorded.*

Raddem: I apologize, Mr. Kloe. In all honesty, my last question was not truly directed to you, but to my colleagues. As such it was improper and I withdraw it.

Lode: Not every expedition that has attempted to pass the various Boundaries has ended in death.

Kloe: No sir. Not every one. But every one has ended either in death or failure. Death or failure. And far more go to death. Far more. Let Captain Dollapan set sail as often as he likes, wasting the money of his ship's owners. But forbid him, sirs, from wasting the lives of men. Lives which are not his to expend.

Poznanek: Captain Dollapan, having heard as we have these comments so far, it sounds as though you are quite an evil man.

Dollapan: Yes, Your Honor, it has sounded that way.

Poznanek: As a man of some fair experience upon the seas, well respected among your peers, and reputedly not one to commonly find himself lacking for crewmen willing to risk their lives by entrusting to your judgment, perhaps you can enlighten us as to where Mr. Kloe has gone wrong.

Dollapan: *No response recorded.*

Poznanek: Captain Dollapan?

Dollapan: I'm not sure he has gone wrong, sir.

Platius: Captain?

Dollapan: I'm sorry, sir. I must confess to being slightly at a loss for words in this matter. The expedition planned is, based on historical precedent, a dangerous one. And were I a bystander, watching the Ammanon Deloré set sail less than two quarters from now, as I pray she will, I must confess I would not be any too greatly surprised to see her fail to return.

Buelle: Captain Dollapan, I trust you have more to add?

Dollapan: Indeed, Your Honor. I stand before you as a man with two convictions that I must share with you. The first one, a fairly weak conviction, perhaps more an inclination: To believe that the Deloré will not return from this quest. But the second is stronger, far stronger. It is a conviction, an absolute certainty, down to my bones: That some day a ship will cross the Boundary areas and return.

Poznanek: Captain, you speak with a boldness approaching that of a prophet.

Dollapan: Your Honor, Your Honors, pardon the presumption of my tone. My conviction does not come from revelation of God. Would that it did. With each passing watch, as Honset draws nearer, I pray for such a revelation. For, if it will put your minds at ease considering the welfare of my men, I do not embark on this mission desiring of death. No, not desiring. Merely defying.

Platius: In some men, that distinction is a fleeting one.

Dollapan: I must leave it to the court to decide how separately I maintain these concepts. But I do, before you, assert that my position is defiance. Death, or defeat, Your Honors, will not claim every ship that ever attempts the crossing.

Usettet: The crossing? Twice now you refer to "crossing". To call it a crossing would seem to assume something to cross into. Something beyond the Boundary Waters.

Dollapan: I know of nothing to rule out navigable waters, or land, beyond.

Usettet: Nor does this Court know of anything that asserts it.

Dollapan: Granted, Your Honor. But one assertion I can make. If anything lies beyond the Boundary Waters, be it water, or land, or anything known or unknown, if there is anything more than just endless Boundary Water engulfing the rest of this globe, then I make this assertion. We will find it. History, Your Honors. History tells us we will find it.

Raddem: Captain Dollapan, you wouldn't be trying to flatter these jurists?

Dollapan: No, Your Honor. Although I have read your book, and admire it, I would make this point regardless. We know there was a time when men feared the sea, and would not live near the coasts. And then there was a time when man would not set sail upon anything but an inland lake. Then a time when he would not sail beyond sight of land. Now we live in a time when men fear to challenge the Boundary Waters that ring us. Some day men will look back. Through history. To us. They will not mock our fear, any more than we mock those who once feared the sea. Their fears were founded, as are ours. Men died going to sea. Men have died challenging the Boundary Waters. And more will die challenging the Boundary Waters. I am willing to risk being one of them.

Lode: For the chance of the glory of being the first to survive?

Dollapan: *No response recorded.*

Lode: Captain?

Dollapan: All glory goes to the God Who Is Silent. Who among us remembers the name of the first man to sail the sea? Or the first to pass beyond sight of land? Whoever survives the Boundary Waters will be lost to memory, crowded out by all those who will rush to follow him, once it is clear that it can be done.

Usettet: Then why, Captain?

Dollapan: Perhaps I might redirect that question to Justice Raddem.

Usettet: Captain, the question was directed to you, and shall be answered by you.

Dollapan: The concept was described, by one wiser than I, as "Historical Inevitability".

Usettet: Is that intended as an answer?

Raddem: Only if you've read the book.

Usettet: I am not interrogating the members of this esteemed panel, but a consultant brought before us, who seems enamored of riddles. Or at least poking fun at those he thinks he can befuddle.

Dollapan: Your Honor, I apologize, and most sincerely so. My humor was not intended at your expense, but more as a private joke between Justice Raddem and myself.

Usettet: A private joke?

Dollapan: Most wholly inappropriate, sir. The question had to do with my motives.   I cite in answer, the concept of Historical Inevitability: that when men's hearts are guided by God, they will move—perhaps slowly, but inexorably—to a commonality. Toward a unifying goal. Sometimes seen. Often not. Over the course of time, it has seemed to me that the best of men have been driven to further and further places, to make common the ways that were once dreaded. It seems to me an affront to history that such a progression should halt abruptly at the Boundary Waters.

Platius: And you would risk not only your own life, but the lives of your crew, for such a philosophy?

Dollapan: I am willing to risk my life. Each man of my crew must decide his own reason, should he wish to risk it as well. But for each man, the risk will be worth taking. Otherwise he would not be aboard.

Lode: And you are confident each man aboard fully understands the risk he will be taking?

Dollapan: *No response recorded.*

Raddem: Captain Dollapan?

Dollapan: *No response recorded.*

Poznanek: Captain....

Dollapan: I stand before this Court of Honor, before God Almighty himself, and declare upon my honor and future, that on this voyage I will lead no man to the Boundary Waters, no man out of sight of land, no man out sight of the safe harbor of Desidomone, without his knowing fully all that I know about what awaits us.

Platius: Captain Dollapan, this court had no intention of extracting from you an oath....

Usettet: Nonetheless, I find the phrasing of that oath interesting....

Raddem: Captain Dollapan.

Dollapan: Yes, Your Honor.

Raddem: Captain. Do you have something to say to this panel?

Dollapan: If it pleases Your Honors, might I make a request?

Raddem: The court is intrigued. And your request is?

Dollapan: That I pose to the court one question, and that I may pose it… in private.

Usettet: Inappropriate, Captain Dollapan. Surely you know all testimony must be given in the presence of both testifiers to a dispute.

Dollapan: With greatest deference to His Honor, I do not propose offering testimony. I only propose offering a question.

Usettet: And do you think it not likely that after you pose your question, whether we answer it or not, that we would have further questions of you?

Dollapan: I humbly submit to Your Honors that I suspect you will feel your questioning of me is, at that point, at an end. But if I am wrong, the court would clearly be free to return all parties to the court and resume questioning.

Poznanek, Usettet, Raddem: *Unintelligible*

Raddem: Mr. Kloe, the court appreciates your participation in this matter. The constable will accompany you to the commons area. Kindly remain there until the court is certain that no further testimony is required.

Ullamar Kloe was escorted out of the Hearing Chamber.

Raddem: Captain Dollapan. This is most irregular. You have a question to ask. A single question. Pose it with care, and alacrity.

Dollapan: Your Honors, owing to your eagerness to bring proper disposition to this case, and knowing that fuller understanding of our voyage might be supplied by the party chartering this voyage, I ask: Would you be willing to inquire of Mr. Anned Islak, now waiting discreetly in the West side chamber to this Hall?

Usettet: Captain Dollapan, kindly explain to this court the reason for these theatrics? Why couldn't this statement, cleverly twisted to the format of question, have been asked in the presence of Mr. Kloe, thereby alleviating any concern of impropriety about this Court that might now be arising in his mind?

Usettet: Captain Dollapan? Captain, am I to deduce from this gesture that you do not intend to answer my question?

Platius: Learned colleague, I should hazard to venture that the

Captain feels constrained by his word to say no more beyond his question. If we are to inquire of him further, we can only properly do so by first recalling Mr. Kloe.

Usettet: So be it. Constable!

Platius   I should point out, however, this one thing. That as the Captain felt the possibility of bringing Mr. Anned Islak covertly before the Temple Court to testify was worth risking the ire of this entire panel— a risk I must say he seems at least two thirds correct in assessing— that it is incumbent upon us to at least consider that course.

Poznanek: Islak's reputation casts an interesting light on this proceeding. I, for one, would like to know how his methods, and way of thinking, come to bear on the question of passability through the Boundary Waters.

Unintelligible consultation

Raddem: Constable, kindly exit through the West door. If you find there a man, escort him in.

Escorted in and recognized by the Court was Anned Islak of Barnable.

Raddem: Mr. Islak. What an odd and twisted set of events brings you to this court. It has been rumored you might shed light upon a pending voyage of the brigantine Ammanon Deloré.

Islak: Honorable Justices, kindly forgive the clumsiness of manner I pressed upon the dear Captain that I might come before you, and come discreetly. I do most eagerly wish to share with you my findings, which have led me to the charter that now awaits launch in Desidomone. However, at peril of inciting you further, there is one last... irregularity... that I would ask of these proceedings.

Usettet: Mr. Islak!

Islak: Your Honors, great lengths were taken to secure secrecy over the Ammanon Deloré's mission. And in all honesty, the fullness of truth is not yet unveiled. I have come before you to unveil precisely those truths. And no matter what happens, I will present these facts to you, here and in this session. But the reason for the secrecy still exists, and it is for this reason that I beg the court to bear with me in instituting the most extraordinary of precautions.

Raddem: What precaution do you seek, Mr. Islak?

Islak: Despite knowing the trustedness of all the court's loyal attendants, specifically the transcriber, the constable, and his three deputies at the doors, I request that these persons remove themselves from the Hall.

Usettet: Preposterous! We would be left with no record of your testimony. Unacceptable.

Islak: Gracious Justices. I have a brief, concise presentation. Although it will raise many questions, the presentation itself has been so rehearsed, I can reproduce it exactly. I propose this. The Hall be cleared of all but yourselves, and me. Even the Captain, I must request, should be excused. I then present the evidence in this folder, and display the contents of this case. If at the end of this presentation any of Your Honors holds that the balance of the proceeding should be recorded, the usual personnel could return, I could re-create my presentation, and the court could proceed to ask questions concerning it.

Buelle: Oh, most generous of you, Mr. Islak.

Islak   If, however, Your Honor. If after viewing my evidence you are all unanimous that this evidence and testimony should appear in no record whatever, then the personnel will not return for the balance of my testimony. You will still ask of me whatever you will, but it will not be recorded.

Usettet: You seriously think I will find in your scribblings and trinkets sufficient cause to upset the pattern of proceedings in this Hall that extends back thousands of years?

Islak: In all honest humility Your Honor, I do so believe.

Usettet: Then you take a fool's stance, Mr. Islak.

Unintelligible consultation.

Raddem: To clarify, Mr. Islak, your view of how this would play out. If the Court disagrees with you, and holds that the proceedings should be on record, the record will resume exactly where it left off? With your short testimony recorded in re-creation?

Islak: That is how I see it, Your Honor. The transcription would carry on as if nothing had happened, and no interruption had occurred.

Unintelligible consultation.

Raddem: Mr. Islak, owing to your reputation with both the people and this Court, we grant a temporary suspension of the recording of these proceedings. Until called back... evidently by Mr. Islak... the transcriber, constable and deputies, and Captain Dollapan will now clear the Hall.

Transcription Ends.

No further testimony exists for the matter of Case 9 of the 7th Hon, in the 3rd Reversal of His Most Honorable Judge Platius.

7H / R3 / P
L Q 3

Receipt of Sale
Desidomone Riggers
Rigging / Outfitting / Clothiers
37 le Connovan Street
Desidomone Harbor, Arquat

Items	Qties	Prices	Ext.
35 pl. Canvass Duffle	1	15 b, 23d	15 b, 23d
Class 5 Log Book	3	2b, 0d	6b, 0d
Pinoae, v 12R/(J5)	2	9b, 98d	19b, 96d
Lyderis Acid, 25cv	1	5b, 12d	5b, 12d

PAID

Total: ~~47b, 31d~~

46b, 31d

59

The 7th Hon, in the 3rd Reversal of His Most Honorable Judge Platius
Resolution of Case 9

Presented to the public by Honorable Justice Platius, during the Fourth Light Quarter

Hear and be advised all in attendance before the Temple Court.

In the matter of the request that the Harbormaster of Desidomone, province of Arquat, be compelled to restrain the sailing ship Ammanon Deloré from departure pending a revision to her current charter.

This Honorable Court concurs unanimously, that neither encouragement nor detraction should be compelled upon the Harbormaster, assuming he is convinced that all parties to this charter have been advised what risks are known and suspected by the principals to the charter.

May God's blessing be upon and protect both those who embark upon, and those who decline from, this endeavor.

To Captain Abbik Dollapan / From Justice E. Raddem
Issued on 7H/3R/Platius
Dear Abbik:

Godspeed on your venture. All the members of the Court, regardless of their disposition, wish for Islak's theories to prove right, at least insofar as his plans will afford you protection.

My young colleague Platius posed to you a question, whether you would risk your life for the philosophy of Historical Inevitability. I noted, though clearly he did not, that your answer lacked a certain specificity. Had Platius noted it, he might even have declared it evasive. I suspect I know that for which you are willing to risk your life. And I understand, though I disagree with, your desire not to speak it before the Court. Islak has made clear to us what he has made clear to you—that the fullness of his reasons for engaging this charter have been kept secret even from you. To my mind, that leaves two possibilities. Either he knows what it is you seek, and for that reason chose you, or he does not know what you seek, and for this reason God has brought you together. Whether this charter will prove useful, either to your goals or to those of Mr. Islak, I cannot pretend to know. I pray success to both of you, for the sake of us all.

I have never known you to be a man disposed to superstition. Yet one recommendation I leave with you, in peril of sounding superstitious myself. This Honset will likely fall near the dawning of Andilla Prime. Do not depart until it arises, I pray, even if it means delaying your departure somewhat past Honset.

The presence of the First Jewel of the Crown will mean no more to you in this endeavor than it will to me. But it may give some heart to the men of your ship. And a voyage of such dire risk is worth starting well, with a crew as confident as her Captain. If they be disposed to such superstition as the blessing of the Coming of the Crown, pray try not to break them of it on this voyage.

May the power of God Almighty guide you. All praise to the God Who Is Silent.

Raddem

P.S.: Mr. Kloe's comment about your "wasting the money of the Deloré's owners" reminds me—do please pass my regards to the staff of the "Shocktele Shipyards". Kindly forward to Vinasa and Lannae an open invitation to stay with me, should they visit the Temple in your absence.

Ammanon Deloré

Shipsmaster's Deck Log

Date *7H / 3R / Platius*

Page **8**

Arrivals	Departures	Gear	Time
		. . .	
——	I. Doel	——	3QL
O. Degg	——	1 medium duffle, standard gear	3QL
A. Degg	——	——	3QL
I. Doel	——	1 bottle possible contraband (confiscated) 1 bottle Ldr. Acid. 1 small duffle, std gear	3QL
Capt. Dollapan	——	——	4QL
A. Islak	——	1 leather pouch/valise, 1 wooden box; inspection waived (Capt's prerogative)	4QL
		. . .	

62

Private Journal of Igren Doel

The dust of Barnable is finally shaken from my feet. I write this crammed into a bunk, below decks of a creaking brig, poised to set sail. Seaman 3rd Class Igren Doel, awaiting his shift topside. The air is foul, the bunk hideously uncomfortable, the character of my crewmates as yet unproven. In short, all is right with the world.

Islak is not currently aboard, being about business with the Captain. But upon his return I will fulfill my pledge of a pint of Pinoae. (And if any gangly Shipsmaster thinks he can relieve me of that duty, he is but half right.)

The last question I must ask myself is whether to tell Anned of the other flask I have brought to share with him. Would he greet my offer with morbid good cheer? Or would I best keep it hidden away, and produce it only if the need should arise? Perhaps I must wait till he reboards, and sense his mood at that time. But the moment is too rich with substance to be pondering such things. I go topside, to take in the sea air.

Log of the Ammanon Deloré

Captain Dollapan recording.

Have advised the Shipsmaster to alert the crew: In deference to the request of Justice Raddem, the Ammanon Deloré shall delay her departure until the rising of Andilla Prime. It is the Captain's recommendation, and request, that all officers and crewmen devote whatever extra time this affords to the pursuit of prayer. May we seek the blessing of the God Who Is Silent upon our travels. Entry ends.

Private Journal of Igren Doel

Stumbled upon Anned returning to the ship, and invited him below decks. The galley being empty, we chose that place to share a discreet toast to the grand adventure ahead. He confirmed certain details of my suspicions about the nature of our voyage, but on other details maintained his silence. Prudent, I suppose. Best not to speak too much truth, to a man imbibing of aged Pinoae, and planning to share bunks with the main body of the crew. It is clear they do not know Islak's true intent. But I construe from his hints that the Captain is advised.

After drawing perhaps one draught too many from our dwindling bottle, I thought the moment light enough to broach a touchier subject, and advised him of the other bottle I have procured, offering to share it with him should the need arise. He took the offer, at first, with the best of cheer, and shared more of the Pinoae. But I detected in him then a sense that he thought my offer to be purely jest. It was then I stepped perhaps beyond the bounds of prudence, drawing out the bottle, and setting it on the table between us.

The change in mood of the moment was, to understate the matter, noticeable. In his eye I caught glimpses of emotion ranging from shock to sorrow to resignation, all in the span of what seemed a single breath.

I was about to speak, to beg pardon for my callous and cavalier attitude, when he silenced me. He stood, thanked me – rather sincerely, it seemed to me – and was off. I will speak to him, and try to mend whatever damage I may have done—but after my head has cleared. Just as well the Shipsmaster found my other bottle of Pinoae.

Personal Log, Abbik Dollapan
Have just concluded a most extraordinary, and unofficial, conversation with Mr. Anned Islak.

He came to my quarters burdened with several books, and his ever-present valise containing charts of land, sea and sky. He then proceeded to recount a most extraordinary conversation with a friend of his, who is evidently one of my new crewmembers.

The point of this discussion was that his friend, though ardently a follower of Islak's work, and vowed to be true to our charter, nonetheless felt it likely that the endeavor should come to evil end. So likely, indeed, that he had brought with him sufficient poison to dispatch himself, Islak (if Islak so wished) and perhaps a half dozen other men, rather than endure the fate of the crew of the Innotek Assan.

The crux of Islak's concern is that if a man, so squarely in his corner as he believes this "Ig" to be, thinks so poorly of our chances, then what will be the mind of our crew, once the true nature of our charter is revealed?

I pointed out there was scant chance of mutiny, as we planned to offer to put off as many men as would have no part of us, as near to Desidomone as Halabae Island. Islak's point, however, was that having a remaining crew of men absolutely true and committed to our course would be of little value, if their number included but Islak, myself, and his friend Ig.

Fearing (or dare I admit it, perhaps hoping) that Islak was suggesting we were at an impasse which would threaten the advent of our departure, I raised my hands in silent frustration. But he launched in then with a renewed enthusiasm, saying:

"Your plan was to set forth, then moor offshore. And there to tell the men the truth which, for now, we whisper only in shadows. So then, this: Launch early, before the rising of Andilla Prime."

I inquired of him: "For what reason would I disregard the request of Judge Raddem, made personally of me?"

And Islak's response: "Consider this. The truth revealed to the men, they are in equal parts dismayed and fearful. They are at what, we believe, will be the emotional low point of our entire trip. That is when I approach them, and make them an offer. A test. To prove the validity of my ways, and the certainty of my predictions, I tell them precisely when Andilla will arise. And Andilla complies, like a dutiful servant. This, dear Captain, I submit to you, the only chance I see to turn them back to our cause."

I inquired as to what degree of certainty he had, that he could accomplish such a feat. He asserted fullest confidence. I, with fair tact, inquired if his certainty was in his knowledge of the heavens, or in some cleverness of presentation. For if such demonstration were based in any part upon deceit, the prospect of discovery would be ruinous. Perhaps the tact with which I phrased my questions was overrated by myself, for I detected a certain measure of hurt in Islak's reaction. The sense of injury fled him as quickly as it came, however, and he said:

"Very well then. I shall perform a similar deed for you, yet this very watch. See if you detect some measure of subterfuge." At once

65

he was immersed in his books, searching for some tidbit—though I could scarcely guess what. I continued about my business for some time when, at length, he exclaimed triumph.

"The time, dear Captain. Pray, inquire of the Officer of the Deck, as to whether he can read the TimeCount upon the collar of Desidomone's lighthouse."

Summoning the Officer via the speaking tube, I asked the TimeCount. As some fair time passed before an answer, I assume the position of our ship was not ideal— that the masts and rigging posed some difficulty. But in time the reply came: Four red, three yellow. Thirty rounds into the fourth watch, I reported to Islak. He flipped hastily through his pages, and in less than a round declared that he had his test. By his request, we now debark from the ship with haste, to make our way to the lighthouse. Entry ends.

Supplementary: Islak has returned from the harbor lighthouse with me. Have advised the Shipsmaster—we depart at Honset, ahead of the rising of Andilla Prime, first jewel of the Crown of God. May the God Who Is Silent then be upon Anned Islak, as he has been upon him this hour.

Activity Log, Lighthouse Master, Harbor of Desidomone

Was honored by a visit from the revered Anned Islak, in the company of a ship's captain, Dollapan by name. They seemed in some fair rush to reach the lightroom, and then hurriedly assembled a mechanism from a case Mr. Islak brought with him. As Mr. Islak was unwilling to describe the nature of his gear, I think it best to record herein what description I can.

It was a wooden tube, or rather two wooden tubes which, attached at their ends, formed a single length, all in all about an arm's length.

From each end, a pair of wooden legs unfolded, to but a handbreadth of length. This whole assembly he placed upon the ledge running the perimeter of the lightroom, taking care to find a place with unobstructed view of the sea to the east.

To this tube, at a place outfitted with an attaching mechanism, he

66

affixed a compass. After some fastidious adjustments while looking through the tube, interspersed with references back to entries in a book he carried with him (a book whose contents he seemed eager for me *not* to view) he hurriedly implored the Captain to look through the tube as well.

Curiously, when Captain Dollapan asserted he saw nothing, Mr. Islak seemed pleased and became much more relaxed in manner. I should think that after such rush and fury to set up his device, a lack of result would be greeted with distress. Yet both men seemed pleased that their efforts had come to naught. Mr. Islak then asked for the precise reading of the time, which I gave him even as I adjusted the display of the lights: Four red and four yellow.

At this point some extended and rather idle chatter became our staple, and I must confess to some share of discomfort on my part, owing to a sense that some matter of import was afoot, to which I was wholly oblivious.

I complimented Mr. Islak upon his development of the Water Clock in the courtyard below, allowing the implementation of the time system he himself had just called upon me to read. His response was both gracious and humble. There then ensued the first of several long and awkward silences, punctuated only by Mr. Islak's occasional return to his mechanism to look through its length. Between these times, when the tube stood alone, I perceived what seemed to be a piece of deformed glass or polished metal in the end nearest the viewer.

We continued in this manner through the posting of R4-Y5 and R4-Y6. As I posted the change of Y7, however, Mr. Islak seemed to grow nervous, and his returns to his tube grew more frequent. And, curiously, the Captain seemed to change in demeanor as well–likewise moving about more. But his attention seemed as drawn to the harbor below (and, I suspect, to his ship) in the same measure that Mr. Islak's was drawn to his tube.

I was in the process of posting eight yellow, when Mr. Islak began to laugh. Both the Captain and myself froze, looking to him. Then he motioned to the Captain, who came and looked through the tube. I perceived some utterance from the Captain, though I could not make it out. The two men stood looking at each other for a time, not speaking, not moving. Then, as if breaking a spell, Mr. Islak laughed again, and began disassembling his toy. Without further word, without so much as a fare-thee-well, they descended and were gone.

After their departure I spent some fair time scanning the sky in the direction their tube had faced. They had been pointing it east, somewhat north of where the First Jewel is due to rise some none too far afuture. I scanned this area, and the horizon north and south of it, even as far as that pending bellwether. Before the God Who Is Silent, and standing within the Temple Court, I declare: There was nothing there.

Log of the Ammanon Deloré
Captain Dollapan recording.

Upon pronouncement from the Officer of the Deck of the commencement of Honset, gave order to light the forward fires, and leave the dock. The charter commencing 7H/3R/Platius is now underway.

Instructed the helm to make way for Halabae Island, but not to pass that point.

Have ordered the crow's nest cleared, for now. Accordingly, have directed that the masts be rigged, at but half sail. Directed the Officer of the Deck to advise the crew we shall assume full haste, after passing Halabae. Entry ends.

Delivered to the Connovan Street dock, after the departure of the Ammanon Deloré. Returned unopened.

Dearest Abbik:

Pray forgive a distraught wife, driven senseless over fear of losing her beloved. Dear Abbik, destroy the letter preceding this one. Think not of it, mention it not. Or, if you will, post it in the Desidomone Center Square, for all to see that I may be scorned and shamed, if you will do but one thing in exchange: Return to my arms, alive, and as whole as the God Who Is Silent permits.

Lannae and I await your return, never more than a thousand beats from the docks of Desidomone.

Forever,

Your loving Vinasa

Book I
Chapter 5: Upon the Winds

Log of the Ammanon Deloré
Captain Dollapan recording.

The Officer of the Deck reports Halabae Island off the port bow.

The order has been given to drop sail, and set anchor. All officers and crew have been called to the deck. This logbook is hereby handed over to Seaman Andril Degg for precise transcription of this Captain's address to his men.

Seaman Third Class Andril Degg recording.
Following is the Captain's address to his men.

Honorable Officers and Crew of the Brigantine Ammanon Deloré, come forth and heed.

It is incumbent upon any ship's captain to be forthright regarding his ship's destination. Due to the most unusual conditions of our destination, and with the full knowledge of the entirety of the Temple Court, that time has not come until now.

Thus it is here, within easy distance of the Isle of Halabae, that I will declare to you the true destination of the Ammanon Deloré. Those wishing to rescind their pledge of service to this ship are free to do so without recrimination, and will be put off at the Halabae harbor cove by longboat. There, a seaworthy schott waits even now to return whoever will to Desidomone; that return will commence once the Ammanon Deloré has left the range of sight of this place, on her way to the glory that awaits her.

The Ammanon Deloré will indeed sail to the Northern DevilsJaws, but she will make no foray against the Boundary Waters there. Rather we will turn East, sailing till the open waters which lie beside the Jaws... good men, hear me out, hear me out... and from there we shall turn again... I say turn again, and with good provision... with good provision that all ships before us have lacked,

71

cross through and safely into the realm of waters marked by the DevilsEye.

At this point Captain Dollapan paused, and discussion continued among the men. The Captain resumed:
Good men. You know me. Many of you have sailed with me. You know I am a man neither of poor judgment nor callous disregard for those under my command. I do not set out upon this mission lightly. One amongst us, Mr. Anned Islak, is known to you all for his soundness of mind. The things he has shown us, the changes he has brought forth, have made better lives for us all. And though we do not all understand the workings of the inventions which have brought him fame, we all understand their effect. The soundness of his devices is beyond dispute. This is because he has insight. Insight into the nature of how God has created this world in which we live, for the time allotted us, until we are called forth to at last hear his voice. Mr. Islak is here, willingly putting his life in the same place as yours. He asks you to do what he himself is doing. Putting aside generations of fear, fear based partly on just cause, but partly on misunderstanding and superstition… superstition, I say… superstition flowing from the minds of men, and not from any passage quotable from The Book. As to the fears that come from superstition, the God Who Is Silent will be at our side to see us past them. As he saw our forefathers past the fears that kept them, generation upon generation, bound to the shores. As for the fears based on just cause, Mr. Islak has equipped us with the tools to protect us. I pray you; hear him now, before I close my remarks to you.

At this point the Captain relinquished the rail to a Mr. Anned Islak of Barnable, whose remarks were as follows:
Brave sailors, all. The intricacies of my reasoning, and the proofs of what I am about to say, are no doubt of little interest to many of you. Yet I say if any man among you wishes to explore them, I will for some fair time be available to explain them in detail. We have many waters to cross before reaching sight of the DevilsJaws. Yet at minimum, each of you should know this. I am

convinced, and confident enough to stake my life upon the conviction, of the following points.

First, the phenomenon, and I do say phenomenon, of the DevilsEye is not of magical or supernatural origin. It is a feature of our natural world, as much as Hon and Dessene in their path above us.

Numerous observations were offered by the crew at this point, but none distinct enough to be recorded here. Presently Mr. Islak continued:

The foremost difference being that neither Hon nor Dessene pose any danger, offer any effect, even, upon the lives of men. But the DevilsEye is not alone in posing danger. Fire, gentlemen. Such as the bonfire lit upon sandy shores by sailors encamped far from home. Fire can pose danger, if one draws too near it. And we are left with two choices. Maintain our distance and live in fear. Or, like the whitesmiths and blacksmiths tending their forges, fashion ourselves protection, protection enabling us to reach into the fire's very lair, with no damage, none I say, to our persons.

I have studied the smiths. I have studied the reports from the fated crew of the Innotek Assan... brave sailors, hear me... I have read the reports. And I have coupled them with observations of our natural world, using devices hitherto unavailable to men. I have seen things, and can demonstrate things, that those before us could not see. Could not hope to understand. But now we can see. Can understand. Can comprehend the reasons for what happened to the Innotek Assan. And we can avoid their fate.

Which brings me to my second point. Defenses. Rain gear, to be worn without a trace of cloud in the sky, to fend off not water, but heat, penetrating heat like a smith's oven. Heavy gloves and boots, so that not an inch of skin will be exposed. And special hoods, crafted by my own hands—to lend that same protection to our heads, while still allowing breath. And special woven gauze, to wrap our eyes. To reduce the light reaching us. Not to cut it off, so we stumble about in a self-imposed blindness, but to reduce the extra light to a normal range, that we might see without being blinded. Blinded as you know some smiths have been, from staring too intently into their forges. Blinded as were the men of the Innotek Assan. These dangers are real. Others are myths, born of tellings and retellings till the original truth is lost.

My last point. There is more lying ahead of us than the DevilsEye. Who among you does not know it? The Eye is a spectacular focus for fear. It draws men's attention, as the needle is drawn to the north end of the compass. And as our attention is fixed there, we ignore what else lies beyond. What mysteries? What wonders? Do you think there are but miles and miles of unending seas? If you believe that, I pity you. But you don't believe that. None of us knows what lies out there, in the realm of the DevilsEye. But I say to you, let us find it out.

Captain Dollapan resumed the rail. His address:
Decide then. Each man for himself. Let no man be pulled against his will, pressed either into service here, or into the longboat ashore. But let each man decide for himself. You are free to inquire of Mr. Islak as to the particulars of the evidences upon which he draws his conclusions. But let me leave you with one observation.

Look to the east. Who among you can see the First Jewel of the Crown? Yes, yes I know, Andilla Prime is not expected, by most of Desidomone's elders, the watchers of things, for yet some five or even six watches.

But it is the declaration of Mr. Anned Islak that the first Jewel will be visible from this ship's nest within....

Here the Captain seemed to draw some signal from Mr. Islak,
...within the passage of time, of forty... say fifty rounds. A Water Clock, modeled after the one in our lighthouse, is hereby started running, upon the rear deck of the Ammanon Deloré. The Officer of the Deck shall be there posted, to watch and ensure no man disturbs the progress of its markers. Each tenth round, marked by a yellow light, shall be called out so all aboard may hear. The crow's nest is hereby reopened, and will be manned. When the jewel is sighted, it will be declared.

74

Mr. Islak has agreed to this display, that you might test his understanding of the workings of the heavens. Before the fifth yellow marker is called, he is sure... that is, he and I are both sure, that you will have all the cause you need to trust his wisdom. Apart from the Officer of the Deck, and the man he appoints to the nest, all other officers and crew are at liberty to discuss these matters among themselves. That is all.

Presentations end.

Supplementary: Captain Dollapan recording.
I retire to my quarters. Entry Ends

Supplementary:
The Officer of the Deck declares the first yellow. Entry ends.

Supplementary:
The Officer of the Deck declares second yellow. Entry ends.

Supplementary:
The Officer of the Deck declares yellow three.
First officer Mennetek and five of the hands came to my quarters. They have pledged to continue on with our charter, regardless of the outcome of Islak's prediction. Good men, all. Entry ends.

Supplementary: Captain Dollapan recording.
The Officer of the Deck declared the fourth yellow marker, and his voice was but faded from our hearing when the call came from the crow's nest. For the span of fifty beats the nestman dithered, as waves on the horizon played havoc with his eyes. But time and the arc of the Crown of God through the heavens willed out. Andilla Prime, First Jewel of the Crown of God, arose ahead of the predictions of all the sayers of the coast, and almost at the command of the man named Anned Islak. The mood on the deck, now that the initial excitement has passed, has palpably changed. A short time yet, for the men to collect their wits. Then I shall call for decision. Entry ends.

Supplementary:
Three men have been set ashore by longboat. Two oarsmen accompanying them will return with the longboat presently. The voyage of the Ammanon Deloré is about, in the truest sense, to begin. Hon has disappeared below the horizon, but Dessene shines nearly from her apex.

Have learned that Seaman Degg, whom I pressed into service as scribe, has been in training for the priesthood. Have asked him to invoke the blessing of God for the ship and crew, just before we weigh anchor. Into the hands of the God Who Is Silent, and into the hands of an artful magician and orator, we commend our lives. Entry ends.

Private Journal of Igren Doel
Several of the crewmen of this brig Ammanon Deloré, having expressed interest in deeper knowledge of the theories, views and opinions of the scientist Anned Islak, Mr. Islak has deemed it worthwhile that some record be made of the matters discussed. As best I can make it out, then, this shall record my understanding of the views of friend Islak, as told to myself and to a handful of sailors likewise interested.

It is Islak's position that:

1. The DevilsEye is in fact a third moon, sister to Hon and Dessene.

2. It is in a "stationary hover" above the far side of Mirrus. This aspect of his theory seems to trouble Anned, though the balance of us do not seem able to divine why. He seems fixed on issues of "constant falling", and "arcing descent". For my part, the fact that the Crown of God, as well as Hon and Dessene themselves, remain above us puts this matter to rest. But the fact that the DevilsEye remains aloft despite being stationary is of definite vexation to him. He made some unconvincing forays into discussions of possible "bobbling" up and down between Mirrus and the Crown of God. In short, this seems a matter of more concern to Islak than to anyone else.

3. The DevilsEye, despite reports of its initial seeming "rise

76

from the depths of the sea", is nowhere near the water's surface. Islak's estimates put it at miles up, perhaps as much as a hundred miles. The reported "rising" is merely the same effect seen as a ship emerges across the horizon—her crow's nest lantern first, then later the forward lamps at her hull coming into view.

4.The size of the DevilsEye has been grossly exaggerated in the reports from Innotek Assan. Anned feels it likely much closer in size to Hon or Dessene, with its size exaggerated owing to its great brightness as well as to the fear it engenders among those who have seen it.

5.On this matter of brightness, he feels it is self-illuminating, likely due to an intense fire on its surface. Owing to this, he fears difficulty in accurately mapping features of its surface.

6.Its tendency to "chase" the observer (so terrifyingly reported by the Innotek Assan and the few others rumored to have seen it more briefly) is an illusion, demonstrable with any distant stationary object. I fear the explanation of this concept was lost on my fellow sailors, but I know it well from passing by the Eastern Highlands. Even the approach to Desidomone harbor affords demonstration, as the road turns parallel to the lighthouse.

7.The DevilsEye is the source of illumination of Hon and Dessene. The phases of the moons are precisely what some have thought—the illumination of the globes by a distant light. His telescopic studies of the moons reveal a pattern of detailed shadows. Shifting as the moons shift, these shadows confirm a light source on the exact opposite side of Mirrus.

This concludes the points of discussion.

We were also granted chance to inspect, and even try on, the head masks of which he is so obviously proud. (None of us felt the courage to tell him—in appearance they are hideous!) They contain a chambered mouthpiece to provide open access to air, though not in a straight line, such that no light might enter. The hood is white, to reflect light and keep cool. The mouthpiece, however, is black; Anned feared light reflecting off white surfaces in the chambers would find its way into the mouth and nose.

The tinted lenses I manufactured for him, as I suspected, will fit into his telescopic protractor, allowing distant viewing even under dazzling light.

All of this, I must confess, is most fascinating. I trust my fellow landward citizens would find it the same. The only tricky bit now will be surviving the voyage, so this report can find its way to them.

After the departure of the other men, Anned passed to me, with some discretion, a collection of papers, saying:

"Read these at a time when your solitude is assured. There are further precautions I have taken, based on what I found in these reports. Read them, and then tell me what measures you would have taken. I am eager to see if you can think of eventualities I have missed."

CORONER'S REPORT SUMMARY
Consolidating Conclusions of Autopsies of Captain, Officers and Crew of the Sailing Ship Innotek Assan
With the exceptions earlier noted, the following points are in aggregate true of those members of the Innotek Assan whose bodies were brought back, or who died after their return.

Primary Causes of Death
Divided as approximately two-thirds of victims due to infection of open sores resulting from unexplained blistering, and one-third of victims due to complications from extreme dehydration. As this latter third also experienced extensive blistering, it is the conjecture of this office, though unsubstantiated, that both fatal effects are tied to the cause, as yet undetermined, of said blistering. This blistering is generally clustered on the arms, legs, shoulders and faces of the victims. See additional skin notations under Attendant Conditions.

Attendant Conditions
Postmortem examinations of the retinas indicate heavy damage to the eyes, beyond levels heretofore observed in this office. The only previous case approaching this level of damage was a metal smith, examined three years previous, long blind, whose death was unrelated to that condition.

Additionally, it was noted that among those surviving the longest was evidenced the greatest amount of clouding of the cornea, a condition very rarely seen, and then only among those surviving to great age.

Furthermore, over most of the skin surface which was not taken up with blistering, there was noticed an unusual reddening, often accompanied with peeling of the outermost layer of skin, to a degree likely more irritating than dangerous.

Conclusions
These observations lead this office toward declaring death to be the direct result of prolonged exposure to intense heat. However, the testimony of the survivors as reported to this office indicates that although heat was experienced, it was far below any extraordinary level. This testimony is thus at odds with this office's conclusion.

It is with some reticence then, that this office offers a qualified verdict of death due to heat exposure, with a note that alternate explanations will be freely entertained, should any be forthcoming.

Book I, Chapter 5: Upon the Winds

Deck Log, Ammanon Deloré
Officer of the Deck Ilbe Rass recording.
Mr. Islak and Seaman Doel requested the main hatch be opened for their inspection. By leave of the Captain, I ordered the hatch opened, and I descended with them. Only two things seemed of interest to them. First, in ship's provisions, our fresh water stocks, along with the extra barrels the Purser requisitioned. Second was our "cargo", such as it was. Mr. Islak opened one of the crates, brushing aside the straw covering. Seaman Doel, upon peering down into it, did but laugh and turn about, exiting the hold without further comment.

As Mr. Islak redressed the straw, and affixed the lid again to the crate, I pointed out to him the copious water that was even now draining from the dozens of boxes. And I inquired of him, what merchant in this far-flung and unexplored expanse would be waiting for a shipment of ice? And if none awaited it here, what chance did he have of returning with it? It was clear that even packed with the additional bales of straw the Purser had ordered, the greater portion of it would be melted by the time we would return to Desidomone, even if we put back during the next few watches.

His only response was that by the time we saw home, the ice would have long since served its purpose.

Although I hardly took that as a meaningful answer, I perceived he wished discuss it no further. I did not press the issue upon him. Entry ends.

Log of the Ammanon Deloré
Captain Dollapan recording.
Continuing due North. Islak has taken to making occasional depth soundings. In an effort to be unobtrusive, he has been taking these readings while we are at full sail—tossing over a weight attached to a rope with periodic markings. By paying the rope out at a very measured speed, he could attain an optimization, as follows. He could sense the moment bottom was hit, because the rope was not played out too quickly, thus not allowed to go too slack.

81

Simultaneously, the weight was not too distantly astern when finding bottom, because the rope was not allowed to play out too slowly. The distance astern at impact was noted, in terms of the angle of the rope, and from this he was able to determine a fairly true measure of depth. All in all, a rather amazing and unnecessary bit of work. Upon discovering his elaborate procedures, and upon observing the number of deckhands who, uncalled by Islak, spontaneously volunteered their services to aid him, I have instructed the Officer of the Deck to periodically tack into the wind, stalling us briefly, that Islak might gain a truer measure. The cost to us in time is insignificant.

These readings seem of some fair importance to Islak, and he notes the results with scrupulous care in his books. As a matter of professional courtesy, I should inquire of him as to the nature of his books. Entry ends.

Anned Islak, DevilsEye Journal

Unease and dread. Have escaped, I fear by the narrowest of margins, an ill turn. My depth soundings awoke in Captain Dollapan a disquiet as to my purpose. This very watch he began prying into both the reasons for my depth soundings, and the contents of the books in which I record them. Foolish, not to have been more discreet. I am now honor-bound by my oath before the Temple Judges to keep from the Captain that which I had, from the outset, felt best to hold from him anyway. But has my carelessness undone both their wisdom and my own? Or has Dollapan deduced my discovery independently? As a seaman of some many years, no doubt familiar with the ocean floor, could he have developed the same suspicion on his own?

Even as I deflected his questions, and steered his attention away from my Master Chart, I was plagued to wonder: Despite the order of the Court, and my own initial instincts, is it right for me to conceal my findings? Abbik's very willingness to captain this charter suggests a mindset not unlike my own. It is clear he shares, in some measure at least, the conviction that everything about us is not random.

Foolishness. Even if we are of one mind, I dare not share my perceptions on this. How can I presume how he will react to it, when I myself have not settled on how to react? When the Temple Judges themselves are thrown into turmoil? Too great a burden. Too great a burden. It is one thing to hold that the God Who is Silent has designed and ordered all of Creation, that he has not turned us over to the whim of random forces, buffeting us in unknowable ways. But it is quite another matter to stare into the very pattern of Creation, as if staring into the very face of God. That is a prospect too frightening—as frightening as the hearing of his voice.

Personal Log, Abbik Dollapan

Have concluded yet another curious encounter with Islak. I am not pleased.

Upon the conclusion of a tour of the deck, I noted he had just completed a depth sounding and was retiring below decks. I inquired as to the purpose of his readings. And I do not think it unfair to say his reaction was such as I have seldom seen in any man who was short of facing peril over his life. All color seemed to drain from him, and he grew nervous to the point of occasional stuttering. And this from a persuasive orator such as Anned Islak!

Presently he seemed to regain himself, and ushered me down, fairly dragged me down, into the chamber we had set him to sharing with his friend Doel.

There he proceeded to scurry me through an explanation, the heart of which—as best I could make it out—was that he was putting finishing touches to a topography of the ocean floor. Evidently he has for some months been booking passage on all manner of ships, sailing a wide range of routes. On each such voyage, he has taken readings such as those he is taking here.

His manner had that peculiar mix of evasiveness and an over-willingness to offer information not called for, such as I have generally seen among those caught in some larceny they wish desperately to conceal. And, though he clumsily disguised it, he took pains to move his valise to an obscure corner of his chamber. This same valise, I perceive, he brought with him to the Temple Court—opening it not during our journey there nor back, and which I can only assume was central to his testimony. The same valise, I am convinced, which he took with us in our climb to the peak of the Desidomone Lighthouse—which he opened there neither, as well. A valise, I begin to sense, he carries with him always. Not that he should find some need of its contents, but that he finds some need of guarding its contents against the advent of prying eyes.

I am now left with a most vexing situation. Anned has, by his actions and words, clearly left me with the impression that the secrets he is keeping regarding this charter are not merely matters of privacy. They are, rather, matters of some fair urgency and even dread. Such secrecy would be tolerable if we were neighbors, confronting each other over a fence. It would be tolerable, barely, if we were still at dock with a shortmonth dividing us from our departure. But not at sea; and not on a voyage such as this. In an endeavor of this magnitude, I can allow no such secrets among my officers, crew, or even with a charter-paying passenger of such high repute as Anned Islak. Before the current watch is at end, I will end this secrecy. God willing, I will end it with tact and professionalism. But even failing that, end it I will.

Supplemental: The matter between Islak and myself has, I suppose, been resolved—though in a most improper and dissatisfying way.   Seeing Islak topside, and noting that Seaman Doel had just begun a shift, I enlisted Mr. Mennetek in a deception worthy of a harbor rat plotting to relieve a widow of her purse. I instructed him to watch Islak, and, upon the slightest suggestion he might return below decks, to engage him in some matter of contrived importance.

This was a duplicitous and cowardly business in which to find a ship's captain engaged, but I was struck by a sense that making a proper and public issue of the matter was ill advised. For part of me had a sense that Anned concealed his secret with good cause, and that it was not wise to reveal it to the crew, or even the officers.

For this cause I lowered myself to ransacking a man's private things.   And to so hollow an end, as well.   For he concealed no terrible secret, no clandestine information.

The charts onto which he was adding details of the contours of the ocean floor were just that. Indeed, they were likely of less value than a standard seaman's chart, cluttered as they were with detailed aspects of the ocean floor far beneath the hull of any ship, treating such irrelevant readings with the same attention of detail as those soundings nearer to a ship's draught.

And as for the valise, it contained but a single thing. It was a broad sheet of vellum, of the finest quality—more than translucent, almost transparent—onto which he had inked a detailed representation of the Crown of God. This was a work of fine craftsmanship, meticulous in its detail, doubtlessly of considerable worth. Yet surely of not much greater value than the precise instruments Islak has manifested no qualms over revealing to both myself and to the lowliest of the Deloré's deckhands.

Chagrined, I returned all to their former estate, and stole like a thief from Islak's chambers, the chastisement of my own conscience no less than any I would have received from Islak had I been caught.

Supplemental: What then *was* it that so haunted him? It was no mere imagining on my part.

Supplemental: Why has he brought his vellum of the Crown of God aboard ship? He has not once taken out his sky-gazing instruments; he thus seems to have no interest in amending the drawing.

Log of the Ammanon Deloré
Captain Dollapan recording.
Disturbance above decks.
Supplemental: May the God Who is Silent be with us now. All ship's hands are topside. Every man stands watch. We may lie at the threshold of a colossal portent.
Supplemental: Nothing. The men's spirits melt away, as does mine. Still, we watch.
Supplemental: Nothing. Have dropped sail, to wait. None among the men speak. We wait, and watch.
Supplemental: Nothing. The men continue to watch. As my spirit calms, I must compose myself to complete this ship's record.

The noise from above decks was the disturbance among the deckhands, as the news spread—the Officer of the Deck had sighted what was supposed to be NewStar.

By the time I achieved the deck, the omen was just past straight overhead, and at first I had trouble spying it amidst the masts, rigging, and sails. But spy it I did. A point of light, just fainter than Andilla Prime, moving far faster across the sky than either Hon or Dessene even at the time of Reversal, yet with a steadfastness that showed it not to be a meteor. All above decks watched the star track across the sky, disappearing into the horizon. Less than two hundred beats passed from my first spotting it near zenith till its disappearance.

Word spread at once to all corners of the ship, and I gave the order that all regular duties were suspended. Each man was under command to watch the sky, North, South, East and West, for the reappearance of the sign. And so each man did, and does even now. And with each passing beat we are dragged down into despair. Why does it not return? Never has any among us seen any sight in the heavens that so nearly matches the prophecies. How can it *not* be NewStar? But if it is, why does it not return? Entry Ends.

Book I
Chapter 6: Arrival

Klaxons. Nausea. Emergency condition. Boten needed to open his eyes. Seconds could matter; he might be about to skip off the atmosphere. Or crash into the Reception Gantry. He needed to open his eyes, but the nausea swelled at the thought. He lowered his head, facing his lap, and cracked open his eyes. His lap grew lighter and darker, lighter and darker.

"Mission Control... Sirocco. Spinning."

He waited a moment for a response, but there was none. Keeping his eyes down, he reached out for the thruster controls.

"Control, am applying thrust to break spin, over." He still could hear no response. He could hear nothing over the warning signals. He began switching off the audio alarms. The capsule grew quieter... quieter... quiet. The slow strobe effect continued. He partly raised his eyes, to get a partial view out the main window. The sun was streaking by. As he had thought: He was tumbling.

"Applying... thrust," he announced. It took a long time to stabilize the Sirocco. He was nauseous, and sleepy, and numb. But in time, the capsule obeyed him, slowing to a halt with the blue, curved horizon steady before him.

"Houston, Sirocco. Come on, boys. I'm in bad shape up here." With a response still not forthcoming, he checked the Comm system. It showed green. His Main Computer was still displaying the status on the launch. Main Effect Power was reading zero. It should have been around ten percent, but he preferred having it too low rather than too high. Departure Angular Deviation read 26.91 degrees, in red. Reception Angular Deviation was blank. Mission Status reading had gone as far as *Departure*, and then had frozen before it had a chance to shift to *Reception*. Reflexively, he reached out and tapped the screen, as if he would somehow dislodge whatever had locked up the system.

"Marky, Marky, Marky," he said. "No more field testing of code for you." Curiously, the Mission Status clock had not locked up. T plus ten minutes, fifty-some seconds. That made no sense to him, but precious little did just then.

"Houston, do you read?"

Then sun broke across the horizon, startling him. Had he dozed off? He flipped down his sun visor.

"Hermes Launch, Hermes Reception. Anybody."

While listening to the static, he did a radar check and confirmed his orbit was stable, and high enough to be clear of any immediate atmospheric drag. His mind was clearing, and he thought about that orbit. He remembered correcting, using the thrusters. But that was just angular correction. He didn't do any orbital adjustment. How did he wind up in a stable orbit? He should have emerged heading straight away from Earth. He checked radar again, to see how elliptical his orbit was, what angle he had emerged at. The word *angle* caught in his mind. He looked back to MainCom. 26.91 degrees, Departure Angular Deviation.

"Point seven one degrees," he could remember Baker saying in the Mission Training sessions. The golden measure. Just over seven tenths of a degree. Within that range, the Reception Tower's field, its Tube, could draw you in. Like Robin Hood's arrow, cheated into the bull's-eye by a magnet. An eleven thousand g.e.k. "magnet".

He reached up to the MainCom screen and hit it again, at the 26.91 degree reading, not so much absent-mindedly this time. The sun had risen to beyond the window's range, and he flipped up his sun visor.

"Houston," he said angrily. He was tapping, almost hitting the display. *Mission Status: Departure.* He formed his hand into a fist, and held it over the screen.

Come on, Alex boy, he thought. *That's not going to help.* He looked up, out the main window, to the ocean steadily appearing and sliding beneath him. The horizon began to glow.

"How fast am I orbiting?" he asked aloud. The glow spread across the horizon, and extended beyond it. It rose higher and higher above the horizon, and began taking a form. He couldn't comprehend it, the size, the shape. And the familiarity of it. He knew what he was seeing. But it was as if his brain refused to connect the image from his eyes to the image he had learned. His heart rate shot up, and his breathing stopped. His brain began to allow the images to associate. He vomited into his helmet, mercifully blocking his view. And as he passed into unconsciousness, he knew what he was seeing. A galaxy, viewed from thousands of light years above the galactic center. And if he were lucky, if the galaxy were the Milky Way, then that was how far he was from home.

Personal Log, Abbik Dollapan
Summoned to my quarters both Anned Islak and the Sailor Andril Degg.

My first question of them, aimed mainly at Islak, was whether the light we saw moving through the sky truly warrants the attention we are giving it. Is it truly so unique as to possibly be NewStar? His answers:

~ He (Islak) has witnessed numerous meteors in his years watching the sky.

~ These meteors have been of great variance in terms of brightness, color, and duration of path.

~ Despite this, none that he has ever seen has ever approached what we saw, in terms of its slowness, and its duration.

In conclusion, Islak is confident in declaring that what we saw is different in nature from any other phenomenon he has ever observed. But as to whether it might be NewStar, he deferred to Sailor Degg. My inquiries of Degg were prefaced by the following observations, which he implored me to include in whatever written record I was making. Degg's declarations:

~ He (Degg) is neither a scholar nor a priest, but merely a young man reared upon farming life, having from time to time availed himself of the teaching of priests and scholars, toward the end that he might one day become a priest himself.

~ His knowledge of The Book, though exceeding the grasp of many a layman, is neither exhaustive nor infallible.

~ His understanding of interpretations of the Mysteries and Conflicts is minimal.

These provisions having been stated, and with the ship's copy of The Book at his disposal, I proceeded with my questions. These resulted in the following observations by Degg, sadly none of which sheds great light on the matter before us:

~ To be declared NewStar, this phenomenon must *repeatedly* cross the sky. Although the expectation of the men is that such crossings would be immediately consecutive, no declaration in The Book mandates this. It thus remains possible that the phenomenon may yet recur.

~ If this phenomenon is to be declared to be NewStar, it must first resolve one of the lesser Conflicts: Although it is written that NewStar will be "steady of light", in the passages about Harbinger it is written that NewStar will be flashing.

But impossible will such resolution be, if the light we saw does not first return to our skies. Entry Ends.

Log of the Ammanon Deloré
Captain Dollapan recording.

Great disturbance on deck. May God be with us.

Supplemental: All praise to God, maker of sky, sea and land. The Ammanon Deloré is blessed to pass directly beneath NewStar. Though Andril Degg would have me wait till the Conflict concerning its constancy is resolved, I am as one with the rest of the crew in celebrating the certainty of it. Now going topside to discuss with Mr. Mennetek (and with Islak) the impact this will have upon our plans.

Supplemental: The Ammanon Deloré is now at full sail. Mennetek is instructing the Officer of the Deck to set up a rotating schedule of three men: one aft, one stern, and one extra man in the crow's nest, to watch for and announce each coming rising of NewStar.

Dearest Aunt Drumae:

I write this letter to you knowing there is scant chance my words will be eventually delivered, and that if they are, the news I now write will, by virtue of our having survived to some known port, be made dated and obsolete. Nonetheless, our extraordinary circumstance and my concern for your son compel me to write, if only to promote the clarity of my own thought.

We have been blessed to see what I trust you have noted in the skies of home as well—a moving star that most among us dare to call NewStar. A great stir of excitement among the men has been aroused at the prospect of a prophecy being fulfilled, and of a Conflict about to be resolved. The excitement is shared by all on board with few exceptions. But notable among these exceptions is Andril. I find this to be a puzzlement, thinking as I did that one such as he, keen of interest in The Book and all the teachings of Mysteries and Conflicts, should be delighted at this prospect. For a time, I thought the matter could be this: If NewStar has in fact appeared, then Restoration must have already revealed himself at the Temple. I thought perhaps his distress was over missing the appearing of Restoration. But I have come to understand that this is not so.

Inquiring of him, I sought to raise his spirits, or failing that, to understand the cause of his dour disposition. What I sensed from him is this:

It is not Restoration that he dreads, nor the coming of NewStar itself, but rather that which NewStar proclaims—the presence amongst us of Harbinger. Harbinger, dear Aunt Drumae, is what I perceive that he fears. Pressing him upon this point, I sensed a darkening of his mood, and I let the issue pass, unresolved.

I will continue to watch him, and to watch out for him, and to seek a moment of better cheer when I might inquire further of him.

The presence in the Temple of Restoration has been yearned for generation upon generation. And once he has appeared, he cannot restore that which was taken from us until Harbinger has come. So

why this anxious dread? Why would one like Andril, so knowledgeable in the writings of The Book, fear the coming of the man with five fingers, the Harbinger of God?
 With all my love,
 Opper

* * *

 Klaxons again. And stench. Alex realized he had vomited into his helmet. Keeping his eyes shut, and his breathing shallow, he reached beside his chair and grabbed the bulky Blo-Vac line. Raising up the triple-bundle line, he plugged its unwieldy head into the receptacle on the side of his helmet. It took him a moment to find the on-off toggle switch. When he activated it, a gentle suction began and grew. Then clean air was pumped in, normalizing pressure. The vacuum and the incoming air both grew in strength, and the vomit clinging to his head and helmet began swirling about.
 "Hold your breath," said the calm digital voice, and he did so. An atomized spray of water began shooting at him, fluctuating around, seeming like a fireman's hose flopping out of control. Abruptly the water spray stopped. The vacuum pressure jumped up, along with the flow of incoming air. "Resume breathing." Which he did. Vacuum and air tapered off, then stopped.
 He looked across his control panel, as best he could through the streaked muck remaining on his visor. He did not look up to the window. He had not deactivated the alarms before, just silenced the klaxons. They had resumed ringing after five minutes. Silencing them again, he began actually deactivating the alarms, one by one.
 The stench of vomit was still strong. Unbuckling himself, he floated up slightly, and then twisted around so his head was at the Cleansing Station. Pulling a plastic bag from the dispenser, he flipped it open with a flick of his wrist. He released it to float beside him. He released the locks on his helmet, and removed it. He drew a breath of clean air—the last he would have for a long time, he knew. Despite the capsule's air scrubbers, the smell of vomit that he had just released would linger, until... until when? Until the cleaning crews

gave the capsule a scrub-down? He began to feel dizzy, and returned his thoughts to the task at hand. Awkwardly, he fought the helmet into the bag, then knotted it and let it drift away. He ripped open a towel pack—an oversized version of a pre-moistened towelette, about a foot square. He wiped his face, then his hair, then the helmet collar of his pressure suit. Crumpling it, he set it on the disposal deck before him. Then, before it could drift off, he hit the contact switch beside the deck. The little doors dropped down, there was a quick blast of suction, and it was gone. The doors snapped up again.

Snaking back into his seat, he grabbed the floating helmet bag, and stuffed it into the helmet chamber on the capsule floor beside him. He removed his gloves, and let them drift. He activated the radio, and switched to broad band transmission.

"Mayday," he said firmly. After a few seconds, he repeated the word in a more matter-of-fact tone.

Who's gonna be listening? he asked himself. *In thousands of years, Earth will receive it*, he thought. *A billion times weaker than anything they'll be able to detect, even by then.*

"Assessment time," he said aloud. "Breathable air: Scrub-able, as long as filters and electrical power hold out." He would check the batteries later; the thought of checking them now brought up a feeling of desperation from his deepest self. How could the batteries last long enough? What could possibly be *long enough*?

"Potable water: Scrub-able. As long as filters… and power… hold out." A recurring theme was beginning to occur to him. He looked down to the ocean below him. He was still in daylight, though the sun was over or behind him, so it did not shine in his eyes. It only illuminated the immense sea. It was very blue. He skipped over the virtual impossibility of a successful re-entry. Even if he pulled it off, what were the chances that there was a breathable atmosphere down there?

What are the chances? he thought. *The chances.* His mind raced over aspects of incalculability. He ticked them off, verbally.

"What are the chances, in *galactic* space, of plopping down even within temperate range of a star?" He didn't bother with the absurd task of running an estimate. "How about," he said, remembering the galactic disk that had risen before him, that would rise again soon, "how about the chances in *inter*galactic space?" For that was what he was on the fringes of. Here, far removed from the neighborhood of stars, the paucity of stellar objects made the emptiness of the galactic plane seem positively crowded.

"Allowing for astronomical positivism," he spoke again, "saying that planets around stars are as common as... as common as... whatever, what are the odds of falling into a stable, symmetric, near-Earth...." Here his voice trailed off. "Or near-Whatever orbit?"

He paused, to allow his propositions to settle in with himself.

"No. Something's going on here. Something's going on." He thought back, to Mission Theory classes. The golden measure. *Within that range,* Baker had said, *the Reception Tower can draw you in. The eleven thousand g.e.k. magnet.* Could 26.91 degrees have aimed him in the general direction of something powerful enough to draw him in?

"Anybody," he said into the broadband. "Is anybody reading me?"

The galactic spiral began to rise again. Boten fell silent before it. This time his reaction was more of awe than of horror. It was beautiful. Something no man had ever seen.

He leaned forward, to keep its scope in view.

"Dear God," he said, "this is not where I want to be. Let it be a dream. And let me wake up now." He had, a very few times in his life, had nightmares he was able to recognize as nightmares while he was still in them. On those rare occasions, he had roused himself from sleep, or even willfully changed the course of the dream. He concentrated on the textures inside his pressure suit, on the lingering but pungent smell of vomit. Too real, he thought. No dream.

"This is not where I want to be," he repeated. "What a waste," he argued. "What a waste of a life. Dear God, don't let it be." But, sensing that no miraculous change of fortune was about to befall him, he shifted his thoughts. "At least, don't let me be alone out here." After a few moments he added: "A verbal response would be nice." The galactic swirl crept out of sight, and he looked back to the horizon. He was edging into night. "Failing that, some unspoken assurance, that you're here, would suffice." A large continental mass was beneath him now, visible either in the galactic glow, or perhaps in the light of some moon out of his range of sight at the moment. There were no massive blobs of electric light, defining advanced cities. If anyone were down there, they were not technological. No experiment, running parallel to Hermes, had brought him here.

Throughout his life, Boten had not always had the sense that God was listening. Just now, he did. Which was a good thing. Because if he hadn't, he might—just might—have blown the emergency bolts on the main hatch and assumed his own private orbit alongside the Sirocco.

Over the next few hours, a certain clarity of purpose fell over him.

First he switched on the automated distress beacon, across the same range of frequencies on which he had spoken when he first arrived. Having set it, he did his best to not think of it. Even so, from time to time the desperation he denied and stuffed down inside himself would spring suddenly to the surface. *Was the beacon on?* His hand would jump to the Com Panel, hovering over the button as he realized that, yes, it was still on. But between such moments of madness, in which he felt as though he were waking from a recurring dream, he fell into a methodical professionalism—gathering all the data he could about the planet below, and the celestial bodies nearby.

The planet had two small moons, in orbits as close to identical as he could determine, circling with a period of roughly fifteen Earth days, give or take a day. The planet was eighty-five percent covered with water, with nearly all the balance divided into two land masses on opposite sides of the globe. Here he observed a most interesting fact. As was true of Earth's moon's travels about Earth, the planet revolved about its sun with a period equal to its rotation. The effect on the planet was that it always maintained the same face toward its sun. The one land mass was always, therefore, in daylight; the other, always in night.

The planet's mass, as calculated by the diameter and period of

Sirocco's orbit, appeared to be eighty to ninety percent of Earth's. The atmosphere was mostly clear, extending to an elevation comparable to the air on Earth, and was punctuated by clouds that were almost exclusively on the sunlit side. At certain points in his orbit, the orange moon revealed, by reflection, a huge lake or inland sea—covering thousands of square miles—in the center of the dark continent.

All these things he deduced in his first ten to twelve hours of orbiting. Sirocco, unfortunately, was hardly an exploratory vehicle. What sensing and measuring instruments she had were geared to help her crew through in a pinch, when information from the ground was temporarily suspended.

Once he had surmised all that he felt he could, and had given another look to confirm the distress signal was still functioning, he set himself to the ugly task he knew he could put off no longer: Assessment of ship's status. Ploddingly he made his way through the system checks, which began converging toward a common conclusion. Although drastic measures could be taken to change the results in minor ways, he had seven to ten days. Seven to ten days to return to Earth, or to descend to the planet's surface, or to die in orbit.

He was surprised to realize what little appeal dying held for him. Intellectually he knew that being permanently cut off from his wife, his daughters, his sister, his home, his life—everything he had ever known—was absolutely devastating. Perfect fodder for a debilitating depression that could easily lead to suicide. But for reasons he did not understand, and that he was happy to not yet explore, he felt none of that. Or, more precisely, when he did begin feeling it, he managed to quickly push it down.

From time to time a nascent claustrophobia would suggest itself. This was something new to him, something never hinted at in his psych tests. He would deny these feelings as well, losing them in sudden flurries of activity. He had to lose them; there was no other option. There was no big, safe, inviting place to run to. Perhaps that was the difference; before, no matter how cramped the conditions, there was always the assurance that he would, ultimately, emerge. That assurance was now gone. This, he thought as he looked around the tiny cabin, could be the rest of his life. Allowing a full-fledged claustrophobia attack, like a fully realized recognition of the separation now upon him, was to invite death. A particularly nasty and pitiful death. Not the kind of death he wanted.

I hope he died well. He could just imagine Bob Jiggs saying it.

"Thanks for the thought, Jiggsy," Boten said aloud. "But I'm not dead just yet."

The mayday beacon was still transmitting. Incoming com lines were very low-level static. The System Distortion meter read zero; nothing else was coming from Earth. If they had any way of duplicating his path, they would have sent something by now. But there had appeared no transponder, no emergency pods with air, water, or (most significantly) power. Power was his shortest commodity. With more power he could keep recycling his environment—at least until the filters began to fail, and he was slowly poisoned. If Sirocco had solar panels, he could draw power from this planet's sun. Until, he remembered, he was slowly poisoned to death. Sirocco was never designed for long-term flight. And that was a mercy. Whatever was going to happen would happen soon.

He would sleep, for now, if he could. And immediately upon waking, he would begin the calculations. With so many factors unknown, the odds of him being able to accurately calculate a safe entry angle for the escape pod were... well, incalculable. But, as he reminded himself while closing his eyes and drifting with strange ease into sleep, the odds of his even being here were far more incalculable than that.

For six and a half hours he slept, and dreamt vividly. But he would never remember any of the dreams.

Log of the Ammanon Deloré
Captain Dollapan recording.

The Ammanon Deloré continues Northward. Slack winds have slowed our pace, but we continue onward.

Seventeen times has NewStar crossed above us, and the men grow tense. By declaration of Holy Scripture, NewStar must fulfill itself before twenty passes are completed. Only three arcs remain. If this is NewStar, as to a man all aboard proclaim, then the chance for resolution of one of the Conflicts is frittering away.

Counteracting the apprehension of the men is the profound advancement of the Crown of God. Only the few having ever traveled this far north (or south) are personally acquainted with the phenomenon: The Crown of God rises faster for those farther to the north. There does, of course, arrive a point in the Crown's arc, where being far to the north stops it from advancing any further. No one this far north has ever had the Crown directly overhead. But for now, we are enjoying a greater view of its glory than those at home. From this, I perceive, the men draw some comfort.

Islak continues his depth soundings, though without need of our adjusting course to accommodate him, owing to our slackened pace. Entry Ends.

Anned Islak, DevilsEye Journal

Just concluded the strangest interview with the Sailor Degg, of whom Captain Dollapan has been inquiring on matters of scriptures. His manner was distressed, but he was unwilling to explain why. Our conversation was so circular in nature, I find I cannot accurately recount it here. What I could come away with were general impressions.

His disquiet, beyond doubt, is over the apparition of NewStar. I misspeak. It is not NewStar itself which disturbs him, but the progression that will unfold: Restoration appearing in the Temple, NewStar proclaiming the arrival of the Harbinger of God, Restoration bringing back to us the voice of the God Who Is Silent. Which step in this process causes him such turmoil? In writing the progression, I have I written the answer itself. Andril Degg, in facing the fulfillment at long last of ancient prophecies, is being struck by a similar dread as that which faces me. Is the peculiarity of his behavior so hard to understand for me, a man who hides his own dreadful discovery from all but the Temple Judges themselves? Had these thoughts occurred to me while Andril was still in my quarters, I might have raised them. It is as well that he left before that could happen.

It was clear that Andril had some matter to discuss with Captain Dollapan. Clear it was also, that he would have preferred to avoid it. It seemed he would rather I afforded him some reason to discredit this phenomenon as being NewStar altogether. I was unable to oblige him. For not only can I see no reason why it should not be NewStar, indeed I sense it must be NewStar. I was a fool not to see it earlier. The whole point of this mission speaks to it. With what will soon come upon us, we must be restored. Restoration must come, and soon. NewStar must appear, and soon. What folly for me to have been surprised, then, at its appearing.

Andril has left me now, though whether to meet with the Captain or to pace the deck struggling for cause *not* to meet with the Captain, I cannot say.

Personal Log, Abbik Dollapan

Have been advised by Seaman Degg that the men should not hang too great an import upon the crossing deadline. He reports there is a divide among the scholars and priests—some holding that ten *plus* ten is the limit for fulfillment, and others holding that ten *times* ten is a more proper reading.

Having now examined the text, I am of two minds as to which sense, twenty or one hundred, is the truer. Will seek the counsel of Mennetek as to whether to spread this word.

Have noticed a change in manner in young Andril. At first I sensed it as a lightening of mood, a cheering. But by the time of his departure, I sensed it might equally well be explained as a sense of resignation; the sense of false peace overcoming a man who has given himself up to his fate. I understand he was inducted aboard by his cousin, with whom he shares a bunk. Will attempt to inquire of this man, Opper Degg, as discretion allows.

Log of the Ammanon Deloré

Captain Dollapan recording.

Twentieth crossing of NewStar has come, and passed. The men are dispirited, but not to the point of despair. Most have taken to heart the observation of Andril Degg of the alternate "one hundred" interpretation.

Wind has picked up, and is now almost squarely astern. Have resumed occasional stalls, to accommodate Mr. Islak. Entry Ends

Log of the Ammanon Deloré
Captain Dollapan recording.
Fiftieth crossing of NewStar has passed. A defining moment for the men, perhaps. For some time now it has been clear that we are no longer directly under the path of NewStar, which is markedly to the South. There is a growing sentiment—reserved, respectful, quiet—that we should hold here and await the one-hundredth pass before proceeding. Word of this reaches me through the most discreet of channels, and I have no fear of rebellion among the men. Still, this is a mood I would not see grow. Entry Ends.

Log of the Ammanon Deloré
Captain Dollapan recording.
Sky ahead has developed a marked red glow. The DevilsJaws are approaching. Have ordered no change in course or speed. Entry Ends.

Personal Log, Abbik Dollapan
Have been given a grim observation by Seaman Degg. Citing several cases of fulfilled prophecies in the past, he thinks it likely that the fulfillment of NewStar will not happen anytime between pass one and pass ninety-nine, but on the one-hundredth pass itself. Although the wording is simply that the designated count will not be exceeded until fulfillment occurs, Andril cited several examples where, in similar prophecies, the specified limit was attained nearly to the point of falsification, before the prophecy was completed.

If that is to be the case here, if no fulfilling event occurs until NewStar approaches the set of its one-hundredth pass, I can expect great consternation from the crew as that one-hundredth approaches.

Perhaps near panic, as the one-hundredth pass has dawned; worse, as it draws near its end.

Andril Degg was accompanied in this visit by his cousin, whom I requested linger with me once Andril left. We were of one mind in our concern over young Andril's mood, yet neither of us had insight into its cause.

Opper Degg offered me one other observation, and it was one I had partly expected. As the arc of NewStar pulls further and further to our south, and as the glow on the horizon approaches, the grumbling among some of the men is that we follow the DevilsJaws, and beyond them, the DevilsEye, rather than following the prophecy of God—the New Star. As I project it, we will have been sailing along the DevilsJaws for nearly half a quarter before the hundredth crossing occurs. We may have even emptied into the passage that leads to DevilsEye. We will be approaching the greatest unknown these men have ever faced, just at the moment they think the prophetic promise is being pulled out from beneath them.

Will discuss this, unofficially, with my officers.

Log of the Ammanon Deloré
Captain Dollapan recording.

DevilsJaws sighted. Turning east to run nearly parallel—allowing a slight closing.

During the turning, the seventieth crossing of NewStar began. Entry Ends.

Personal Log, Abbik Dollapan
As we draw slowly in toward the DevilsJaws, I am struck by their terrible appearance. Only once in my days as a sailor have I seen them, and then it was the Western Jaws. These of the north seem to me more grim, more threatening. The ragged spikes of rock jut forth from the sea, illuminated by the red glow beyond them. The glow is almost enough to see by, without aid of lantern. Eightieth crossing of NewStar is ending. I hear no grumbling from the men. But I would not blame them if I did. Did courage or foolishness bring

us to this point? Will courage or madness drive us on?

Log of the Ammanon Deloré
Captain Dollapan recording.
End of the DevilsJaws are in sight. Redness of the sky reaches almost up to the tips of the jaws. We are in the eighty-first crossing. Little is said amongst the men, beyond what is needed to perform their duties. Entry Ends.

Log of the Ammanon Deloré
Captain Dollapan recording.
The DevilsJaws are far astern; nothing but a vast shallows, and the reddened sky, are to our port. The order is given to turn due north. We now head into the region reputed to be occupied by the DevilsEye. The Crown of God holds steady behind us, starboard astern. Perhaps it is well the men are so fixed on NewStar; I think none have noticed that although the Crown has nearly half-risen, it continues to rise barely at all. Entry Ends.
Supplemental: Islak has suspended depth readings while we are in the shallows. Entry Ends.

Log of the Ammanon Deloré
Captain Dollapan recording.
Ninety-Eighth crossing now at zenith. Horizon ahead too bright to watch. Temperature rising; Islak confirms via his instruments

Dearest Aunt Drumae:
I fear our voyage is near its end, whether by mutiny, or the DevilsEye, or by the vengeful hand of the God Who is Silent. We traverse where men ought not. Common among the men is the sense that NewStar was given to us as a sign not to proceed, but to flee back to waters more properly the domain of men who fear God.
Among some is even spoken the notion that if we do not turn back now, the God Who Is Silent will be silent evermore.

Light. Everywhere is light. Behind us, the Crown of God fades as if washed away by the pervading brightness coming from ahead. If someday, somehow, this letter reaches you, know that some among us, your son and nephew in part, implored their captain to return home.

Op

*　　　*　　　*

For several days, Alex dedicated himself to the running of the numbers. The Sirocco's computers were not loaded with any re-entry calculation software; all of those numbers were run from the ground. If she were so equipped, the programs would be useless anyway—so many constants about Earth's atmosphere and gravity were built into them. So he began with reconstructing his basic understanding of re-entry principles from memory. The first Day of Numbers he spent just re-teaching himself the calculations based on Earth constants, trying to hone in on the answers he knew were correct for Earth. His first results made no sense, and he beat through the equations repeatedly till he jogged up the memories, one by one, of the facets of the problem that he had been forgetting. The hardest point came when he first came up with an answer for Earth re-entry that was, within accepted margins, correct. Was the answer correct because the equations and formulae were, at last, correct? Or had he made two, three, or four errors in the formulations, which by chance had canceled each other out?

If so, then the numbers he would enter for this planet's constants would certainly not cancel each other out; his calculations would be fatally wrong. He had to tear apart and reassemble his equations, looking for some error. But before, he had the psychological advantage of knowing that there was an error. The final answer was wrong, so the equations had to be wrong. The confidence that there was an error helped him find the error.

Now a sort of intellectual jujitsu worked against him. Subconsciously he resisted any change to the equations; any change would lead, in the short term, to the wrong answer—until he could

103

uncover a mating error, and bring the answer back to its target. With no certainty that there must be an error, finding an error seemed impossible. Frustrated, he gave up and slept.

The next day he began with a decision: For good or ill, the equations would stand. He would live or die by the formulae he had thus far developed.

Now he began settling in on the numbers to plug in. He took his original estimates about the planet below, and refined them. And refined them again. And again. Eventually, the figures seemed more guesswork than calculation.

The escape pod's extremely low mass, the most recent generation of foam ceramics, plus the balloon-chute recovery system, gave him a wider margin of error than the old hard-shell re-entry schemas of manned re-entry. But not as wide as the variations in his guesses about the planet's specs. Not by a long shot.

After two more days, he had settled on a set of numbers that resulted in specific re-entry parameters: Heat shell angulation. Descent angulation. Orbital speed. Heat shell ejection point. Balloon-chute flair rate and flair size. A perfectly concrete set of guidelines to program into the emergency pod's computer.

He toyed with the idea of just changing one or two of his guesses with alternate numbers, numbers he felt would be well within the realm of possibility, to see how the descent parameters would be affected. But in the end, he decided, what was the point? Such an exercise could only serve to convince him not to make the descent. And that would leave him waiting to die, orbiting in the capsule, like one more piece of lost luggage. He smiled as he thought of Hammond, calling the Command Capsule the "Cargo Bay". That's all he was up here now—just a lost piece of orbiting cargo. Better to die like a pilot than some piece of jetsam.

He settled himself in for sleep. Knowing that when he awoke he would begin the departure protocols, he figured the tension would keep him awake. Again, he surprised himself. The ship's clock revealed eight and a quarter hours' uninterrupted sleep.

<u>Log of the Ammanon Deloré</u>
Captain Dollapan recording.
Helm reports the compass needle as slow in responding to changes in our course. Expected. Advised the helm to monitor the compass, but to use the red sky as a general director northward.

<u>Personal Log, Abbik Dollapan</u>
Ship's compass becoming erratic. Have reconfirmed with Islak that this is predictable. Among those who have ventured along the Boundary Waters either to the far east or far west, it is known that traveling north leads to a common area—the vicinity of the northern DevilsJaws. Therefore, presumably, there is, somewhere beyond the DevilsJaws, some single point of attraction for the compass needle. Any ship reaching that point, as it now appears we are doing, will find its compass of waning dependability. Indeed, Islak is of the mind that, were we to scuttle about in search of the precise point, we might find a spot upon which our compass would actually spin.

Although I would look upon it with some amusement, and Mr. Islak would look upon it as a matter of scientific curiosity, I doubt such a sight would be well received among the men. Although they seem to be taking pains to hold their tongues near the officers and myself, it is clear they are vexed to distraction with fears, both named and nameless. The apparition of a spinning compass needle might well cross for them a threshold that would bode ill for us all.

Book I
Chapter 7: In the Gaze of the DevilsEye

Awaking to his last day in orbit, Alex Boten ate, evacuated his bodily wastes, and began the EmEvac procedures. Most of the procedures he followed, but there were some exceptions. He emptied the last of Sirocco's foodstuffs into a bag to bring along. If he survived, there might not be any food readily at hand. Although he could have transferred the balance of the Sirocco's air to the pod, he did not do so. If the atmosphere were not breathable, then the added minutes he could gain would be minutes he would rather not have. Protocol also called for him to wear his helmet during descent. Two factors dissuaded him from this. First was the fact that it had been locked in its compartment, bagged, with vomit residue, for some days now. Second was the rationale for wearing it during descent. If something went wrong, a pressurized suit with helmet in place could give an astronaut a little more survival time until a rescue crew could save him. There would be no rescue crew. If something went wrong, then a few minutes more to figure out just what it was that went wrong was worse than useless.

He bumped up the power on his outgoing distress signal, and left it running. He switched off Air Cleansing, and adjusted the environmental controls so Sirocco would allow her interior temperature to cool to around forty. This would save on battery power, thus keeping the beacon up as long as possible, while still keeping the interior from freezing, which might adversely affect the radio or computer systems. He kept the mission clock running. Unlocking the releases on the floor panel, he swung it up and revealed the escape pod's narrow dual-passenger space. Casket-like. He pushed the bag of foodstuffs in, and let it float there.

Punching the go-code into the EmEvac system, and turning off the audio, he watched the seconds tick off on the display. He had decided to try for an ocean landing, near the daylight continent. He had about twenty minutes to go before Sirocco would be over the proper point. He was just beginning his ninety-ninth orbit. He patted the control panel.

"Sorry I can't stick around for one hundred, old girl. You'll just have to enjoy it for the both of us."

Watching the ocean sliding by beneath him, he wondered if Sirocco reflected enough light to be seen. Probably, he thought, at least to an observer on the dark side. Any intelligent life on the light side would have no idea he was here. And there would be no intelligent life on the dark side; who would choose to live in the dark, when light existed so close by? Still, it gave him some comfort to imagine someone down below, looking up at him circling, waiting for him to descend.

After fifteen minutes, he switched off the emergency beacon. "Commander Alexander Boten," he said into the mike, "of the Sirocco, to anyone listening. EmEvac in process. Hoping to land on the planet below." He paused to think. "Say 'Hi' to Bob Jiggs for me." He paused to think again. "No hard feelings, guys. Everybody did their best." He paused one last time. "Bye, Katie. Love you. My love to the girls. Boten out." Switching the automated beacon back on, he crawled into the pod, nudging the food bag into the copilot's space beside him. Lying on his back, he reached up and pulled down the pod lid, twisting the engagement handle. The pod automatically locked the lid down, and closed the environmental connection to the Sirocco capsule. Snaking his arm up by his head, Alex entered the go-code. A small screen lit up just above his eyes, displaying the mission status. The electrical umbilical detached. All of Alex's information from the Sirocco now came by radio. Again twisting up, he switched off the audio, so he would be spared the countdown. Keeping his hand by the audio switch, he watched the display. Everything remained nominal.

"Jesus, please get me down there." The display remained at nominal. Three minutes. He prayed for forgiveness, for every sin, recalled or forgotten, real or imagined. He prayed for Kathy, and for a full and happy life for Maddy and Ella. He prayed for Abbey, alone at their father's bedside. He thought of his father, but he couldn't bring himself to pray for him. He was likely dead by now. Was that the reason he resisted praying for him? Because in his traditions there were no prayers for the dead? Or was it because he just didn't *want* to pray for him? What an idea to end on, he thought. Ten seconds.

He remembered a line from an old war movie. A soldier, about to begin a mission drop: "One-way express elevator to hell. Going *down*." He wished he could remember which movie; he wondered whether it had turned out well.

Log of the Ammanon Deloré
Captain Dollapan recording.

Ninety-ninth crossing has begun. All topside lanterns have been extinguished, the air about us being bathed in this cursed reddish glow emanating from straight ahead.

The order is given to fold sail and drop anchor. Without order or suggestion, all of the Ammanon Deloré's officers and crew have gathered on the top decks. They are sprawled out, watching the skies. Only myself, Islak, and his friend Igren Doel wander the decks. No one speaks, save those engaged in prayer.

Supplemental: NewStar sets, unmarked by any event..

Supplemental: Ig Doel has joined the men in their watch.

Log of the Ammanon Deloré
Captain Dollapan recording.

NewStar dawns, on its hundredth arc. I sit beside the unmanned helmsman's wheel, this log astride my lap. Should NewStar set with no sign or event suggestive of its fulfillment, I think fear should drive me back. Whether it is fear over the abortive omen, or fear of the reaction of the men, or equal parts of both is a question I would gladly wrestle with on the trip back.

The budding priest, Andril, joins Anned and myself about the helmsman's wheel. He announced himself by simply saying, "It comes". Beyond that he has offered no conversation, nor have we been inclined to illicit from him anything more. Have had my fill of cryptic utterances.

Forgive.

NewStar has completed one fourth of its tracing of the sky.

*　　*　　*

The clamps released, and there was a slight sense of weight as the maneuvering thrusters moved him away from the Sirocco.

Balance. He had recalculated for the mass of only one passenger, but the weight was supposed to be even. Wrenching up his hands, he unbuckled his harness—there really was no place to go, anyway—and wriggled over to straddle the spaces.

It was harder to see the Flight Status panel, but he could read it. Nominal. Unbelievable stupidity. He waited, and watched.

The Ceramic Shell temp was due to rise. It didn't. The deviation from mission norms widened. Alex smiled slightly. "Oh well," he said, and then swallowed. "Not long now."

The shell temp climbed at last, but it was too far behind the curve. The pod was coming in too steeply now, having not been buoyed by the atmosphere. As the air thickened, the heat would catch up, with a vengeance. The angle stabilized, but still too steep. The shell temp began to climb, passed Mission Norm, and approached RedLine.

At least, thought Boten, *I won't burn.* Before the heat would penetrate the inner Ceramic Shell, the outer Ceramic Shell should undergo catastrophic failure. The entire pod would explode, in essence. Shell temp reached and crossed RedLine. This was not unexpected; RedLine was not an absolute. The temperature began to stabilize, at four percent over.

Cruel, Alex thought. *That's cruel. Don't dangle a hope in front of me. Just finish it.* The temperature crept down.

Briefings... discussions... Ceramic Shell could hold up how long at RedLine? Ejection point was approaching. The balloon-chute should melt at this temperature. Could it exceed RedLine by as much as the shell?

The escape pod ejected its spent heat shell. Chaos and tumbling. Audio warnings overriding the silent mode he had ordered. He had a sense of weight; the balloon-chute had deployed. The tumbling subsided, but there was still a rocking sensation. The ceramic shell had been successfully sloughed off, and the balloon-chute had survived, but the pod was twirling. That might be nothing, or it might be fatal. It depended on how tightly the chute cords got wrapped.

He was only a few kilometers up, now. But a few kilometers from what? With the change in angle, he could be coming down anywhere. Thousands of miles from land, in a sea whose currents he knew nothing about. Or worse, on land. The Ceramic Shell and balloon-chute systems were predicated on an ultra-light payload. The pod was not designed to survive anything harder than water.

An irrational confidence overcame him. If he had survived all this, he couldn't possibly be crushed on a pile of rock.

As his altitude melted away, so did the confidence. Sliding back into position, he rebuckled his harness. Contact: Rapid deceleration, then reacceleration upward. Momentary weightlessness, and then another, lesser deceleration. Water—or at least liquid.

He had survived. The balloons deflated, settling the pod into the water. There was a gentle rocking. The pod seemed to have maintained its integrity, and there was no indication he was sinking. There was, therefore, no urgency about exiting. Neither, however, was there any reason to wait.

His defiance of the helmet protocol began to seem childish. It was borne of the assumption he would not survive the descent. *But no*, he told himself, *the rationale still carried weight*: If the atmosphere was poisonous, the helmet would only delay the inevitable.

He began punching in the release codes. As his hand hovered over the button labeled Main Hatch, he reflexively held his breath. Closing his eyes, he hit the button. Staying hinged at one side, the other side of the door blew out with enough force to flop fully open.

Boten took a short, tentative sniff.

Salt air. He breathed again, to confirm it, then looked up. Beyond the open hatchway, he looked up to a red sky. He had expected blue, from his observations. Beyond the hatch, the signal strobe was flashing; perhaps it was affecting his vision. He began regular breathing. Crawling up to a sitting position, he looked around. He saw nothing all around but gentle sea, and to one side a red sun hanging motionless, its lower third below the line of the horizon. A quarter turn from that, the ghostly pale apparition of the galaxy filled half the sky, forever half-risen.

Log of the Ammanon Deloré
Captain Dollapan recording.

May the gracious God who stands by our side be lifted up in praise.

Before reaching zenith, a flash of light, a shimmering green iridescence, appeared below NewStar and streaked downward. But two or three beats in duration, it seemed to grow in size before disappearing in a yellow flash.

None among us knows what it means. For the moment, none among us cares. Ten crossings, and ten upon those, were not completed before some augury shone down upon us. Whatever its meaning, NewStar has been given us, and has fulfilled itself as prophesied unto the ancients.

Those whose strength has not failed them dance upon the decks. As I write this, NewStar sets. For a time, we celebrate, and rest. Soon and very soon, we press on.

*　　　*　　　*

Alex would have preferred to switch off the irritating strobe light—or to rip it out with his bare hands, if that were the only way—but he needed it now. He needed the incredibly slim possibility it afforded: The possibility of being spotted.

Based on the sun's low aspect on the horizon, he had splashed thousands of miles from his target, thousands of miles from any major land. Any dry soil closer than the lit side's continent would have to be less than a hundred miles across, or else he would have seen it from orbit. And so his only prospect for survival was that this planet bore some intelligent life—life that was now searching for him based on his fiery entry into the atmosphere, or that would stumble across him by accident as they traversed the sea en route to some distant destination.

On a teeming earthly ocean, his chances would be slim. But here? He prayed for land. It embarrassed him; providence had already granted him ten thousand times more good fortune than he could expect.

"Whatever you give," he conceded, "it's never enough. Even so, please God, let me find land."

The sea was becalmed; there was no discernable wind. Barely noticeable swells, just a few inches in height, hinted that somewhere far away there might be winds churning up waves—waves which had dispersed to virtual nothingness by the time they reached here.

The waters were clear. He guessed he could see to a depth of fifteen or twenty feet. But there was no trace of bottom, or of tall reaching weeds. The ocean floor could be fifty feet, or fifty miles. The sky was cloudless, the sun, of course, motionless. He had nothing by which to gauge if he were in a current.

He had thought of the faded galactic spiral as motionless, but it occurred to him that this was not entirely true; over the course of this planet's "year", the half-risen swirl would creep around the horizon, growing brighter as it moved away from the sun, then fading again as it approached the sun on the opposite side. Eventually it would disappear in the red glow, slowly emerging again to repeat the cycle.

Would he live to see a full cycling? Not with the provisions he now had.

Examining his food bag, he concluded he could comfortably go four days. This estimate was based on three criteria:

First, there was no point in living on bare minimum subsistence levels; why starve yourself, just to put off the inevitable?

Second, there was no point in gorging. It made sense to space the food out, to give himself whatever chance of finding land, or of life finding him, that might exist.

And third, the escape pod was equipped with two days' water for two men—four days' water for one. Since water can't very effectively be stretched (the human body is far less tolerant of water deprivation than it is of food deprivation) his situation was going to turn desperate in four days, no matter what.

He apportioned the food into four groups, and each of those into two. He had never been very much on lunch. Looking to the sun, still hanging in the ocean exactly as when he had first seen it, he laughed. No point in keeping track of days in the traditional sense. He climbed into the pod and noted the time on the control panel. Topside again, he settled himself into a comfortable position, and began to scan the horizon.

For hours, he saw nothing. For hours, he thought of nothing, but home. He thought of Katie, and of his girls—old enough to understand he would not be coming home, but not old enough to understand, really, why. He and Katie had been trying for another child, hoping for a son. It chilled him to think they might have succeeded; she could be pregnant even now, and he would never know. He thought of longsuffering Abbey, alone by their father's deathbed. He thought of his father, no more distant from him now than if Alex were at his side, staring into his comatose face. Perhaps, in some ways, no more distant now than ever. Was he even still alive? Sometime, before the ever-shortening arc of Alex Boten's life drew to its close, Jeremy Boten's life would reach its own sadly unremarkable end. But Alex would never know.

He shifted to try to find a more comfortable position.

Why did he care just when his father passed? What difference would knowing make? So he would know the precise moment in which to make the accepted motions of mourning? Or so he could mark the event with a silent satisfaction? Or—down deep somewhere, in a part of him he didn't want to admit to—did it bother him that somehow the old man might just hang on, and outlive him?

He had become just like his father. Pitiable and helpless, waiting for an ignominious end. The only difference was that his father, even if he should awaken, was surrounded by medical staff that would prevent him from ending his own sad drama. There were no medics here, no tending nurses. If he felt he had taken all he could take, there was no one to stay his hand.

He sat up and looked off to the horizon, in no particular direction. For the first time since splashing down, he spoke to God in a manner more than perfunctory:

"Jesus, don't let it end like this. Give me land, or give me some huge swamping wave. Live or die. Don't let me waste away. Don't leave me with the choice of ending it myself, or slowly going mad from drinking saltwater." Lying back, he gave up his horizon watch. Closing his eyes, just four hours into what his biological clock told him was his "day", he slept.

Log of the Ammanon Deloré
Captain Dollapan recording.

At the suggestion of Mr. Anned Islak, and with the consultation and full concurrence of the Captain, the following orders are given to all hands, officers, and passengers aboard the brigantine Ammanon Deloré:

~ All men not specifically and vitally needed topside, and not under specific, limited instructions otherwise, are to remain below decks.

~ All portholes part of occupied chambers are to be left open for ventilation, but loosely hanging cloth is to be affixed over them such that any light entering in is diffused.

~ Water rations are immediately doubled for all hands.

~ To each man, be he above or below decks, is to be issued at once the following gear, to be worn at all times above decks, and kept close at hand at all times below decks: Rain jacket, rain pants, hull scrubber gloves, boots.

~ All hands are directed to not look to the brightening sky ahead, but to at all times keep their eyes averted therefrom.

The only exceptions to these rules are for the crowsman, as

follows:

~ He is given to wear one additional item of clothing, the special white headpiece designed by Mr. Islak, to be worn at all times. Over the eye holes he is to wrap repeatedly layers of gauze, supplied by Mr. Islak, sufficient to reduce his visibility such that the glowing sky is dimmed to comfortability. That his vision is thus impaired to the point of being unable to distinguish plain objects on the horizon is to be of no concern to him.

~ He is instructed to *at no time* look away from the redness ahead, watching only for such change as he may perceive through his protecting gauze. The goal of his watch is to be the DevilsEye. Should it appear, he is to look away at once upon announcing it, that Islak may advise us on how to further protect his eyes at that point.

This concludes all special orders. As to general orders, the following are given:

~ Hoist anchor
~ Set three-quarters sail.
~ Set main course dead-on to the center of the horizon's glow.
~ Tack alternately 10 degrees port and starboard.
~ All hands are instructed to pray for the guidance of the Almighty God, and to prepare themselves for what glory awaits us.

Entry Ends.

Log of the Ammanon Deloré
Captain Dollapan recording.

By order of the Captain, the ship is turned into the wind. Just after the changing of the third watch since setting sail, the report from the nest is made of a great light breaking on the horizon.

Islak has fitted the crowsman's eyeholes with additional gauze.

We turn to catch the wind, and set full sail. Same course maintained, but order to tack is suspended. With all due haste we lunge forward to our destiny.

116

Supplemental: The phenomenon is visible now from the deck. Having been fitted, as has Islak, with the hoods and gauze, I have granted the two of us exception to the crew's special orders.

Supplemental: The point of light ahead broadens, and a shape is manifesting itself, according to the following sketch:

We are met with the Devil's Eye.

Book I
Chapter 8: Landfall

Log of the Ammanon Deloré
Supplemental: Have turned aside to the wind, holding position.

Supplemental: Upon Islak's advice, all men topside are hereby ordered to don masks and eye gauze. All are ordered not to look in the Eye's direction, as excepted: The crowsman, only so far as is needed to alert us to any changes, and Islak only so far as he deems necessary for his readings.

Three-quarters sail is set, course dead-on for the DevilsEye, without tack. Entry Ends.

Log of the Ammanon Deloré
Captain Dollapan recording.

The DevilsEye expands in girth as we press on. The men of the Ammanon Deloré amaze me; the coming of NewStar has invigorated them, and given them courage beyond their means. Entry Ends.

Personal Log, Abbik Dollapan
The brightness of the Eye has extended across the sky, paling NewStar to where it cannot be seen—even by those men who violate standing orders and briefly unveil their eyes to seek it. But present or not, visible or not, NewStar has served its purpose. There is consensus among the men that the Conflict of NewStar has been resolved: That its constancy defined it, and that its flash marked the moment of its fulfillment. There is now eager anticipation among the men to return home, anticipation that Harbinger is now in the midst of the people. Some hold that he is at the Temple, some hold that he is at the Temple Adjunct. But all hold that he has come. And regardless of where Harbinger is—surely Restoration stands at the Temple.

Yet despite their desire to be at home, to witness the mystery of Harbinger's unfolding, they are loyal to the mission. Almost to a man, there is a sense that the timing of this mission was not random, that we have reason for being here at so momentous a time.

As for myself, surely the appearance and fulfillment of NewStar must answer all of my questions—must cancel all of my doubts. But why do these thoughts yet persist? Now that the thrill of NewStar's fulfillment is passed, I find myself the same man I was. I find the Deloré still the same ship, the ocean and the sky unchanged.

Why have I come out to this place? If such a sign as NewStar cannot change me, what do I hope to find ahead? Into the hand of God I consign myself. Despite all that I feel, despite all that I do not feel, in him who is silent will I trust.

Supplemental: Have just been visited by a disturbed Anned Islak, whom I comforted as best I could. The DevilsEye has not met his predictions so closely as he would have liked, and it is a source of much vexation. Of greatest concern is its girth. Although I pointed out to him that the limits of its width seemed obvious (as the sketch below reveals)...

...he seems intent upon berating himself for having misjudged its size. Indeed, it seems to be roughly the dimension that the survivors of the Innotek Assan reported: Nearly a thumb's width at arm's length. It was this report that Anned had dismissed as exaggeration.

I fear my efforts at cheering him, by pointing him to our successes so far, were for naught. Perhaps it is this drive for perfection that has brought him to the place of high esteem he enjoys among the populace. Yet at the same time I fear that such a drive must, in the end, destroy him. Although I do not understand the depth of his concern over this, I do not dismiss it. I know what it is to be plagued by a dread that another cannot reason away. Dear sweet child Lannae, how I need your assurances, your arguments, and your certitude now. Beloved Vinasa, forgive me—should I survive to return to you.

Anned Islak, DevilsEye Journal

Dollapan is a fool. My warnings to him were met with deaf indifference. He seems convinced my anxiety is over pride, over what others would think of my miscalculations. Cursed trivialities. The fulfillment of NewStar seems a heady brew, from which even our esteemed captain has taken too generous a draught.

We approach a danger that no man in history has survived—and the sheath of knowledge, with which I felt we were guarded, is now clearly stripped away.

The DevilsEye cannot be a moon. No moon, either so large or so near, could remain suspended above us.

The DevilsEye is not what I had supposed. And if that is true, it could be anything. And if *that* is true, the defenses I now employ could be equally erroneous—and utterly useless.

A burning moon. Dollapan knows that was what I had declared it to be. And if he had but eyes to look, he would see it is self evidently not a burning moon.

I have brought necessities to guard us against dangers which I now understand that we do not face. And against those dangers that we *shall* confront, I have no provision.

May the God Who Is Silent forgive me, if my arrogance costs the lives of this crew.

Resuming my depth measurements. I almost despair to note the water is shallowing as I expected. If this continues, we will likely find land ahead. And if we find this growing chain of islands? Do I celebrate my cleverness in foreseeing it? Or shudder over the fact that it will ultimately help change the view that I, and every Mirran, holds of the world about us?

Log of the Ammanon Deloré

Captain Dollapan recording.

Land is sighted! Although it appears to be but a speck, we are tacking slightly to starboard to approach it. Mr. Islak is taking continual rough depth soundings to ensure we do not run aground on shallows. While the depth is lessening, we are thus far in no danger.

Even as I am writing this, word has come down from the nest of another speck of land, further to starboard. We press on.

Supplemental: It is confirmed the first sighting is but a tiny plot of land, perhaps a dozen yards across, a mere rise of sand and rock. We are not bothering to put ashore. Headed for the second sighting. Per Islak's request, we are plotting a tacking course, crossing repeatedly and broadly across the line between these two tiny isles. I suspect that by mapping a contour of the ocean floor, he intends to deduce whether these are isolated islands or part of some longer chain.

Log of the Ammanon Deloré
First Officer Mennetek recording.

Captain is topside conferring with Mr. Islak. More land spotted ahead, roughly in line with the first two islands spotted. The second was of the size of the first, but the third appears larger. My understanding from overhearing Mr. Islak's discussions is that there is a ridge along the bottom connecting these islands, a strong indication that more will appear ahead.

Log of the Ammanon Deloré
Captain Dollapan recording.

We have now passed nine plots of land. Although some are smaller than the ones preceding them, they in general are growing larger. A tenth, yet ahead, seems considerably larger than any we have passed thus far. The lay of the islands has been curving steadily away from the DevilsEye, and we are now sailing nearly at right angles to it.

Islak continues his depth measurements to monitor our safety, but the existence of a ridge (of which these islands are but the manifest evidence) is in no doubt. We have assumed a course parallel to the line of the islands, rather than directly in their line, so as to minimize any risk of running aground.

Supplemental: The tenth island is substantial, and appears to have permanent plant growth, including trees. Planning to put ashore.

Log of the Ammanon Deloré
Captain Dollapan recording.

Still approaching island ten, and the crowsman has sighted a massive island in the distance. Would otherwise abandon plans to set ashore on island ten, but Islak is most urgent about putting ashore just briefly.

Supplemental: Islak has put ashore with two crewmen, shovels, ropes, and a tall pole with a flag. All he seems to have done is to have planted the pole, and tied three support lines to it, anchored by rocks. This seems to have satisfied him, though what he can deduce from it is beyond me. We are on course now for the massive island before us.

One of the crewmen who went ashore on isle ten returned with several types of leaves, all unlike anything I have seen before, all in varying degrees of the most brilliant green.

DevilsEye Experiment Journal
Anned Islak recording.[1]

Have put ashore with nine men on what Captain Dollapan has graciously allowed me to dub Valor Island. Although there is much excitement about the plant life—all of which is completely new to us— my attentions are elsewhere. The spacing of these islands is such that they afford me a chance to take measurements upon the DevilsEye itself. Nothing can be of greater import now.

Will first attempt to obtain precise ranging on the flag we set down earlier. Then will use sightings both here and there to calculate distance to the Eye.

> ~ Setting markers at one-hundred-yard spacing along the beach.
> ~ Using sighting protractor to gauge the distant marker.
> (Fortunate, that I elected to raise the flag as high as I did; the

---

[1] At various points, diagrams and tables of data have been inserted into the Experiment Journal. Although these did not originally interrupt the actual flow of notes, they may be helpful in understanding the experiments conducted.

curve of the sea blocks half the height of the pole. Fortunate as well that Ig's lenses are of the quality they are, elsewise I should not even be able to spot the marker, let alone measure it. Must remember also to pay bonus to Steffik for his precision metalwork on the protractor.)

~ Measured angle A as 49.912 degrees, angle B as 49.783 degrees.[2]

Blank Form:

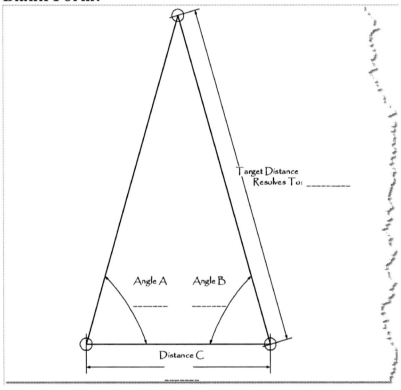

Target Distance
Resolves To: _____

Angle A   Angle B

_ _ _ _ _   _ _ _ _ _

Distance C

---

[2] The degree system employed by Islak involved a two hundred degree circle; under this system, a right angle would be fifty degrees.

Form Filled In For Marker:

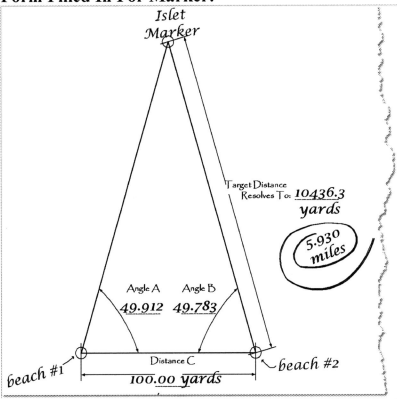

Islet
Marker

Target Distance
Resolves To: *10436.3*
yards

5.930 miles

Angle A   Angle B
49.912 *49.783*

beach #1

Distance C
100.00 yards

beach #2

~ Computation plus references to tables yields a distance of
10,436 yards, or just over five point nine miles.

A six mile separation between a marker here and the marker on
the islet should be sufficient, either to allay my fears or to confirm the
worst. I can take detailed measurements on the Eye from here, but I
must then convince the Captain to return to the islet. I sense he is
keen both on exploring Valor Island, and upon pressing on toward the
Eye. Returning to a small snub of land already passed by will likely
not be among his priorities. But convince him I must.

Private Journal of Igren Doel

Anned grows progressively more agitated as our journey wears on, although I cannot perceive the reason. Although the men complain over the heat around us and the amplification of that heat due to the protective gear, we are nonetheless suffering none of the effects that destroyed the crew of the Innotek Assan. The extra water rations are adequate, and the Captain has given orders for the ice blocks to begin being chipped, for distribution. We are as comfortable as could be hoped.

It seems to me the DevilsEye itself, rather than its effects, are more the source of Anned's fears.

He called upon me to join him in entreating the Captain to indulge his experimentation further by returning to one of the lesser islands, the one where he took such care in mounting his flag pole.

Before meeting the Captain, he enjoined me—in tones so serious as to almost be comic—that I must under all conditions back his position, on the utmost necessity of our making this return. All this, while refusing to explain to me the precise reason why. Fortunately the Captain did not call upon me to explain a rationale for my support of Anned's position. He was, rather, amenable to leaving a small contingent to explore Valor, while the Deloré shuttled briefly to our previous stop.

DevilsEye Experiment Journal

Anned Islak recording.

~ Refitting one side of sighting protractor with colored lenses Igren Doel produced.

~ Have completed a reading on the DevilsEye, with one of the Valor beach markers as a reference. 51.033 degrees. We are now sailing back to our first marker. Am dealing with a lingering afterimage of the DevilsEye, but it is fading.

Form Partially Completed For the DevilsEye:

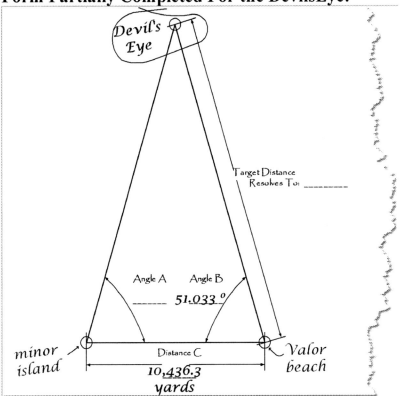

~ Have put ashore, and made reading of 48.969 degrees. *Technically impossible*, as these add to more than one hundred degrees—the maximum for an infinitely-distant object. Error either in measurement made here or in measurement at Valor Island. Completing series of measurements for averaging.

Readings:	1	2	3	4	5	6	7	8	9	10	Average
Angle B	48.969	48.967	48.967	48.968	48.969	48.966	48.966	48.965	48.969	48.970	
Angle A	51.033										

~ Returning via Ammanon Deloré to Valor Island. Persistent afterimage of the Eye becoming more troublesome. Seems to be fading more slowly, now after the series of readings. Must take care to make each of next sightings as short as possible. Also, will do some sightings with left eye, so effect is not concentrated solely in the right.

~ Taking series of readings, to refine initial result.

Readings:	1	2	3	4	5	6	7	8	9	10	Average
Angle B	48.969	48.967	48.967	48.968	48.969	48.966	48.966	48.965	48.969	48.970	
Angle A	51.033	51.033	51.030	51.035	51.036	51.032	51.033	51.035	51.031	51.030	

~ Am resuming the ship to perform calculations, while the Captain cycles men ashore to continue exploration.

~ Afterimage effect so intense in right eye, cannot properly read my numbers. Have fitted right eye with makeshift patch; am beginning calculations now using left.

Readings:	1	2	3	4	5	6	7	8	9	10	Average
Angle B	48.969	48.967	48.967	48.968	48.969	48.966	48.966	48.965	48.969	48.970	48.9676
Angle A	51.033	51.033	51.030	51.035	51.036	51.032	51.033	51.035	51.031	51.030	51.0328

Minimum readable variance a given, at .0008 degrees. Separation established as 5.93 miles. Computation results in minimums: Distance 235,947 miles, diameter 3,067 miles. Minimums. Actual figures may be larger, by unknown amount. God have mercy. What have we found?

Must find Mennetek, have him signal somehow for the Captain. Must turn for home. Must turn for home _now_.

*　　　*　　　*

Later—he would never know precisely how much later—Alex awoke. To his right, the sun hung exactly as it had before. The sky remained the steady red of frozen dawn. He scanned the horizon ahead of him, waiting for any sign of cloud or land to appear. None did. From time to time he looked to the right, confirming the sun, and to the left, toward the darker horizon. He never looked behind, to the ominous, looming galaxy. As long as all he saw was sun and sea and empty sky, he could pretend. He could forget.

Once, in a leftward glance, he saw something new. Near where the pod disappeared below the waterline, a bird floated. It nibbled at the metallic edge of the pod. Alex stared at it dumbly for nearly twenty seconds. It was white, vaguely gull-like, but with a longer neck. Its bill was a yellowish gray with a red spot at the end.

Abruptly, he sat up. The bird looked up, startled by his sudden move, but seemingly unafraid of him.

"Hello," Alex said, reflexively.

The bird did not reply. But its companions did. High overhead, a flock of nearly a dozen called back and forth to each other with a soft, high pitched squeak. In response, the bird beside him turned and launched itself awkwardly into the air, struggling against the water for some fifty feet.

"Don't go," Alex said whimsically. He spun around. Behind him was land. His guess, and a wild guess it was, put it at a mile off. An island, it seemed, rising almost as high as its girth, standing at the right edge of the galactic spiral.

In a flash, the possibilities clicked through his mind. If the current (and clearly, now, there must be one) was heading him toward the island, he could either stay with the pod or abandon it. The pod would find its way to—or at least closer to—the island. If he were now drifting abreast of the island, or worse, away from it, abandoning the pod was the only course open to him.

Abandonment won, by acclamation. Diving halfway into the pod, he hit the raft eject. Outside, a small compartment popped open, and a two-man inflatable sprang to life via compressed gas. Inside the vacated compartment he found one of the three-piece collapsing paddles, and assembled it. He piled into the raft, leaving it attached to the pod, and began to paddle like a madman. One thought filled his mind: Not crossing the line of straining any part of his body. A pulled muscle, a strained back, they could mean the difference between life and death, now. Just as surely as not paddling hard enough could, if the current was drawing him away. He concentrated on the front edge of the raft, on the paddle, on the water. He kept the island just enough in his field of view to maintain his direction. Behind him, the pod pulled at him, but he dragged it along. Eventually, he looked up. He could discern no progress.

He worked through the arithmatic simplicity of the options once again. If the current was toward the island, the pod would come, eventually. If not, retaining the pod was not worth losing landfall. He climbed back onto the pod, took his bag of foodstuffs (now thrown back into one pile) and removed the jug of water. All these he piled into the raft, along with the pieces of the second oar. Untying the mooring line, he left the pod behind without so much as a farewell.

Paddling with the same intensity as before, he could feel himself making progress now, each thrust lurching him ahead as much as casting water behind him. Periodically he forced himself to rest, which became harder and harder to do as the island loomed before him. It was green. A strange green, an oddly flat green in the red dawn, but green. He made no effort to study the types of foliage coming into view. He didn't care what it looked like. He wouldn't let himself think about what it looked like, or about whether anything would be edible. It was land. It was coming. Stroke by stroke it was coming.

He thought about the bird. He thought about how strangely... *birdlike* it was. Thousands of light years from home, and here was a bird that he wouldn't give a second thought to if it alit next to him on a San Francisco pier.

He could see features on the bottom. His early estimate was generous; ten feet or so seemed the maximum viewable depth. But he was at less than that now. Still a long way from shore. The bottom contour seemed gradual. But what was the bottom? Some coral-like growth that would puncture his raft while he was still thirty or forty feet from shore? Forcing him to wade in? In reach of some shallow-water shark, or whatever equivalent this planet had to serve up for him?

Paddle, he thought. Paddle. Just get there.

At five feet of depth, the bottom resolved itself into sand, with occasional fist-sized rocks. Motion. He froze. It was beneath and ahead, huge, as big across as his raft. Bigger. It moved. Fast. Too fast. He realized he had stopped breathing. He began breathing again. It was a school of... of something. Finger-length fish.

He spun around. Fish in schools sometimes dart about to evade a predator. He watched. He saw the end of the school approach, then pass under him. Beyond, at the edge of what he could see... nothing. Still nothing. More nothing.

A thousand horror films suddenly raced through his mind, and he cautiously looked forward, half expecting some monster to be lunging over the front of his raft. There was nothing but the beckoning beach, a hundred feet off.

He bit his lip, and then stifled a self-deprecating laugh. He could sit here all day, looking first fore, then aft, as the current slowly dragged him back out. He resumed paddling, a slower, more deliberate paddling. He forced from his mind, by sheer will, the sense of impending doom.

At thirty feet from shore, the gentle swells caused him to occasionally touch the sandy bottom. Quickening his pace, he brought the raft to a fairly firm grounding twenty feet from the shore's farthest reach. One last look around, to confirm the absence of unspeakable monsters, and he jumped out. Towing the raft by the mooring line, he dragged it beyond the waves' farthest reach by some twenty feet.

He dropped the line, looking into the jungle-like growth fifty feet ahead of him. He looked each way along the beach, a beach like any tropical beach of home. He looked out to sea, and spotted the low profile of the pod. He guessed it was moving parallel to the beach.

He flopped into a pile on the sand. His hands grasped the sand and lifted it. He let it sift out. Not knowing what manner of nasties might crawl through this beach, he climbed, exhausted, back into the raft. Lightly, ever so lightly, he dozed.

In time, the sound of waves awoke him. He startled to full waking, for a moment terrified that he had fallen asleep, been set adrift by a tide, and that he did not know where his paddle was. He realized, in this order:

He was on shore, exactly where he had deposited himself.

His paddle was in the raft beside him.

As this planet's moons were small, and its sun effectively motionless, there were no tides.

Dragging the raft the rest of the way to the foliage, he tethered the line to the first small tree he found. No point in taking chances. Looking into the foliage, he saw fruit. Or what he took for fruit. He did not let it sway him. He would remember it, but there was no point in eating anything until his own food ran out. Along the beach, there were flowers. Not many, but some. Driftwood. Other islands? He shook off the notion. There might be other islands, but the wood could just as easily have come from this island—washed out and then washed back up, as the winds changed.

He began a hike of the beach, of the entire island's perimeter, if the terrain would permit it. His attention, though, was continually drawn to the sun. He began to realize what an annoyance, what a distraction, what an abominable frustration this endless dawning would come to be. If there were other islands, he hoped they would lead away from the sun. He would rather live his life in a perpetual pre-dawn twilight, whose "time" in Earthly terms he could imagine ranging over a period of several hours, than to live with his day stuck, forever, at some precise point of solar elevation, whatever that point was.

Stopping, he watched the boots of his pressure suit settle into the sand. He craned his head back, looking into the sky.

"This is a beautiful place," he whispered. "Beautiful world. Beautiful sea. Beautiful island. But this is not the course I planned for my life." He recalled what he had said to Jiggs: *No ticket. No ticket for this flight.*

"This," Alex said aloud, "is not where I'm supposed to be."

God offered him no argument.

Alex climbed up and down a low ridge of rocks that extended out into the sea. He could see no reason for their being there. On the beach beyond them there was motion—a broad, swarming motion. A curious lack of fear, a lack of caution, had befallen him, and he raced ahead. The creatures, small crablike creatures, fanned out away from him. Each was the size of a thumbnail; there were, perhaps, two hundred. He would pursue them later. He continued walking.

He pondered the broad expanse of beach that seemed to encircle the island. What did he know about beaches? What had he heard,

132

what had he read? Beach sand was the result of endless pounding by the surf, reducing rocks to tiny fragments. So this calm was not the natural state of things, or at least not the permanent state. There had to be periods of strong, crashing waves.

Walking onward, he became aware of the sound of water—unlike the sound of the gentle swells playing with the shore. This was a more rapid, frenetic sound. And it was not from the ocean. It was landward. Stepping toward the sea's edge, so he could see better over the foliage of the island, he scanned the slopes of the island's summit. He had moved far enough around the island so he could see both the sunward and the shaded side of the summit. There was what seemed to him, initially, a curious divide. The foliage on the sunward side was a normal, earthly green. But the shaded side was different. It was sparser, but the difference was more than that. Although there was green on the shaded side, it was a far more subdued green, a duller green. Other colors fought for prominence—browns, yellows, oranges. And as he considered it, it made sense to him. On the island face exposed to the sun, chlorophyll was the clear winner in the race to draw energy from the environment, as it had been across the entire globe of Earth. But here, the sun never moved. On the shaded side, the only light available was what was reflected down off the atmosphere. Other strategies prevailed. What, he wondered, would it be like further on into the darkness? The non-green plants suggested life might find a way to survive there, but the sparseness he saw suggested it would be a barren existence, a hardscrabble, difficult existence. As he continued to scan the slopes, at last he saw the source of the sound he had been hearing—a stream of water.

Now he abandoned all caution, and tore through the jungle-like growth, heading for the slope. This was the last piece to his puzzle. Fruit would be good, if it did not kill him, but it would likely not provide enough moisture to survive. If there was a source of fresh water, however, he might survive as long as his wits, and his fortune, and the providence of God allowed. He might actually have a life.

Valor Island Exploration Journal
Abbik Dollapan recording.
Have set out as leader of second of two parties of five. Will take notes in transit as conditions permit. Foliage on the island appears dense, though several natural breaks in the growth appear to afford passage. Everything here seems riotous shades of green. No evidence yet of animal life, although several types of bird songs can be heard.

A stream can be seen rushing down from the highland summit of the island. My guess would be that some natural depression has formed a basin to catch rainwater. The source of this stream is our party's goal.

One of our group is Islak's friend, Ig Doel. He seems most intent on gathering specimens. I perceive it is not so much a natural interest for him, but an effort to provide Islak the samples Islak himself would otherwise have gathered, so that he might study them once his DevilsEye measurement mania has passed.

In the shadow of Valor Island, particularly under the canopy of vegetation, the light is far less bright. We have stripped off all but a single layer of gauze from our masks. We must make for a humorous sight. Were it not that I knew the masks had been originally formed into their current state, I should think the grayish white globs of rubber were melting in the heat.

Are taking frequent breaks to rest and drink. These protective suits becoming a cursed nuisance. But the fate of the Innotek Assan has thus far been adequate to keep us all in line.

Bird life confirmed. Have spotted three species—am familiar with none. First was an all-white bird, over a fathom in wingspan, long of neck and leg, traveling in a group of five, high and silent. Second was a swarm of small brownish birds, each small enough to fit inside a man's hand, nondescript save for a black mask and a single black bar on each wing, moving about in the treetops, chittering incessantly. Third was taken by myself at first for some ground animal. It moved ahead of us through the underbrush until we closed too tightly upon it, when it took flight. My view was limited, but the other men reported it as either brown and black mottled, or brown with black bars. The head was some bright combination of blue and red, but owing to direction and motion, nothing more specific can be said. Beak to tail it was over a foot, less than two.

The route we are following through the foliage seems clearly to be an animal trail. Occasionally there are traces of tracks, but they are too fragmentary to yield clear description.

Have now found one clear track. Five toed animal, small claws, entire print slightly wider than a man's thumb.

Have come to the stream. The water is fresh, but am only allowing myself and Doel to draw from it for now. If, by our return, we still feel no ill effects, the rest of our party will partake as well.

Climb is steep now. From time to time, can see the Deloré anchored offshore. We have climbed to an elevation level with her crow's nest. She is a magnificent sight, as the crew rolls up her white sails aglow in the red light of the DevilsEye. Behind her, the faded Crown hangs as if frozen, half-risen.

Have spotted small animal, party is chasing it up the slope—am joining them.

*   *   *

The terrain changed, as did the plant life. On his way to the stream Alex noticed numerous types of fruit, of varying degrees of appeal, and began recognizing types of plants he was encountering over and over again.

"I'll spend a lifetime," he panted as he ran "just thinking up names for everything."

At last, under a canopy of leaves so dense it was almost like night, he came to the stream. It was a yard across and racing past him downhill, undoubtedly emptying into the sea. But that was not the end that interested him. He followed it upward. In some places it snaked through nearly flat areas, in others it almost became a waterfall, and he had to move like a rock climber to continue. Several times the climb got the best of him, and he had to stop to rest.

He had neglected to bring water with him. He ached for water.

135

Lying on his side, he watched the rushing stream bubbling beside him. It smelled clean, and fresh, and sweet. It might contain anything. Microbes, viruses, poisonous minerals. But the same sense that had overcome him previously, overcame him again. If this were deadly, what hope would he have? That some other rushing stream would appear, free of such toxins? Besides, he had no way of testing this water—beyond observing, as he had, that the native plants flourished along its edges.

Perhaps it was a form of suicide without stigma. Perhaps it was recklessness from exhaustion. He rolled over and submerged his face in the stream, drawing long and deep. When he grew short of air he snapped his head back so his hair slicked back across his scalp. He savored the mineral sweetness, and he did not die. Unfastening his gloves, he clipped them to the waist of his suit. He ran his fingers through his hair. Lying back, he looked up through the broad green leaves, and into the red sky above. He could learn to live with this, he thought.

Not sleepy, but desperate to rest his muscles, he lounged for perhaps half an hour. Then, rousting himself, he pressed on, upward. His pace was leisurely now. No longer a man in desperation, he was the de facto king of his new domain, proudly surveying all that he ruled.

In time he reached the source of the stream—the three streams, actually, for he could see three places where water escaped the twenty-yard-wide depression that evidently captured rainwater. The clouds he had seen from orbit would bring rain, he surmised. Unless this island possessed the most incredible natural hydrological system imaginable, pumping water up to a height of....

Just how high was he, he wondered? From his current vantage point, trees blocked his view of the ocean. Across the pool was the final rise to a treeless point, maybe thirty yards to traverse, amounting to another ten yards of elevation.

He slogged knee-deep through the water along the edge of the pool, and up the last mount. Pacing himself, he reached the peak barely winded. Looking out he saw the great sun, barely changed in aspect for all his elevation, and the vast red shimmering sea spread out before him, and in that calm expanse a single, massive, three-masted sailing ship.

He fell to his knees. His breaths came in short, explosive bursts. If it were an illusion, it was not some fleeting trick of light; if it were an illusion, it was borne of madness, for it persisted.

"Men" he said aloud. Maybe not men like me, he thought, but men. Explorers, or travelers. They build ships, like ours. He squinted to make out details. He knew little of Earth's old-style sailing ships. But from what he knew, this seemed identical.

It was distant, but creeping his way; the meager wind was barely playing with her massive sails. The sails. Every sailing ship he had ever seen had white sails. These... these were something else. Each of her mainsails was the same: Jet black, with a bright yellow streak. The yellow began as a point along the top edge, near the left corner; from there it slashed to the right and down, widening to nearly a fourth of the sail's width at the bottom, reaching nearly to the opposite corner.

The pattern could mean anything. But it was clear that it meant *something*. And whatever the message was, Alex sensed, it was not a happy message.

Piracy. That was what the sails said to him. Then he tried to shake the thought off. *Just cultural norms*, he thought. *Thousands of years of human tradition—these beings must have a completely separate sensibility. These colors and shapes might evoke anything in them. It needn't be bad.*

"Alright," he said aloud. "So if you really believe that, why aren't you gathering wood right now for a signal fire?"

Scuttling feet first and face down along the slope, he reached the pool. Only one thing made sense. He had to hide. Until he knew more, he had to hide. What things exposed him?

His footprints on the beach—nothing he could do about them without exposing himself further.

His raft at the trees' edge—if he snuck through the overgrowth, he might manage to safely drag it out of sight.

And the drifting escape pod. It could be near the ship. They might have found it already. Nothing he could do there.

The raft, then. He began a controlled scramble down the hill descending mostly the way he had come, along the face hidden from the ship.

His hands were scraped, and he stopped just long enough to put his gloves back on; the gloves made it awkward grabbing onto handholds, but their protection allowed a more rough-and-tumble descent. Mostly he followed the stream, but here and there he departed from it to move downward more quickly. Eventually he lost track of the stream.

Panic welled in him. He had no time for getting lost; he had to hide that raft. Recklessly he tumbled down, till he heard something that froze him. He heard voices.

Log of the Ammanon Deloré
Dollapan, humble servant of Almighty God.

All praise and glory to He Who Is Silent. May the God of land, sea and sky forever receive glory.

This log is recorded by the hand of a mere man, but by the grace of God I pray that every word may be blessed and approved by God Most High as an accurate recounting of what we each have seen, and felt, and heard.

I begin my account from where I have left off in my exploration journal of the place we have elected to call Valor Island.

Spying a small animal of uncertain nature, we pursued it up a steep rise some one hundred feet, covered mostly in a yellowish dry grass. There, the ground leveled but the heavy green vegetation resumed. The animal was still ahead of us, and we continued pursuing it. It became clear that a steep rise, nearly a vertical wall of some thirty feet, would soon block the path of the pursued, and so we closed upon it with renewed vigor.

Two of our party lagged slightly behind, and thus Ilbe Rass, Igren Doel and I burst together into a small clearing at the foot of the wall.

Whatever we had pursued had vanished, perhaps into some small hole, perhaps into the overgrowth to the left or the right.

138

But before us, standing at the base of the rise, was a blessed vision. A man, if one dare call him a man, dressed in clothing of brilliant white, and of a form never before seen by any among us. He turned to face us. Upon his breastplate was writing in some marvelous and unknown script. About his neck, his garments gathered into a ring of silver.

He spoke to us, in words we could not understand. Those who had lagged now folded in behind us, confronted by this incredible sight.

Beside me, Igren Doel, craftsman of Barnable, spoke: "Who are you?"

At first, the blessed vision gave no response. Then, drawing off one of his bulky gloves, he held high his holy hand and extended it to us.

We fell in terror before him. We knelt before the glory of the most blessed, the Harbinger, the man of five fingers.

*   *   *

Below him, obscured by foliage, there were voices. Excited, agitated voices. Nearing voices. He turned and scrambled back up. He could not recognize any words, though the voices were distinct enough. It was a language he had never heard. The inevitability of this should have been obvious, but in the rush of the moment, the strangeness of their language terrified him.

There were many voices, and they were closing. He knew their tone—they were in pursuit. He stumbled into a rock face. Not the way he had come down. No way up. He spun back to the way he had just come. The foliage rustled, and then burst aside.

Three hideous creatures stood facing him.

"My God," he whispered.

They seemed human in shape, but shape only. They had clothing, odd clothing, but his attention fixed on their heads. Repulsive, sickly white heads, of no discernable form. Their lumpy white flesh glistened. They were like some malformed genetic mutations. Their mouths were black, irregular. And eyes... they

139

seemed to have no eyes. Where a human would have eyes they had horizontal bands, bands encircling their heads.

Two more appeared behind the first three. Outnumbered, five to one. They all stood motionless, Boten and the five.

They seemed ready to lunge. He imagined them swarming him, overpowering him, devouring him with their misshapen mouths. Eaten alive, by horrors such as these.

There was a sound—speech, it seemed. But none of their mouths had moved.

He wouldn't wait for them to attack. He had to act, to do... something. He remembered what had been described as the universal sign of greeting. Time to find out how universal 'universal' was. Slowly, he unfastened the glove of his right hand, and slid it off. Then, gently, he raised his right hand.

There was no change in their faces, not the slightest change. But their bodies changed at once. First one dropped to its knees, then another. After a moment's pause the other three dropped together. Most seemed to be facing down, but two continued to face him. Of those two, one began to make sounds, words, it seemed. Then it went silent.

Alex spoke, knowing his words would be as unintelligible to them as theirs were to him: "Step aside, boys," he said gently. Then, in an ever-so-slightly sterner tone, he said, nodding: "Let me pass."

One of the creatures reached up slowly and clasped the sides of his own head, as if covering his ears to block out Alex's words. At least that was what Alex thought. Grasping the lumpy white flesh-like surface, it lifted off its mask, revealing the entirely human-looking face of Abbik Dollapan.

BOOK II - Harbinger

(Author's note: For a time in the story, the language differences pose a problem. The Mirran tongue will be expressed in English, and presented in normal font. Boten's spoken English words will be displayed in italics, and the reader must recognize that the Mirrans are incapable of understanding it.)

Book II
Chapter 1: Contact

He became aware of a rocking, a gentle rocking. He must have passed out. The last thing he remembered was a face, a human face. Still half asleep, and with his eyes still closed, he tried attuning himself to his surroundings. The rocking was slow and mostly steady, but with occasional variations. It was accompanied by deep, wooden creakings. He might be aboard a wooden ship.

He listened for other sounds, for engine noises. He heard no mechanical thrumming of a steam engine, no whine of turbines. There were voices, but he could not make out what they were saying. Some spoke in an odd tonal pattern, almost like singing. But if it were singing, it was so off-key that no melody was discernable. Yet there was a rhythm to it; whatever it was, it flowed in three-four time. There was a splashing of waves, not loud, but steady. And there was a fluttering of wind—like wind on sails. He remembered the pirate ship, or what he had taken to be a pirate ship; he remembered the black and yellow sails.

With a start, he was fully awake. He was on his back. Looking up, he saw a ceiling of finely fitted wood planking. Beyond the foot of his bed—for that is where he now perceived he was lying, a comfortably soft bed—was mounted to the wall a lantern, burning just brightly enough to illuminate the room. The lamp was a finely detailed metal and glass affair, with the ignition point for the oil or gas hidden behind a dispersing metal shield, probably to guard the eyes. To his right, across the room, was what he guessed was a window, though it was covered by a hastily attached blanket or sheet. But the occasional waft of air animating it, and the reddish light penetrating it, revealed a window's presence.

He gently fingered the shirt he wore. His pressure suit was gone, replaced by an oddly woven but quite comfortable shirt and pants.

The fasteners were a bar-and-loop equivalent to buttons. He must have been deeply, deeply out— to have slept through the removal of his suit, and being dressed in new clothes. The entire room rocked again, ever so slightly, and he realized he was aboard a ship. A sailing ship. He sat up abruptly, and his head began to pound. To the right of the window, a figure slumbering in a chair stirred.

Seeing that Harbinger was awake, Captain Dollapan rushed to his side.

"Most holy one, have mercy on us," he said, kneeling beside Alex's bed. "How can we be of service to you?"

Alex turned his head slowly to the man, pondering his incomprehensible language. The man's nose seemed to have been broken at some time in the past. His right ear had an oddly scarred fold near the top. His face was weathered by years of salt air. It was a seafaring face, an utterly human face. It was the same face he had seen on the island, the man beneath the mask. Unless they all looked alike here, he thought.

"There's no way you speak English, right?"

The man cocked his head a moment, then lifted his palms and shrugged. Alex smiled. So there really are some gestures that are universal. The man's hands—or, more specifically, his fingers—caught Alex's attention. The little finger of his left hand was missing, as were the little finger and ring finger of his right. Here was a man, thought Alex, who had a long history upon the seas.

"Français?" Alex asked. *"Deutsche?"* He had retained his German as easily as he had picked it up, but his French was broken. He shook his head. It was a stupid inquiry. The idea they would speak French or German was as absurd as their speaking English. But it was the only thing he could think to ask. The man continued to shrug. Looking around, Alex saw a table near the head of the bed, and on it, a cup in a recess. He was thirsty. He motioned toward the cup, and the man handed it to him.

It was half full of some dark liquid. He drank. It was either a fruit juice that had gone bad, or a mild alcohol. Moving it from his face, he rolled his tongue around inside his mouth. He began to understand the reason for his headache. It was likely they had been hydrating him with this, and that he had a twinge of a hangover. Smiling, he handed the cup back and shook his head.

Mortified, Dollapan took back the cup.

"One moment, kind sir," the Captain said, and sprang to the door. "Tell Mr. Mennetek," he told the seaman outside, "that... our guest... is awake. But first, have someone chip some ice and bring it with a pitcher, at once. And," he added, handing him the cup, "tell Seaman Doel to heave overboard the rest of his Pinoae, bottle and all. Run, man!"

Turning, Dollapan found the newcomer at the porthole, with the blanket pushed aside. Dollapan joined him there.

It was clear to Alex that they were under sail, and away from the sun. But it would take time for him to develop the language skills that would allow him to inquire as to their destination. His pitiful bag of foodstuffs was gone now, and just as well. This was his life now. If there were any food on this planet that would sustain him, people who seemed identical to him would have it. And as for his raft? The raft he thought of as some old snakeskin he had shed. The ship shifted again, and he braced himself. Alex returned to the bed, and sat with his legs hanging over the edge.

His benefactor managed with some success to pantomime that the cup had been disposed of by being cast overboard.

This can't work, Alex thought. Smiling, he told his companion: *"We're like a bunch of monkeys, gesturing to each other."* The man was visibly distressed over not understanding, but Alex broadened his smile, thus putting him at ease. Either he had to learn their language, or they had to learn his. So, either several thousand, or million, or billion of them would learn English, or else one reasonably intelligent earthling would show what he could do.

He made a gesture like writing. His companion helped him up and led him to a small desk. There he laid out a sheet of paper—a fine, linen-like paper, and what seemed to be a fountain pen. He dipped it in an inkwell, and handed it to Alex. Alex examined the tip. Surprisingly like the antique fountain pen Mark Grossman kept at his desk, he thought. Only so many ways to build a mousetrap.

The man pulled up a small bench, just broad enough for them both to be seated. Pen in hand, Alex wrote the words *"This is English"* near the top left. Then he drew a vertical line dividing the paper. Handing over the pen, he pointed to the blank right hand side. The man looked at him, confused. Alex pointed back to his bed, to the window, to the logbook on the desk, and then he shrugged. Again, he pointed to the white space.

The man held the pen near the paper, and hesitated. He looked at the unreadable words Harbinger had written.

Alex saw where he was looking. Taking the logbook, he laid it over what he had written. Then waving his hand toward it, he tried to convey dismissal of what he had written. Again, he pointed to random things about the room, and again, to the paper.

Dollapan puzzled over all of this. How could the Harbinger of God not know how to speak their language? Or how to write it? Nonetheless, it appeared as though that was what confronted him. Adjusting the pen in his hand, he wrote with painful precision "My name is Abbik Dollapan."

The newcomer's delight in having convinced him to write was unmistakable. Taking the logbook away, the newcomer took Dollapan's hand, still holding the pen, and moved it below the three strange words he had earlier written on the left. The newcomer moved Dollapan's hand to create a few strange letters. Then he stopped, and caused the Captain to cross out what he had just written. Dollapan looked at him. The newcomer pointed to the words on the left, and shook his head. Then he took the pen in his own hand and crossed off everything on the left. He moved his hand to the right, below what Dollapan had written. Laying Dollapan's hand upon his own, he gestured with an open palm.

Dollapan was flabbergasted. It seemed he was asking to be taught how to write. Could he be understanding correctly? Could Harbinger be asking for lessons, like a schoolchild? He used his hand to move the newcomer's hand, to spell out the first three letters of the Mirran alphabet. Then he stopped. Again, the newcomer's pleasure was obvious.

Captain Dollapan leaned back, and thought. Looking over to the man, he saw what he took to be a hopeful smile. Dollapan nodded, and the man's smile broadened. There was a sharp knock at the door. "Come," said Dollapan. A sailor entered with a tray holding a glass pitcher filled with ice water. Dollapan took it from him. "Advise Mr. Mennetek that Andril Degg is to be hereby relieved of all duties. Have Sailor Degg report to these quarters at once."

*   *   *

Before his language lessons began, Alex learned things about them from pure observation. Most startling was their hands. Although the first man he had met—the man he came to perceive as the captain of the ship—had in fact lost his right ring finger to an accident, his missing little fingers were another matter. On both right and left these beings lacked the little finger. This in itself was not strange. Indeed, if anything were strange, it was that this seemed the only significant way they differed from him. But what was odd was the structure of the hand, for it contained all the precursors of the missing finger. In examining their hands, he could clearly feel that there were five sets of metacarpal bones extending from the wrist to the knuckles. But in these people, the fifth metacarpal ended without a finger. Visually, it suggested the little finger had been chopped off. Indeed, it was his assumption initially that this was precisely the case—that all had undergone some ritualistic childhood amputation. It was some time before his language skills would develop to where he could understand that this was a genetic condition, one that had arisen within the time of their recorded history.

Other differences between these people and himself were trivial. The hairline along their scalp was recessed, an inch or more. He had taken it to be the beginnings of balding, till he had seen it was universal amongst the crew. He wondered if it was true, as well, of their women.

For that matter, of course, he had to wonder if they *had* women. It seemed almost a given; everyone aboard ship bore the clear traits of human maleness. Could they be so humanlike, and yet not have a male-female schism? Still, he was making assumptions. So much

147

would have to wait for his understanding of their language to develop.

Their eye colors were somewhat different from what he was accustomed to. Brown eyes existed, and were mostly indistinguishable from human brown eyes, but they were a rarity. Blue and green seemed more common, but there was something odd about those colors. One man, named Islak, seemed less self-conscious over being stared at, and Alex was able to examine his eyes. Although they were basically blue, they were flecked with violet.

These people grew no beards, though that was common among some earthly races. The Captain, once he had recovered from the shock of Alex's emerging beard, quickly arranged tools with which Alex could shave often, and in private. Neither of them could guess how the crew as a whole would react to their new guest growing hair from his face like some wild animal.

The rhythmic vocalizations he had heard upon first awakening were, in fact, singing. He had thought it atonal, but he began to realize it possessed its own tonality. It was simply not a Western European repeating-octave tonality. It was to him as skewed and random as traditional Chinese music had always been. The sailors used it to help synchronize their actions, mostly for raising and lowering sails. His initial assessment of three-four time was correct; all the songs repeated a one-two-three, one-two-three pattern. As he heard more of it, the intonations carried more and more sense. The songs became less grating, and almost pleasant.

As Alex's language lessons began, one fact quickly emerged—and it had nothing to do with language. The Mirrans operated on a sleeping and waking schedule utterly different from his own. With no earthly timepiece, the closest he could reckon time was based on his own heart rate being seventy-two per minute. With that as a baseline, he figured the typical Mirran cycle involved almost exactly four hours awake, and two hours of sleep.

In theory, with no solar cycle to function as a referee, every individual could operate on a completely separate schedule. However, he soon learned that people bound together (such as a ship's crew) would coordinate to a common waking-sleeping schedule. This difference in their schedules, eight hours versus twenty-four, posed no great difficulty between Alex and the Mirrans—once, that is, it was understood. Initially, Alex had been frustrated over Andril Degg's frequent "naps" as he perceived them. And the Mirrans were greatly concerned over Boten's apparent comas, lasting three or four watches (six to eight hours) at a time.

Captain Dollapan learned to schedule language lessons by cycling between Andril Degg, Ig Doel, and Islak (all of whom proved excellent teachers) and also to simply allow the newcomer ("Boten", he called himself) to sleep as long as he wanted. Both Boten and the Mirrans were intrigued to note that, in the long run, they all spent the same ratio of time waking to sleeping.

As his understanding of the Mirran tongue improved, the first topic that emerged was the ship he spotted at the island. For although he had at first assumed he was now aboard that three-masted ship of fearsome black and yellow sails, he had since learned that this ship had two masts, rigged with all white sails.

"This ship is what? What name?"[3] Alex asked Andril.

"Ammanon Deloré," he answered.

"And what is other ship?"

"Other ship?" asked Degg. "We have longboats. Two longboats. A longboat brought you from Valor Island to the Deloré. We thought you were unconscious... asleep. Do you remember the longboat?"

"It was a long boat. Longer than Deloré. What was her name?"

"Longer..." echoed Degg, "...longer than the Deloré? No. Smaller. Much smaller. And the longboats have no names."

"No," said Alex, as best he could muster in Mirran, "this was bigger than Deloré."

Degg called for the Captain, and called for Islak to be roused from his sleep. When they had gathered around him, Degg explained what had been said so far, and then pressed on:

"You saw another ship, larger than the Ammanon Deloré?" To

---

[3] The broken nature of Boten's speech reflects his limited understanding of Mirran, in which he is speaking.

149

this, Alex nodded.

"When?" asked the Captain. "When did you see her?"

Alex struggled, and then threw up his hands. He still found Mirran timekeeping confusing.

"Before or after you came on board?" Islak asked.

"Before boarding," Alex said. "Before seeing... before meeting... you all."

Dollapan leaned against the wall, thinking. "There's no other ship scheduled to be out this far," he said, mostly to himself. "And no other that has been lost at sea off the northern coast for at least... there must be a mistake." He turned his attention back to Boten. "Where?" he asked. "Where did you see her?"

"On the sea, drifting."

"But where on the sea?" Dollapan pressed.

"Between..." Alex said, "...between island, Valor Island, between island and... *the sun*... the DevilsEye." Inwardly he smiled. He had learned what they called their sun. And, knowing they had always lived in the shadowed side of their planet, he understood why they had so dubbed it.

"Beyond Valor Island?" Islak said, in wonderment. "What ship? What ship has ever been beyond Valor Island?"

"Only one," Dollapan said vacantly. "Only one I can imagine." His attention sharpened, and turned again to Alex. "Three masts? A galleon?"

"Three masts..." Alex repeated, nodding.

"Before the Deloré," Dollapan reaffirmed. "Long before?"

"Long?" Alex asked.

"Much time before?"

"Some time before."

"Ab, what is it?" Islak asked.

Dollapan turned to him. "Twenty-one years before." He turned again to Alex. "Innotek Assan," he said gently. "Her name was the Innotek Assan." Andril Degg turned away in horror.

Dollapan spoke in hushed tones to Islak: "Twenty-one years. Could he have been out here all this time? He would have been but a child when the Assan sailed."

"If," observed Islak quietly, "he ages as we understand aging. He could be... eternal. Nothing in Scripture says Harbinger must be a man, as we understand men."

"But if he were more than a man," Dollapan said, "could he not have done something? Intervened, on behalf of the Assan's crew? Rescued them somehow from their fate? He is said to have powers...."

Alex sensed the change that had overcome the room; all his questioners grew silent, and were clearly filled with dread. Perhaps he had been right, about the meaning of the ship's sails.

"Where is Innotek Assan? Where now?"

"Where?" said Dollapan. "Gone. The ship is dead. Her crew is dead. Innotek Assan is no more."

"Dead? Why dead? How, dead?"

Islak answered: "The DevilsEye. They could not survive the DevilsEye."

"But you survive the Eye. Why you, and not Assan?"

The Captain turned aside, and spoke to Andril Degg: "He saw them, but had no idea what was happening to them?"

"Good Captain, the Harbinger is not God," Degg reminded him. "He is not omniscient. His learning of our language shows us that."

"Protection," Islak explained to Alex. "We have protection, and the Assan did not. That is why we survive. And why they did not."

"Why did they have not protection?"

"They left long before us, before anyone knew. They came back to us... dying... and dead."

How long was I out? Alex wondered. Maybe the black with yellow slash was some sort of distress or disaster sign. He could see in their faces, in the very way they stood, that the whole matter was terribly painful.

"No more," Boten told them. "We need speak of it, no more."

Book II
Chapter 2: Fluency, and Understanding

Over the watches that followed, Alex learned quickly.

He preferred his lessons with Anned Islak who, he came to understand, was a scientist. The profession being newly developed, he appeared to have the reputation of a Da Vinci or a Galileo. As Alex's fluency improved, so did the sharpness of their conversations, and Alex perceived that Islak's reputation was likely deserved. Islak was hampered, however, by a limited knowledgebase. Things Alex knew simply because generations upon generations before him had thought them through, these things were but recent discoveries, or even yet undiscovered for Islak. Alex constantly held himself back from explaining concepts; there was no way to know what a sudden influx of scientific knowledge might do, what dangers he might thrust upon these people. He would need to learn much about their science, and their culture, before he could consider revealing mysteries that might propel them forward technologically. Once he nearly overstepped himself. When inquiring further about the uniformity of waking and sleeping schedules, Islak was able to communicate to him that the coordination of schedules shipboard also applied to whole cities. There, the close proximity mandated a common schedule. However, between cities of considerable distance, there was apparently no coordination. And none seemed needed. From this Alex deduced that the Mirrans had neither instant communications nor fast transport. On Earth, all time had been local time (noon defined as the sun being straight overhead) until the advent of the train and the telegraph. Only then had a system of time zones and uniformity of timekeeping across broad distances been established. He was about to inquire if this were true, when he stopped himself. The very posing of the question: "Do you have instantaneous communications?" or "Can you travel hundreds of miles over the span of a single watch?" would inherently suggest that such things were possible. And that suggestion would lead a man like Islak to, for good or ill, achieve such feats.

Alex's lessons with Andril Degg had their own interests and dangers. Degg was in training for the Mirran priesthood, and it was clear that religious beliefs were a vital part of their society. Clearly they were monotheistic, which suggested a fascinating commonality that he was excited to explore. But this brought him to a danger he feared even more than revealing too much to Islak. For it quickly became obvious that Degg, as well as most of the crew, were convinced that he, Alexander Boten, was a fulfillment of some ancient Mirran prophecy. The dangers here were almost incalculable.

First, if he could not dissuade them of this notion, they would look to him for spiritual leadership, and divine revelation. What right would he have to lay the template of his own beliefs across theirs? Endless rounds of Select Committee hearings, held over concerns about the implications of the Hermes project, had hammered that into his head. On the other hand, what right would he have to withhold from them what understanding of God he had? How similar, or how different, would their concepts of God be? Where they differed, would he defer to theirs, or they to his? Or could they stand side by side? These were questions that the powers-that-be back on Earth were just beginning to struggle with, in anticipation of the later stages of the Hermes project. Until now, Alex had only thought of such questions as an amusement. But this—this could be deadly serious. Although Andril Degg constantly pressed him for his understanding of God, Alex resisted. He had to learn all he could about Mirran beliefs before he could consider saying anything. The one thing he had said from the outset, and that he felt compelled to stand by, was that he was not this figure they all assumed, this "Harbinger". The problems of discussing science with Islak seemed trivial next to discussing religion with Degg.

One other distinction between his teachers became evident. Degg seemed far more intent on written exercises, whereas Islak focused purely on the verbal. At first, Alex thought the peculiarity was Degg's, spurred on by the prospect of Alex's being able to read their holy scriptures—The Book, they simply called it. But in time he came to see the prejudice as being on Islak's side. For although Degg merely weighted his lessons strongly toward the written, Islak's slant was absolute. It seemed impossible to believe his first thought—that someone as articulate verbally as Anned Islak might be illiterate. He began to observe Islak more closely; his motions, his actions, his perceptions of things around him. Alex began to suspect that Islak was going blind. He mentioned this to no one.

Although Alex was able to pick up some of the Mirran's written language, he found the spoken tongue far easier. Their grammar and syntax were not greatly different from earthly languages with which he was familiar. But their alphabet, and the way written words mutated in context—ways not reflected in the spoken word—made their written language a nightmare. This concept—that the written and spoken languages would be distinct—had only the faintest parallels in Alex's experience. There was "conversational" English and "formal" or "technical" English, but compared to this, those differences were trivial.

Most frustrating for young Andril Degg was Alex's utter inability to grasp the writings of Mirran scripture. The Book was written in a long-defunct form of their written language, even more complex than the current form. Passages recounting what some person had spoken—or what God himself had spoken—would be comprehensible. But the rest might as well have been written in Sanskrit. All Alex could deduce about their religious beliefs had to come verbally.

His most relaxed lessons were under the tutelage of one Igren Doel, a glass smith from Islak's home town of Barnable. At first Alex was alarmed by Doel; Doel's close-set eyes gave his gaze an overstated intensity. But in time Alex came to see that Ig Doel, alone among his teachers, had no agenda whatsoever, but was fascinated merely to be in Alex's presence. In time, Alex came to view Ig's close-set stare, together with his abrupt motions and his tendency to cock his head when listening, as rather bird-like. The intense gaze, from then on, was less threatening and more amusing. These lessons he found breezy and most enjoyable.

Alex was shown the utmost deference, by all members of the

crew, and he was given free run of the ship. This was extended to him in ways he sometimes felt were wholly inappropriate. When asking to see the Captain, he would be escorted to the Captain's quarters—and left there, unattended, while the Captain was called away from his duties to meet with him. On one such occasion, while awaiting Dollapan's arrival, Alex noted standing on the Captain's desk something that had escaped his attention when they had embarked on their initial writing lesson. Or perhaps, he thought, it was something that had not been left out at that earlier time. It was a framed picture, a portrait of sorts. There were three figures; the central one he guessed to be the Captain. On either side of him were what Alex took to be two women. The style of the portrait was curious. It was done as a line drawing, without shadings. And it seemed almost mechanical, rather than artistic. Then he remembered seeing something once that had a similar effect. It had been created with a device that was a precursor to a camera: A large box with a pinhole opening on one face. And on the opposite face of the box, the image of the subject, after passing through the pinhole, was projected. There the image was traced by the "photographer". Picking the picture up to look more closely at the corners, he found the initials of the artist. He half expected to see Islak's initials there, but it had been signed by someone else.

His eyes lingered for a time over the two outer figures. He couldn't say just why, but they definitely struck him as female. Perhaps this was his first hint that these beings' humanity extended to separation of sexes. The three figures, even in the lifeless, soulless format of the drawing, seemed to him to exude a domestic solidarity. He envied the Captain—but not, he fancied, in any resentful sense.

As he was about to set the portrait down, a folded paper caught his eye. It lay on the desk, and had evidently been mostly obscured by the picture. Without thinking, he picked it up. It seemed to be a letter, for the ink of handwritten script had partly bled through. He noticed then a scent, which he could only think of as a perfume. It seemed to be upon the paper itself and was very faint—so faint, it seemed to him, that it might have accidentally been transferred from the writer's skin. Quickly he laid the paper back down, and replaced the picture atop it. He was intruding, too deeply, too quickly, into the Captain's life.

*   *   *

The language lessons went smoothly. Before long, Alex was fluent in a practical sense, and his lessons focused on refining his skills. Their sentences tended to be long and expressive, and he enjoyed growing more adept at mimicking their style.

Between his lessons, he preferred to spend time on the deck. There, he could let his mind flow with the waves, and the rocking of the ship, and the gentle fluttering of the sails. The sea-shanties sung by the sailors made perfect musical sense to him now, but this understanding came at a price; he found himself having more and more trouble recalling the music he had always lived with. Pop songs got scrambled in his memory first. He remembered the singers' faces, but he could no longer hum the tunes. Soon classical pieces were harder to recall. He clung to one, a clarinet concerto by Mozart. By humming or whistling it to himself daily, he was able to preserve his memory of the octave scale. There was little else left to him of Earth.

The prevailing winds were against them. He understood from the crew that it had been a long journey out; it was shaping up to be an even more arduous journey home, tacking broadly to maintain some forward gain. The DevilsEye, as they called it, had long since set behind them, leaving just a red smear on the horizon. Ahead and to starboard, still out of sight, was a large rock formation they called the DevilsJaws. They might or might not pass near enough to see it. To port, in the eastern sky, was the galactic swirl, which they referred to as "The Crown of God". The status of this object in their sky was a curiosity. Although it was, technically, rising, this was only true for a stationary observer. The farther south they traveled, the lower on the horizon the galaxy appeared. In essence, by moving as fast southward as possible, they were causing the Crown of God to appear to be setting. He reasoned, and the Captain confirmed for him, that this action would lessen the further south they went, and that by the time they reached land, the Crown of God would be strictly rising, no

157

matter what their direction. He thought back, how near the Mirran pole, where they had picked him up, this Crown of God was perpetually half-risen. How throughout the Mirran year, from that vantage point, the galaxy crept along the horizon sideways, and was eventually lost in the sun's glare. And how, much later, it would reappear gradually on the other side of the sun, as it moved far enough from the brightness to again be seen.

But he realized that for those farther south, nearer the Mirran equator, a completely different effect would be had. For a large part of their year, the Crown would be completely hidden. Then, as it rose, it would climb to straight overhead. Unfaded by any trace of sunlight, he imagined it must be beautiful as it reached its zenith.

Only part of one arm was currently above the horizon, but seeing it reflected in the calm sea, he could imagine what a glorious sight it would be. The Crown of God. How could it have been named anything else?

And, every hour or so, a faint point of light would crawl across the sky. Everyone's attention seemed riveted on it. Islak was curious as to what Alex could tell him of it. Degg was certain Alex could tell him of it, and seemed fixed on getting him to admit that he had some connection to it. All Alex felt he could do was to refuse to discuss the matter.

Holding firmly to the Deloré's midship railing, Alex watched it now, just past its zenith. Its radio beacon was no doubt still transmitting, although everything else about it would be lifeless, cold, and dead. He found himself wishing that its orbit would decay, so that it might burn away in a flash just as the outer shell of the escape pod had. Some day, he thought. Some *day?* Some *time*, was more appropriate. After some incalculable time, maybe hours, maybe years, it would disappear. But until then, its course through the constant night would be an endless reminder of home.

"It is important to you," Islak said behind him, "isn't it?"

The sudden voice did not startle him. Few things startled him these days.

"What's important?"

"It is NewStar you are watching, is it not?"

Alex did not reply.

"Offer no vague evasions," Islak suggested, "and I will press the point no further. Poor Degg will hound you enough."

"My connection to this new star is important to him."

"He has his own private nightmares that haunt him. He dreads the coming of Harbinger, for reasons... well, for reasons which are his own."

"Are others... disturbed, about the coming of this 'Harbinger'?" Alex asked.

Islak did not answer at first, seemingly lost in thought. "Had you asked me that before we set sail, or before we spotted NewStar in the sky, I would have laughed at the thought. For generations we have longingly looked forward to the coming of Restoration, and of Harbinger." Then a darkness came over his tone. "But looking forward to something, even striving after something, is not the same as receiving that thing."

"Speak to me, my friend," said Alex.

"You are connected with NewStar," Islak said. "You deny this," he added with a smile, "but I detect a lack of conviction in your denials." The smile left him. "It does not matter. But I would ask you this. From the vantage point of NewStar, have you looked down upon the world?"

"Islak," he said, hating the deception, "there is nothing on this matter I can tell you."

"If it matters," Islak said, "if it is a part of the reason you do not wish to discuss this, I can assure you of something. Despite Andril Degg's reactions, I can assure you that if you prove to be Harbinger, no harm will come to you. Not by his, or any other Mirran's hand."

Alex did not reply, but simply watched the Sirocco draw near to its setting.

"I have many toys," Islak said, "for peering in where men's eyes fail. If any of my instruments would be of use to you in learning something of this NewStar—which seems to interest you, as much as it does us—I should gladly lend you their use."

"Thank you," Alex replied. Sirocco disappeared.

"Ig and I have talked about grinding a new glass," Islak said, as if changing the subject. "A fine glass. A massive glass. What do you think, friend Boten? If I were to mount such a glass, and attach to it some mechanism to pan through the sky at great speed? Say at the speed of something like NewStar? Were I to turn its gaze upon this heavenly apparition, what do you suppose that I should see?"

Alex turned and looked at him squarely. There was a notion that had never occurred to him.

"How many others on Mirrus work with glass the way you do? In the making of magnifying lenses, I mean."

"None. Not a one of whom I know. Igren Doel is the only producer. I am, as far as I suppose, the only user."

"Then," said Alex, looking out across the ocean, "all that I can think to say is... I should wish that you would not pursue this idea."

Islak nodded. "Very well, then. As long as I manage to keep my curiosity at bay, I shall not pursue it." Receiving no further reaction, Islak walked away.

Before he had moved beyond earshot, Alex spoke toward the sea: "You, sir, are a man neither accustomed to, nor long capable of, keeping your curiosity in check."

Stopping, Islak turned back to him. Then, with a silent nod, moved on along his way.

Alex sighed. If he were right about Islak's vision, the danger was minimal. He suspected Islak could no more view the Sirocco through a lens, of any power, than he could see his own hand held out before him.

Alex moved to the starboard bow. There, just below his reach, one of the twin lamps mounted to the ship's sides burned a hundred or a thousand times more brightly than the soft cabin lights. Within the lamps, polished reflectors directed light ahead; around them, opaque shrouds guarded all ship's eyes from their direct intensity. The light they threw ahead was only a pin's prick in the night. Or rather, what Alex Boten perceived as night. To the Mirrans, the darkness they fended off with their oil lamps was the simple order of things.

He marveled at the Mirrans. So human, so very human. Too human, it seemed, to be coincidental. So little separated them from himself.

Even the missing fifth finger seemed almost a triviality, especially as Islak had confirmed to him the underlying bone structure of the Mirran hand. Alex concurred with him; it seemed likely the writings in The Book were correct—Mirrans had once had five fingers. Something had changed them. Here Alex had kept his speculations to himself. A birth defect, perhaps, propagating among the population. A virus attacking a very specific part of the genetic code. Intervention by an omnipotent God. Alex favored the last two, if for no other reason than that they fit the history recorded in the Mirran scripture.

As Andril Degg relayed it to him, the loss of the fifth Mirran finger had begun abruptly, with all children born after a specific point in time. A genetic defect, even a dominant one, would have taken generations to wend its way—to insinuate itself through the whole population; a genetic virus was more plausible. But even that was a stretch; the effect was reported to have no exceptions, and thus must have spread with lightning speed. Conceivably, an airborne infection, with no noticeable indicators, could propagate quickly enough to infect everyone within the birthing of a single generation. Yet he had never heard of a genetic virus having such a profoundly clear physical effect, and yet no secondary effects whatsoever.

If the Mirran texts were to be believed in this regard, the intervention of God seemed at least as likely a proposition. A virus of such selectivity and potency was easier to imagine being designed, than being a random happenstance. Alex's inclination was to think of God's hand being at work. But if it were, then the reason for it and the meaning of it were as much a mystery to the Mirrans as they were to him.

As for the texts, if Andril was conveying them accurately, they seemed to Alex more an orderly history that some superstitious allegory.

In terms of his own experience, a more mathematical tack led him to the same end: Regardless of the likelihood of earthlike planets, of the commonness of carbon-based life, of intelligent life not only resembling but nearly copying human form, a greater factor remained. Even if human-like (or Mirran-like) life existed on planets circling every sun, the odds of random chance depositing him in orbit around a sun, let alone around a planet orbiting a sun, were beyond reckoning. Some form of reason, design, and plan seemed to have brought him here. The inexorable sense of divinity seemed to confront him on both the visceral and intellectual planes.

Leaning on the bow rail, he drew deeply of the sea air. The divine hand on his life was all that was left him. Everything else had been ripped away. Initially he had thought just of himself, of what had become of him. In time he had begun to think of those he had left behind, mostly of Madeline, and El and Katie. *Oh Katie May*, he thought. *What was it like for you, when the news came?* He had fallen, uncontrolled and at a wild angle, down the tower and into The Tube. The most likely conclusion would be that the Sirocco had been destroyed. And Alex knew what they had said more or less: Had the Sirocco somehow survived, his power (and thus his air and water) would have been long gone by now. She had found her way through the denial and anger, and by now considered herself widowed. In the truest, most fundamental sense, he realized, she was. She would have to move on with her life. She was not the living-single type. Certainly not the single-mother type. She needed a husband as surely as the girls needed a father. She would remarry. He hoped she would choose well.

And if she remarried, and Maddy and El forgot him, as he knew they must, and they bonded to the new man? And if they had a dozen children of their own? What if then, in some fantastic way, he should return—to Earth, to home? Then the problems to be resolved would be ones he would gladly face, no matter what he had to give up to do so. To hold his girls. To touch Katie's hand, even if under the watchful eye of a new husband. To fall to his knees and touch the soil of Earth. Just... once... more.

He closed his eyes. The idea of return, toyed with even tangentially, was too painful, only for its utter impossibility. He couldn't think of such things; they would drive him mad.

He faced astern, and the forelamp beneath him warmed his back. His eyes moved across the decks, straining in the faint orange moonlight. Amidst the occasional crewmen tending to their jobs, a lone figure was walking the deck. It was Captain Dollapan. The Captain seemed neither to approach nor to recede. He seemed to be casually checking various aspects of the ship in a way that suggested to Alex that he was maintaining a purposeful distance. Alex approached him, meeting him amidships.

"I am not well versed in ship's operations," Alex admitted, "but perhaps I might assist you?"

"Thank you, but no," said Dollapan. "The things I am tending are of no great consequence."

"Indeed." Alex's eyes locked on his. "That's what caught my eye. It seems a ship's captain's energies could be otherwise employed."

Dollapan gazed back at him, considered protesting, but then resigned himself to having been detected.

"Walk with me, Alex Boten." Dollapan turned and headed for the bow, to the very place from which Alex had spotted him.

Alex followed him, as if in tow. Dollapan seemed entirely in place here. His bearing was that of the absolute seaman. It wasn't only his face that showed his time at sea; his hands betrayed the years as well. And it was more than just the missing ring finger lost in some long ago accident. Two of his fingernails had been damaged, and had grown back skewed and wavy. His left hand bore several scars.

The Captain stood at the rail, and Alex stepped up beside him. Standing in the reflected glow of the forward lights, the Captain ran his hand along his hair. It was sandy blond hair, beginning to gray, pulled back into a ponytail—a not uncommon style among the men on ship. The forelight seemed to change his face. To Alex, it suddenly seemed less weathered than... tired.

"I was not spying on you, Mr. Boten."

"It was not my intent to level such a charge against you, sir."

"Yet you perceived the matters I was attending to were a sham."

"'Sham' might be a bit strong," Alex offered. "But tell me, my Captain. What is it about me that concerns you?"

"Not you, in the truest sense," said Dollapan. His voice grew muted: "My concern is more with... my crew."

"Sir?"

"They are a fine crew, do not misunderstand. Many have sailed with me before. And the rest come highly recommended. They have braved dangers from which most men would shrink. But they are faced now with a prospect that none of us imagined when we set sail."

"The appearance," Alex ventured, "of the new star."

"More than that," Captain Dollapan added. "The appearance of one whom many herald as the Harbinger of God."

Leaning over the rail, Alex looked behind the lamp, into the dark water sliding by beneath them.

"You understand by now, I trust," Alex told him, "that I am not, that I cannot be, this thing you at first assumed me to be."

The Captain did not reply.

"This 'Harbinger'" Alex told him. "It is not what I was meant to be."

"Indeed. And what were you 'meant to be', Alex Boten?"

Still leaning over the rail, Alex turned his head back, looking across the ship, through the rails and rigging on the opposite side, to the rising arm of the galaxy.

I am an astronaut, he thought. *But there are no words to express that here.* Even if there were words, he knew, it would still be best not to express them. At least not yet.

"Well," Alex said. "Let me rephrase myself. Being the 'Harbinger of God' is not what I had envisioned for my life."

"I respect your denials," Dollapan told him. "But many of the crew still hold that you are he. And that is the point that concerns me. There is arising among some… a disquiet over the prospect."

"Islak assured me shortly ago that no one among Mirrans would bring any harm to me."

"And he is right, I am certain. I cannot imagine anyone harming you. Least of all because they believe you to be the Harbinger of God. But still…." Dollapan gazed out to the sea, "…these are strange times, filled with strange events. I feel more at ease with my eye upon you."

"Captain, as needless as everyone assures me it is, it gives me

164

comfort to know I have a protector such as you." As he was speaking the words, his intention had been merely to ease the Captain's embarrassment over having been caught watching him. But as Alex finished speaking the words, it occurred to him that there was deep truth in them. He felt cared for, protected, in a way he had not felt in a long time.

"Good, then," the Captain said. "Good."

The Captain did not move from his spot. He still stood, looking out over the water.

"But," Alex said at last, "there is something else." The Captain did not respond at first, and Alex waited for him.

"I understand there is much you cannot say," the Captain observed. "And yet, I find myself with a question."

"Islak and Degg have already asked me everything imaginable."

"Degg is a budding priest; there is much he takes for granted. And Islak bases all he does on certain assumptions. Why don't we… step back a little?"

"Captain?"

"To something more basic."

"Very well. But I'm not sure I will be able to answer," Alex warned him.

"I see," said Captain Dollapan, his eyes shifting slowly across the waters.

Alex felt wrong, holding back without even knowing the question.

"If it is important," Alex said, "there is no reason not to ask."

"Some questions are best left unasked," Dollapan said.

Dollapan's words left him uneasy, conflicted.

"That," Alex said, "is not an attitude of which Anned Islak would approve."

"True enough," the Captain conceded. "But it is not Anned Islak whose opinion concerns me now. It is yours. The truth, Alexander Boten, is that I am not sure what you should think of me, were I to ask this question."

"Indeed?"   There was vulnerability in that observation, vulnerability that took Alex aback. He was unsure what tone to take to draw the Captain out. He decided to gamble that a man used to taking charge, to dealing with challenges, might respond well to aggression: "And what would I think of you, Captain Dollapan, if you had not the courage to ask it?"

Dollapan understood the psychology at once. He willingly let it manipulate him, let it drive him toward the place he wanted to go—the place he needed to go. He looked around. Convinced no one could hear, he spoke: "You cannot say whether God has sent you. I understand this. But perhaps you can answer a more core question." His voice grew softer. "Can you say... whether God... is?"

Here was a question Alex had not expected, not from Captain Abbik Dollapan. He had understood the Captain and Islak to be of virtually one mind, that this was part of why Islak had chosen Dollapan to master the charter. The existence of God was fundamental to all that Islak did, to all that he was. For Islak, it was no unchallenged assumption; it was an inevitable conclusion. Curious it now was to learn that Islak had chosen as captain, of so dangerous a charter as this, a man who would pose such a question.

'Can you say whether God is?' The question brought him back—far, far, back—to the congressional closed-door hearings on the future of the Hermes project. Alex hadn't gone there to testify, only to observe. Everyone who had applied and had a serious chance of one day going on a Hermes interstellar jump was at the hearings. A few of the top candidates actually did testify. But mostly, testimony was from the Agency's top men, and from whatever theologians and philosophers some Congressmen thought qualified as experts.

A consensus had emerged, in time. If the crews did encounter intelligent life, and if communication could be established, no declarations of faith were to be made. This had been the consensus, but it had been a consensus by only the thinnest of margins. A cynic might have concluded it was a consensus engineered by the selection of those chosen to speak. Those who dissented did so vociferously, but futilely. Alex remembered the last day of the hearings, and the closing exchange between the Select Committee's Chairman and the Agency's Director.

166

> Representative DeLibri: Mr. Director, I am inclined to agree with most of my fellow committeemen. We should limit all of these hypothetical, potential discussions which might one day occur. Limit them to matters of fact.
>
> Director Jackson: Congressman DeLibri, it occurs to me that by limiting discussions to what you label as *fact*, we will be completely bypassing issues of *truth*.
>
> DeLibri: Conceded, Mr. Director. But would you want to promote discussions of truth? If so, whose truth? Your truth? My truth? Some astronaut's truth?
>
> Jackson: Well, Congressman, as someone once said, 'What is truth?'
>
> DeLibri: Indeed, Mr. Director. A wise observation, indeed.

Alex smiled at the memory. Fortunately for the Director, no one advised Congressman DeLibri of the source of the quote until after the session had ended.

"Have you posed this question," Alex asked, "of your friend Anned Islak?"

"Dear Anned would blanch to hear me speak so. In truth, Alexander Boten, I leapt at this charter, not because I *believe* that Anned Islak *is* right. I took it because I *want* him to be right. I would be a happier man if I were sure, as I was in years gone by, that there is order to the world—order to the land, sea and sky. I would be more at ease without this creeping sense that all about me is chaos and randomness. This sense that plagues me... it is not how I have lived my life, not how I have raised my family, not how I have commanded my ships. It has been upon me too long. This is why I venture to ask that which I know is inopportune, what I suspect you will even decline to answer."

Matters of fact, the panel had decided. *Limit them to matters of fact*. Alex was not bound by oath to follow that edict. Only astronauts chosen for the final phases of Hermes would one day be asked to commit to it. But it was clear that a commitment to the edict was Congress' intent. Clear that they would have insisted Alex commit to it, had anyone thought he might end up in such a place as this. *Matters of fact.* He watched the Captain staring out over the waters. 'Can you say whether God is?' Dollapan had asked. How many times had this man asked himself this question? How long had it haunted him? To what lengths had he gone to conceal his uncertainty from those around him?

For Alex, debate over philosophical and theological contamination crumbled in the face of compassion.

"There is much I cannot say," Alex repeated. "But there are two things I can say."

Captain Dollapan turned to face him squarely. "I am prepared," he told Alex, "to hear you. Whatever you may say."

"First," Alex said, "it is a matter of fact that I have never seen God, never had tangible sensory proof that he is. And second, it is a matter of fact that I do believe that he is."

"I see," Dollapan intoned. The sails fluttered briefly, and the Ammanon Deloré continued slicing smoothly, slowly through the gentle swells. Captain Dollapan drew in a breath, deeply. "What a curious thing you are, Alexander Boten, to have been set into the midst of us."

*   *   *

Once, when passing by outside Anned Islak's cabin, Alex heard a voice which caught his ear. It was familiar, but he could not place it….

"You see order about you. I grant you, I see it as well…."

Mennetek, Alex realized, the ship's first officer. Now, the line between hearing-in-passing and eavesdropping is easily crossed, and Alex crossed it almost before he knew it. Almost.

"…but as for what you see in that order," Mennetek went on, "that is where we depart."

"Order is order," said Islak. Alex sensed equal parts of annoyance and confusion in the scientist's tone. "How is it that you look at the same things I look at, Mr. Mennetek, and in them see no sign of the creator?"

"'The heart of the wicked is dulled' they say." Mennetek's tone

168

was more teasing than sarcastic. "Perhaps the mind of the wicked is dulled, as well?"

"Rubbish," was Islak's retort. There was a silence. "Not the scripture," Islak said, as if apologizing for himself. "Your application of it."

Alex found himself leaning closer to the door with each round of banter, and feeling progressively embarrassed with himself as he did so. Without allowing himself an internal debate (which he might lose) he knocked.

Upon opening the door, Islak's face at first showed surprise, and then a wry amusement.

"Come in, kind sir," he said, stepping back and to the side. A shift in the ship's orientation spilled Alex forward, as if on cue.

Mennetek's face paled, which pleased Islak to no end.

"Now, dear Mennetek, you were saying...."

"Another time, to be sure," Mennetek said, arising from the small table built into the wall.

"Nonsense," said Islak, closing the cabin door. He slid a chair to the table for Alex, and in so doing, effectively blocked Mennetek in. Then Islak sat at his original position, opposite Mennetek. "Come, Alex Boten, sit with us. Philosophize."

Alex saw the discomfort in the First Officer's eyes. Having no desire to embarrass him, he stood his ground so that Mennetek might slide aside the chair and move out.

But Islak's hand went to the chair before Mennetek could make his move. His large hand wrapped around the chair's arm.

"Arken," Islak said, almost in a whisper. "You know this man disavows what we have claimed him to be. He claims not to be sent from God. He declines even to discuss God. How would you think you could offend him?"

With a creaking of timbers, the Ammanon Deloré shifted again, this time impelling Alex toward the door. He resisted, intrigued to hear what Arken Mennetek would say.

"Besides," Islak added, in a tone now intended for all to hear, "if the view to which you claim to hold should be true, then this man Alexander Boten would have to be a mere man." Islak's hand slid from the chair's arm. "And there would be no God to take offense."

Mennetek's lip curled slightly on one side, and for a moment Alex thought he would receive a brief lesson in some new aspects of the Mirran tongue. Mennetek checked himself, however, and eased back down into his chair. Alex sat down, as well. Arken Mennetek was thin, especially compared to Anned Islak. He was thin in the body, thin in the face, even his features—his nose, his eyebrows. And since his thinness was not offset by inordinate height, these features gave the impression of his being a small man. But Alex had seen him on deck, commanding the men. In action, there was nothing slight about him.

"Mr. Islak and I have been exploring the concept," Mennetek said, without ever taking his gaze off of Islak, "of whether the natural world offers proof of God."

"More precisely, Mr. Boten, whether the natural world suggests God, to a point nearing plausible exclusion. Proof is a word I reserve for certain very specific conditions." As with Mennetek's words before, these words from Islak were not directed at Alex Boten, but directly across the table.

Mennetek turned to Alex. "I should ask you, sir, to be frank with me. Does such a discussion disturb you? Or... offend you?"

"Our estimable First Officer wishes to know if you intend to strike him dead for blasphemy."

Mennetek shot an angry glare at Islak, giving Alex just the moment he needed to settle into the tone of the discussion.

"It would be rude of me indeed," Alex said, "having proclaimed to no end that I am merely a man not unlike yourselves, to now suddenly reveal myself to be... an *angel* of God." Alex knew of no Mirran equivalent, and so used the English word *angel*. "No, Mr. Mennetek, you may speak freely in front of me... at least as freely as you would speak in my absence. I am not here to hold you to account."

"So," Islak said, in a tone now free of playful jabbing, "how is it you see the order all about you, and yet you do not see the handiwork of a creator?"

Mennetek's eyes wandered about the cabin, though not in search of any specific item. His mind was searching; the traveling of his eyes was merely a sign of that. Suddenly, his eyes snapped to Islak.

"Parket," he said. "You've played Parket with the Captain. On this voyage."

"Yes."

"Your set, or his?"

"Mine," Islak said.

"You have it here, in your cabin?"

Islak nodded, arose from his chair, and turned to a wall cabinet.

"Only the stones," Mennetek said. "No need for the board."

Islak laid on the table a pouch filled with clanking stone objects. Mennetek untied the pouch.

"We look about us," Mennetek said. "We see many things." He reached into the pouch. "Some things clearly have order to them." He pulled out three flat stones. On each was a letter of the Mirran alphabet. "Most things," he said, laying the stones out in a row, "have no obvious order." Pulling another set of three, he lined them up beneath the first three. Both sets spelled gibberish. Four more times he pulled out stones with no meaning. Alex noted that many of the stones repeated; he guessed they were part of a word game, a spelling game. Finally, Mennetek pulled out a set of stones that gave him what he wanted. He arranged them at the bottom of the array so that they spelled TUR.

Turning to Alex, he said: "I don't know how far your language lessons have gone, if they have taught you spelling. These letters spell 'tur', a small fresh water shoreline animal." His attention turned back to Islak. "Now, I had to arrange the order of these letters; they came out of the pouch U-R-T. But you will grant me, that had I continued pulling letters, entirely at random, in time I would have pulled a T-U-R, in that order."

"Granted," said Islak. "In time, and with enough stones to draw from. 'Tur' would have come up."

"There, then, is your universe, Mr. Anned Islak." Mennetek's hand swept across the grid of stones he had laid out. "You look at it, and see stretches of randomness. And here and there you see order. A word, a meaningful word. A true and legitimate word. Yet I

171

submit to you, it is every bit as random as the nonsense that was drawn before it."

Islak looked at the array, then at Mennetek, and again at the array. He looked to Alex. Alex widened his eyes, and gave a slight turn to the head. He hoped the gesture was interpreted on Mirrus as it would be on earth: 'Don't look at *me*.'

Islak smiled. Again, he looked to Mennetek. "There is something wrong. With this." He waved his hand at the stones. "With this argument."

"I would not dispute that," the first officer said. "It is entirely possible I have made an error in reasoning. I await your kind assistance in pointing it out to me."

Islak looked again to the stones, leaning back in his chair.

"I will give you some time to ponder my folly," said Mennetek, rising. Alex got up and cleared a path for him.

Without moving his eyes from the table, Islak spoke to him as he opened the cabin door: "It is so intuitively obvious that it is wrong... on such a basic, fundamental level, that it seems to defy disproving. You are good, sir. Very good."

"I may be good, kind sir," Mennetek answered. "But am I right? Being clever need not be the same as being right."

Now Islak looked up to him, as did Alex. Both saw an unexpected expression in his face.

"I..." Mennetek began. "I have never used this argument before." He glanced at the table. "Had never... imagined it, before." He needlessly adjusted the fasteners on his cuffs and collar, using them as a delaying tactic while he marshaled his thoughts. Then, with the door open and his hand on the knob, he brightened: "If you find the argument disturbing... you are not alone." He slipped through the doorway, and was gone.

Alex looked to Islak, but Islak's attention was on the bottom row of stones, on the magically, randomly appearing sequence.

Forgetting himself, Alex said: "It is a silly argument. You know that."

Islak nodded, without shifting his gaze. "It is silly," he agreed. "Silly, and wrong. But that does not matter. Not until I can say to him, or say to myself, precisely why it is wrong."

"He doesn't even believe it himself. The whole discussion was a game to him. An intellectual wrestling match."

"He did not believe it at first," Islak observed. "But he stumbled onto something. Something unexpected. When a man sets his mind, sets his life, upon a certain course, he becomes comfortable with it. Everything he encounters seems to conform to it. It becomes a way of life. The two most disturbing things that can happen to such a man are that he comes upon strong evidence contradicting his view, or that he comes upon incontrovertible evidence proving his view."

"Mr. Islak?"

"At such times, a man is forced to consider all the ramifications of the views he has so blithely held. It can come like a terrible weight, suddenly."

"Well then," Alex said brightly, "the kindest service we can offer to our fine First Officer is to formulate a solid argument proving what we know instinctively, that his spelling argument is meaningless."

"Yes, we must do him that kindness. But another time, Mr. Boten. I grow weary just now."

Islak did not look up from the table, and Alex slipped quietly out of the cabin. The walls, the ceiling, the floor, all softly creaked as the Deloré shifted. Anned Islak fancied he could hear the water slipping past the hull. Probably just the blood rushing through his own ears, he mused. His hand reached to the leather satchel along the wall under the table. He laid his fingers along its top edge. He remembered the disturbed look on Mennetek's face just before he left.

"Oh, Arken," he whispered, staring nowhere in particular. "How can two men, of such diametrically opposite views, be so equally worn down by the same effect?"

*   *   *

During their trip the winds grew and faded repeatedly, but there was an overall trend to increasing calm. This, Alex learned, was the way of things. For some time, since the coming of the drought, there had been virtually no wind (and no clouds) over the land. Gentle

173

breezes played along the ocean shore, and winds picked up the further out a ship sailed. The last leg of their journey was at a crawl.

When the Desidomone lighthouse at last broke the horizon ahead of them, Captain Dollapan ordered the Deloré into a position between Halabae Island and the harbor, and there he anchored.

Via signal lights, he ordered the following message sent to the tower:

"Ammanon Deloré at anchor. Crew safe. Wish medical exams before docking. DevilsEye met and survived."

Presently, a message was sent back: "Request received. Arranging medical. NewStar is come. Any word of Harbinger? Any word of Restoration?"

This was troubling. All aboard the Deloré (save Alex Boten) had assumed Restoration must have appeared in the Temple during their journey out. How could it be otherwise, if Restoration were to precede NewStar? The suggestion that he had not yet come was mystifying. Dollapan ordered that the crew not be informed of this message.

The only reply Dollapan ordered was "Awaiting medical."

Meanwhile, he prepared a letter. He began writing it three times. The first two opened with references to the last letter he had received, but these he destroyed before completing their first paragraphs. It was the third—composed as if that previous letter had never arrived—which he sent with First Officer Mennetek, in a longboat, to deliver by hand:

Most beloved Vinasa,

By the grace of the Most High God, we are brought to the shores of home, each man safe. I pray you speak to no one of this, nor about that which I now request.

With utmost dispatch arrange for a funeral coach. (No, my dear one, no one has died. Patience!) Inwardly, without thought to a casket, it should accommodate myself and two other men. It must have full drapery to close off any windows, a driver of the highest discretion, and two horses. The horses must be well rested and prepared for a journey at least as far as Barnable, and possibly beyond.

I beg of you to have this coach within sight of the Fannest Street dock, no later than the lighthouse signaling Red Twelve, Yellow One.

Eagerly yearning your embrace,
Abbik

Book II
Chapter 3: Desidomone

A funeral coach stood along Fannest Street, a block from, and facing away from, the disused dock. Her driver attended the horses, but nothing else. The curtain of her rear window, drawn closed for all but the scantest corner, never moved.

The harbor lighthouse time lights progressed, through Red Eleven and into Red Twelve. Within the twelfth Red, the first, second, and third Yellow lights came to shine. Before the fourth Yellow appeared, three men scuttled forth from under the dock, across Harbor Road, and up Fannest Street. The door of the coach opened a crack, and as the men approached, the tiny open corner of rear drape was tugged shut.

Into the dark chamber climbed Dollapan, then Boten, then Islak. The moment the door closed behind them, a dim lantern was uncovered to illuminate the inside of the hearse in a faint yellow glow.

The first thing that met Alex's eye was the Captain, in a passionate embrace with what he took to be the Captain's wife. Turning discreetly aside, Boten noticed the only other thing in the coach besides Islak: another figure dressed in the same black garb as Mistress Dollapan. This second figure he took to be the Captain's daughter, whose presence none of them had expected.

Reaching up, she unhooked the corner of the veil covering her face, and drew it away. Boten felt as though he had been struck. Her pale face seemed to float in the black framing of her hat, veil, and dress. The yellow lamp caught and reflected in her eyes, eyes of an almost fluorescent green. Among the men of the Deloré, he had seen a remarkable range of new eye colors. But nothing like this. Perhaps among the women of Mirrus, it was common. But on Earth he had never seen anything like it. Her features were most delicate, as if made of porcelain, and she startled him when she spoke:

"With Mr. Islak," she said, "I am acquainted. But the man of ill manners is new to me."

Boten removed his hat, tipping his head toward her in the same motion.

"My lady," he said, and then could think of nothing further. "Forgive me," he continued at last. "I am... new... to this place. And sadly unfamiliar with your ways." What ill manners was she referring to? Was it his staring? His delay in removing his hat? Some other slight he could not yet guess? She gracefully removed her black gloves. He was already on her wrong side, he figured; may as well make a go of redeeming himself. Based on the femininity of her attire, and upon the nature of everything that surrounded him, he hoped that a provincial sexist gesture might be in place. From his right hand, he surreptitiously removed the four-fingered workman's glove Dollapan had provided him, keeping his little finger still rolled into his palm. He reached up and took her left hand, holding it so the nature of his own hand was concealed. He raised her hand to his lips, and kissed it. On all the Mirran hands he had seen since his arrival, the missing little finger of each had seemed odd, even disturbing. This was the first hand on which it seemed natural. Her fingers were not as delicate as her face. They had the feel of fingers that had seen work. Not logging or hammering, yet not idleness, either.

As his lips paused, hovering over her hand, he smelled perfume. The same perfume, it seemed to him, he had smelled upon the letter in the Captain's cabin.

He was just beginning to come to terms with never seeing Kathy. And now, this woman... this girl... stirred feelings within him that surprised him, disturbed him. Embarrassment, and guilt, washed over him. He released her hand, and drew his own hand cautiously down and out of sight.

Now it was her turn to stare at him, which she did with her hand hovering where he had released it.

"Father," she said, without looking away from Alex. "What manner of man have you brought to us?"

Dollapan looked to them, and glared. "A madman, I think, Lannae." Then, with Alex's attention on him, Dollapan mouthed the words: *Your glove.*

Alex began sliding his hand back into it, but Lannae snatched the glove from him. A quick glance revealed nothing unusual about it. The glove's only peculiarity, a stretching of the material in the palm where his fifth finger had lain curled, escaped her notice. Holding the glove before her, she turned to the Captain.

"Father? Too much is going unsaid here. Why are we sitting in a funeral coach when no one has died? Why are we stationed at a pier decertified for use due to disrepair? And who is this oddly mannered man?"

The Captain leaned back, as though resigned.

Lannae saw that Alex was holding his bared hand out of sight. Turning her head slightly askance, she set her jaw. She reached out for his hand, slowly but with determination.

"Or what manner of treasure does he...." Her hand had found his, and in an instant she knew his secret. Her hand shot up to cover her mouth. "What manner of man...."

"Just a man, my lady. Miss Lannae Dollapan, if I understand correctly."

"Surely, sir. More than just a man. NewStar has appeared, to the North and East. After ten crossings, and ten upon those, it has flashed brilliantly. And now, from that same North and East, my father returns to us in the company of a man we have never seen, a man of five... merciful Heaven, forgive me." Then, looking straight into him, even through him, she said: "Most holy sir, I am your servant. Ask of me what you will." Then she lowered her gaze from him.

With his ungloved hand, he reached out and touched her beneath her chin.   Captain and Mistress Dollapan gasped, and Lannae Dollapan lifted her head.

"This," Boten said with determination, "must stop. I am not the 'Harbinger' you seek. I am only a man."

"I foresee," said Islak, settling back in his seat, "an interesting journey ahead for us all."

Captain Dollapan pushed up the driver's hatch but a crack, and hissed: "Barnable! With haste!"

Within a Sheltering Darkness

*   *   *

During the first leg of their journey, two compromises were soon reached.

First, Vinasa and Lannae Dollapan would stay, if Alex would not touch them. For although he had, in fact, breeched no aspect of Mirran etiquette by touching Lannae or kissing her hand, the idea that Harbinger might have an interest in his daughter caused Captain Dollapan acute distress, even beyond that expected from a father whose daughter was attaining marriageable age.

Second, of a more private nature, Captain Dollapan agreed to serve God in any way, yielding any service and sacrificing any or all measure of his modest wealth, if God would dissuade his Harbinger from interest in the Captain's daughter. No acceptance of the terms of this second point was forthcoming, but Dollapan left the offer open.

Within the limits of Desidomone, Alex was struck by the brightness of the city. Oil lamps abounded, on each street corner, at the front of every business and home, everywhere people traversed with any frequency. It had seemed to him aboard ship that a great deal of oil was being burned, but here it was riotously magnified.

Islak explained that Mirrus had two great marshes, bubbling forth with an oil—an odorless, tasteless brown substance, almost impossible to burn in its natural state. But after a simple refining process had extracted a sludge, the remaining clear liquid burned brightly, though with a slight yellow cast, and gave off little in the way of choking gases. This refining process was a major component of the Mirran economy. The sludge extracted, Islak went on to explain, was a potent fertilizer, which itself fueled the second and greater part of their commerce—agriculture.

This afforded Alex the chance to pose more straightforward questions around which he had danced for some time. Never once in the meals he had been offered aboard the Deloré had he been given anything he took to be meat. Two possibilities had occurred to him— first, that they were vegetarians, and second, that preserving of meats on long ocean voyages posed problems. It was not a question he

180

could put to them in a straightforward way, however. If they were vegetarians, then asking if they ate meat (which would have to be spelled out rather graphically as eating the flesh of animals) would itself suggest that such a thing were an option. His interest in the question might betray him as a carnivore. And were they vegetarians, such a concept could be quite shocking.

But Alex took his chance now, plying Islak with questions about the nature of their agriculture, pressing him to rattle off the full litany of things produced for consumption, taking care by his questions not to inherently limit the discussion to produce, but to keep the topic generalized. Although his vocabulary was already extensive, it grew during this portion of the trip as he learned the names and descriptions of a wide range of edible crops. And crops they all were. Not even animal milk or bird eggs of any kind entered into the discussion. When once animals did enter in—the topics of what Alex took to be a sheep-like animal raised for its wool, and of the breeding of horses—he tried to leverage the discussion into the raising of other animals. He got nowhere, apart from mention of several small species bred as pets.

For a long time they rode on without stopping. Although Vinasa and Lannae Dollapan had been alerted to the peculiarities of Boten's long sleep, Lannae, at least, did not entirely believe it. For when he at long last settled into sleep, the jostling of the carriage would, from time to time, rouse him to the edge of wakefulness. And after he had slept through two whole watches, every time a bump stirred him he became aware of her hovering over him, looking down on him with concern. Her apprehension over his well-being amused him at first, and comforted him as it wore on. After seven hours, he roused for good, with some regret she would no longer linger over him.

The carriage stopped for the first time, halfway to Barnable, so the horses might drink from a natural spring. Everyone emerged from the hearse to stretch. They were in the middle of nowhere, as far as he could discern. The land was featureless and flat as best he could make out. The Crown of God had continued to climb, and gave more light now. The orange Dessene had set, but its yellow twin, Hon, now added some light. However, what light there was revealed little. He had heard that Mirrus had numerous highlands, but he could make out no sign of them near here. They seemed to be in a broad wasteland.

Walking to the front of the carriage he stood beside the driver, who scrupulously ignored him while tending to the harnesses of the horses. 'Horse' was doubtlessly the closest animal to which to compare these creatures. They stood the height of a horse at their shoulders. Their necks were shorter; their heads, broader. Their tails were not longhaired like earthly horses, but shorthaired, except at their ends, which were tufted. Like Clydesdales, their legs were longhaired—but had been trimmed back to reveal their hooves. The hooves were not smooth, but rippled and ridged, as if made of overlapping layers of frilled clamshells. Alex assumed, initially, that they were painted. He later learned that they were, by nature, as colorful as they were textured. Predominantly red and yellow, they had splashes of iridescent blue and violet, as well. Their coats were a shiny black, though these two had been chosen to match the coach.

Curious, he thought, that black would be the color of mourning in a land where blackness was the normal state of things. But then it occurred to him that blackness—or more precisely, darkness—was only the normal state far from civilization. Here, between cities, or on the open sea. But the Mirrans brought constant light to anyplace practical. Through their own efforts, a warm yellow was actually their normal state.

Distant hooves drew his attention back the way they had come. Running lights were slowly approaching. Occasionally carriages, wagons, and individual horsemen had passed them heading back toward Desidomone. But now that they were stopped, for the first time a vehicle was passing them in their own direction. Instinctively, Alex stepped around the hearse so as not to be seen as the wagon passed. He found himself facing Lannae Dollapan.

His earlier repeated denials of identity, mixed with his now obvious desire to stay hidden, re-emboldened her.

"I never imagined," she said, "the Harbinger of God shying from a feed wagon."

"Keep that thought," he said, smiling. As quickly as it came, the smile left him. "You must disabuse yourself of this notion," he told her, "that I am some sort of fulfillment of prophecy. As I understand it, this Harbinger you seek will come to you for a reason. I am not here for any reason. I am here by a mistake. A ghastly, damnable mistake."

She watched as a darkness came over his expression.

"This…" he said, looking around, "…all of this… is a mistake. I shouldn't be here. Why is it no one seems able to believe that simple fact?"

Clearly, she thought over her next words with care, delivering them after some lengthy pause, and then with slow deliberation: "Might I see your hand?"

Glad to free himself of the awkward glove, and to flex his neglected last finger, he held out his hand. She took it in hers, holding it palm up. He thought of his pledge to touch neither Dollapan's wife nor daughter. This contact was not his doing, he told himself somewhat self-servingly, but rather her doing. With her index finger, she traced the line where the little finger met his hand, the place where a Mirran hand would end. She almost seemed to be examining it, as if searching for some seam or stitching. Never in her life had she seen such a thing, yet she marveled at how natural it seemed—the continuity of the outside edge of the hand, the smoothness of the arc of the points defined by the fingertips. Although it was considered poor taste, some artists had depicted what the hand of the Man with Five Fingers would look like. None had captured this simple beauty. All were in one way or another awkward. As awkward, she now perceived, as her own hands. Beside his hands, her own seemed to her misshapen, ugly.

"Thank you," she whispered, releasing his hand and turning from him. She returned to the interior of the carriage.

"Could we…" Islak said from behind him. Alex jumped at his voice and spun to face him. "Dear Sir," said Islak with alarm, "are you alright?"

"Fine," Alex said. "I'm fine. What did you say?"

"I wished to inquire, before we are all thrust again into such tight confines, if you and I might take some private counsel."

"Certainly," Alex said, stepping away from the carriage. Then he stopped, looking back at Islak, who did not follow him. Returning to Islak, he stood close so that they might speak in hushed tones.

"If you seek private counsel," Alex observed, "Shouldn't we move off from the others?"

Islak bit his lip, and seemed unprepared to respond.

Realization hit Alex. Taking Islak's arm in his, he said: "Come, my proud friend. Walk with me." Together they moved from the light of the hearse's running lamps, into the relative darkness of Hon and the slow-creeping arm of the Crown.

"I perceive I have not been so clever as I thought," Islak said. "I must look a fool, to everyone."

"You look a fool to no one, including me," Alex told him. "And I suspect that only I have deduced your secret. But why a secret? Why do you conceal this condition?"

"At first, when I began to suspect that my vision would not return, it was for fear of the safety of the crew and the mission. It was before we had met you, when I was making sightings on the DevilsEye. The lenses Ig produced for me met well my specifications. Alas, my specifications were not up to the need. Either the darkening of the glass was not enough, or of a sort that allowed some harmful agent to pass."

Ultraviolet, thought Alex. Dear Islak, ever near the truth. Always with insight into possibilities most would never imagine.

"I knew," Islak went on, "that I alone was in danger, for I alone was staring directly into the magnified Eye. Even so, I used what vision remained for me to conduct eye tests among some of the men. Everyone seemed safe. But what if my condition should become known to the men? What reaction, to news that the designer of all their protections had himself been struck down?"

"Panic," Alex agreed. "Perhaps a mutiny springing spontaneously, before the Captain could give the order to turn about."

"I resolved to convince Captain Dollapan to turn for home at once, revealing to him my condition, if need be. Your arrival, however, eliminated my dilemma."

"The Captain wanted to rush me back to home."

"Indeed. It seemed to me best to maintain my pretense until the

184

Book II, Chapter 3:   Desidomone

DevilsEye had disappeared below the horizon. But by then…."

"By then… "Alex continued, "…you had learned you could pull it off."

"Pull it off?" Islak asked.

"You could maintain the illusion. You could make everyone think you still had vision."

"Indeed. And of course, up to a point, I did. Even now I can make out shapes and motion around the periphery. Enough to fill in the gaps. Aided by hearing, and a familiarity with my surroundings. And if the room is brightly lit enough. I had fancied myself able to maintain the pretense. I liked being thought of as a sighted man. Is it, as you say, pride?"

"That's not for me to say." Alex stopped them, some fifty feet from the carriage. The horses had finished their drink. "You asked me for private counsel. But it was not to discuss this. Surely you sensed for some time that I knew your secret."

"Yes, I did. And your discretion was noted with appreciation. What I wished to discuss is this. It is clear that, while you are reticent to discuss the details, the circumstances of your arrival on Valor Island posed what you feel is a great unlikelihood."

"Yes, that is fair to say."

"To a point suggestive of divine intervention."

Alex thought over the suggestion with care. It was safer to admit this to Islak than to Andril Degg. "It seems to me the most logical explanation."

"Then," said Islak, with an edge of urgency, "consider a proposition. That although you know nothing of The Book, or of the prophecies given by God to us—notwithstanding this, might you not *be* the Harbinger?"

"I think that unlikely," Alex said.

"As unlikely as your standing here, now?"

Alex looked aside, and down. "Friend Islak," he said, "you have a way of framing a question…."

"Is it not possible that you are he?"

"It could be possible. But you have not called us out here simply that I might concede that point."

"Young Andril Degg has spoken to you much of Harbinger, of what the prophecies say. Including, I trust, that he shall be able to heal."

Alex exhaled. "My dear Anned Islak...."

"My condition progresses, and I soon face a dual prospect. Both that I shall be unable to conceal my condition, laying me open to the pity of my fellow men. And that I shall be unable to care for myself in even the most basic of ways. I am a man driven by insight and knowledge, who has now come to be driven by fear. Despise me not, for that. One thing I ask of you, speak the word that I might be healed. Let me not watch the last of my sight fade, thinking there was some avenue I did not pursue. I know you are versed in the ways of science. Think of it as an experiment."

Alex raised his hand to Islak's lips, and stilled him. In other circumstances he would have felt honored to be called upon to pray for his friend. But not like this. Not under the shabby pretension of being the "Harbinger" for whom these people yearned. Yet, before him was Islak's face, set in desperation. It was withering. Alex swallowed. *Please God*, he thought, *forgive me.* Laying the fingertips of each hand upon Islak's closed lids, he said softly: "Be healed."

Islak drew his head back, opened his eyes, and looked around. He blinked several times. "It is in the nature of the scientific method," Islak said, "to develop a theory, devise a test, and use whatever results—positive or negative—to refine that theory as needed. In that sense," he said, putting his arm around Alex and directing them back in the general direction from which they had come, "no experiment is truly a failure. No matter what the outcome."

"I am sorry, my friend," Alex told him. "If ever I encounter this Harbinger, with his healing powers, it is to you I will first direct him."

*   *   *

During the final segment of their ride to Barnable, a single horse with rider came up from behind them, passed them at full gallop, and disappeared ahead.   Alex watched him pass, through a corner of a curtain.   The Dollapans seemed keenly aware of the rider, but said nothing about him.

Sensing Alex's curiosity, Islak asked: "What was he wearing?"

"White, it seemed.   Something light-colored.   He had a cape or cloak, flowing back behind him."

"A very light gray.   Pants, boots, and a hat to match?"

"Who was he?"

"A courier," Mistress Dollapan said, staring at the curtain, as if looking through it.   "Carrying some urgent dispatch."

"We have a standard message delivery service," Islak told him. "Wagons deliver written correspondence routinely between cities. But for something more urgent, a courier will carry it directly."

Standard mail, thought Boten, *and a Pony Express.*

Mistress Dollapan looked to her husband.   "Some important news," she said, "has broken somewhere behind us.   News which needs conveying somewhere to the South."

That declaration hung heavy in the air for some time, with no one seeming inclined to either expand upon it, or to change the subject.   For a while, Lannae watched Alex prepare to speak and then stop himself several times.   She looked to the window, and back to them.   Finally, she could stand his discomfort no more.

"There has been a distress across the land for some time.   The great joy over the spotting of NewStar gave way to a general unease, once word spread to the outer lands that no sign of Restoration had been seen in the Temple Complex.   This grew to a sense of dread, once NewStar flashed to no effect."

Alex knew these last words were directed at him, to elicit some response, but he feigned ignorance.

"Holy scripture," she implored him, "clearly states that the fulfillment of NewStar marks the journey of Harbinger from the Adjunct to the Temple.   News spread from the North, where NewStar could be seen, to all parts South—via urgent courier.   Soon inquiries from all quarters flowed in to both the Adjunct and the Temple, and between those two shrines.   And when all word returned that no trace of Harbinger was to be found, or of Restoration, who was to precede him, dismay settled upon our people."

Another rider passed them, though this one did not wear the uniform of a courier.

"Of late," Vinasa added, as the hoofbeats faded, "a dirge has been heard in the streets of Desidomone. Its words say: 'Misery upon us / For NewStar is fulfilled / And Harbinger is not come'. One last hope was pinned upon the Ammanon Deloré; since she was sailing to the North at the time NewStar appeared in the North, many hoped she would carry some news."

"Upon her return to port," Lannae said, "couriers fanned out at once with the news of her homecoming. All of Mirrus awaits word from her officers and crew."

"I instructed the crew," the Captain told Alex, "to say nothing of you—of our suspicions that you are Harbinger, or of your denials of the same. But knowing the limits of secrecy, I used the ruse of medical exams for the crew to delay their return to the general population—thus providing us a chance to reach the Temple, to consult with the Temple Judges, before word of your presence circulated."

"And now, dear Alex," Islak added, "with us just short of Barnable, and far from the Temple, some news has broken forth from the direction of Desidomone, rushing in the direction of the Temple. I suspect the Dollapans fear, as do I, that word of a Man of Five Fingers is loosed upon the land. If so, every man and woman of Mirrus will be searching for you."

Book II
Chapter 4: Barnable and Beyond

During his next round of sleep, voices stirred him. The carriage wasn't moving. He looked around. The carriage was empty. Light poured in around the edges of the curtains.

Must be morning, he thought, forgetting. Groggily, he stepped out. They were in a barn, ringed by oil lamps. His riding companions milled about, talking happily, and sharing embraces with someone. Alex spotted the beak-like nose emerging from beneath a pair of close-set eyes; Igren Doel.

"Our Harbinger awakes!" Ig announced, seeing him emerge.

"I thought," Boten said, yawning, "you were held up on the Deloré."

"By the Captain's kind command before his departure, I was the first to be declared fit to depart. And by a fine steed, I arrived in time to make arrangements for your arrival." He stepped up to the hearse, and slid his hands across its woodwork. "I think," he said, "that I remember passing you. I did not know what manner of transport you had employed. It never occurred to me this hearse might be you." He turned his head to Captain and Mistress Dollapan: "And for that reason, it seems to have been an excellent choice. But come," he said, moving over to a quartet of horses, fitted with saddles. "I fear we have little time for self-congratulation." He adjusted the fittings of the saddles. "Shortly after debarking from the Deloré, some fair noise erupted on the ship, and thereafter on the docks. Word of our subterfuge may have escaped. I suspect couriers may have been sent out even ahead of me, as I endeavored to secure a horse."

"A courier passed us on the way here," Boten told him, gently handling the bridle. "It has been a long time since I rode," he said, looking the saddle over. "And it wasn't on one of these. Not exactly."

Ig Doel looked at him with a wild-eyed grin. "Then," he said with relish, "this shall be an adventure!"

Vinasa and Lannae resumed the funeral coach, in which they would, at a more leisurely pace, return to Desidomone. Their departure, Lannae's departure, brought on a mix of sadness and relief for Alex. He needed, he knew, to not be in her company for a time, to clear his head. The Captain bade goodbye to his family, and swung open the broad doors of the Barnable Livery. Meanwhile, Ig Doel gave Alex the most rudimentary refresher in riding, focused almost exclusively on mounting.

Ig sidled up to Alex's mount, and said covertly: "We ride with the Captain in front. Islak straight behind him. You and I on either side of Islak."

Alex looked at him squarely. Ig gave him a firm nod. For a moment Alex's heart sank; knowledge of Islak's secret had widened. But then a smile crossed his lips, and he nodded assent. These beings, he thought, might be human in form. But they were better than human in their dealings with each other. Moving into position around their near-blind companion, they tore off into the night.

*   *   *

After nearly a full watch, they stopped at a small stream, which fed into a major river not far ahead. While Dollapan, Islak, and Doel settled in for a watch's sleep, Boten prowled the area on horseback. He was amazed at how well he could see, though he imagined the Mirrans' eyes were even more adept.

Back on the island—Valor Island, as they called it—he had imagined what vegetation would be like here, in the depth of darkness. He had imagined a sparse, borderline existence. He had pegged it. What he saw here reminded him of New Mexico. It was almost like looking out across the high desert. There were few trees, mostly just patches of shrubs and grasses. He saw nothing like a cactus, but it would not have surprised him to encounter something along those lines. Most of his memories of New Mexico were daylight memories, but even in this dark, dark twilight, he felt himself returning to the days of his youth. He and Abbey had grown up in a place much like this, far from cities, far from people. Their father had wanted it that way; he had always been more comfortable in isolation. But the isolation was not complete for the children; Alex and Abbey had always had each other.

Alex moved his horse off the path. Not everything was desert-like, he realized. Here and there, in low areas, the ground was cracked. It appeared water had once been standing, perhaps not that long ago, but had now evaporated. This place was not the high desert, he reminded himself. It merely resembled one. It was not dry, necessarily. It was sparse because of the darkness. The plants that thrived here were those few drawing on some source of life other than sunlight. They had found some chlorophyll equivalent to draw life from the air, or the soil. Or perhaps from the now-scarce water—for the current dryness appeared temporary. He turned his horse back to the path.

Exploring the road ahead, he found it soon dropped away. This was the beginning of the lowlands of the river. Far ahead and level with him (on the opposite rise, he surmised) he saw a cluster of lamps. Several rose up higher. He guessed a building was under construction.

Not wanting to stray too far from his companions, he decided not to ride down, but rather held his place on the ridge. Another, brighter band of galactic arm had arisen, and a glow on the horizon hinted that before long the galactic core would follow.

Below him, he became aware of the sound of the river. Two pairs of lights—one pair nearer, one pair farther—shone steadily. Lighted markers, he assumed, for both ends of a bridge.

A new sound caught his ear; a scuttling of some small animal just before him. He dismounted. He listened. Silence. He released thereins, trusting his horse to stand its ground, and moved ahead. He heard it, and this time saw it as well—something small, moving awkwardly from shrub to shrub, desperate for cover. It had stopped within a scrub that lay within the indistinct shadow he cast, the shadow powered by the Crown of God. Moving slowly to one side, he let the Crown's light fall on the scraggly bush. He could see it; it

191

was a small crested bird with an almost absurdly large glimmering tail plume. Puffing furiously, its eyes locked on him. One wing hung down on the ground.

"*Well, my friend,*" Alex said, reverting to English. "*And what is your story?*" He knew birds sometimes feigned injury, to draw predators away from their nests. Giving the bird a knowing smile, he turned from it and walked away, back towards his horse. If the bird were protecting a nest, then retracing the path on which it had led him would be the surest route to that nest. Halfway to the horse he stopped and listened. He waited. His ears strained. The distant river was the only sound he heard. Turning again, he returned to the bird, finding it hidden in the sorrowful scrap of growth where he'd left it.

"*No ruse then, my friend.*" There was no diminution in the bird's breathing; it seemed destined to burst at any moment. He stepped back, trying to seem less threatening. It was only a bird, but he did wish he could save it. He wished he could save it, but he knew he could not. He knew.

An old memory sprang upon him. He had been perhaps ten when he found the bird, a small non-descript bird with a broken wing, a bird whose species he never did determine. He found it in the desert wastes, in a place not altogether unlike this. Taking it at once to Abbey, they had consulted each other, with the gravity of Emergency Room doctors. Ultimately, there was no course open to them but Father. He had counseled them that they had only two alternatives. This was a living thing; they must either kill it now, or pour themselves into caring for it.

For Alex, there had been no option. The thought of rescuing it, nursing it back to health, had a heroic feel. Their father drove Alex and Abbey into Gaton, some fair journey of almost an hour, to seek out a vet.

The wing was set, a makeshift splint attached, and they were off for home. It did not occur to Alex till sometime afterward that there had been no discussion of a bill, no hint that Alex should pay anything. Just another of the many paradoxes that were their father. In many ways, he did the outward things. All those things Alex would have given up in a moment, in exchange for the things that were missing.

His thoughts returned to the present. He looked again to the bird, and he sighed. Craning his neck around, he looked to the rising Crown of God. He imagined the place where Earth was, within the sea of stars. He looked to it, and looked back in time, to when he was ten. He looked back to this wounded bird's counterpart, then in his care. Within a week of finding it, the bird had abruptly died. There were no hints preceding the event, and no clues that trailed after. One morning it was simply dead.

He had cursed God over it; cursed him bitterly. To a ten-year-old, a wounded bird being nursed back to health was the entirety of the universe. And death, to a ten-year-old, was not an inevitability; it was an unjust cruelty. His rant against God was predictably heartfelt. When he had grown old enough to understand just what he had said, just what it had meant, his words haunted him. They haunted him for years. In truth, they still bothered him some even now, from time to time when he recalled them. He had asked for forgiveness many times, and had no reason to doubt forgiveness had been granted. But the words were still there. They had been spoken. They always would remain, historical fact.

Buoyed by their father's reaction to the bird, by his contribution to caring for it, they tried to share their grief with him. But true to form, he had been dismissive. *Only a bird*, after all. *Everything dies.* All of which had been true. But none of which they needed just then. All they had needed was a touch of human compassion. What they got was *Let it go, move on, grow up.* If not in those words, then clearly in that spirit.

"Why does he have to be that way?" Abbey had asked when Alex found her, under a scraggly pinon that had grown out of a boulder outcropping over a mile from the house.

"He is what he is," Alex said.

"Somebody ought to tell him. I ought to tell him. That he shouldn't say stuff like that."

For the first time, Alex used the words that would guide them to surviving the years until they were old enough to leave: "There are some things," he told her. "Some things, that you just don't say to him."

After all the years, those words still resonated. Turning back to the bird at his feet, Alex weighed the dichotomy his father had impressed upon him. Kill it. Care for it. Despite everything he held against the old man, he could never assail his logic. In this, as in so much else, Jeremy Boten had been right.

He hadn't the heart to kill it. He hadn't the resources to care for it. Then, whether it was because neither of the choices seemed viable, or because part of him wanted to reject his father's cold rationality, he turned and left the bird there.

Now speaking in Mirran, he gently called back to it: "Best of luck to you, my friend."

Climbing back on the horse, he decided that whatever would happen to the bird, would happen. If the wing was broken, it would die. If the wing was sprained, or out of joint, perhaps it would live. Whatever would happen to it, it was the same thing that would have happened to it if he had never noticed it fluttering in the brush.

He looked both ways along the path: West, the trail down to the river, and East, the way back to his companions. He had diligently avoided looking to the North, but his eyes found their way there now. No sign of the Sirocco greeted him. She was on the far side, or too low, or, by the grace of God, had descended far enough to burn. By the grace of God, he thought. The grace of God. There were weightier things upon him, weightier things than whether one bird lived or died.

"So," he said, initially to himself. "What am I supposed to do?" As he spoke, the direction of his words grew less inward, and more outward. "These people are looking... to me. I'm in the middle of this, and there's no way out. I can't just... just... recuse myself, like some judge with an inconvenient self-interest. There's nobody to step in... nobody to take over... nobody to clean up this mess. My being here has caused a crisis for them." There was, he sensed, a note of accusation in his words. He changed the direction of his thoughts, ever so slightly. "Did you give these people a prophecy?" he spoke to the sky. "A promise? A sign? Or did they make it all up?" He was rewarded with silence. He stroked his mount's mane. "Alright then,"

194

he prayed. "We'll cut through all the crap. I'll assume you spoke to them. But if you spoke to them once, why did you stop? Why are you 'The God Who Is Silent'? Why don't you speak to them now?" Then, lowering his voice, he added "Why don't you speak to *me* now?"

The God Who is Silent offered no response.

"Alright, then. I'll ask the question." Boten's mount shifted beneath him. He realized it was disquieted by his tone. He patted its thick neck. "Alright then," he echoed more gently. "I'll ask the question. What is this 'Harbinger'?"

Although no answer came, another question arose in his mind.

"Harbinger," he said, "means omen, or sign. What is this Harbinger supposed to foretell?"

"Never," came a voice from the darkness, "let young Andril Degg hear you ask such a question." The voice was Igren Doel's. He approached Alex on foot. "The lad would throw a fit over your not understanding."

"It is known, then? It's not one of your 'Mysteries'?"

"No," Ig said. "There are many passages from The Book compiled into the book of mysteries. But Harbinger's mission is not among those." He took Alex's horse's bridle in hand. "It is known. And before departing the Deloré, I learned that Andril's dread over your appearing hinges on that very point."

"What then, am I to be the harbinger of?"

"There is a chain of events. Restoration appears in the Temple Complex. NewStar announces Harbinger. Harbinger portends Restoration's act...."

"What is he the restorer of?" Alex asked.

"Of the first and only thing you should expect to be of concern," Ig said whimsically, "among people whose references to their Creator as 'the Most High God' and 'the Most Holy God', are outpaced only by their references to him as 'the God Who Is Silent'."

"So Restoration is to bring the voice of God back to the people? And Harbinger portends this happening. But what you're saying then... is that Andril Degg fears hearing the voice of God."

"To see the face of the Most Holy God is to die. How nearly as

195

terrifying the prospect of hearing his voice?"

"But I thought that when God went silent, it was a terrible thing. I thought the people longed to hear his voice again."

"So thought we all," Ig said. "Andril simply has more imagination and foresight than most of us. The thing we have been taught for generations to yearn for—it is something we have grown accustomed to being without. Some... many... have begun to perceive they are comfortable in their current estate."

"And you, Igren Doel? Are you comfortable in that estate?"

Doel seemed to struggle with the question, as if the inquiry bore more weight than Alex had intended. Finally, he scoffed the idea away:

"I am comfortable in no estate. That is why I run off to pursue mad adventures." Here he lifted his arms up from his sides, and wiggled his fingers: "I am the wind." The horse turned its head to look at him, considered him, and then looked away.

"I'm not certain I believe you," Alex said. "Not entirely. You are a businessman. You run a glassworks, yes? That makes you a solid, stable citizen."

"Oh. Does it, now? Oh, my." He laughed to himself. "Don't be fooled by appearances. My business was not begun by the labor of my hands; it was inherited. The soundness, the stability—they were my father's, not my own." Looking off across the wasteland, he added: "Were there any frontiers yet to explore, I would have declined the inheritance, and pursued them to their end. But everything around me has been discovered, been explored. There is nothing left to discover." He turned back to Alex. "Or so I thought," he added, smiling, "until Anned Islak enlightened me. A few mysteries remain, it seems. I may be living in a portentous time, after all, if the God Who is Silent is preparing to speak."

"How long has God been silent to your people?"

Ig began to walk, leading Alex's horse.

"Long," he said absently. "Long. Long before the Adjunct. Generations upon generations without number."

"I've heard of this Adjunct before. It's part of the prophecy."

"All tied in," Ig said, "with the first Harbinger."

"There was another?" Alex said, his interest acute.

"Long ago, in the Southern wastelands. A child was born, born with five fingers. And God spoke." Igren stopped, and sighed. "So they say. So The Book records. I have no cause to doubt it. God spoke in an audible voice, to the elders of the village where the child was born. He gave instructions, and the Temple Adjunct was built. And when the child was grown, he... completed it."

"And what became of him, this man of five fingers, after he had completed this Adjunct to the Temple?"

"By the time he completed it, he was an old, old man. He removed himself from the company of men. Retreated into isolation. In a short time, he died. The last thing God said to us, was that he again would be the God Who Is Silent, until Harbinger returned."

"I should like to see this Temple Adjunct. See this Harbinger's handiwork."

"It is a forbidden place," Ig said. "We are only allowed to see it from the outside. Only Harbinger was allowed in."

Alex thought over his next question with care. He almost did not ask it, but in the end, he gave in to himself.

"Was only the *first* Harbinger allowed in?"

Ig let the bridle slide from his hand. "Come," he said, walking away. "The others are stirring. Let us hasten to the Temple Court, if you wish to pose questions such as that."

*   *   *

The river crossing was unsettling for Alex. Although the wooden bridge seemed built solidly, the river raged wildly beneath them. Either it had swollen well beyond its normal banks, or the Mirran bridge builders liked playing with disaster; the water nearly reached the spanning structure, and seemed to be washing away at the supports where the bridge met the banks.

After crossing the river, they chose a slow, less-used pathway up to the far crest. Implicitly, Alex knew they were maneuvering to avoid the workmen at the construction site. The project was a tower, thus far two stories in height, apparently made of brick or stone. Although the riders spoke little, in an effort to not disclose their presence, Alex understood it was a project with which Islak was connected. The workmen were thus likely to recognize the scientist/inventor among their group. And, knowing of his inclusion in the Deloré voyage, his being spotted by them here and now was not in Alex's best interests.

Later, Alex would learn that this was one of many towers arising between Desidomone and Shelaemstet, the great Temple City. This was the second string of towers being built. The first had been completed some time before between Shelaemstet and the eastern port city of Mej Moribor.

A cupola at the top of each tower was to be visible to those towers ahead and behind, with the aid of simple fixed-position telescopes. Signal lights within the capping dome of each tower allowed those manning the towers to relay communications at speeds never before dreamed—virtually instantaneous communication. Now that the east-west line had been completed and was running successfully, it was to become just one of many tendrils reaching in all directions from Shelaemstet, paid for by each of the cities serviced. The network would be directed and managed by Islak— until operations had grown sufficiently routine to allow him to relinquish control and turn his mind to fresher challenges. Alex marveled at it; instantaneous communication was coming to them ahead of the discovery of electricity.

A second bridge met the riders not long after the first, and then nothing was between them and Shelaemstet but a vacant plain.

Alex began to make out, in the distance, the centerpiece of Shelaemstet. Their pace prevented easy discussion, so he kept his evolving observations to himself. At first, there was only a point of light on the horizon. In time it grew and took form, looking like an Egyptian pyramid, with its top third sliced off.

Closer still, and the lights of the surrounding city manifested themselves. It was then for the first time that it struck him that the entire geometric structure seemed to be aglow. As they drew nearer, he began to sense that the structure was being bathed in flood lamps near its base.

The city had no discernable limit—no wall, or gate, or even sign

198

that he noted. But homes and soon businesses began appearing more frequently, eventually in clusters, and finally in a continuous flow around them.   Mostly of wood, occasionally of stonework, they were—as in Desidomone— all well lit. What little he had seen of Barnable had been the same.

The hundred and fifty foot tall structure looming before them (not the Temple itself, he picked up from his companions, but rather some attendant structure) soon manifested a curious trait. It was not stepped, like South American pyramids, nor was it smooth like the Egyptian versions had originally been. For a time he thought that it resembled the final state of the Egyptian, a de facto series of "tiny" steps formed by the building materials themselves. But then the steps began resolving into a series of scalloping curves.

It was at this time that the Captain began checking at inns for lodgings, and at their second stop he had success.   Dollapan negotiated terms with the woman innkeeper. She was the first Mirran woman Alex had seen who was not wearing a hat, and he was intrigued to see that she, like the Mirran men, had a recessed hairline. He tried to imagine Lannae Dollapan without her black hat and mourning veil, tried to imagine her with this same hairline revealed. He smiled at the thought. He could not envision it.

While Captain Dollapan arranged care for their horses, Igren settled Alex into his room on the second floor, above the commons room and dining hall.

The room was an odd mix of the familiar and strange. It was plain in appointments, though fastidiously clean. It had a simple chair, table and bed, such as one might expect of some pre-Victorian hostel. There was only one window, a tiny one barely large enough to fit a man's head, covered by a drape that could be pulled aside but not permanently drawn open. This was not a window designed to admit light from the outside nor to afford a view to the lodger as he lounged about—for neither light nor view were there to be had. It was merely a convenience to see out and speak down into the street, should the need arise.

There was no toilet facility in the room. Those accommodations were evidently downstairs. He could only hope they were somewhat more advanced than the predictably spartan shipboard procedures, and the utter lack of any conveniences on the road.

"The watch is but half finished," Ig said in the doorway, preparing to leave him, "but we'll sleep as best we can. I want to move upon the Temple Court as soon as we can."

"Ig, I'm sorry," Alex said. "I've been up for ten watches so far. If I don't take my sleep soon, I'll not be of much use before the Judges."

Igren dropped his forehead into his palm. He had lost track of Boten's bizarre schedule. "How long this time," he said, without looking up.

Alex smiled. It wasn't like he was picking random periods of waking and sleeping. Then he thought again. To the Mirrans, no doubt, that was just how it seemed.

"Give me three watches," Alex offered, "and I should be able to handle myself." Six hours would do him, if he slept soundly. And after sleeping in a rocking funeral coach, and upon a hardscrabble plain, the bed beside him held great promise.

Book II
Chapter 5: Before the Temple Court

He had only one false awakening. Stirring due to no cause he could discern, he sensed he had not slept a full shift (for that was the term he now used, "a full night" being a hopeless anachronism). Nonetheless, he ventured downstairs, to confirm by the display of lit and unlit candles that only between one and two watches had passed. When next he awoke, he did not need to check downstairs. He felt within himself that he was rested. The inn had provided him a basin for washing. He used it, along with a rather dangerous-looking knife Igren Doel had provided him, and a bladder of pulpy vegetable gel—also by Ig's grace—to shave. It was a particular concern now, being in the close company of many strangers, to avoid any appearance of beard. To avoid the appearance of anything, for that matter, that would set him apart.

As he finished his shave, Captain Dollapan joined him. The Captain tossed a pair of new gloves upon his bedside table.

"The workman's gloves you have been using," he explained to Alex, "will not do for someone entering the Temple Court." Sitting down, he watched Alex's last few passes with the blade. It always fascinated him. "So I have purchased gloves for us all. Not identical, lest we draw attention to them. Yet a pair for each of us, lest attention be drawn to you as the only man wearing them."

"Pardon the observation, dear Captain. But you are a man adept at… what is the Mirran word for *skullduggery*?"

"*Skullduggery*," Dollapan echoed in English. He smiled. "I surely do not know. But it is a fine sounding word indeed. I thank you."

Their party gathered downstairs and ate, the first regular meal any had enjoyed in some time. Alex and Islak retained their gloves, seated into the corner so that Doel and Dollapan could more effectively screen them.

From the inn they moved, on foot, to the huge stone structure that, they confirmed to Alex, was their goal. Nearing it, his suspicion about illuminating floodlights was confirmed. A nearly continuous ring of lamps, hooded by reflective screens, shone light upward onto it. As they passed between lamps to approach it, Alex became aware that they were walking on flat stone. Without stopping, he scanned it. The stone was continuous, and did not bear any tool marks. It appeared that they walked upon an enormous, naturally occurring flat piece of exposed bedrock.

The huge stonework ahead of them had no obvious stair. At various, seemingly random places, Alex saw Mirrans scaling it. Some were alone, most were in groups of two or three or four.

Like a pyramid, it had four faces, and they approached it near the center of one of those faces. The scalloping effect now resolved into one last level of detail. Each scallop was a group of nine steps, of varying rise, yet equal run. The first step was nearly two feet high, but the next just over a foot. Each step was shorter than the one before it, but the amount of change grew less and less, till the ninth was only a few inches. But since the horizontal run was constant (at about the average for an earthly stair) the full set of nine gave the appearance of a curve.

After each ninth, the tenth returned to the height of the first. And so the pattern repeated, more times than he could count at so close an angle—for they were now at the base.

As if choosing a point at random, his three companions began climbing the stone rows as if they were stairs. Alex hesitated, but before they could note that he was lagging, he sprang up and assumed a position behind Islak. With Ig Doel and the Captain on either side of Islak, he wondered if Ig had spoken some covert word to the Captain about Islak's location in the party during the climb.

The height of the climb posed no great challenge to Alex. His physical training equipped him well to climb the height before them. But the irregularity of the stairs was vexing; smaller and smaller, to the point of absurdity, and then a step too large to be taken with grace. Over, and over, and over. He felt as if he were climbing a graph of logarithmic paper. He found it impossible to establish timing to his steps. He did, however, manage to retain a count. And by the time they neared the summit, he could see that there were twenty full sets. But at the top, almost as if in affront to his sensibilities, a final twenty-first set was incomplete. Only the first three steps of a set were there to cap off their climb.

Without speaking, all turned and sat on the top edge, resting. They looked at the city below as best they could, faced with the dazzling floodlights.

"Why," asked Alex, between large breaths which he struggled to not make sound like gasps, "the last three."

Someone around him grunted inquiringly.

"Twenty sets," he said. "Twenty full sets. Each one identical. Each one complete. Why this last set. Why just three."

"Twenty sets of nine and three," Islak said, matter-of-factly. "So God spoke it to us. So we built it."

"God spoke this?" Alex said. "So this structure... goes way back."

"Before the Adjunct," said Dollapan, standing and breathing deeply. "Before the city itself, perhaps. The records are not clear that far back. But yes, long ago. Long ago enough that God spoke to us. Each aspect, each detail. God spoke clearly, how he wanted it built." The Captain knelt, and ran his hand along the final cresting edge. "It certainly looks as if we built it well. It looks as if we built it the way that he asked us. It looks like it has no flaw, to displease him."

"Abbik," said Islak wearily. "Do not walk that road again. The Book records that God himself told us—His silence is not for punishment over any wrong we have done."

"Then why?" Alex asked. "What is the reason for God's silence?"

"Come," Igren said, standing up. "These questions are not for us to answer. Let him ask of the Court." With that, Ig Doel moved away from the edge, toward the center of the flat top.

"The reason," Islak whispered to Alex, "has never been given. Some feel the need to invent a reason. Others are content to wait."

The top of the structure was a square, over a hundred feet on a side. In the center was a rectangular pool twenty feet by ten, recessed into the surface, the water's edge almost even with the stone top.

Near opposite corners, bracketing the pool, were two round metal basins over six feet across, apparently filled with oil, or oil floating on top of water; the oil was aflame. Upon reaching these huge torches, the men removed their shoes and unwound the long strips of cloth, one strip per foot, which served as socks. Proceeding barefoot, they sat at the edge of the pool, washing their feet.

Alex slowly followed them. Although he was reluctant to join them and risk breaching some point of etiquette, he was certain that not mimicking their actions would be the greatest taboo of all. Eight other men and three women where in various stages of approaching the pool, washing in it, or departing. No one spoke during this process, even though the party of four drew some fair attention for not removing their gloves to wash.

After a few minutes of cleansing, those who had come to the pool would retrieve their shoes and wraps (though they would not resume wearing them, carrying them instead) and then they would begin the climb down.

Dismayed that the entire climb had been only for a ceremonial washing, Alex nonetheless held his tongue. Never once during the approach nor during the climb, when conversation was obviously allowed, had any of his companions spoken the slightest word of discontent over the task. It was obvious that for them, this act was a given.

After retrieving their shoes, the four began the climb downward as well. Not, however, the way they had come. Their descent was clearly aimed at a cluster of buildings near the base, on the opposite side from their ascent. The largest of the buildings, a broad structure with open patios, was the Temple itself. He had learned that there were many ceremonial steps to be accomplished if one were to move from the outer areas to the inner ones. From the centermost patio, a constant curl of smoke arose. A burnt offering, Alex surmised, likely of grain or fruit. The only thing inward of that was a tall enclosed structure, what his companions had called The Most Holy Place. Alex had not pressed the point, and thus he did not know if there were any ceremonial procedures that could clear him to enter there. He hoped there were. With no idea what was there, even of what he hoped would be there, he nonetheless felt drawn to it.

But if such an exploration were to be, then it would be some other time. A lesser building to one side, he learned as they descended, was their current objective—the Temple Court.

In the distance ahead, a mile or more, the city lights ended abruptly. The same was true to the right and left. He had understood that a great lake surrounded Shelaemstet on three sides, but he had not understood it to be a Great Lake, on the order of Superior, or the Caspian. It extended in all three directions, with no far shores visible.

By the time they had descended a third of the way, Alex was in pain; the stone of the steps was wearing into the soles of his bare feet. This pilgrimage was evidently a common one for the Mirrans, and their feet were accustomed to it. He focused his attention on the buildings below them. The Temple and the four other light gray stone buildings all faced a common courtyard. Although columns lined the front of each, they seemed, at least at a distance, oddly plain. Even the utilitarian communications towers which they had seen Islak's crew erecting had more artifice than these.

With three full sets of steps remaining, Alex stopped and sat. His feet were raw. Hoisting one upon his knee, he examined it. It was bright red at the ball and heel, and hot. The outer dead layer of skin was peeled away. His companions gathered around him.

"I'm alright," he said before they could ask, setting his foot back gingerly on the cool stone. He motioned them on ahead, and then followed them awkwardly. By the time he reached the bottom, he could feel blisters forming.

Outwardly the Temple Court building was all stonework, without a sign of any other materials. Inwardly it was all woodwork—floor, ceiling and walls—with no hint of stone. A constable led them down a short hall, lined with empty benches, to a great pair of wooden doors. The constable entered, closing the doors, and left them waiting.

"Normally," Ig told Alex, without turning back to him, "there would be petitioners here, waiting for appointments to present their cases to the Judges. But evidently the message the Captain sent on ahead of us was sufficiently detailed to cause them to clear their schedule."

Alex nodded, but did not speak; the pain on the soles of his feet was sharp. He looked to the wooden floor around and behind him, fearing he might be bleeding. He was not.

He looked up. The ceiling some twenty feet above them was adorned with square cloth banners, ten feet across, hung by their corners. Four banners, each of white, surrounded a central one. It was the central one that held his attention; a black banner, emblazoned with a streak of yellow.

"Why is that hanging there?" he asked of no one in particular.

"They are flags of judgment," Dollapan answered. "What better place for them?"

"Judgment?" Alex echoed.

"Four flags of acquittal, and one of... condemnation." Dollapan turned to him. "The sign of condemnation. It... troubles you?" Dollapan was nervous.

"I thought," Alex said, "that the center flag indicated distress. Disaster."

"No...."

"If it means condemnation," Alex said, "why did the Assan fly sails emblazoned in this way?"

Dollapan spun to him. Reaching out with his paw-like hands, he grasped Alex by the shoulders. In a moment Dollapan remembered himself, and remembered who was before him—or at least, who he believed was before him. He slackened his grip, but kept his hands on Alex's shoulders.

"The Innotek Assan," Dollapan said levelly, "never flew such a flag as that."

"Not a flag," Alex said. "Her sails. That was the pattern of her sails."

Dollapan's weathered face slackened, draining of color. "No proper sailing ship," he said, almost in a whisper, "has ever sailed... with sails such as that." He nodded upward, as if unwilling to look at the symbol hanging above them.

"The Assan," Islak said, "flew no such sail, neither on her departure from us, nor upon her return. She carried no such sail, nor would she have carried provisions to fabricate one."

Alex's mind raced. "Could she have stowed the sails below decks, before her return?"

"No such banner was anywhere aboard her," Dollapan insisted, releasing him. "The dock crews would have found it."

"Dock crews?" Alex said.

"The crews," said Dollapan, exasperated. "On the docks. When she wandered into port."

"She followed us into port? I never saw her behind us."

Ig Doel threw back his head. "We are about to appear before the High Court... to present to them a madman."

"The Innotek Assan," Dollapan said gravely, "fell victim to the DevilsEye some twenty years ago."

Alex digested that bit of information. "Then it was not the Assan that I saw," he said quietly. "Then what ship did I see?" asked Alex firmly.

"If you saw a sail such as that, it was not on any proper ship." Dollapan would say no more.

"Not on any *proper* ship?" Alex asked of Islak. It was obvious from Islak's expression that he hoped that no more needed to be said. What emerged next was clearly painful for Islak to say:

"We have tried to be a people worthy of one day again hearing his voice. We have tried to live according to the instructions, as well as the intent—as best we can divine it—of The Book. But chaos and disorder," he said, "enter all systems. We are not perfect, in the way that he is perfect."

Again, Alex had the sense that Islak hoped he had said enough. But Alex's silence encouraged him to continue.

"This whole Court," Islak said, sweeping his hand about him, "and those lesser courts like it, are confirmation of this shortcoming. If we lived as we should, each man at peace with his brother, each child in harmony with his parent, each citizen on good terms with his neighbor, what disputes then would we have? And what need of courts?"

"For what value it may have," Alex told him, "I find no shame in a people needing courts."

"This," Islak said, "is not our shame. The court itself was established in The Book. As were punishments... for specific... crimes."

Ig Doel and Captain Dollapan moved over to the benches placed for waiting petitioners. It seemed to Alex that they were avoiding looking at him, like disobedient children dreading a coming punishment.

"Anned," Alex said firmly, laying his hand on Islak's shoulder. "You of all people must understand that I am not the Harbinger you seek. And I have surely not come here to condemn you. Don't confess to me. Rather, simply explain to me. What is this about?"

"The crimes laid out in The Book are far ranging. They cover many things. When a man is careless, and his recklessness causes the death of another, for this there is a punishment. But when a man dies, neither by age, nor disease, nor the foolish act of himself or another, but rather by willful design... for this, no punishment is prescribed. No such occurrence is contemplated. Yet it is to this that we have descended."

Alex ached to console him. But what could he say, without revealing that he himself came from a world so savage that murder was commonplace?

"Five times, within my lifespan," Islak said, "has this Court, the highest court in all the land, concluded that deaths were willful acts."

"Five times," Alex repeated, unable to choose between laughing and crying, that his companions should be torn apart by a murder rate as low as this.

Islak raised his face to the flags overhead. He stood as if looking at the center flag firmly, resolutely, like a condemned man facing his executioner.

"For a crime not laid out, we have devised a punishment not prescribed."

"Those who kill," Alex ventured sympathetically, "you kill?"

Islak turned to him with horror.

What have I done? thought Alex. *Will he think it a wild speculation on my part? Or something I would consider natural?*

"No," Islak whispered. Not that." Now, though, Islak seemed

209

freer to discuss the matter. "God has said, 'I alone shall avenge the slayer of man,' and we have abided by his command."

The ancient debate arose in Alex's mind, now framed in a new reality: Had God given them this command to affirm their respect for life, and thereby keep their murder rate so low? Or had he blessed them with a disposition that kept their murder rate low, thereby enabling so sweeping a declaration to be made? On Earth, both sides would take this idyllic world as proof of their opposing views.

"Yet I fear," Islak continued, "we have pressed the limits of the command God gave. When a man is convicted of this crime, he is borne by a sailing ship, to Boundary Waters. He may choose. There are shoals, there are DevilsJaws. He may even be brought to the waters leading to one of the DevilsEyes." In this moment of distress, Islak fell back upon the long held belief that the various DevilsEyes were separate phenomena, rather than a single distant object. "Whichever he chooses, there he is set adrift. In a small boat, with provisions that might last a Quarter, if he is sparing. One leg is chained to the transom, that he should never leave it. The other leg is chained to a bottom plug in the boat, that by one swift kick he might end his sentence, choosing instead to be dragged under with his sinking vessel. And on this tiny boat is mounted a single mast, and on that mast hangs a sail, both to carry the guilty off into the Boundary Waters to the death that awaits him, and also to warn any other ship that might happen across him, should he attempt to return. It is a black sail, with a yellow slash, declaring 'This man, condemned'."

"These boats," Alex said. "They are always one-man affairs? Tiny boats, with a single mast and sail?"

"This is what we have chosen to do."

"And no such boat has ever found its way back to the mainland?"

"None. A journey of such distance, in such a craft, cannot be accomplished."

But someone, Alex knew, had survived. Survived to reach land. Perhaps some island or island chain. Perhaps even the huge mainland positioned directly under the Mirran sun, the huge plot of land toward which he had aimed his escape pod—the continent now directly across the globe from them, some seven thousand miles directly under their feet.

But the ship he had seen was not the product of some tiny band of old men. Only five had been set adrift, within Islak's lifetime. Most of those would have died while drifting, or upon encountering the Mirran sun.

"Sometime," Alex said with conviction. "Sometime long ago. A woman was so condemned, as well."

Ig and Captain Dollapan forgot their shame for a moment, intrigued by Alex's knowledge of their past.

"More than once," Islak said. "But if you are not a prophet, nor an agent of the most high God, if you do in fact know nothing about us as you have professed, how do you know something from so distant in our past?"

Alex's mind raced through the possibilities. Australia had begun as a prison colony. But all manner of prisoners had been sent there, for a wide range of crimes. And others had settled there, without criminal pasts. These had had a leavening effect. But that was Australia. Here, there would have been no such leavening effect. If there were a genetic predisposition to criminality—even if it were only statistical and not absolute—then what sort of people would be bred from a small population completely composed of murderers? Perhaps the sort that, when they produced sailing ships to ply their new homeland's waters, would proudly adopt an emblem that was the symbol of their condemnation? A people steeped in bitterness over their exile into a land of endless burning sunlight? A sunlight that had no doubt killed most of them from the outset. But a few, the hardiest, the most desperate to cling to life, these might survive. And with one survivor a woman, they could reproduce. Reproduce and flourish, perhaps even enough to build sailing ships that were at least the rival of those of the peaceful Mirrans Alex had come to know. And perhaps even now they were exploring, out at least as far as the edge of darkness marked by Valor Island. But could mere darkness, conquerable by lamp or torch, hold them back forever as surely as scorching daylight had held back a people used to perpetual night?

211

Or was contact, between people separated by generations, imminent? Perhaps the others had evolved peacefully. But if the worst nightmares of eugenicists were correct, then those now lurking at the threshold of this dimly lit hemisphere might be ruthless and bloodthirsty, and with a generations-old score to settle.

Beyond the wooden doors, there was a stirring. The Judges were entering the chamber. Alex had come here uncertain how much to say, but feeling that this was the place to begin speaking the truth. Now he had to decide how to deal with a whole new set of truths that, a few minutes earlier, he could have scarcely imagined.

The constable admitted them, closing the door behind them and posting himself to watch the door. At first Alex thought they had entered a chamber of stone, but soon he realized that it was completely finished in a very pale wood. Doing his best not to hobble, he moved forward with the others. They approached a semicircle of seven chairs, not raised, as he had imagined, but at floor level. In fact, with the Judges seated and the petitioners standing, as it appeared they would, the Judges were actually below eye level. One of the chairs, the rightmost, was empty. Passing by a court official seated at a table to the right (he would come to learn this was a transcriptionist who recorded all words, as well as comings and goings of petitioners and Judges) they approached a broad waist-high rostrum, which stood roughly at the center of the circle defined by the Judges' chairs. The four stopped several feet short of it. Directly across on either side of them were lesser, plainer doors. Presumably the Judges had entered by one or both of these.

Book II, Chapter 5: Before the Temple Court

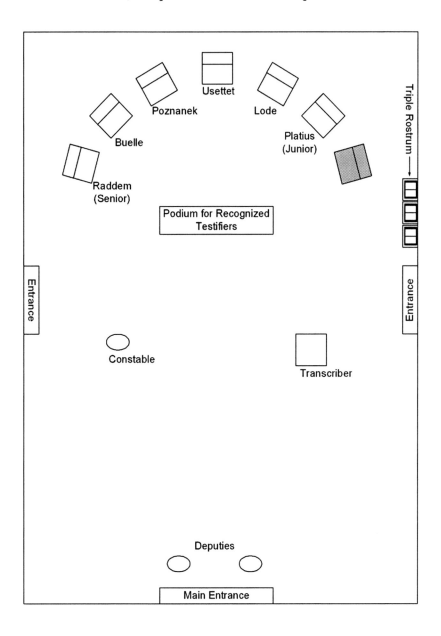

The petitioners were asked their names, and their relevancy to the proceeding. Their responses, as given and recorded:

"Abbik Dollapan. Captain of the brigantine Ammanon Deloré; discoverer of… of him whom we accompany before you."

"Anned Islak. Scientist, and sponsor of the mission in question."

"Igren Doel. Craftsman, and personal aide to Mr. Islak."

After each addressed the court, they approached and stood behind the podium. That left only one man before the court, unidentified, undefined. Alex cleared his throat. With authority, he said:

"Alexander Boten." He paused, mulling his options. "Traveler," he added at last. All the Judges' eyes were on him. The Judge on the far left reached down beside himself, took up a piece of paper, and spoke to them.

"Captain Dollapan. This court is in possession of a most extraordinary correspondence, purportedly from you. The claims in this letter are… of such a nature that I am reluctant to read them into the record. Do you claim authorship of this letter, and do you stand behind its contents?"

Dollapan answered: "I claim authorship, and stand behind its assertions. Begging the court's indulgence…." He removed his gloves, and laid them across the front edge of the rostrum. Looking sideways at Islak, he saw no reaction. "Gloves," Dollapan whispered, without turning to him.

"I know, I know," Islak muttered, tugging his glove's fingers outward. "I'm not totally blind, yet. It was a pause for dramatic effect." He laid his gloves beside Dollapan's. Ig's soon followed. Several of the Judges leaned forward in their chairs.

Alex sighed. For better or worse, it was time to face the music. Methodically he removed his gloves, laid them next to the rest, and held his hands aloft, almost in a gesture of resignation. Save for the Judge immediately in front of them, the reactions were obvious. Mixed, but obvious. The first three seemed, to varying degrees, pleased. The fifth seemed uncomfortable; the sixth, fearful. Only Judge four—Usettet, he would learn, was unchanged.

The first Judge, Raddem, spoke again. "Are you then the

Harbinger?"

Alex struggled with a response. He had a plan of what to say; he was simply amassing the courage to say it.

Beside Raddem, Buelle spoke: "Pray tell us. Are you the Harbinger of God?"

"Learned Justices. I come before you as one unfamiliar with your ways—with your customs or your laws. Forgive me if I overstep propriety. Pray give me correction if I offend. If it be allowed, might I speak with you… in total privacy?"

Dollapan rolled his eyes; another round trip spent as excess baggage.

Islak leaned forward. "Alex," he whispered, "surely after making me wait all this time…."

Dollapan nudged Islak: "Well, Anned? Quite a kick in the pants, eh?"

Ig spoke, gathering up their gloves: "If it please the court. I and my companions can withdraw to the lobby just beyond, and be available at a moment's call."

The Judges conferred in tones that were hushed but not suggesting total secrecy, and they quickly concurred. Soon, only the Judges, Alex, the transcriber and the constable remained. Alex looked to the constable, and the transcriber, and then to the Judges. The center Judge, Usettet, looked at him with eyes that conveyed a simple message: *Do not ask it.*

Alex decided the transcriber and the constable would be alright. The main thing was to keep from Islak those bits of information he would now reveal. The only concern that Dollapan and Ig Doel posed was that they might, either with intent or by accident, reveal something to Islak. The men before him might, he had once thought, put him to death. Now he understood that at most they might banish him to a more or less certain fate. He could accept that. But Anned Islak would take inside himself the knowledge of Alex's origins, and what it meant about the Crown of God, and it could change his view of the heavens. Where those insights would lead was unknowable. Revealing information to the Judges might cause problems as well, but he was not as concerned about them. The risks to Mirrus in speaking to the Judges seemed to be, in his mind, acceptable.

"This court," said the stern looking Judge Lode, one seat to the right of center, "repeats its question. Do you claim to be Harbinger?"

"Your Honors. I have, at various times, denied I am the Harbinger, and questioned myself as to whether I might be the Harbinger. I have, in fact, conducted an impromptu test, which suggests I am not the Harbinger. And although this answer will be less definitive than you or I should like, it seems the only one I can reach: I must leave it up to you, sirs, to decide my identity, and my office—if any—within the framework God has prophetically given you."

There was a generalized grumbling among the Judges at this.

Usettet arose. "Alexander Boten," he said, moving off to Alex's right. He continued to speak as he walked away: "If you are Harbinger…" and then, as if to dismiss objection, he waved his hand, "…even if you are not Harbinger. Whatever you are." He reached the side wall of the chamber. There along the wall were three podiums, each with a book. Usettet opened the book to the right. "Answer me, if you can, this Conflict. The Holy Book tells us many things about Harbinger. About the true Harbinger, who is to come. But reconcile for me these three. First, we are told, from the very lips of God: 'The Harbinger shall come to the Temple's Great Stone from the Temple's Adjunct, without infirmity, whole in body, a man of five fingers.' So it has been written." Now he looked back to Alex. "Not merely with five fingers. But without any infirmity. Elsewhere we are told in God's own voice: 'The Harbinger of God will come forth from the Temple's Adjunct blind and mute, led toward the Temple tended by those who pity him.' And yet elsewhere, this: 'Once Harbinger leaves the Temple's Adjunct, he will never return to it, nor will he see it, nor will he touch it; his feet will never be upon it again.' So then, Traveler Alexander Boten. Tell me how this can be? Without infirmity, yet blind and mute? If the journey from the Adjunct to the Temple is made only once? How can these all be true of you? For true of you they must be, if we are to believe you are the Harbinger of the most high God."

"I understand," Alex said, "that you have many questions. Many conflicts, puzzles, within The Book. One, concerning NewStar's constancy and flashing, seems to have been resolved. Others, like this one, seem unsolvable."

Disgusted, Usettet returned to his seat.

"What I *can* tell you," Alex continued, "is what I am, and what I am not. As for what I am not? I am not an *angel*, nor any other heavenly being. I come to you, not from heaven, but from a place in many ways very much like this. It is heaven to which I aspire, as surely as do you, not heaven from which I have come. I am also not one who has come to give you insight into your Holy Book, nor into the Mysteries and Conflicts you have noted surrounding it. In truth I know nothing of your Book other than what has been taught me since my arrival."

This brought forth widespread dismay, and Alex quickly moved to address it:

"I am of a people who believe, as do you, that there is one God, maker of all things. He has given us a book of holy writings as well. But they are writings crafted for my people, and for the purposes he has for my people. I do not know to what degree his purposes for my people and for your people align. I would not presume to say to what degree they should align."

"The people you come from," asked Platius, farthest to the right, "are they from some island nation, beyond the Boundary Waters?"

"No, your Honor."

"Then where," snapped Usettet, "do you purport to come from?"

"Learned Judges, I will answer you. I will answer fully, and in truth. I will answer without condition. One thing I ask to be allowed to say first, and I pray you heed my concern. It is for precisely this question that I have asked the court be cleared. I say with utmost certainty that none in my party would wish harm upon anyone in all the land. Nonetheless, there is one in my party who, though not intending it, might set in motion by this knowledge certain chains of events which could bring ill."

"Islak," said Raddem. "You fear Anned Islak."

"If it is not too presumptuous," Alex offered, "might I inquire of the Judgeship? How has Your Honor deduced this?"

217

Raddem mulled the question. "Perhaps because of this. Of all those who have been in this chamber for this proceeding, he is unique. His way of thinking, and the changes he has brought about. Most admire him. A few fear him."

"I count myself in both camps," Alex said. "I admire him for what he is, and does. I fear him for what he might unintentionally do, if told too much before he is meant to know it. My point in saying this is not to bring any condemnation down upon him, but to beg the court's highest care in protecting, from all ears outside this court, what I am about to say."

"Alexander Boten." The only Judge who had thus far not addressed him, Poznanek, just left of center, was speaking. "I hate to distress this court with my next suggestion."

"No!" shouted Usettet, his voice startling them all. "I will not have it! I will not abide it! This court becomes a free-for-all... a cartwheeling travesty! There will be order. There will be procedure."

Poznanek raised a calming hand, and whispered to Usettet. After a moment, Usettet resettled himself in his chair, facing away. Poznanek arose and approached Alex. They stood on opposite sides of the podium. Poznanek smiled, and leaned forward. He whispered, so the transcriptionist could not hear.

"You have long been in the company of Anned Islak?"

"Yes, sir."

"You have discussed... many things?"

"Yes, Your Honor."

"He has discussed with you the matter he discussed with us... during his last visit here?"

Alex searched his eyes. "No, sir."

Poznanek looked at him blankly. "No?"

"No, sir. I'm sorry. I know he has been here before. Sometime before the Deloré sailed. But I know nothing of what he may have discussed with you."

"I see. This is most awkward." Poznanek now leaned in even closer. Alex felt the warmth of the Judge's breath upon his ear as he spoke: "I am honor bound to reveal nothing regarding previous conversations. So I will pose this in the most general way. The thing you are about to tell us. Does it relate to... the order... the structure... of this universe in which we live?"

Alex weighed the question. "That would be... a fair characterization."

"Indeed," the Judge said, nodding. "I test the limits of propriety, I fear, but one last question. Does this matter concern... both Mirrus... and the Crown of God?"

Alex leaned back, that he might look at Poznanek squarely. Had he said too much to Islak? Had Islak figured something out? But Poznanek was discussing something Islak had said *before* the Deloré had sailed.

"Yes... it does concern them both," Alex whispered cautiously.

With a knowing nod, the Judge said: "Have no fear." He then turned to his fellow Judges. "Gentlemen. Consultation, please." They gathered in a tight knot before him. There were a few vigorous gestures, mostly from Usettet, it seemed, but consensus came quickly.

Raddem spoke: "The constable will escort the recorder to the outer chamber, where they will both await their recall. Transcription is briefly suspended." All the Judges reseated themselves. Once Raddem's words had been written, the transcriber and the constable were gone.

Poznanek spoke to him: "Traveler Alexander Boten. You have said there was a matter you wished to discuss in private. A matter that might bring some fair turmoil to us, and to our people. Pray, assume discretion among this panel. Proceed." Poznanek gave him a knowing nod.

Alex looked at him, puzzled. All he could think to do was to proceed, along the lines he had planned.

"Honorable Judges. There appears periodically in your sky a vast display of light, which you call the Crown of God." Alex noted that Poznanek continued to smile, and nod. Alex tried to ignore him. "Upon close examination, you may have noted that there are, within this display, many tiny points of light." At this, Poznanek cocked his head unconsciously, as though hearing something unexpected. Alex gave up wondering, and continued. "I tell you now that this entire Crown of God is at an unimaginable distance. And that each of these points of light, in addition to being unimaginably distant, is likewise unimaginably huge." Poznanek was leaning forward now, perplexed. "Further, one of those points of light has near it a world much the size of your own, but utterly invisible due to its remoteness. It is from this world that I have come."

The Judges appeared thunderstruck. This was clearly not what Poznanek, not what any of them, had expected. Raddem whispered to Buelle, who then left by the door to the left. There was much discussion amongst the Judges, but no questions for Alex. He waited at the podium, leaning on it to lessen the weight on his throbbing feet.

Buelle returned with what seemed a large roll of paper. He handed it to Raddem, who brought it to the podium. It was vellum, like a map of the sky that Islak had once showed him aboard the Deloré. Unrolling it, Alex saw that that was precisely what it was—the finely inked drawing of the Crown of God, the galaxy.

"You are in possession," Alex asked, "of Anned Islak's map?"

"This is a copy," Raddem said carefully, "that he made for us to keep here, after his last visit. You have seen it before, then?"

"Briefly. On the Ammanon Deloré."

Raddem waited in silence, as Alex looked over the inked lines. When Alex looked up at him, Raddem narrowed his gaze, locking on to his eyes. His next words were delivered slowly, methodically:

"Why did he show it to you?"

"He never said why. I had the impression he expected it to elicit some response."

"This was all he showed you? Nothing else? Nothing else with this?"

"He showed me many things," Alex said. "I don't remember what he showed me just before or just after this. It wasn't a significant event. It didn't make much of an impression on me. I mean, it is a fine drawing, a fine piece of work, but...."

"Where," asked Raddem, seeming not to pay attention to him. "Where, on here, are you from?"

Looking at the map, he tried to orient himself. Locating Earth from a viewpoint above the galactic plane was something with which he had little experience, but he found what he assumed was the right point, on one of the spiral arms. He pointed to it.

Raddem looked at the point, as if gaining his own bearings. Then, over the course of but two rounds, Alex watched a most disturbing transformation. The color drained from Raddem's face. His sturdy frame slumped, and it seemed he would collapse. His eyelids hung low, but his eyes did not close. He began to speak, to no one in particular: "Everything. All of it. Every passage. All changed. Everything...."

Alex reached out a hand to him, but he moved away. Raddem allowed the vellum to re-roll itself, and left it on the podium. Walking back toward his chair, he said: "We need to speak to Islak. Alone."

Alex was concerned, but decided to leave Raddem to the care of the other Judges. He turned to leave, but as he took his first step, one of his blood blisters burst, staining the floor. He stopped, looking down at the red smear he had left.

"What?" demanded Usettet. "Are you bleeding? Where are your wraps?"

"Outside," Alex answered. With the others, he had left his foot wraps and shoes outside the final door to the Court.

With a contemptuous sound, Usettet rushed to the wall beyond the Judges' chairs, where each Judge had left his wraps and shoes. Taking one of his own wraps, he rushed to Alex.

"Off of your feet,' Usettet demanded. "Get them up. You're getting blood everywhere. Come." Alex sat on the floor. Raising Alex's foot, he began wrapping it, not as a standard footwrap, but as a bandage. After four turns, he abruptly stopped. The other Judges, including Raddem, had gathered around them. Without looking up, Usettet asked him, his voice a whisper: "How did this happen?"

"It was the climb down from the... whatever it is. The huge stone, outside."

"You washed your feet. You climbed the Mirran Stone, and you washed your feet?" Usettet asked. "Why? Why did you do that? Did someone tell you it was a law, that you were required?"

"No," Alex said, taking the wrap and continuing to dress it around.

Gently, Usettet took it back, and continued the winding himself. "If you didn't think it was a law, then why did you do it?"

"Everybody else was doing it," Alex said, almost apologetically. "It seemed like it was important to them."

Another Judge, Alex could not tell whom, spoke: "He was 'Honoring the ways of old'. Not 'Honoring the Law', but 'Honoring the ways of old'."

Usettet's hands trembled. "The Mysteries," he said. "Bring me the Mysteries."

Platius went to the trio of books, returning with the one from the far left. Buelle and Lode held it, while Platius flipped through the pages.

"The Mystery of the Shedding of Blood," he recited. What followed was a quotation from the Mirran's Holy Book, and Platius labored haltingly to translate it down into the modern Mirran tongue, for Alex's benefit, as he went. "'Restoration will come to the halls of power / Shedding blood before the wise / To honor the ways of old / And the powerful will make himself low before the infirm / Binding up his wounds'." Platius stopped. "We always thought…. But we were wrong. All of us, for generations, have been wrong. Restoration is not 'the powerful'. *"We* are 'the powerful'. We, the Temple Judgeship."

Absently tucking the end of the wrap into one of the folds, Usettet said: "Read it all." He exhaled it, like a dying man's last words.

"When you see these things…" Platius began. He was unable to finish.

"When you see these things," Raddem spoke, with re-found vigor, "Know that the Harbinger… is not far."

Usettet looked Alex in the eye, looking through a curtain of his own tears. "The Restoration… and the Harbinger…" he said, "…are one." Shaking his head, he said: "Forgive me."

"Most honored Judge," Alex whispered, reaching out and wiping away Usettet's tears. "I am drawn deeper and deeper into things I do not understand. You assume… you all assume… too much. Don't proclaim me this Harbinger. Not based on this simple turn of events.

And as for 'Restoration', it is not within my power to restore to you anything you lack. Least of all, to restore to you the voice of God."

*   *   *

With Alex sequestered outside, the Judges conducted one last session, a private, unrecorded session, with Anned Islak. In that session, enough was revealed to Islak that he henceforth guarded his maps with an obsessive mania which put his previous precautions to shame.

At the end of the session, three resolutions had been decided amongst them.

First, the Judges would vacate the Temple Court, making arrangements to travel by the fastest coach available to the southern coast—to the Adjunct.

Second, Boten and Islak would tarry in Shelaemstet only so long as needed for the Traveler Alexander Boten's feet to heal—not heal completely, but enough that he might be able to ride the fastest steed to be had. By these horses, he and the Scientist Anned Islak would journey with utmost haste, to the southern coast, to the Adjunct.

Third, Islak would take with him all the copies of the maps he had earlier left with the Judges. And somewhere between Shelaemstet and the Adjunct, some time between now and when they all rejoined, Islak would tell his riding companion all that Islak knew, all that Islak suspected. Before they all stood together facing the Adjunct, the Traveler Alexander Boten was to know who, and what, he was.

Book II
Chapter 6: Crossing

Igren Doel left them, to tend what shambles remained of his business interests in Barnable. Alex resumed his room at the inn—for less than ten watches, Islak assured him—to give his feet a chance to heal. Captain Dollapan, in his own room, would remain there even after they had left, awaiting word from them. And, if there were developments in Shelaemstet, forwarding that news to them.

While changing the dressings on Alex's feet—proper dressings now, not footwraps pressed into service—Alex implored Islak that they should move on, but Islak was resolute.

"It was the Judges' command," he said firmly, "that we go with all haste to the Adjunct... *once you were well enough to travel.* Your feet are doing well," he observed, smearing on a salve before rebinding them. "Ten watches, perhaps a little more."

"I think that by now they would do better exposed to the air," Alex protested.

Islak glared at him with mock sternness: "Young man, I have some fair experience in the healing arts. Now, mind your doctor." Then, resuming his true demeanor, he continued: "Soon you will be ready for a gentle horseback ride, south to the Great Lake. There we book passage, horses and all, crossing south to the refining town of Ohlmont. And by then you should be sufficiently healed for the more strenuous ride—south, to the Adjunct."

Outside, the Captain's voice raised—excited, but not alarmed. Pleased, it seemed to Alex. Islak poked his head out the window, and thus remained for a time.

"Well," Alex said. "Come along. What is it then?"

Islak could see little; the illumination of the street was not enough for what was left of his eyes. But he recognized the voices. Islak pulled back into the room, still staring out the window, through

225

the drape that had settled back into place. Then he turned to Alex. "Opper and Andril Degg," he said absently. Then, belatedly, he smiled. "I wonder what brings them here." Then, as if forgetting Alex's presence, he left the room without bidding goodbye. A moment later he leaned back into Alex's room. "You know of Andril's fixation. About you, about Harbinger. Say nothing to him about what has happened. Nothing about the Judges... about Restoration."

In the lobby, while the Deggs were negotiating terms with the innkeeper, Islak slipped outside to where the Captain was temporarily securing their horses to a hitching post.

"Why have they come?"

"Why do you think?" Dollapan said, keeping his eye on the inn door. "Because of Alex Boten. To find out what the Judges say. About him. That's why Andril has come. His cousin, I should think, has come to keep an eye on young Andril."

"What have you said to them?'

"Nothing of consequence. 'Welcome', 'Let me tend your horses'. Mere pleasantries."

"Good. Offer nothing of our interview before the Temple Court. If pressed, admit what you must. But resist all but the most basic details."

"Certainly nothing," Dollapan suggested, "about the Mystery of the Shedding of Blood."

"Indeed. Mr. Boten's feet are 'injured', that is all. One of us must occupy Andril whenever the other changes the dressings. We leave in ten watches. Less, if Andril is prying. We can say 'south' if we must, but explain no further about our destination."

"He knows your destination," Dollapan said.

"What? How?"

"They didn't say. I gather they picked it up from whoever told them we were staying here."

"Too much information," Islak complained, "is spreading too freely."

"If you can handle things here," Dollapan said, "I'll go ahead and take these mares down to the stable."

Inside the inn, the lamps provided better viewing for Islak, but his sight was still limited. One of the two cousins stayed with the innkeeper; signing in, Islak surmised. The other was headed for the stairs. Islak approached him.

"A long ride?" he ventured.

"Mr. Islak!" came the answer. It was a young voice, but not so young as Andril. It had a slight rasp from years of salt air. And the hand that grasped his was a weathered hand.

"So tell me, Opper," Islak proceeded confidently. "What brings you to the shadow of the Mirran Stone?"

The handshake stopped, and there was no reply. For a moment, Islak thought he had misidentified the man before him.

"Come," Opper said, climbing the stairs. Reaching the summit, he stopped. When Islak had passed from the stairwell, Opper stood where he could look down.

"I am here," he said, "because my cousin seems unstoppable. This Harbinger business... it is an obsession. It is all he speaks of. It is better since we have come ashore, now that he knows that Restoration was not manifested in our absence. But still, he remains fixed on this Alex Boten. He wouldn't be still until he found out what the Judges ...."

Hearing Andril approaching, Islak cut him off. As Andril reached the top of the stairs, they engaged in a final round of greetings as they moved to Alex's room. Then Islak and the elder Degg left Alex and Andril to visit. Down the hall, their furtive discussion continued.

"I cannot stay long," Opper told him. "But I wanted to speak with you. Information is scant and unreliable. Rumors rule. You have been to the Temple Court?"

"How much do you need to know?"

"No more than what I have just learned from your evasion. But the Judges have made no declaration?"

"Not yet. I am not certain they are all convinced. But it is clear which way they lean. I suspect they have some final test in mind."

"So you are headed to the Adjunct, as we were told. I see. Very well. Just know this: If this Alex Boten is not the Harbinger, then

fine. Even if he turns out to be some clever pretender, with all of his
denials a mere ruse. Whatever he is, for good or ill, if at the end of it
all he is not the Harbinger, then so be it. But if the Temple Court
rules otherwise...." He seemed reluctant to continue.

"If he is..." Islak prodded.

"My cousin is a fine young man. But he is consumed with dread
over Harbinger, and what Harbinger is said to bring in his wake. If
the Judges declare this man Harbinger... I do not know what Andril's
reaction will be."

*   *   *

"Tell me," said Alex, "about the Book of Mysteries."

"The Mysteries?" said Andril, shedding his coat. He sat in the
chair beside Alex's bed. "You know the basics. Only The Book is
divine, sent by God. The Mysteries and the Conflicts quote from it.
The Mysteries are segments of The Book which, by themselves, seem
to make no sense. The Conflicts are groups of quotations—at least
two, in some cases as many as six—which seem to make no sense
when taken together. Seeming contradictions. But what is it you are
asking? What about the Mysteries?"

"There was a mystery about NewStar."

"A Mystery, and a Conflict." Andril's face grew troubled. If the
light that still streaks our northern sky is, in fact, NewStar, it may
have solved them both. The prophecies spoke of NewStar having a
fulfillment, but never said what that meant. This was the Mystery.
There was also a Conflict; it was said it would shine steadily,
elsewhere it was said it would flash. The light that now circles us was
steady, and then—in the tenth upon tenth crossing, when it was to
fulfill its task—it flashed. At the time, it seemed obvious: The flash
was the fulfillment. Mystery explained. Conflict resolved. But
now...."

"Now," continued Alex, "what?"

"Now that explanation seems more... a convenient
rationalization. Like a people eager to see a prophecy fulfilled,
contriving to see a meaning. Like a people afraid to see a prophecy

228

Book II, Chapter 6: Crossing

fail, desperate to patch together unrelated events."

Alex resettled himself in bed: "Tell me of other Mysteries."

"Well," Andril smiled. "There is the Mystery of the Mirran Stone. The Mystery of the Southern Boundaries. The Mystery of the Shedding of Blood."

"Hmm," Alex said, feigning a mere passing curiosity. "Tell me about the Mystery of Blood."

"The Shedding of Blood,' Andril corrected. "I have pondered that Mystery much, of late. It was largely that which persuaded me to heed your protestations. A figure named Restoration is to appear in the Temple complex. Perhaps on the Mirran Stone, perhaps even in the holy Temple itself."

"And what will this 'Restoration' do?"

"There, the mystery. He is to shed blood, and thereby honor the ways of old. But none of our ways, as far back as anyone remembers, as far back as any written record, had a tradition of shedding blood. Some think this refers to some ancient practice, before recorded word, of bleeding people ritualistically. But no evidence exists of this. God never commanded this. So what 'ways' will he be honoring?"

"But you don't doubt The Book."

Andril laughed quietly. "Some have doubted it. But Mysteries continue to be revealed. Conflicts continue to be resolved. The doubters are made to look like fools in the end."

"But how do such things resolve?"

"Different ways. To generalize? Two main ways. What is said in The Book proves to be more complex than we had imagined. Other times, we have made foolish assumptions. Sometimes, when the understanding comes, it is like a blindfold being suddenly removed; we are amazed we had not seen the truth."

"Tell me more, about 'Restoration'."

Andril cocked his head. "There is more," he said. "One thing more. When we see the shedding of blood, we are to know that Harbinger is not far. This was the key thing for me, as concerns yourself. While we were still at sea, I considered it possible that you were Harbinger. And that therefore, back here in Shelaemstet, somewhere in the halls of power, Restoration had already come. But

229

once I was freed of the ship, I found that no news was abroad about Restoration having come. In all honesty, I did not believe it until I reached Shelaemstet itself, and inquired of those who live here. No Restoration."

"And Restoration must come before Harbinger?"

"Forgive any error in my phrasing, but roughly: 'When you see Restoration shedding blood, know that the Harbinger is not far'."

"I see," Alex said. "I am, then, as you see it, no longer a threat?"

Andril smiled. "I am sorry, Alex Boten. Even if you had been Harbinger, it would have been wrong of me to fear you. I will devote myself to correcting my thinking. When Harbinger does come, I want to be able to welcome him, with more courtesy than I showed to you."

Alex took his hand, wanting to relieve Andril's conscience, but he was unsure what words to use. *Later*, he thought to himself, *I'll say something to him later*. And he left the words unspoken. His silence in that moment would prove to be one of his life's greatest regrets.

*   *   *

After Alex slept next, Islak changed the dressings on his feet. This time he applied no salve, and left the wrappings loose to admit air.

"Your people call this figure 'Restoration', Alex said.

It took Islak a moment to sort though the unexpected statement, with its implied query. "Restoration," he said. "It is understood that he will restore Mirrans to communication with God. That he will cause God to again speak to us."

"Yes, but how?"

"In all honesty," Islak confessed, "I have never pondered that. Curious. It seems a fair question." Then, shrugging, he added: "I guess he simply… will."

"But if it is Restoration who brings back God's voice, why doesn't Andril dread the coming of Restoration? Why does he dread Harbinger?"

"I suppose," Islak theorized, "it is because Harbinger was thrown

230

in his face, before he had time to grapple with the thought of Restoration appearing. He assumed Restoration had already come. We all did, when New Star appeared. Besides, Harbinger is the final key. He is, after all, what his name suggests—a sign, an omen, that the time is close. Restoration appears. Harbinger comes. Restoration restores. Harbinger is the final moment, the final event before God's voice is heard"

"They are closely tied, this Restoration and this Harbinger. It wasn't so much of a jump for the Judge to say they are one."

Islak flinched, looking helplessly toward the door. He could hardly tell if it were open or shut, let alone if anyone were there. He spoke in a hushed tone: "Do not discuss this with anyone, especially the boy." Now his voice returned to its fullness. "I am off, to book our passage; I will return with our horses. In one watch, two at most, we are off."

"Do you think," Alex asked, "that Andril would want to accompany us?"

Islak laughed. "He would do anything." Then realization hit him. "What?" he demanded. "What are you saying?"

"Andril Degg has, from the outset, feared that I was your Harbinger. Despite this, he was a model of decorum, and invaluable in teaching me to speak your language. Now some of the Judges suspect what for young Degg would be far worse: That I am both Harbinger and Restoration. Word of this could get out at any time, Anned. You know that. And if it does, then Andril Degg's torment will be tenfold. This all must be put to rest. Whatever the Judges have planned for our gathering at the Adjunct, that should be the end of it. That should establish finally that I am not what Andril has feared. I think I owe it to him to allow him to be present for that."

Islak pulled up a chair, close to Alex's side: "You told them something. The Judges, in the Temple Court. When you were alone, you told them something. And it changed everything about their attitude. It convinced them that you are the Harbinger."

"What convinced them," Alex corrected, "was that business about Restoration. I pop a blood blister at an opportune moment, and suddenly everybody is ready to re-interpret Mirran scriptures in ways no one has ever read them before. This whole thing has become an obsession."

Alex Boten was the second person to suggest obsession. Islak shook it off. "You forget," Islak said. "I spoke with the Judges after that. The Mystery of the Shedding of Blood was important to them, but it was what you told them... that was what turned them."

"And you," Alex said, "told them something as well. Earlier, before the Ammanon Deloré sailed, you told them something. Something you were ordered to tell me."

Islak stood up. "Something I was ordered to tell you before we meet with the Judges at the Adjunct. We have a voyage, and a long ride ahead of us, before that deadline is upon me."

"You'll have longer than you bargained for," Alex told him, "unless you book passage for three. Unless Andril Degg joins us, I'll not be leaving. And I will leave it to you to explain to the Temple Judges our failure to appear together."

When Islak returned to the inn, he brought with him crutches to aid Alex in moving about, and the horses—three horses. Two were the stallions he and Alex had ridden, black with gray banding. The third was the more solidly built mottled mare, a farm mare, a workhorse. Andril Degg's horse.

Clearing their things from their rooms, they paid their bills with the innkeeper, and were off. Captain Dollapan and Andril Degg secured Alex as best they could in his saddle, without placing his feet in the stirrups. Alex's protestations that his feet were not in need of such gentle care drew renewed inquiries from Andril as to the source of his injuries, and thereafter Alex quietly submitted. Better, Alex knew, to direct attentions elsewhere.

"Go with God," the Captain told Alex, as Andril mounted his own horse. "May his hand protect you."

"And may his hand protect you as well," Alex returned, "as you have protected me, since we met."

Dollapan laid his hand upon Alex's: "He shall guard us both, and we shall meet again."

Alex turned his hand over, grasping the Captain's. Their eyes locked.

232

"Alex? Are you alright?"

Alex could not respond. Leaving Abbik Dollapan seemed wrong, terribly wrong. But he could voice no reason why.

"I'm fine," he said, releasing the Captain's hand. "Sorry. I'm fine. And you, dear Captain? How are you?"

Dollapan cocked his head.

"What we discussed," Alex said quietly, "aboard the Deloré. Your question. Do you find yourself... any closer to resolution?"

Adjusting Alex's saddle straps, the Captain smiled, and quoted from Mirran scripture: "'The mind of man is like a wave upon the waters; / It changes course for reasons it does not understand.' Don't worry about me, Traveler Alexander Boten. These thoughts... I do not know where they came from. In their own time, they will likely pass of their own accord."

"If these thoughts linger, dear Captain, do not grow too comfortable with them. I'm taking Islak from you, but surely there must be others you can speak to about this."

"There are two," he answered. "They have sustained me thus far. So shall they continue."

"Greet Vinasa for me," Alex said. *And Lannae*, he knew he should add; it was mere courtesy. But mentioning her name to Captain Dollapan felt awkward. And after a moment's hesitation, it was too late to add mention of her without drawing attention to that awkwardness.

The Captain studied him for a moment, and then nodded: "I will pass your message along." Their eyes held on each other for a time, and within Captain Dollapan a subtle change began. He still feared the Traveler Alexander Boten, feared his interest in Lannae. But Boten's reluctance to mention her name touched him. It might have been a reluctance born out of Boten's respect for him, or born out of confusion over his own feelings, or born out of a dozen other things. But it seemed clear that the Man of Five Fingers felt some need to keep himself in check, and he did hold himself in check. Of all the confusion of feelings Dollapan held toward Boten, fear over his interest in Lannae moved backward in the crowd.

Andril moved his horse ahead, and Islak moved along beside

him. Alex prodded his horse ahead, pulling up on Islak's other side.

Although this inland lake appeared in dimension to be a sea, the docks were a simple affair, unable to handle more than three or four ships of the size of the one that they approached. She was odd to Alex's eye, basically an overbuilt barge. A single main mast, and a line of oars protruding from both sides. The sails were stowed elsewhere, not even wrapped in their places. It was clear that the calm that was now on the water—a windless, waveless stillness—had been upon the place for a long time, causing the Shipsmaster to give up with keeping his sails at the ready.

At the dock they dismounted. After Islak had confirmed their booking, they split up. Islak helped Alex maneuver toward the stateroom the three would share, and Andril led the horses down the special ramp for large cargo loading. Massive double doors swung out at the ship's rear, a short way above the waterline. It would be an impossible design for a seagoing vessel, but for the Great Lake it posed no hazard. Even in normal times, the waves would not reach to the bottom of the doors. And in a time such as this, one could leave the doors open and not be at risk.

Handing the bridles to the Cargomaster, Andril found himself in a place where, by chance rather than design, the ship's lamps cast no light. And from this darkened corner, he had a line of sight up to the main dock, the well-lit dock. There Islak—in an effort to aid Alex Boten—was in fact slowing him, nearly tripping him, in a comic earnestness. And whereas other passengers moved around the two men, one person seemed to be holding back. But not holding back as might some polite stranger, immediately behind them, reluctant to pass them lest he make them self-conscious. This figure stood back a fair ways, clearly making an effort to match their progress and not close upon them. And although Andril's view was partly blocked by the railings of the dock, it seemed to him that the man's clothes were those of a Shelaemstet constabulary.

*　　　*　　　*

"Explain to me," Alex said, as they settled their things into the room, "about the sails. Why oars, and no sails?"

"The drought" said Islak, in a tone suggesting no further explanation would be needed.   Eventually he realized Alex was waiting for some deeper explanation.

"The Great Lake has been calm for a long, long time. Normally it is active. Bubbling."

"Bubbling?" Alex said, with concern.   "Just what do you mean, 'bubbling'?"

"The Great Lake is mostly shallow, considering its breadth. But the eastern and western lobes each contain an area of immeasurable depth. From these areas emanate, normally, a bubbling turbulence."

Volcanic, thought Alex. *The whole lake could be volcanic.*

"Over these two areas is a powerful updraft of air," Islak continued. "Clouds form high overhead, from there moving outwards in all directions, watering the lands near and far."

"So a prevailing wind blows outward?"

"Up high the winds blow outward; the motion of the clouds is evidence of that. But closer to the ground, in the realm of men and sail, the winds blow inward."

"Replacing the air," Alex said, "that was displaced by the updraft."

"It is a constant and predictable wind that men can sail by. It was on the Great Lake that men learned the skills they would later use upon the sea. The two active areas themselves are turbulent. But it is a random, non-directed turbulence, which actually has a calming effect on the rest of the Great Lake. But now, no activity, no winds... and no clouds. A great stillness, and a drought. And ship's oars, once a last-resort precaution, are now the mainstay of crossings."

With a few shouted commands, their ship's mooring lines were cast off. Dock hands pushed her away with poles, and the dockside oars were extended. Slowly, they maneuvered out into the Lake, where they picked up an admirable speed.

"How," asked Alex, "does the lake replenish itself? The only rivers I have seen, those we crossed between Barnable and here, flowed away from the lake."

"All rivers flow away from the Great Lake," Islak told him.

"Then what is the source of the water?"

"I cannot say with certainty. But what I can tell you is that since the action ceased, the Great Lake's level has risen."

"Risen?"

"Indeed, yes. The rivers flowing out from it are becoming dangerous torrents. But it is this great increase in the rivers that has preserved us. Those northwest farms along the rivers, if not so close as to have been washed away, are the only farms blessed with water, since the rains stopped. We have food, but life is uncomfortably spare."

"You must have some kind of bizarre hydrologic subterranean system. It must be returning water via deep underwater springs. I suppose the water is then dispersed by runoff, through the rivers, and by evaporation from this bubbling action."

"And with the bubbling stopped," Islak continued, "the evaporation decreases. More water is left to run off in the rivers."

A disturbing thought occurred to Alex. "Has the Great Lake ever gone still before?"

"Never," answered Islak. "Never that has been recorded."

"Is it growing cooler?"

Islak smiled. "Interesting. My first thought when the churning ceased. I took measurements. Within the variances that are to be expected, I did not detect a temperature change."

"Then it may not be going dormant," Alex said to himself.

"No," said Islak. "It is dormant. The activity has stopped."

"I mean a different kind of dormancy," Alex said. "Are there places, anywhere throughout the land, where smoke rises from the ground?"

"No." Then, thinking it over, Islak added: "Not that I have seen. There are stories, from some of the eastern and southern Boundary Waters. I have always dismissed them. But of late, I am less dismissive of sailors' tales. What would it mean to you, this smoke rising from the ground?"

"This entire Great Lake could be a massive double... *caldera*." He had to struggle for the English word. He doubted there was a Mirran equivalent.

"And this *caldera*," Islak said. "What would it mean for us?"

"Nothing," Alex said. "Nothing we could do anything about for now. But when we're done at the Adjunct, I'd prefer an all-land route."

*   *   *

On the main deck, with the docks receding and the vast expanse of the Great Lake ahead, Andril moved about the ship in a course designed to look random. It was not. Had his people been sport fishermen, they would have had a word for trolling—and that was precisely the business Andril was now about. If he had been correct about the uniform of the man shadowing Misters Boten and Islak, then it seemed likely he had been following them since they passed the Temple Complex—that he had, therefore, been following all three of them. And so Andril used himself as a lure, wandering the most heavily trafficked areas of the deck. He would step into an open area, and then move to somewhere more secluded, seeing if someone would follow. In time, someone did. Andril endeavored to keep his eyes from the man's face, avoiding confrontation. He led him on a path that seemed not unreasonable for a curious shipgoer familiarizing himself with the deck, while circuitous enough to allay any doubt that he was being followed.

Passing through the door that led down to the cabins, Andril closed the door behind him and at once snatched the lantern from the wall. He turned the knob down to where the light almost extinguished, then held it behind him. He waited.

After nearly a round, the door opened again. The figure, confronted by the unexpected darkness of the passage, stood in the doorway. He was silhouetted by orange light from Dessene as it set upon the lake.

Andril drew the lantern around in front of him.

Seeing the point of light of the near-extinguished lantern, the figure backed out of the doorway. "Sorry," he said. "Wrong passageway."

Andril eased up the control knob, illuminating them. "No," he said. "This is the passageway you seek." The man wore workmen's clothes now, not a uniform.

"I am sorry sir," the man said. "You are mistaken."

He wasn't in uniform, but the face was the same, the same that had followed Andril's companions on the dock. "You, sir, are mistaken," Andril corrected, "if you think I do not know when I am being followed."

The stranger did not reply. He stood, weighing his options.

Andril spoke: "Does the Temple Guard have interest in a farmer, a cripple, and a visitor from the north? Or is your interest personal?"

"I am the Chief Constable of the Temple Court. And my interest is personal."

"Please, kind Chief Constable," said Andril, in a tone conveying utmost gravity, "share with me your interest."

The Constable looked around the deck behind him, and then stepped in through the door and closed it. He reached for the lamp, but Andril held it away. The Constable flipped his gaze to the wall, and Andril hung the lamp back in its place.

"Know with whom you travel," the Constable said.

"I know them," Andril said.

"No," he replied. "You do not."

"Enlighten me."

"This thinker," said the constable, "this inventor, this Anned Islak. He revealed something to the Temple Court. I know not what. And this other, this Traveler Alexander Boten, he revealed something to the Temple Court. This I know, but am honor bound not to speak it." Here he paused, looking down the passage, to the stairs leading below deck. "These two things, taken together, have convinced the Temple Court that the Traveler Alexander Boten is Harbinger."

"They have not declared him," Andril scoffed.

"All six of the Temple Judges will meet him at the Adjunct. There they will declare him. I am certain of it."

"The Judges," said Andril incredulously, "journey to the Temple Adjunct?"

"By land, around the western lobe of the Great Lake, yes."

"What you are claiming," Andril countered, "would mean the Judges believe Restoration is already here. That he has somehow been missed."

"The Judges believe," the Constable said evenly, "that he is both Harbinger and Restoration."

Andril did not respond. But he remembered Alex's interest in Restoration. He remembered Alex's interest in the Mystery. The Mystery of the Shedding of Blood. And he remembered the bandages, the injuries to Alex Boten's feet. Andril remembered how whenever Boten's injuries needed tending, Andril was always conveniently otherwise engaged. He leaned against the wall, and closed his eyes.

"It need not be this way," the Constable said. "If Harbinger does not arrive at the Adjunct."

"What are you suggesting?" asked Andril, snapped back as if from a trance.

"Nothing improper. Only this. If it is within the range of God's will that things remain as they are, then God will afford an opportunity. It only then remains, for those who wish things to remain as they are, to encourage and develop that opportunity. To steer circumstances toward it. After we dock at Ohlmont, anyone wishing to reach the southern coast must pass through marshes— miles and miles of marshes. Farther south is the crossing of the Adjunct Highlands—a crossing treacherous in places, if a certain route is chosen."

"You speak of man's will, not God's will," said Andril.

"I know that we are of one mind," said the Constable. "When first you arrived in the City, you came directly to the Temple Complex. The questions you asked were reported to me. I know…" and here his tone lowered, "…that you fear the things that I fear. The things that many fear, now that they are upon us. Do you want to face what lies ahead, if he is Harbinger? If he is Restoration? Do you want to end up like Anned Islak—blind or mad or worse?"

"What do you mean?"

"Don't suggest to me," said the Constable, "that you did not know God has struck him blind."

"I suspected his blindness. But what of it? We have journeyed to the DevilsEye. Is it so strange that one among us lost his sight? Why should Islak's blindness give us license to...?"

"Do you not know why God struck him blind? Do you not know what it is he carries with him in that valise of his? Anned Islak has looked into the face of God, and has dared to draw what he has seen. And for looking into the face of God, he has been struck blind."

"How would you know what he carries in his valise?"

"Watch him. See how he carries it, how he guards it. Offer to hold it for him. What he has seen, what he has recorded, terrifies him. As it should you. We stand at the edge of a new prospect, of hearing the voice of God Almighty. Not through prophets. Not through wise men. But every man and woman, hearing his voice themselves. Hearing the very voice of the God Who Is Silent. Mortal man cannot endure it. We are doomed."

The Constable had the advantage over Andril in both height and weight, but Andril grabbed him and swung them both around, trading places and throwing the Constable against the wall. Then he backed out through the same doorway the Constable had entered, stepping into Dessene's orange afterglow.

"Stay away from Alex Boten," Andril said, and he was gone.

*   *   *

Andril Degg joined Alex in the common stateroom, ill of mood and restrained. Islak was above, on deck. Alex watched Andril settle in and arrange his things. It seemed to Alex that Andril's attention kept returning to Islak's things, as if he were searching, but not wanting anyone to know that he was searching. Whatever Andril might be covertly seeking, he was evidently not finding it. The only thing Islak had taken with him, other than the clothes he wore, was his ever-present valise. And, Alex thought, if Andril were to fix upon a thing in Islak's possession, what better candidate than the mysterious valise? Once Andril had seemed to have settled all of his possessions, and moved on to merely rearranging them so as to seem busy, it seemed to Alex a good time to shift the young man's focus.

"If I am going to the Adjunct," Alex said, "I should know something about it. What can you tell me?"

Andril was startled, partly at hearing his voice after the prolonged silence, and partly at the nature of the question. Then, the grim determination of his face softened. His aspect changed from that of a worried man to an enthusiastic youth. It was a change that pleased Alex.

"What shall I tell you?" asked Andril, drawing a stool to Alex's bed.

"I know God once suspended his silence, and told people of the first Harbinger. And they built a temple, or a structure... something, by God's command. The Harbinger was born with five fingers. The Harbinger worked inside the structure for years after the workmen had finished. When he himself was finished, he became a hermit till he died. And, I take it, no one has been inside this 'Adjunct' since."

"It is a forbidden place," Andril said. "None but Harbinger may enter."

"But tell me about it. About its appearance."

"It is made of chelsit stone, inside and out, quarried from the highlands just north of there. The place God chose was an expanse of smooth bedrock."

"Like the Mirran Stone, at the Temple Complex," Alex suggested.

"The very same, in color, texture, and evenness. But into this rock, the people were instructed to burrow."

"Through the rock?" Alex asked.

"It was a massive undertaking. The rock extended down to the height of a man. But they were instructed to dig far deeper. The area carved out was nearly that of the Temple Stone. And with this expanse of the bedrock opened up, the people dug, through the dirt, setting as they went a series of stone steps."

As Andril described the spacing of the steps, Alex recognized it: "The same steps as the Mirran Stone."

Andril dithered. "Similar. Yet different." He struggled for awhile to explain the difference, and then gave up. "When the steps were completed, to the depth God had specified, the chelsit stone was

241

brought down and the Temple Adjunct built."

"It is all stone, then?"

"Mostly stone. The Book records that logs of sedres and tersa were brought in...." Andril saw he was not familiar with these words. "Fragrant and durable woods, resistant to decay. Also a block of black orbid, a hard, glassy rock. It's found mostly around the Great Lake. The best pieces are actually submerged in the lake itself. Other things went into the construction of the Adjunct—bolts of the richest cloth, and things that are just summarized as 'other items of finery'. But no further details on them are recorded."

"And that's it?" Alex asked.

"Mostly. Dimensions are given, for the outside. But we don't know what is on the inside. The interface between the walls and roof was unusual. The walls aren't solid all the way up. The final foot or so are pillars of chelsit, so there is an almost continuous open air passage."

"Can't you see in, then?"

"The roof is steeply angled, and extends well out beyond the wall. The view is blocked."

"But if someone climbed up along the wall...."

"Why would one do that?" Andril asked, confused.

"To see in," Alex said.

"If one wanted to see what was inside, one could walk in through the entrance."

"The door isn't blocked off?"

"The door? There is no door. Just an opening. A baffle obstructs the view." Andril produced for him a sketch:

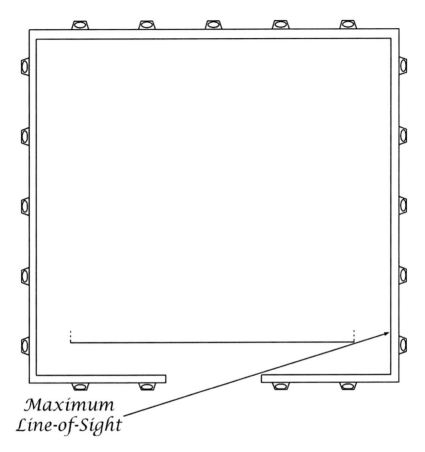

Maximum
Line-of-Sight

"Then anyone could just walk in."

Andril cocked his head. "It is a forbidden place. No one enters."

"For a curious and exploratory people, you have a strong respect for the prohibitions of God," Alex observed.

"Mr. Islak would tell you that those respecting God *are* the curious, the exploratory. Those who believe we are ruled by randomness have nothing to search out. For them, all that is beyond what we now know is mere chaos. Chaos and futility."

"So for all these years, everyone has respected the prohibition. No one has walked through that open doorway. Nobody has seen the

243

inside, except the men who built it."

"The workmen only built the walls and roof," Andril reminded him. "They knew what we know, from reading the dimensions. There was nothing inside to see, until after their work was done."

"Alright," Alex conceded. "Nobody has seen it except this first Harbinger."

Andril looked at him strangely. "Harbinger never saw what was inside."

"I thought he completed it."

"He did," Andril said. But Harbinger, the first Harbinger, was born blind."

Alex turned to look at him squarely: "Would you say that again?"

"The first Harbinger of God, he was born with five fingers, and blind."

"How did he do his work? How did he know what to do?"

"You are not the first to ask that. Harbinger's parents, and the elders who heard the voice of God, felt the same way. Hold on...." Digging through his things, he produced a copy, slightly ruffled, but thoroughly serviceable, of the Mirran scriptures. Presently he found the passage he sought, about what God spoke to the prophet, to be told to the people:

"I have chosen him, and by me was he chosen.
None other have I consulted; from none among the ranks of men has my counsel been drawn.
Know that if man scorns my harbinger,
Even if the harbinger scorns himself,
Yet your God has not despised him.
Your God has chosen him, has set him at the Temple's Adjunct;
Has set him at its very door."

"The construction," Andril told him, "continued as the Harbinger grew to adulthood. After the twenty-ninth reversal of his life, Harbinger went to the Adjunct, and declared construction complete.

The workmen were to leave, leaving their tools behind. The lamps were to be lit, and forever maintained."

"The lamps?"

"Oil fired lamps. Five per side, twenty in all. Mounted on the exterior walls of the Adjunct."

"You said 'forever maintained'."

"To this day," Andril told him. It is not hard. The entire Adjunct is recessed to where wind can scarcely touch it. The roof extends over, protecting it from rain. The keepers merely maintain the oil levels."

"The keepers? That's somebody's job, just keeping the oil full?"

"It is a rotating service," Andril explained. "But there is a waiting list."

"This Adjunct is an important thing."

"It is central," he declared quietly, looking Alex squarely in the eye, "to the coming of Harbinger."

"And so, Harbinger declared the Adjunct completed..." Alex encouraged him on.

"He declared the exterior completed. Harbinger entered the Temple Adjunct, and he remained there for forty reversals."

"Forty reversals? Forty crossings of the Crown of God across the sky?"

"The priests tended to his needs, but they never entered the Adjunct. Only Harbinger would come and go. After forty reversals he emerged, never to re-enter, and declared his work, the work of the Almighty God, to be completed."

Islak entered the cabin, with his valise.

"And what became of him?" Alex asked

"Thereafter he departed the company of men," Andril explained, "retreating into the southern highlands to live alone."

With a sigh, Islak realized of whom they were speaking. He slid the valise between his bed and the wall.

"The priests still tended to his needs," continued Andril, "leaving him food and clothing in a certain place. But he never would return to civilization. He remained alone, unwilling to bear the company of men, until he died. Some say, and perhaps with cause, that his work drove him mad. The priests buried him in the highlands, in a place unmarked and unknown."

"You are a charmer, young Degg," Islak said. "Now off to the ship's galley with you. And fetch us something while you are there."

Before Andril returned, Alex had fallen into sleep. It was a deeper sleep than he had become accustomed to, aided by the slight rocking of the ship, and the rhythmic creaking of the oars. For four solid watches he slept.

Book II
Chapter 7: Disaster

When he returned to consciousness, seemingly in exactly the position he had fallen asleep, he found Islak hovering over him. Islak had been wanting to redress Alex's feet, but had waited so as not to wake him. Now he wasted no time.

Alex swung himself over to the porthole while Islak unwrapped his feet. There were lights, out across the water.

"Ohlmont," Islak told him. "Two watches at most, and we will be astride our horses." He began wrapping fresh bandages.

"No," Alex fussed. "Enough of this. Leave them to the air."

"You cannot yet wear your boots. Let me at least wrap them so much as to protect them from whatever you may chance to walk upon while still aboard ship."

Alex consented. He breakfasted on the dried fruits Andril had brought up from the galley.

"Where is Andril?" Alex asked.

"In the hold," Islak told him, "checking on the horses." Islak leaned over him, looking out the porthole, to the shoreward lights. "Oh. Farther away than I thought."

"From Ohlmont? How far can we be? It's so bright."

"Ohlmont is a refining town. Of one thing there, there is never a shortage. And that thing, you may be sure, is oil."

Islak began losing his balance, nearly falling on Alex. Alex reached out to steady him, and then he felt it himself: The ship was shifting—lurching backward. They could hear others aboard ship, calling out in surprise and distress. The backward motion changed; now they were moving down. Boten had never actually experienced it shipboard, but in an instant he sensed what was happening. A swell was approaching, was upon them, perhaps even about to break. Their ship was caught in the undertow of the trough. He pulled Islak down onto the bed. There was no time to speak. Shouts and screams of passengers and crew were silenced as they shot upward. When the upward thrust had passed, they immediately fell—not like they had before, not with a sense of lightness as on a descending elevator—but in a virtual weightlessness. Weightlessness was nothing new to Alex, but it caught him off guard. He nearly vomited. Their descent ended abruptly. Alex found himself on the floor, Islak beside him. There were muffled shouts around the ship, everywhere the chatter of voices, and sobbing somewhere nearby. But nothing with the urgency they had heard just before the wave hit. Climbing across his overturned bed, Alex pulled himself to the porthole. The wave that had swept under them moved like a gliding giant toward the shore; the lights of Ohlmont were obstructed by it, but its top edge glistened under the Crown of God. As best he could tell, it did not seem to be curved around them. Rather, it appeared to be formed along a nearly straight line. The epicenter was far, far behind them.

"Your Great Lake," Alex said, "is active again."

Islak pushed him aside. "A wave?" he said, disbelieving. "This is not how the lake behaves. This is not in its nature. It is a churning, a bubbling. Not this."

The tallest lights of Ohlmont were visible above the crest now, as the wave moved away from them. Alex guessed it had been ten to twenty feet. Whether it would stay that height or climb as it crested depended on the changes in depth as the wave neared shore.

"All the activity that has been stopped for so long," Alex explained. "All that energy. It's been stored up. If we're lucky, it's all been released."

"Andril," said Islak. "He was checking the horses."

"I'm alright here," Alex said. "See if you can find him."

But before Islak reached the door, all the voices stopped. The talking, the shouting, all went silent, except one or two people crying. Islak looked to Alex. Both knew: It was not a good silence. Alex was closer to the window, and looked out. He could hear a hissing, now. Everyone else had heard it already. The water seemed to boil. Then a deckhand or a passenger, someone behind his field of view, directed a lantern's light to the water beside and below. The water was churning, all around them, and it seemed to be throwing debris

248

up to the surface.

"There were two active places," Alex said to Islak, without looking to him. "Could we be near one of them?"

"No," Islak said. "The center of the western lobe is over a hundred miles from here."

Alex turned from the window. "This is bad," he said. A deep rumbling began, and grew louder. "You had best hold onto something."

"But Andril...."

The rumbling grew louder, to where the planking beneath them began vibrating.

"I don't think you'll make it to him," Alex observed. "Grab something."

Islak's head snapped to his bed, which lay overturned against a wall. He leapt upon it, pulling it away. Alex watched him, puzzled. Islak dug through his bedding, and pulled out the valise.

"Anned, something very, very bad is happening. Deadly. Forget the papers." Alex moved into a corner, and slid down to the floor. The vibrations pulsed through him.

Islak had torn open the valise, and dug out what seemed like a streamer of dull white cloth, which he laid on the floor. Then he pulled out his vellum drawing of the Crown, and other maps of paper, and hurriedly twisted them into a single roll. The bow of the ship kicked up suddenly, and settled back down.

"That might be it," Alex said. "That might be all." But even as he said it, he knew he was wrong. The rumbling, now nearly a roar, continued.

Islak stuffed the roll of maps into the streamer, which Alex now realized was a long thin bag. Animal intestine, he guessed. Treated and cured. And waterproof?

"Islak, don't be stupid! Brace yourself, man! Whatever that is, it's not worth your life!" Alex doubted if he heard. He could barely hear himself. Islak tied the end, and tied it again. The ship began rocking, swaying unpredictably. Islak pulled a second bag from the valise, sliding the first into it, tying it.

There was no further building, no escalation. The blast hit

abruptly, and Alex would remember little of it. The ship was thrown upward, initially. But after a moment, everything was chaos and tumbling. Water shot in through the porthole like a blast of rocket exhaust, then ceased, then shot in again. The room was filling with water. Alex had hoped the interior of the ship would afford some protection. It began looking like a tomb. Independently, Alex and Islak struggled out the door, and then were washed down the passageway. Alex tried to swim, but the bandages on his feet hindered him. By grabbing protrusions in the corridor, he pulled himself along. Islak was ahead of him, his precious maps nowhere to be seen. Islak kept looking back to Alex, and Alex kept yelling "Go!" to encourage him on. The passageway ended in wreckage. A blast of water from behind propelled them through it, and they were out of the ship, floating in the water.

The ship was on her side, sinking slowly.

"Andril... and the horses..." Islak gasped. "They could not have made it."

Alex did not reply. His mouth was only intermittently above water. As he kicked to maintain himself, the waterlogged bandages seemed to be pulling him down. They were loosely wrapped, and coming undone—but as they did, they tangled about his legs. He could kick less and less. He dog-paddled with his arms. It wasn't enough. He knew he would go down. Taking a breath, he reached down. The bandages were a hopeless tangle. He came up for air, but took in water with it. His mind raced through the options; the last moments of his life would come to one of these:

— Take a breath before you go down. That would give a few seconds longer, but would end with the agony of air-starved lungs. But, he had heard, there was a peaceful moment as the brain's oxygen level dipped.

— Keep your mouth open as you go down. Quicker. Just the revolting sensation of taking in the water.

— Flail wildly in panic. Easiest, because it required no planning or thought. Undignified, but with the virtue of coming naturally.

Stupid, stupid way to die. Where was his mistake? Not getting out of the room faster? Not unwrapping his feet before the big blast had hit? That was it. Maybe he could go back, redo that part. For one curious moment, he realized he was being irrational. Lack of oxygen? Was he underwater already? Waving his hand before his face, he felt the drag of water on it. Yes, he was under. It was all done. Sad. Wasn't there something he was supposed to do first? Something....

A hand grabbed his and pulled him up. Although he did not realize it, his head was now above water. He would have kept holding his breath, reflexively, except that he crashed into something. It was firm, but with some give to it. Familiar. The impact forced the used air out of his lungs, and he drew in more air automatically.

Andril slid off of the saddle on one side, dragging Alex across from the other side. There was no time to tend to him, so Andril left him there, trusting to God that he was breathing, and that the horse would keep him afloat. Andril followed the hastily tied line that connected the saddle of the first horse to the saddle of the second. The horses were struggling, but managing to keep above water. The horse across which Alex had been flopped was Andril's own. She was not as fast as the two stallions, but she was sturdier. And, Andril fancied, a more powerful swimmer. Reaching the second horse, Andril spotted Islak nearby, flopping like a lame bird. Although he clearly knew nothing of how to swim, he seemed to be having no problem staying up. Andril swam to him, and pulled him back to the second horse. As Islak dragged himself partway across the saddle, Andril understood Islak's ability to stay afloat; he had been riding astraddle some long, thin balloon.

The third horse had come detached, and Andril looked around for it. There hadn't been much time, between the first wave and the disastrous explosion. Not enough time to tie proper knots, just ones that he hoped would serve.

He spotted the third horse, thirty feet off. It wasn't doing well. There was no way he would be able to hold it up, but maybe if he could calm it... maybe if he could calm the creature, it would stay up.

Alex gradually became aware of his surroundings. He was facing down, a few inches above water. He was lying across a saddle.

Nonsensical. Looking up, he saw Andril swimming away, toward a horse struggling in the water. He tried to speak, but instead heaved up some water. Exhausted, he laid his head against the saddle, his hair awash in the lake.

"Alex!" He recognized it as Islak's voice. "Alex?"

Alex waved his hand, irrationally hoping Islak would see him and calm down. Looking around, he couldn't see Islak. Andril had reached the horse. It was responding to him, calming. Andril was busy with something. Removing the saddle, Alex guessed. Andril kept stroking the panicky animal.

Only a farm boy, thought Alex, could have saved that horse. Good animal sense. Grabbing onto the saddle, Alex pushed himself up to look around. The bow of the ship had risen, and was just now going under. The cargo doors in her stern, thought Alex, had probably been her doom. He spotted Islak, on the horse tied to his. He looked for Andril. He could not find him. Andril and the second stallion were gone.

Sliding off the saddle, he used the horse for flotation as he pulled at the bindings entangling his legs. Stripping to the waist, he let his clothes and the bandages drift away. Afraid he might panic the horse, he decided not to cling to its bridle as he moved around it, but to swim around in a desperate effort to get to where he had last seen the boy. By the time Alex had circumvented the horse, however, he was exhausted and breathless. Reaching the opposite side of the saddle, he clung to it, unable even to pull himself up.

Alex could effect no rescue. Andril Degg was gone, forever gone. Whether struck by a flailing hoof, or entangled in the bridle or the victim of a half dozen other possible fates, Alex would never know.

Alex was moving, through the water. He and the horse, together, were moving. With the carcass of the ship gone, the horses could now see the lights of Ohlmont—which had apparently survived both the first wave and whatever effects had hit it from the blast. The lights were like a beacon, leading the horses to shore.

Book II
Chapter 8: The Temple Adjunct

Ohlmont proper escaped major damage from the waves. The docks were destroyed, as were the small number of homes and businesses directly on or near the water's edge. But owing to the contour of the land, a hundred feet from shore most of the effects were nuisance water damage.

Islak's money was lost in the wreck, but he was able to ply his reputation into some generous advances, providing all they needed. The stallion they sold to a livery; the owner was certain it would recover with adequate rest and feeding. With the proceeds, and some of the money Islak had borrowed, they purchased another. The mare, which had been Andril's horse, seemed fit for travel as soon as she hit the shore.

Alex and Islak rested for two watches at an inn. (The innkeeper, a devotee of Islak's discoveries, inventions and theories, refused to accept payment for their stay.)

As they left Ohlmont, they approached the southwestern city limit, and it was a double sorrow for Alex. The first was leaving what Alex had come to think of as the City of Light. Their mounts stood at the crest of a hill, with the town below them ablaze with wildly excessive oil-fired lighting. The refining process produced differing grades of oil; the lower grades were not profitable to transport, but were usable for burning. Thus everywhere in Ohlmont were brilliantly blazing lamps—indoors, outdoors, where there seemed some need, where there clearly was none. The residents of Ohlmont were used to the brilliance, but visitors often found it uncomfortable to the eyes. For Alex, it was like strolling about at dawn. Andril's mare was restless under him, pawing at the ground, eager to move off into the relative darkness illumined only by Hon, and the ever upward creeping arms of the Crown of God.

These reflected in the still waters of the Great Lake, the waters that held the body of Andril Degg. This was his second and greater sorrow; Alex wished there were a grave, some place he could visit now or in the future, to pay his respects. Looking around him, he realized this spot would serve that function. From here he could look out to where Andril had saved him.

He wondered how long the waters would wait before stirring again— whether they would stir as they always had in the past, thus restarting the hydrological cycle, or whether they would erupt with even more violence than they had just seen, perhaps even wiping away Shelaemstet itself.

Without a word, Alex started his horse down the hill, away from Ohlmont, and away from the Great Lake. Islak followed.

As they approached the lowlands, now at a gentle trot, they passed through growth unlike anything Alex had seen before on their journeys. The long sloping hill was lush with vegetation, but it seldom grew high enough to block their view of the vast oil marshes that spread out before them in the bottomlands. Each refining station was like an island of light along the marsh's outer edges. You could not traverse the oil marsh itself, Islak explained. The oil seeped up and mixed with the soil, making a shifting goo. Plants grew in boggy clumps upon the surface, but nothing of substantial size could grow without collapsing back into the muck. As they entered the bottomland, on a trail that led along the solid grounds around the marsh, they approached a massive forest. They slowed their horses to a walk. The trees were huge, like massive elms. As best he could make out, though, they did not have traditional leaves. They seemed to have streamers, like massively overgrown weeping willows. The two of them passed into the forest, and, it seemed to Alex, into another world.

It was within this world that Alex learned to quell an incessant inner voice that had long complained of the perpetual night of Mirrus. He had not known night on this planet, not until now. The huge trees around them blocked off all light from the moon, and the glow from the Crown of God. This was like the deep night of Earth, the new moon night at midnight, with clouds blocking the stars; utter darkness.

Each of them carried a lantern, casting a forward shaft of light. And the refinery workers, whom they occasionally passed on the trail, maintained a series of lanterns marking major turns and hazards. But all of these were like pinpricks in the massive, unstoppable dark.

The vast canopy of branches above them was alive with birds. Or perhaps bats. Or perhaps something else he could scarcely imagine. He opted not to inquire of Islak. Better not to know, he felt.

Islak wanted them to resume a trot, but Alex resisted. He was uncomfortable moving quickly with so little vision. For Islak, forging ahead and trusting the animal had become second nature. But Islak deferred to his companion. After they had stopped for Islak to sleep, however, Alex began to feel the forest would last forever if they did not push ahead more quickly. When they started off again, it was at a trot. Before long, they had moved into a canter.

Alex slept once in the forest, a double watch. They stopped several times for Islak to sleep, and when their sleep schedules did not coincide, Alex did not wander about exploring.

Emerging from the forests, with the oil marshes behind them, they stopped to feed, water and rest the horses. Then, under the blazing double moon (for Dessene had now risen, as well) they were off at a gallop.

South of the marshes lay a broad prairie, now dangerously dry, which allowed them to cover ground quickly. Despite the delay at Ohlmont due to the disaster, Islak hoped they might yet arrive at the Adjunct before the Judges. If the Judges had any delays in leaving Shelaemstet, and if the coach they booked was chosen less for speed than for comfort, then he and Boten might reach the Adjunct first.

An elevated ridge began to take shape before them. The southern Adjunct Highlands, Islak explained. From this side, the people of old had gathered the sedres wood for the Adjunct. From the far side they had chopped the tersa and mined the chelsit stone that comprised the bulk of the Adjunct structure. It was probably along the path they now rode that the block of black orbid had been carried.

There was not a single path to follow; various crisscrossing pathways had been beaten into the prairie ground. From time to time they would stop; Islak would have him describe the pattern of the ridges on the nearing highlands, until Islak recognized the description. They would then ride ahead until the next path crossed theirs. And from there they could turn right or left, or continue ahead. In this way, they zeroed in on the place Islak had in mind—a pass that seemed to his mind a fair compromise between its alignment with their objective, and its ease of travel.

They arrived at the foot of the pass, with the Adjunct Highlands reaching up before them. *Not the Rockies*, thought Alex, *but formidable*. After a bit of wandering, they found the final feature that had caused Islak to choose this place: a well.

"The tenders of the animals use it," Islak told him, "to water their charges before and after the climb. The best feeding grasses grow high."

Alex lowered a rope and bucket by hand; there was no overhead cranking system. "The tenders of animals," he echoed. Undoubtedly horses, or load-bearing oxen. Still, a last desperate vision of cattle flitted through his mind—and with it, an illusory whiff of grilling steak. "*Not their way*," he said to himself in English. "*It is not their way*."

"I'm sorry," Islak said, "I didn't catch that."

"Just a lost dream," said Alex, handing him a full bucket. "What animals?"

Islak told him, but Alex did not recognize the name.

"What do they do?" asked Alex. "What do they... provide?"

Islak poured the bucket into a trough, which the horses attacked. "Their coats. They are sheared periodically." He fingered the lapel of his coat. "They are processed, into cloth."

Alex nodded. Nevermore—pot roast, lamb chops. All past. "I see," he said.

Islak mistook his unintended tone of sorrow for confusion. "Is this not done among your people?" he asked.

"What?" said Alex. "Is what not done?" He had been thinking of eating slaughtered meat. What had he said? Had he said something aloud?

"Your clothing," Islak said, cautiously handing him back the bucket. "Is it not made in this way?"

"Some of it," Alex said, smiling. He hadn't felt guilty over eating meat since he was ten years old. He didn't feel guilt now, not exactly. It was more... embarrassment. But the reaction of the Mirrans was still unimaginable to him. How would earthlings respond to an alien visitor, if they discovered he was a cannibal?

When both the horses and the riders were rested, they began the ascent. A clear, well-worn pathway led up into the highlands, snaking around to ease the climb, and leading past numerous exhausted quarries. Most of the galactic bar had cleared the horizon, and its brilliance caught and reflected in the highland peaks, reflecting down into the quarries. The chelsit that remained within them was nearly pure white.

The path crested and began leading down. But before they had descended far, the path led them out of the concealing peaks, giving them a view of the plain to the south. Far in the distance, Alex could see a thin edge of ocean. But on the land just this side of the sea, there was a glow.

"There's light," Alex said, pulling back on the reins. "A city, maybe near the Adjunct?"

"There is no city near the Adjunct," Islak told him. "No one wants to build near the forbidden place. There are a few buildings, to house those who tend the lamps, and for the storing of oil. But no city. The light you see is the Adjunct itself."

"It must be incredibly bright. How do your people stand it?"

"Personally," said Islak, easing his horse past Alex, "I don't anticipate difficulty." His horse navigated the downward path. Although Islak urged it to go faster, the horse obeyed only to a point. But once the path emptied onto the flat, they were off at full gallop. There was only one path now. From the highland pass there could be only one destination, for hundreds of miles on either side.

Without benefit of elevation, the view of the sea was gone. From what Islak had told him, the Adjunct was far enough inland that they likely would not see the sea again, unless they proceeded south after their business at the Adjunct was completed. And as for their business at the Adjunct, Alex grew in equal parts annoyed and concerned. Annoyed with Islak, for his refusal to comply with the Judges' command until they had reached the Adjunct, and concerned with the Judges, who seemed prepared to coronate him somehow—all on the basis of coincidental events. Powerful, strange coincidences, he was willing to admit. But not as powerful as the Judges seemed to think. He was sure that if the Mirrans were willing to change the interpretations of other prophecies, he could probably fulfill them as well. Anyone could. It was a question of how far you stretched the accepted understandings. And that was a matter of how far you wanted to stretch them. But whatever little surprise Islak had for him, likely rolled up in the maps he carried in his saddlebags, and whatever rationale the Judges would thrust upon him, he knew that the time had come to be resolute. The glow of the Adjunct was close now. And unless he wanted to be god, or king, or fill some other outrageously pivotal role in their culture, he had to draw the line. It was true that these beings were too human, down to the tiniest aspects of physiology, to be explained away as anything other than the handiwork of God—the same God who had created him. But that didn't mean God had Alex Boten in mind when he gave them their sacred writings. What a monstrous evil it would be to usurp the place of the true Harbinger, whenever he would come. It was then that a terrible thought occurred to him. Maybe Sirocco had been the prophesied NewStar. Maybe Harbinger was among them even now—but with their eyes set on him, on Alex Boten, the Mirrans would not recognize the one who truly was to fulfill their scriptures. Alex Boten, the great false prophet—now there was a fine ambassadorial title.

He pulled up beside Islak, and slowed him down. They had arrived. A hundred yards before them was the gaping crater-like depression into which the Adjunct had been built. Light streamed up from it, from lamps below their line of sight. They approached some outbuildings, and two men came forth to meet them.

"You have come to a forbidden place," one said, though his tone was not confrontational; more curious. "Who are you? What business do you have?"

"Our horses," said Islak, dismounting, "are in need of water,

258

Book II, Chapter 8: The Temple Adjunct

food, and rest. For now, this is the extent of our business." He drew out the long double bag from his saddlebag. "As to my name, I am Anned Islak, of Barnable, in Arquat."

"Mr. Islak," said the man, taking the horse's bridle, "you honor us. Come with us, please." The men led them to the nearest building. It was a single large room, some sort of commons room, evidently for cooking and dining. While one man took the horses, to tend to their needs, the other invited them in to sit, as three more men joined them. In time, Alex learned that the Adjunct was surrounded by four clusters of buildings, roughly to the north, south, east and west. Each compound had two men. One man from each of the other three compounds had come to see what manner of visitors had come. No one visited the Adjunct; their presence here was an event.

Islak was polite, especially since the keepers of the Adjunct were serving them food, but he was elusive about the nature of their visit.

"More will come here, and soon," he told them. "They will likely come via a coach, and almost certainly from the west, looping around the Adjunct Highlands. It would be well if you could prepare accommodations for them. Six, in addition to ourselves."

"Respected sir," the man said, "these facilities are not intended for such an end. The nearest inn...."

"The six," Islak interrupted gently, "are arriving from an arduous journey from Shelaemstet. From the Temple Complex itself. The six who are coming, whose arrival may at any moment be upon us, are the Temple Judges."

It took nearly a full round for the implications of this—of all six Temple Judges coming to the Adjunct—to sink in with the man. As it did, he became visibly shaken. Speaking no more, he left them to their meal and hurried off to consult with the others, and to make what preparations they could.

Alex and Islak spoke no more during their meal—Anned Islak, because the task that he had been given was now unavoidably upon him; Alex Boten, because he knew Islak needed to collect his thoughts for that very task. Throughout the meal, the rolled maps lay on the table before them.

Islak finished eating, and arose without speaking. Taking the

259

maps, he carefully found his way to a lamp hanging on the wall.

"Come," he said, taking the lamp in hand. "Let us go to the Adjunct."

Alex moved to the door, and Islak followed his lead. As they emerged from the building, the two keepers of the north compound were upon them, offering to help in whatever way they could.

"No," said Islak, forging ahead to the Adjunct's bright glow, "focus on your preparations. We must be alone."

Side by side they approached the edge, walking on the same smooth bedrock that surrounded the Mirran Stone at the Temple Complex. They stopped when they reached the edge. They stood at the perimeter of a huge, carved hole in the ground. The hole seemed like it formed an inverted pyramid, like the Mirran Stone—but extending down rather than up. It was almost as if the Mirran Stone had been quarried from here as a single block, lifted out, flipped upright, and deposited hundreds of miles to the north.

Like the Mirran Stone, it was formed into scalloping steps. But these were different, and he understood now what Andril Degg had once tried to explain to him. The scalloping effect was reversed.

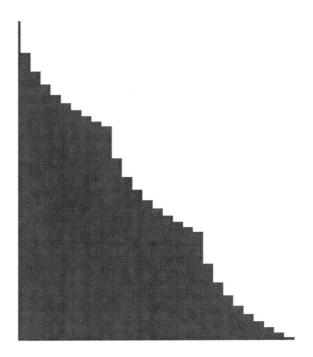

Its magnitude was the same; it seemed to extend nearly as far down as the Mirran Stone extended up. But all of this was mere approach; mere presentation. At the square bottom was a ring of brightly burning lamps, and in the middle of those was a simple stone building, itself ringed with lamps on its outer walls, though these were blocked by the building's overhanging roof. It seemed, from this distance and elevation, to be a simple four-sided building, with a four-sided roof rising to a point.

"You have something to tell me," Alex observed, without looking to him. "No more games, Anned. Talk to me. What is it you told the Judges, back before the Ammanon Deloré sailed?"

Islak sat down on the smooth stone, untying the long thin bag. With some fair difficulty, he coaxed the rolled-up papers out of it. Extracting from the roll the large vellum, he laid it out upon the stone. It kept trying to re-roll itself, and Islak finally removed his shoes, placing them on opposite corners. He removed his coat, and wadded it into a bundle to hold the third. The fourth, he held with his hand. The finely detailed galactic map had been slightly damaged—some creases and tears, a few places where water had encroached and caused the ink to run—but it was still a masterful and beautiful work. The vellum was sheer enough that Alex could see the stone beneath it.

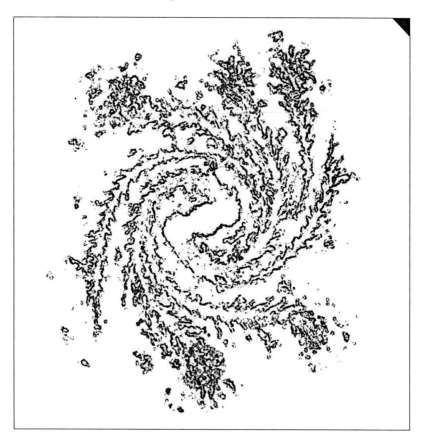

Islak sighed, holding his head as if examining it, though Alex doubted he could see much of it. The scientist/inventor said nothing.

"I have seen this already" Alex reminded him. "On the Deloré. You showed it to me. It's a fine piece of work, but…."

"My life's work has been," said Islak, ignoring him, "to discover the workings of...." He paused, and stretched out his arms. "Of everything, if that is not too grandiose an assertion."

"A worthy task," Alex said.

"Always, behind everything I have attempted, has been the belief, the assumption, that God has designed the universe in an orderly way. That he has not left us to the whims of randomness, to chance."

Something in Islak's words, or perhaps his tone, touched Alex. He felt compelled to say more than his reason told him he should: "Your assumptions are true. There is great order. Order that you have found, order that yet awaits your discovery." Alex sat beside him.

"A man's fingers have many tiny ridges in them," Islak said. And then he smiled. "Although you were not aware of it, I long ago confirmed that your fingers are the same. On the Deloré, when we tended to you, when you slept. I examined your hands, your fingers. You have these ridges as well."

"I know you're going somewhere with this," Alex said.

"I first became aware of them as a child, after touching glass. They left a residue, a print, upon the glass."

"You could call them 'finger-prints'," Alex suggested, with some private amusement.

"Have you ever examined them, examined them closely? With a curved lens, to amplify their size?"

"Yes," Alex said. "I suppose I have."

"That, in essence," said Islak, "has been my life. I have seen shapes. Patterns. Swirls. Things that suggest some larger pattern. As if I were the tiniest of insects, even smaller than the eye can see, I have scurried about on God's thumb, trying to deduce what I believe to be the 'finger prints' of God. And in all my life, in all my explorations, in all the rules of order that I have deduced, I have mapped out perhaps only a half dozen lines of God's finger's 'print'."

"You have to remember where you started from," Alex consoled him. "You have made all your discoveries from scratch."

"I do not lament," Islak said, "how little I have yet learned. I am proud of my discoveries. And I will discover more. In fact, my problem is that I *have* discovered more. Much more. More than I was ready to receive. You would think, would you not, that one such as I, dedicated to finding evidence of God through his creation, would be overjoyed in finding, not mere evidence, but actual proof."

Alex looked across the galactic map, trying to understand what Islak thought he had found. There was nothing drawn on the map that any Mirran couldn't see in the sky, at the right time of year.

"I feel," Islak said, almost choking on his words, "like poor Andril Degg." He began crying, half his tears landing on the stone, half on the vellum. "All his life he looked forward to the coming of Harbinger, to the return of the voice of God. But when hearing the voice of God drew too near, he panicked. It became too fearful of a thing. Now I feel that I am he. That I am young Andril Degg. We might as well have been twin brothers, bound together in the womb. For I struggled to see the evidence of God in the world around me. Like some tiny bug, I mapped out God's 'finger print' in the ordered laws of motion and weight, and the properties of light. I developed that sense of a 'fingerprint' all about me. And then, in a flash, was revealed to me not the gentle curving dip of a ridge on a fingertip pressed into the mud of the universe, but the entirety of a massive hand. An all-encompassing proof of creation. And I am overcome by it."

"What, Anned? What have you seen?"

"Take up the map of the Crown of God," Islak told him.

Alex stood up and lifted the sheet off of the stone. Islak began unrolling another map, a paper map, of roughly the same size.

"I have gathered together many maps, of varying accuracies. I have consolidated them, ignoring portions inconsistent, accepting portions that have agreed. I have added considerable detail, after performing considerable examinations, during considerable travel. To the traditional maps of land and sea I have added features of the ocean's depths. Features more than one ship's captain has thought me daft for examining. Sailors care for what may scrape their hulls. I have consolidated that information, but also information of greater depths." He secured the corners of the paper map as the vellum's corners had been. "I have brought all this information together, into one master map."

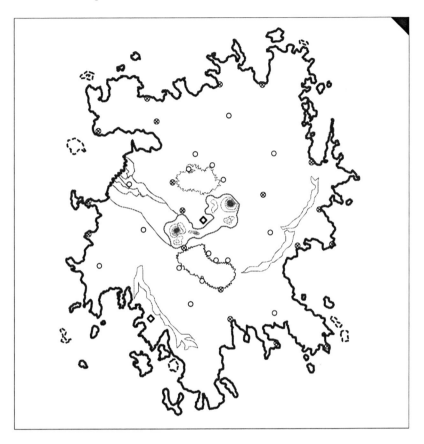

The map spread out before them was indeed a master map of the Mirran continent; its lakes and streams, its highlands, the twin oil marshes bracketing the Great Lake, and contours of great underwater shapes in the ocean. Several cities were mapped, as were the Great Temple and the Temple Adjunct, but none were labeled.

"It is beautiful," Alex said with admiration.

Islak began weeping again. "It is terrible," he said. "The map on the ground, it has one corner, darkened with ink."

"I see it."

"The map you hold," Islak said. "It has the same."

Alex looked. He found it, a one-inch wide triangle inked in. He looked down to the paper map. His mouth moved, forming one word without sound: "…what?" He held the vellum up, so the lamp Islak had brought out shone through it. He shook his head.

Then, moving down to his knees, he laid the corner of the vellum, the corner with the triangle, over the matching mark on the paper. The association was more than unmistakable; it was inarguable.

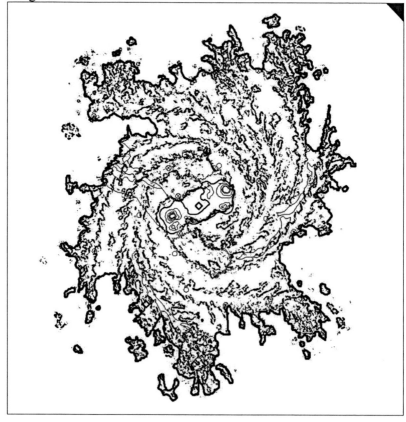

The Great Lake traced out the galactic core and bar. The oil marshes traced major swellings in the galactic swirl. Highlands and underwater ridges defined portions of the spiral arms. Halabae Island, where the Deloré had anchored so that Dollapan could inform the crew of their true mission—it was a globular cluster. Even the towns seemed to conform. Apart from the coastal towns, which would naturally grow up to service sailing ships, the inland towns were clustered. They grouped themselves along the spiral arms. Probably indicative of some natural quality of the soil, or underground springs, that the great spiral arms delineated.

"Behold," said Islak, "the hand print of God."

Alex was without words.

"There is a place in the scriptures," Islak told him. "In it, God says: 'Ask not to look upon me, / For to look upon the face of the living God / is to wither and perish / like green shoots in the smith's fire.' I feel as if I have looked into the face of God."

In the distance, a team of horses could be heard.

"At times," Alex said, "I have thought of the heavens in different ways. Usually as a great emptiness, with occasional pockets of gas and light, and a smattering of rock. But sometimes as a great, complex machine, with gravity pulling things in circles like a vast timekeeping mechanism. Other times, I've thought of it as a work of art, with sweeping strokes and patterns."

"And now, Traveler Alex Boten?" Knowing what you know now, how do you think of the heavens?"

Looking up, Alex saw the enormous Crown of God—saw its shadings of light and dark, and saw the outline of Mirrus overlaid upon it.

"It is… a message."

"But what message, Alex? What does it say? To you?"

Alex felt as if he were embarking upon a psych test. *Now, Mr. Boten, I want you to tell me the first thing that comes into your mind.* He drank in the image above him, drank of it deeply. Ideas came to him. Perhaps they were the message God was communicating. Perhaps they were echoes of his deepest inner self.

"And you, Scientist Anned Islak? What do the heavens say to

you?"

"Alas, Alex. The fullness of their meaning escapes me. But it does seem to me that God is saying the heavens and this world are connected—intimately connected. And that therefore either the heavens can reveal this world, or this world can reveal the heavens. And that it must... *must*... be now."

"How so? Why the urgency?"

"Coastlines change, Alex. Slowly, but unstoppably. The oldest records refer to islands, isthmuses, peninsulas, all that no longer exist. Over the span of a single Reversal you can see the change to a shore. What must happen over thousands? But no change has ever been noted in the Crown of God, not in generations upon generations." Islak stopped, drew a deep breath, and continued: "Either God formed the Crown in anticipation of the shape our world would at this very time take, or he has been steadily shaping our world up to this very day to conform it to the Crown. Either way, the time for this message is now."

"But you do not know what that message is."

"No," Islak confessed. "But I do know that it is important. That all that is about us, and all that is above us, was designed to deliver it—this shows how important it is. I have to know. I have to understand. I was willing to risk all, to understand."

Alex lowered his eyes from the Crown, to survey his friend. Then he looked down to the maps.

"This is what you showed them. What you showed to the Temple Judges."

Islak did not reply.

"And this is why they approved your charter, isn't it?"

"Why they declined to stop it, to be more precise. But yes."

"What was it all about, Anned? What were you hoping to find?"

Again, Islak said nothing.

Alex waited.

"You don't know," Alex offered softly. "You never knew what you were looking for."

"I didn't know what we would find. I couldn't even guess what we *might* find. I was hoping. The Judges and I, all of us were hoping. For more of the message."

"More of the message?"

"If all of Mirrus is a map of the heavens, then if there is anything beyond the boundary waters, it must reveal something of the heavens and their connection to this world, something of the mind of God. Something. Something of what God intends to communicate with this portent my maps have revealed."

"And? Did your voyage reveal anything to you?" Alex asked.

"A better understanding of what the DevilsEye truly is, I suppose. But how that fits into this, I cannot fathom. My fears, Alex. My fears made me turn back. My fears, plus finding the Harbinger. Once we found you, turning for home was inevitable. But I cannot help but wonder: What more might we have found, had we pressed on?"

A whole continent, thought Alex. And what meaning would that have held? A relationship between that continent, and the Mirran sun always above it?

"There was another urgency as well," Islak said. "An urgency not measured in decades. But in months, perhaps even quarters. Perhaps even less. Because of the other maps."

"Other maps?" said Alex.

"The maps that a hundred other mapmakers were doubtlessly working on. Mapmaking is moving out of the realm of art, and into the realm of science. The depiction of landmasses and shorelines grows less fanciful, and more precise. In time, in very little time, I suspect, the realization I have made will be made by others. And once the nature of... of all things... becomes clear to all, once it is thrust suddenly upon them, I do not know what their reaction will be. But if Andril and I are any measure, it will be troubling."

More troubling than you could know, Alex thought. His mind raced across the theological implications. Was it actually stated in scripture, or was it just human interpretation of scripture? Man could choose to believe in God or not. God had given man the freedom to make that choice. But at the end of all things, when God would dwell with man, it would be impossible to deny God. At that point, no choice would be possible—at least, not for sane men. The choice to believe in God or not would be, by the mere fact of God's presence, taken away.

Alex looked across the maps. On Earth, the revealing of such a truth as this would almost certainly herald the end of the age, the imminent appearing of God, and with it, the judgment. Because on Earth, the revealing of such a truth as this would remove man's freedom to choose or reject God. Judgment Day would be all that was left. Did the same apply here? If word of this got out, would it, by necessity, mean God was about to move in some undeniable way? Was that why a man such as Anned Islak was born to live at just this time? To reveal this startling aspect of creation to the Mirrans just before, or just after, some shattering move of God?

These were questions, Alex knew, that were best considered carefully before being offered for discussion.

"I have seen too much of his handiwork to doubt," Islak said, "and so I believe in him. At the same time, I have seen too little of him to be adequately assured. And so I have sought him, finding more bits of evidence in every investigation. But now... now what I have seen. A thousand times more powerful that what I had sought after. A hundred times more powerful than what I had hoped for. I look into the face of this... and I am undone. Even I do not fully understand my reaction. But I long for the veil against which for years I have struggled."

"The Deloré's journey—to find what lay beyond the Boundary Waters—it was all just... an act of desperation."

"Desperation?" replied Islak, in surprise. "Desperation. No, I do not think so. I acted in keeping with my established methods."

"How so," Alex challenged.

"Once I had found that the heavens and Mirrus were connected, I needed more information. Information either about the heavens or about Mirrus. Such information, it seemed to me, clearly must lie beyond the known horizons—the portions of Mirrus as yet unexplored, and the portions of the sky visible from those areas as yet unexplored. I merely set out to gather that information."

"I see." Alex paused to digest the idea. "But how could you be sure that such further information would be there, to find?" Alex persisted. Islak seemed flummoxed.

"I can only say," he said tentatively, "that to me, the proposition seemed intuitively obvious. If what we see of Mirrus is connected to the heavens, then what we cannot see of it should be connected as well."

"I'm not sure," Alex offered playfully, "that this is so much a matter of scientific insight, as it is a matter of faith."

Islak cocked his head.

"My dear Alex," he said in wonderment. "Scientific insight is a matter of faith. I explore everything I do through science, because I have faith that God constructed things with a sense of order."

Alex nodded. "Very well. So you would consider the voyage of the Ammanon Deloré, with no aim more specific than to cross beyond the Boundary Waters, to be a matter of scientific methodology."

"If you please," Islak conceded. He pondered the phrasing. "I prefer to think of it as a matter of faith," he countered, with a feigned indignity. Then he sighed. "But I suppose I must concede: On that voyage, Desperation and Faith sailed hand in hand."

Alex struggled for the words to describe it, but the Mirran language failed him in this. In English he muttered:

"*A Hail Mary pass.*"

"But on that voyage," Islak said, ignoring him, "Faith won out over Desperation."

The absoluteness of Islak's tone surprised him. "By what standard of measure?" Alex asked.

"On that voyage, we found the Harbinger of God. Unless you still cling to your early protestations that you are not he. That all the signs pointing toward you are mere coincidence. Built upon coincidence, and again upon coincidence. And if you cling to that, you are more a man of desperation than I have ever been."

Islak cast his hand dismissively toward the maps. "I have fulfilled the Judges' command," he said. "I have revealed to you what I earlier revealed to them. There was no such command on you. Even so, I ask you now. What did you say to the Judges?"

Far off to the West, Alex thought he could see the running lights of a coach.

"I had resolved," Alex said, "not to tell you. But what you have already seen here...." He looked down to the overlaid maps. "What you have already seen here will affect your thinking far more profoundly than any news I could bring. Alright then. I told the Judges where I come from."

"It is somewhere," Islak ventured, "on the far side of the world? And in some way this relates to my maps?"

Alex took him gently by the shoulders. "Dear friend. Did you not suspect at one time, early after we had met, that I came from some place beyond your world?"

Islak nodded.

"I thought you suspected it. Clever. Very well. I do. I come from a place within the Crown of God."

Islak closed his eyes, an instinctive reaction to not wanting to look at Alex. "Oh," he exhaled. "I have been so exalted as wise, by so many. How then is it that I am proven to be so stupid?" He stood up and turned away. Then he laughed. "Yet I perceive that you, Alex Boten are perhaps not so much wiser. God forbid I should say such a thing."

"What do you mean?" asked Alex, kneeling beside the maps.

"Show me the place, from which you come," Islak said.

Islak was still facing away from him, facing neither the map nor the actual Crown of God in the sky. Alex didn't know how to respond.

"On the map, Traveler Alexander Boten. Point out the place." Still, Islak wasn't facing him.

Alex looked over the map. This was the same thing that Judge Raddem had asked of him, the same question whose answer had shaken Raddem to the very center of his being. Alex knew roughly Earth's distance from the galactic core, that it was embedded in one of the arms, that it lagged somewhat behind the central bar. As he had before the Judges, he guessed as best he could. "Here," he said, touching the map.

"And what is there, in the place you have touched? On the map of Mirrus underneath, what place?"

"It's near the coast, the northeast coast. In a chain of islands."

Islak turned, facing down toward him, confused. "Islands? In the northeast?"

"Yes. There aren't any towns nearby, at least none that are marked here."

"No, no, no." Islak said. Then realization hit him. "How sure are you of the spot?"

"I don't know. Fairly sure. My people have never been outside of the Crown. Our mapping has been by extrapolation, not observation."

"The Crown of God is somewhat symmetrical, yes?" asked Islak.

Alex looked down at the map. Islak was right. Earth could be on either one of the main arm systems that had been drawn. He looked down to the southern edge, to the other place that Earth might be. In his mind now, the two maps were one. The Mirran continent, the Crown of God. It was all one. And on the southern edge of the Mirran continent, slightly to the west, the place corresponding to Earth on the galactic map, there was only one thing, only one feature. There was only one thing precisely at the place he suddenly knew corresponded to Earth; there was nothing else for hundreds of miles.

Shaking, the Traveler Alexander Boten rose from his knees. As the carriage carrying the Temple Judges pulled to a stop some fifty yards off, he looked away from the map, down into the stonework shell that had been fashioned untold generations before.

He looked away from the place on the map marking the Temple Adjunct, away from the place corresponding to Earth, and down to the actual place itself.

He looked to the small stone structure which, as revealed by Anned Islak's maps, had been labeled by the very hand of God to be Earth.

As he stood staring down at it, the Judges filed in around him. For a time, no one spoke. Eventually, Raddem stepped up beside Islak.

"You have complied with the order of the Court?" Raddem asked softly.

"I have told him," Islak said, not caring who heard. "And he has told me. No more secrets."

Judge Lode stepped up to Alex. He studied the Traveler's ashen face for a while, before daring to speak.

"You know," Lode said at last, "who you are?"

"I know…" Alex ventured, "…where I have come from." His eyes never left the Adjunct.

"Then if you accept," said Usettet, stepping next to Lode, "what seems clear to us, that everything around us serves as a map of the sky, can you help us?"

Alex looked to him. "Help you?"

"Can you help us understand the prophecies? Understand the Conflict? Is there something in all of this, that resolves the Conflict of Harbinger?"

Alex shook his head. Nothing was clear to him now. All his thoughts were in a fog. "What? What isn't clear?"

"We were told that Harbinger would come from the Temple Adjunct to the Temple, whole and without infirmity. We always thought this meant from the Adjunct," and here Usettet pointed down below, "to the Temple." His arm swept northward. "The conflict with other places in scriptures disappears if this passage refers instead to your traveling through the sky—with the places of origin and destination, in the sky, identified by allegory with the names of places here on Mirran land."

"*Okay*," Alex said in English. From his tone, Usettet inferred assent.

"But if this were what the writings in The Book meant, then you would have traveled from your home, near the edge of the Crown of God, to the center of the Crown. The journey written in the Book as being from the Temple Adjunct to the Temple, would be from the edge of the crown to its center. Not to here, not to our world, so far away from the Crown of God."

Alex closed his eyes, tightly, and tried to shake of the fog enshrouding his mind. He looked down to the map.

"Let's stop," he said, crouching. "Let's look at this. *Earth*." He touched the map. "*Earth* is here. In terms of elevation, it's practically within the map itself. Fifty, sixty light years above or below the galactic plane. But Mirrus," and here, he stood, "Mirrus is

274

up here, waist high." He held his fist out, above the center of the map. "Mirrus is far above the galactic plane. You are centered above the core, but at a great elevation." Alex let his fist dissolve; his hand hung limp. He whispered: "A great elevation." He looked to the Adjunct steps, to the different heights of the steps. A smile crept across his face as he closed his eyes, visualizing the step pattern he had climbed and descended at the Mirran Stone. Step by step, set by set, he had climbed up and down it all. And he had never seen. Until now. Still whispering, he said: "I understand."

Islak leaned into him. "Pray, inform us."

"What does it say?" Alex asked. What does it say, exactly? About the journey, from the Adjunct to the Temple?"

Platius had The Book with him, and had the passage marked: "The Harbinger shall come to the Temple's Mirran Stone from the Temple's Adjunct, without infirmity, whole in body, a man of five fingers."

"From the Adjunct, to where? Read it again?"

Platius quoted: "…to the Temple's Mirran Stone…."

"Not to the Temple," Alex said. "To the Stone. To the Mirran Stone."

"The Mirran Stone is right beside the Temple," Raddem said. "In terms of this map, they are indistinguishable."

Alex looked him squarely in the eye. "The Temple is built level on the bedrock. But the Mirran Stone rises up. Elevation. The peak of the Mirran Stone is far above the bedrock."

"A few hundred feet," Lode said. "No more than that."

Islak spoke: "Justice Lode is right, Alex. Even on the scale of this map, the height of the Mirran Stone is negligible. A mere wrinkle in the vellum. Not waist high, where you say Mirrus is."

"Elevation," Alex interrupted, taking Islak gently by the shoulders, "was not given on a linear scale. It couldn't be. Whatever feature here on this world that was meant to represent Mirrus itself, it would have needed to be at a fantastic height. Above your... *atmosphere*." Alex released Islak. "Elevation had to be shown a different way. And it was. On a completely different kind of scale. Not a scale meant for you to understand. But on a scale meant for *me* to understand. These steps." He turned away from them, and jumped down the first, tallest step toward the Adjunct. "I saw them, at the Mirran Stone. I thought about it then, about the pattern of the steps."

"Pattern?" Raddem asked.

"Yes. The heights of the steps. Every step of the way up, and every step of the way down, there is a pattern. A meaning." He ran his hands over the stones. "A big step, then smaller, and smaller, till the tenth step becomes the size of the first. Then smaller and smaller again. Repeating. Every tenth step returning to the full size. The Mirran Stone, and this approach to the Adjunct. They are *logarithmic* scales."

"*Logarithmic*," Islak said.

"The first step, it is an actual, non-scaled dimension. A foot or two. The second step...."

"Which is shorter," Islak continued.

Alex corrected him: "Which is only depicted as shorter. It actually represents the same distance. Each of the first nine steps represents the same distance. But their depiction grows more and more compressed."

"Until the tenth step returns to the original size," ventured Islak.

"No, my friend. Not really. The tenth step continues the compression of scale, at the same rate."

"Of course," Islak said, climbing down beside him, and feeling the ninth and tenth steps. "The tenth step is not a single step. It is ten steps, combined into one."

"And the next step, shown slightly smaller?" Alex prodded.

"The next step represents twenty, then thirty, then forty...."

"Each one compressing smaller."

"Until the shortest of the set, ninety. And the next step, a large step, is one hundred," Islak said.

"Two hundred, three hundred, four. Each set of steps, a multiple of ten. On downward through hundreds, thousands, tens of thousands, hundreds of thousands. On this kind of scale, the first step is exactly what it measures. But by the end, each step represents huge distances."

"Did you not say," ventured Lode, that your *Earth* was almost even with this plane of the Crown of God? That its elevation was negligible?"

"Comparatively, yes. Maybe fifty light years."

Poznanek muttered, to himself more than to anyone else: "Light... years?"

"Why then," Lode asked, "would the Temple Adjunct be recessed so far below the bedrock? It is nearly as low as the Mirran Stone is high."

"Nearly," said Alex. "Nearly." He turned to look down. "How many steps, how many sets of steps, are there here?"

"Seventeen sets," declared Platius with conviction, "and seven steps toward completing an eighteenth."

"And the Mirran Stone," said Alex. "How many sets there?"

"Twenty. Twenty sets, plus three steps."

"And these three sets," said Lode skeptically, "even less than three full sets, these make the difference between the almost imperceptible lowering of your *Earth*, and the immense elevation of Mirrus?"

"Yes, these three sets," said Alex. "Do not forget the compression of scale. Just under three sets of steps mean just under one thousand times the distance."

"Would God have given such a riddle?" protested Usettet. "Would he have tried so hard to hide from us his meaning?"

Alex shook his head. "This scale was not set up this way as a sign to you. It was meant as a sign to me."

Islak spoke: "This riddle of elevation. It could not even be pondered, until someone recognized the pattern—the pattern of Mirrus and the Crown. And once that pattern was recognized...."

"Then I appeared," said Alex. He turned to look at Usettet. "That passage, it *is* referring to a journey through the sky. A journey from Earth to Mirrus."

"Earth," said Islak, smiling. "Curious name."

"The second passage of the Conflict," said Platius, "must therefore apply to this place, must mean what was always assumed, so that it does not conflict with the first."

"Please," said Alex. "Read."

Platius paused, reading ahead to prepare an impromptu translation. He began: "The Harbinger of God will come forth from the Temple's Adjunct...." Here Platius' voice trailed off.

"Read it to him," Usettet urged. "He has a right to know what is written."

"...will come forth from the Temple's Adjunct blind and mute, led toward the Temple tended by those who pity him."

Islak wondered what reaction that phrase had stirred up within his companion. "I should simply like," Islak announced, "to observe one point. If you do not enter the Adjunct, you cannot leave it. Nothing commands you to enter."

"The comings and goings of Harbinger are his own affair," said Raddem. "He is only a sign of what is about to happen. He has no tasks to perform, inside or outside of the Temple Adjunct. But Restoration is different. Restoration, we are told, will stand outside the Temple Adjunct and speak to us. We always thought Restoration and Harbinger were two different figures. Now that we suspect they are one, we have a new problem."

Alex climbed up the top step, rejoining them. "And the problem is?"

"Judge Platius, read for us the third aspect of the Conflict of Harbinger."

"Once Harbinger leaves the Temple's Adjunct, he will never return to it, nor will he see it, nor will he touch it; his feet will never be upon it again."

"As Harbinger," Raddem observed, "you can never return to the Adjunct once you leave it. But as Restoration, if Restoration you are, it is written you will come to the Adjunct many times to address the people, preparing to restore them."

"There is, of course, a solution," Alex said.

"The *same* solution," said Raddem. "That in one of these passages we have read, this physical building is not referred to, but rather your home, your world, your Earth. So tell me, Traveler Alexander Boten, which do you think is meant? That as Restoration, you will many times go to your world, your Earth, and there address the people of Mirrus?"

"Or," said Alex, "that as Harbinger, having left my world, I will never return to it. Ever."

Raddem laid his hands upon Alex's shoulders. "I am sorry."

"I knew," Alex said. "From the moment I arrived, I knew. There was never going to be any going back." He drew in a deep breath. "Still, it seems different now. I'm not sure why." But he knew why. Even if he could not admit it to Raddem. Even if he would not admit it to himself. Kathy, Maddy. Ella—he had tried to adapt himself to the belief he would never see them again. But somewhere in the depths of himself, there was always the unspoken thought, the shadow of hope.

Now, Platius' recitation echoed through him: *Once Harbinger leaves the Temple's Adjunct*, once Alex left Earth, *he will never return to it, nor will he see it, nor will he touch it; his feet will never be upon it again.*

Everything he had known and loved—or more precisely, the distant and unspoken and irrational hope of returning to it—was swept away in an instant. Without even recognizing it existed, he knew now that it was that hope that had kept him grounded. A sense of weightlessness was upon him, more profound than what he ever felt in orbit, more terrifying than what he had felt during the Great Lake—crossing disaster. He was grateful for Raddem's steadying hands, still upon him. Without looking up to the Crown of God, he remembered seeing it the first time upon waking up in Mirran orbit. The sensations of terror as he realized what it meant crawled upon him again.

Alex looked down to the small stone building, the only echo of home left to him. *Whatever is inside of you, it is as close to Earth as I am ever going to come*, he thought. And then he wondered: *If you are Earth, what secret do you hold? What is it about you that has kept you forbidden?*

"Your law," said Alex, "holds that no one but Harbinger may enter."

"Correct," said Raddem, withdrawing his touch.

"Are you prepared to declare that I am Harbinger?"

"There has been much discussion on the way here—many stops,

as we pondered and debated issues too weighty and too complex to delve into while in motion. We are not prepared to declare you Harbinger. But we are prepared to declare you exempt from the prohibition."

Alex turned to him and smiled. "You are worthy," he told Raddem, "of earthly judges."

Raddem bowed graciously, "Thank you, sir."

They moved together to the coach that had delivered the Judges, in order to make some final preparations. On the way, Islak moved in close to Alex, and spoke covertly: "It was not a compliment, was it?"

Alex said nothing, but reached his arm around, and patted Islak on the shoulder.

Book II
Chapter 9: Forbidden

Within ten rounds they stood at the front of the Adjunct. It was the closest Islak and two of the Judges had ever been to the forbidden place. Except for Alex and Islak, everyone kept a hand shielding their eyes from the lamps.

A long rope was tied to Alex's waist, so as to deal with both of the predominantly held beliefs. The first, held by most of the Judges, that Alex would be struck blind, and thus fulfill the prophecy of The Book. The second, the minority view, that Alex would be struck dead, and thus confirm the prohibitions of The Book. Either way, the rope would help extract him without necessitating anyone else's entry.

Without speaking, Alex turned from them, facing the open entrance. It was generous of width, but short of height—barely six feet of clearance. Five oil-burning lights were on each side, including the front. The center light was mounted just above the lintel. They were not lamps, like he had seen elsewhere—no metal nozzle, or adjusting knob. They were too high to see into, but it seemed that each was just a bowl of oil, burning off as fast as air could rush in to feed it. Wildly flickering flames swirled up from each. But there were enough of them that they evened each other out, giving a fairly stable glow to the white chelsit rock.

Islak stepped up beside him. They faced the doorway together.

"The Judges who refuse to declare you," Islak said quietly, still facing the doorway, "are fools trapped in tradition. They refuse to consider that they may have read the scriptures incorrectly."

"Granted," Alex said.

"Then you know who you are. You know that you are Harbinger."

"I… suspect it."

"Nothing commands you to enter," Islak said levelly.

Alex turned his head to look at him. "You have said that before. Why do you keep repeating it?"

"Because it is true," Islak said firmly, still facing ahead. Then his tone softened: "And because when Harbinger emerges, he will be blind. You don't know, Alex, what it is to be blind."

"If it is to be my fate, I will at least have a well-trained companion to lead me through it."

"Do not assume too much," Islak said.

Alex waited, not wanting to prod him on, wanting him to continue in his own time.

"When Igren Doel signed on as a deck hand on the Ammanon Deloré, he brought with him something. Something for us to share."

Alex smiled. "That vile Pinoae. Truly, Anned, I may never understand the Mirran palate."

"Not the Pinoae," Islak told him. "Something else. In case the mission went badly, in case we wound up like the crew of the Innotek Assan. He brought for us a bottle of Lyderis. Of Lyderis acid."

"And the reason for this?"

"Lyderis has many uses, but the most relevant one in our case was one which the manufacturer never intended. Lyderis acid is a most potent, most fast-acting poison. We survived the DevilsEye. The Mirran *sun*, as you call it. But I retained the bottle of Lyderis. I have carried it ever since. I carry it even now."

"Because you have been blinded? You have found blindness to be so great a burden?"

"My life's work, in all its facets, in all the many ways I have pursued it, has all been one thing: Observation. A scientist who cannot observe... is no longer a scientist. He is a fond memory of what he once was. He is a recollection, to those about him, of his former glory days. The innkeeper in Ohlmont...."

"The one who would not let us pay."

"Yes. That was homage. It was gratitude. It was tribute. All for what he perceived me to be. But as time goes by, I will come to be known, not for what I am discovering, but for what I *have* discovered, in the past. Then that will change."

"Islak, your people are not so transient in their memories, or their loyalties."

"Oh, they will not withhold their money. They will be free with that. I have no doubt I will survive, both on the proceeds of my inventions, and upon the kindness of those about me. But it is the kindness itself that will change. No longer tribute, or homage. Only charity."

"And for this you would end your life? For pride, over charity shown to you by those you have served?"

"No, for more than that, though for that in part. I am... I was... a scientist. An observer, Alex. The Scientist Anned Islak died in the glare of the DevilsEye. It is just his body that lingers on, like a footprint on the sandy shore, waiting for the next wave to reclaim it."

"Then wait awhile. Linger just a little longer, so that you might complete one more task that the Almighty God, the God of land, sea and air has set before you. If I emerge from here blind, as you fear I will, tarry long enough to teach me the finer points of surviving without sight. Teach me the memory tricks that allow you to navigate a room. Teach me how you divide voices in a crowd, when you cannot match sounds to the motions of a given man's mouth. Teach me a hundred other things that you have learned in so short a time, and that I would otherwise take a lifetime to master." Alex reached down to the rope piled at his feet, and found the loose end. He handed it to Islak. "Wait for me here, in case I need you."

"I cannot dissuade you," Islak said.

"I've already given up my entire existence, all that I was living for, against my will. I would have refused, had I been given the chance. It's time I gave up something willingly."

Alex turned to face the Judges. He did not speak to them, did not gesture to them. Again he turned to the doorway.

Without turning to Islak, he told him: "Prepare yourself, to hear the voice of God." Alex took the rope in hand, so he could pull it along rather than having it drag from his waist. He stepped in.

He stood practically touching the inner blocking wall, which for generations had shielded the view of anyone peering in from outside. It was a short wall, just over seven feet tall. Had he wished, had he dared, he could have reached up and grasped the top edge, then boosted himself up to look over it.

He stood staring point blank at the stone surface. Nothing happened. He decided to turn left. The blocking wall and the outer front wall formed a narrow passage before him. As he neared the corner, the rope dragged slightly on the edge of the main doorway; he could see peripherally (for he steadfastly kept his eyes ahead) that the blocking wall turned off to the right, paralleling the outer side wall. He turned to the right. The blocking wall paralleled the side wall all the way to the rear. He began to understand that the inner blocking wall formed an inner square, within the outer square of the Adjunct's walls. Now with just the slightest confidence, he walked down the long hall formed by the inner and outer walls. The rope was dragging across several edges now, as he came to the rear corner. Looking around to his right, his suspicion was confirmed; the inner wall formed an inner box. But on this, the rear wall of that inner box, there was an opening leading further inward. He pulled twenty feet of rope to him, piling it in the corner where he stood, and then he approached the rear opening.

His heart sank. Through the opening was another, more inward, blocking wall. He began to imagine an endless series of inner squares, like a maze. Or, he thought, like Russian egg-shaped nesting figures. An endless shell within a shell. This next, more inward wall was the same height. Pulling the pile of slack rope to him, he re-coiled it at this second entrance. Then he pulled along another ten feet, and coiled it, as well.

He moved in, to the next shell. At the first doorway, he had turned left; this time, as if to break some jinx, he turned right. Now, as he neared the corner, he saw that this latest blocking wall was just that—a single blocking wall. It was not part of another inner square. He had reached the center. Looking left, around the edge of the innermost blocking wall, he saw a large open area.

There were no ceilings anywhere in the Adjunct, only the roof; he looked up to where the four sides of the stone roof came to a peak. Down near their bottom edges, where they interfaced with the upright supports from the outer walls, the roof stones positively glowed. They were reflecting the light from the lamps on the outside of the walls. On all sides, the roof stones served like huge reflectors. Within the outer supporting walls, within the inner blocking walls, at the center of the Temple Adjunct, there was only one thing—what seemed at first to be a huge reddish block, as tall as it was wide, with rippled sides and gold edges. He stood for a time, staring at it. In the end, his mind made sense of it. It was a curtain, a red, four-sided curtain. Framed by rods of gold, or brass, it was set up around some object in the very center of the room.

He approached it. The curtain-stands were on a raised platform of squared logs—two layers of squared logs, the first layer all facing one way, the second layer laid perpendicular. The bottom layer was darker; the upper layer, lighter. Sedres and tersa, he guessed. The upper layer covered a lesser area, effectively forming a step. Walking around the platform, he examined the curtain. To his eye, it appeared seamless. It was secured to both the vertical and the horizontal rods by metal rings, spaced every few inches. The curtain was either continuous, or was secured at the vertical rods in such a way that no view could be had inside. He completed his circuit. Then, so the rope that secured him to the outside world would not get hopelessly tangled, he walked back around to the point from which he had started. Looking around, he puzzled over the emptiness of the interior. Not the spartan nature of the design, for he had seen this sort of sparseness in the Temple Complex. But nothing had invaded this space. No animals had built nests in its shelter; no birds had nested atop the dividing walls.

Within a Sheltering Darkness

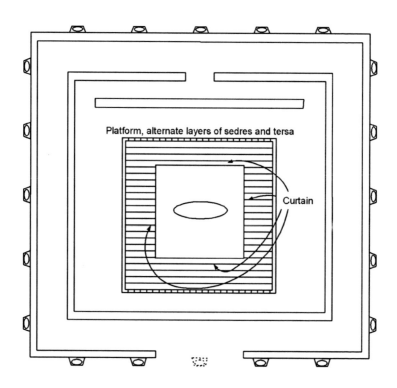

Platform, alternate layers of sedres and tersa

Curtain

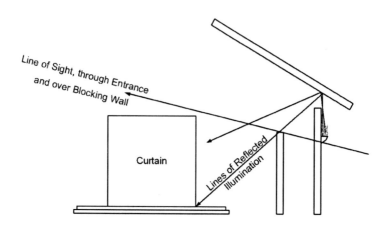

Line of Sight, through Entrance and over Blocking Wall

Lines of Reflected Illumination

Curtain

"This is a forbidden place," he said aloud. Even the animals had obeyed. There was no sign of rust or decay. The rods and the rings, he surmised, must be gold, or some gold-silver alloy; some metal that would not tarnish. The site was not that far from the sea; he thought he could smell a trace of salt in the air; salt that would be powerfully corrosive, especially over years, over generations.

He set his foot upon the wood platform. Both layers seemed sound. How had someone described them? Fragrant woods, resistant to decay? Even so, it had been a long time.

He stepped fully onto the platform, up to the curtain. Running the back of his hand along it, he disturbed dust that rose in gentle swirls. He looked to the floor, to the finely hewn square logs. There was no dust there. He felt very uncomfortable. Everything here seemed... unnatural. Non-corrosive metals were fine. Aromatic woods not decaying, he could accept. But the curtain itself? These people did not have synthetic textiles. They wove their clothes from wool, or the closet thing to wool they had here. What natural cloth could survive—suspended, hanging—for more generations than these people could remember? And the dust—clinging to the cloth, but not forming on the floor? It was wrong. It was... he kept coming back to the word... unnatural.

Kneeling, he examined the bottom edge of the fabric. It appeared to have been folded under and sewn; hemmed. Pinching it with both hands, he tugged at it. It tore apart, more easily than the finest tissue paper. Startled, he dropped it. As he did, a ripple ran upward, like a wave across a calm pond, leaving a trail of swirling dust behind it. His heart raced; he stood, as the ripple reached the top. A gold ring shifted on the horizontal pole, absorbing the energy of the upward wave. The dust settled downward. His heart began to slow.

And then, from the top, another disturbance began. At the gold ring, the one that had shifted, the curtain came away—came away in two pieces, as if the top button of a shirt had let loose, and the ends of the collar had flopped down. They hung there for a moment, and then they shifted again; the curtain was tearing, under its own weight. The shifting weight accelerated the effect. A plume of dust formed; as the tear spread downward, the disturbance spread. The curtain, essentially, dissolved. Like a calving wedge from a glacier, it dropped to the floor. There was a virtual explosion of dust.

Alex stumbled backward, falling off of the platform, and landing on his back on the stone floor. Through the swirls of dust he heard the metal poles and rods clattering to the floor, and here and there metal rings rolled away—until their momentum slowed, they began arcing, and they finally rolled into death spirals and clanked down.

"Alex!" He recognized Islak's voice. "Alex Boten!"

Alex tried to call back, but immediately began choking on the dust.

"Alright!" he finally managed to croak. "I am… alright!"

"Come out to us!"

Alex did not try to answer. Pulling up a corner of his coat, he breathed through it. The lamplight reflecting in from outside danced madly through the dust. He thought he saw shapes, but they dissolved before him. Crawling up onto the platform, he crossed over rods and rings of gold, and over patches of the surviving red cloth. He came to a wide piece of black stone. The stone was glassy and smooth, about six inches thick. As he felt around it, the dust began to settle. The broad square of black orbid before which he knelt was merely a base, a support structure for the main black stone arising at its center. He reached out and touched it.

He began to understand. He began to understand why he was here at the Adjunct, and why he was here on Mirrus. His hands followed the curves of the stone as he arose. The curtain dust was settling; he could see the shaped stone more and more clearly.

*　　*　　*

At the entrance to the Adjunct, Islak struggled to restrain himself from calling out again. He knew Alex had survived the terrible crashing sound, and the plume of dust that Raddem described to him as escaping the Adjunct; he had heard Alex's voice. Now he had to wait.

Some of the Judges conferred, some paced. Raddem sat silently on the stone floor from which the Adjunct arose, responding to no one. Thousands of years of history were reaching their pivot point; even those who denied it outwardly knew that this was true. For good or ill, things would change. If this man were Harbinger, they could trust God that the change would be for the good. But if he were an imposter....

A sound arose from inside the Adjunct, echoing off the stone walls. It was a sound that seemed at first not living, like a scraping of one surface upon another. But as it grew, it became more human—more desperately, horribly human.

"Pull him out," Platius gasped.

Islak stood with the rope in his hands, unable to move. Raddem leapt up, and he and Platius snatched the rope from him. They pulled. At first the rope came freely, and they feared it had come untied. The sound escalated, grew louder, more distressing. And then it stopped. Raddem and Platius froze, as if they were of one mind. They listened. Inside the recesses of the Adjunct, Alex Boten caught his breath. The sound which next escaped the chelsit walls was unmistakable: It was a scream.

All the Judges swarmed the rope now. As they pulled, the line went taut. They could feel a thrashing, a struggling on the other end. They pulled as the screaming continued, desperate to extricate him, but fearful they would topple him and greatly increase the difficulty of easing him out. In fits and starts the rope tightened and slackened, as if Alex were moving randomly. With each slackening, they drew the rope toward them; with each tightening, they firmly resisted.

Islak and the cluster of Judges found themselves nearing the doorway. Those in front pushed back on the group as much as pulling in the rope.

Alex Boten shot out from the Adjunct, as if propelled by an explosion. He fell into their midst. They pinned his arms, keeping his hands from his eyes, for he was clawing at them as he screamed. Islak and one Judge sat on his legs, holding him down from writhing.

At great length the twisting of his body and his screaming exhausted him, and he began to relax. Although they tried speaking to him, they could elicit from him no response. Although they could see no sign of damage that he might have done to his eyes, neither

289

could they see any sign that he recognized, or even saw, any of them. Together they lay there, in a heap, before the opening of the Adjunct, while the keepers of the Adjunct looked down from above in horror and fear. After nearly a full watch had passed, he was sufficiently exhausted that they could move him. Then these seven men half-carried, half-walked him, blind and mute, from the Temple's Adjunct. They led him into their coach, heading off in the direction of the Temple.

BOOK III – Restoration

Book III
Chapter 1: Awakening

I spent a long time, a long time, in nowhere. As had happened when the Hermes 9 launch tower had twisted everything before me to a dot and then shot me through it, in a similar way my world had collapsed in upon itself, shrunken into a dot, and I had once again been fired through an impossible place. What had swirled and condensed before me was a stone place, a white stone place. But it was more than just that, much more. That was all I could remember. And then I was floating.

There were voices—some calming, some urgent—but I had the sense that they all cared for me, and that I was safe with them. They seemed to guide me as I floated in the darkness.

The darkness; that was... something. Something important, I was sure. Where I was had to do with darkness. But this darkness that I was in now, that was different. I had grown comfortable in a darkness, but this was far deeper. Not threatening, not fearful, just deeper, and more complete.

I wasn't asleep—at least not always. I walked sometimes, although it always seemed someone was at my arm. Sometimes I sat, and I ate. I could taste the food, feel it crunching in my mouth. It smelled delicious. It tasted delicious. I wished there were meat. I tried asking for some, but I didn't seem to be able to get the words out.

There were times when I did sleep. I am sure of this. Not because it felt much different from the other times, but because the strangest things happened. I assume they were dreams, so I assume I was asleep. I saw people; this was something I never did when I was awake. People I had known a long, long time ago. A lifetime ago. I saw an old man, a sick man, lying in bed. I think he was dying. I'm sure I was supposed to know him, but I never tried to remember how I knew him. I don't think I wanted to know. I wanted to see him, but I did not want to stay with him.

There was a lady, a beautiful lady, with a young girl. No, two young girls. Or was it one? They looked just the same. I would have to give them names, to tell them apart. *Ella*, I called one. *Maddy*, I named the other. And the lady, the beautiful lady, she was holding a baby. A fine, strong young boy. I held him, and played with him, though for some reason I could think of no name to call him. These people I *did* want to stay with, but I had to leave them. There were other people here to see, too. Jiggs. Bob Jiggs was waiting to see me. And Marky Grossman. I had something to tell Mark, something important, something he needed to hear. He was upset, and I was the only one who could tell him what he needed to hear. But I did not have time to see any of them. I had somewhere to go, something to do.

Someone was stroking my head, washing me. I was awake now. I felt a warm washcloth sliding across my forehead. It was a woman tending to me. I smelled a perfume, a faint but distinctive perfume. I knew it, and it pleased me. It made me think of sailing, though I was not sure why.

There was singing. As she wiped my forehead, the woman was singing. The song was strange, in a way I could not define. It reminded me of sailing, as well. As I listened to the notes, they seemed to be in conflict—fighting against some other song I remembered. The other song was from an instrument, a long dark wooden instrument, with silver keys. What was it called? Why couldn't I remember what it was called?

I slipped into a dream; as the lady sang, each note seemed to push and distort the silver keys, as if they were made of clay. Soon, the dark wood instrument was unplayable, unrecognizable. The instrument faded away, and I faded back to wakefulness.

"That's very nice," I said. My voice was raspy, and it surprised me. The singing stopped, and with it, the wiping of my forehead. "Oh..." I said. I missed the stroking touch. I missed the voice. "Kathy? Abbey?" I felt a tear forming in my eye. The stroking resumed.

"Alexander?" This was not a voice I knew. But it was a nice

voice, a comfortable voice. A voice I trusted at once.

"Thirsty," I said. That was it. That was why my voice was raspy. Yes, I was thirsty. A hand moved behind my neck and eased me up to sitting. I was in a bed. I had been sleeping. It was nighttime; that was why it was so dark. A cup of water touched my lips, and I drank from it.

"Could you turn on some light?" I asked. No response was forthcoming. Shortly thereafter, she eased me down.

"You should rest," she said.

Talking about the light made her uncomfortable. It made me uncomfortable, too. There was something about turning on the lights, something bad. I rolled onto my side, and I slept. As best I recall, I did not dream.

*   *   *

I awoke to the sounds of birds calling; bright, chirping calls. There were voices, chatting voices, beyond a door, or a wall. I couldn't understand them. It was still dark. Don't think about the dark, I thought to myself. Sitting up, I oriented myself, made sure I wasn't dizzy. I had been asleep a long time, I knew. I turned, slipping my legs over the edge of the bed, touching my toes to the floor. Was I strong enough to stand?

I tried. I was. The sounds of the birds were coming from straight ahead of me. And other sounds, animal sounds. Horses, I thought. I was on a farm. Carefully, I felt my way forward. Coming to a wall, I followed the sounds to a tiny window, covered by a drape. I had seen this kind of window before. At the inn, with Islak, and the Captain. Reality, and a stern wakefulness, rushed in on me. Like water shooting in through a sinking ship's porthole. I shook off that image. Grabbing the drape, I pulled it aside. I saw nothing. I wouldn't see anything. There were no lights to be lit, not for me. I was blind.

Short of breath, I dropped to my knees. The curtain came down with me, clutched in my hand. There were sounds, somewhere behind me. A door?

295

"Mr. Boten," said the woman's voice. Rushing in behind me, she firmly helped me up. "Are you with us, Mr. Boten?" She sat me down on the edge of the bed.

"I have been... drifting, haven't I?"

"Well nigh onto two shortmonths now. I was coming to despair."

"Forgive me if I should know this, kind lady. But who are you?"

She laughed a reassuring laugh. "It has been a disorienting time for you, kind sir. No, you should not know me. But now you shall. My name is Drumae."

"Madame Drumae, it is a pleasure."

Again she laughed. "No, no. Just 'Drumae'. It is my given name."

"And this place?"

"Just a humble farm. They thought it best that you be in a place... more secluded."

"They thought... the Judges thought. That I should be in a place more secluded than... the City. Shelaemstet. Anned. Anned Islak...."

"Anned Islak tended to your side for a long time indeed. But for now he has returned to Barnable. I will send word of your awakening, and he will be here as quickly as he can."

I slid my hands across my eyes. "Has a doctor been in, to see me?"

"Yes, but he will want to come again, now that you are more lucid. There were limits to what he could learn, with the curious responses you gave him."

"But he will confirm the obvious. There is light here, is there not, Drumae?" She did not reply, thereby saying 'yes'. I was blind.

The realization was neither startling nor disturbing. I had known it in my half-waking haze for some time.

I smiled, in what I took to be her general direction. "I should like to bathe," I told her. "A steamy, soapy bathing, with scratchy pads or brushes." She laughed heartily. "And then," I added, "if I might impose, I should like a meal. A meal akin to the ones I have only partly been aware of eating these two shortmonths. A meal for which I shall at last be able to express my proper appreciation."

"I shall direct you to the bath, and get you started. By the time you are finished, Lannae should have a meal prepared that will satisfy well."

"Lannae," I said. I remembered a perfume, a perfume I smelled in my delirium. I had recognized it from somewhere. I knew I had. "Lannae?"

"Ah," said Drumae with a sigh. "The Captain feared I should see such a reaction in your face."

"The Captain? Then it is Lannae Dollapan of whom you speak?"

"She has tended you along with me, since about the time of Mr. Islak's departure. Now come. Let us make you presentable. For whomever you may encounter."

* * *

The meal was delicious, though Lannae Dollapan had left the house before I finished my bath. Fetching the doctor from his rounds in a nearby village, Drumae said. I was disappointed she didn't greet me before leaving; I wondered if my blindness troubled or embarrassed her, or if she feared it embarrassed me. I began to understand some of what Islak had gone through, wondering about the reactions of others.

The doctor arrived, on horseback, as I finished eating. At the sound of his approach, Drumae laid her hand upon mine.

"Your name is Ellig," she told me, calmly but firmly, and then she went to the door to let the doctor in. I perceived that Lannae came into the house also, behind him, though she said nothing. But there was an additional set of footsteps, and the occasional sound of someone moving about, someone other than Drumae and the doctor. Whoever it was seemed to be staying near the door. I felt certain it was her; the perfume I had smelled during my delirium, the perfume I remembered from inside the coach from Desidomone, had returned.

"It is surprising," the doctor said, "to see you so mobile after being bedridden so long."

"I'm a little shaky," I admitted.

Right at the dining table, he began a series of routine checks: respiration, heart, reflexes. He checked me for swollen glands; it struck me that he checked in the same places an earthly doctor would check—a suggestion that our anatomic matching extended beneath the skin.

I began to feel warmth near my face; I suspected he was using a flame to test my eye reactions. "Do you see anything?" he asked. I felt the warmth shifting; he was moving it right to left.

"I feel it. But I don't see it. Not at all."

"Hmm. The man who brought you here said you might have been exposed to some fair amount of dust. What can you tell me about that?"

I remembered the curtain's collapse, and the dust being all around me, choking me. I hadn't felt irritation in my eyes, but some of the dust must have settled there. How had Islak known about the dust? Had I been able to tell him? Or had he and the Judges come into the Adjunct to rescue me? If they had, they might know something about what happened, about what I could not remember.

"Young man?"

"I'm sorry. Yes. There was dust. A great deal of dust."

"Any unusual smells with it? Any hint of mold?"

"No. No mold. Definitely no mold...." I was remembering how strangely preserved everything in the Adjunct had been. "No mold," I repeated. "And I'm not really sure about the dust. It may have been dust. Or it may have been fabric... disintegrating."

"Disintegrating fabric?" the doctor asked.

"You seemed unsure," another voice said. Lannae. "During your delirium. We asked you about the dust on your clothes. You didn't seem sure where it had come from." Her tone was leading: *Don't discuss the dust.*

"You were able to answer questions?" the doctor prodded me. "You didn't seem responsive when I first examined you."

I wasn't sure what to say. I didn't remember any questions during the haze of the long sleep; I certainly did not remember giving answers. Maybe that was just as well; since my name was being kept secret, it was likely that the events that landed me here were being concealed as well.

"He has grown more responsive with time," Drumae said, ending an awkward silence.

The warmth near my face ended, and I heard the doctor closing up something, likely a pouch or a bag.

"I should like to see a sample of this fabric," the doctor said.

"He had nothing with him," Drumae said, "save the clothes he wore, which you examined when you first were called."

"Might I obtain a sample somewhere?" asked the doctor.

I opened my mouth as if to speak, then shook my head and shrugged. "Miss Dollapan? Might there have been something I said during my convalescence that might shed some light on where this all happened to me?"

"You do not even know where this event happened?" the doctor asked.

"I am sorry," I said. Actually, there was little I could have told him, had I wanted to—for although I remembered entering the Adjunct, my memory broke apart there. I had observed things, important things, I was sure. But I could not recall them. I remembered the curtain, the crumbling curtain. That was the center of everything, I was sure of it. There were sounds; there was a clanking of metal. Something metal was there. Everything inside the Adjunct doorway was unlike memories; it was like echoes of memories. What I had seen inside was lost, or blocked. But from what I could gather, even the location being the Adjunct was more than I should reveal. I tried to redirect his line of thought: "Is it not possible to deduce anything from the dust itself? I understand you examined it on my clothes."

"Yes," said the doctor. I felt I could look through the utter darkness, that I could see his face and read it as clearly as I had ever read anyone's. He did not believe us; he knew that we knew more. "Yes, I examined the dust. There was nothing remarkable in it. And nothing about your eyes suggesting they had interacted with it in any way." He stood up. "I see no damage to any vital portion of your eyes. Your corneas and the fluid in your eyes are clear. Your retinas show no sign of damage."

"Which just leaves me with one problem," I said. "Why can't I see?"

"There is a remote chance of nerve damage between the eye and the brain, or of damage to the brain itself—which I consider even more remote. All of your physical reactions are sharp. Your hearing is obviously acute. The condition of your sense of taste and your appetite are evidenced by the empty plate before you. My best guess—and it is only a guess, mind you—is that we are looking at what one might call an hysterical blindness."

"A psychological reaction?"

"Yes..." said the doctor. I could tell by his tone that I was showing I knew too much. Hysterical reactions leading to physical manifestations must be a new, and highly advanced concept, unfamiliar to the common man. "If this is the case..." and here I suspected he was speaking to Lannae and Drumae as much as to me, "...then his sight could return at any time. More likely abruptly rather than gradually. Remembering the circumstances that led to this condition will likely be helpful. But remembering may be... uncomfortable. Remembering, when it comes, may come in pieces. I should check back with you in another quarter. In the meantime, if your sight begins to partially return, contact me at once. That would suggest a more physiological problem, which we should try to address that way."

Drumae led him to the door, and Lannae sat beside me at the table. She laid her hand upon mine, patting it. I wanted to turn my hand, taking hers in mine, but without being able to see the expression on her face, I couldn't. Was she giving me a look of smiling affection, or of dour pity?

From the open doorway, the doctor said: "I shall see you soon, mister...." He paused, as if trying to remember the name Drumae had told him. Had he forgotten? Or was he fishing, to see if I remembered it? I did not. And if the doctor really did remember, I could not afford to improvise.

"Yes, soon," I dodged awkwardly. "Allik," I added. Not quite right. "Ellig. I'll see you soon doctor. Thank you."

He was gone.

Drumae joined us at the table, and Lannae withdrew her hand.

"Mr. Boten, forgive a foolish old woman," said Drumae. "There is so much I should have told you while you were eating. Before the doctor came."

"There is a great turmoil among the people," Lannae said. "There is nearly total agreement that the light to the north is NewStar."

There was a definite 'present tense' to her statement. "It is still there?" I asked. "Moving through the sky?"

"Yes," she said. I wasn't sure how I felt about that. The Sirocco was like a bridge to my former life. Somewhere between a keepsake carried in the pocket and a millstone tied around the neck.

Drumae continued: "With NewStar accepted, and fulfilled, Harbinger must be amongst us. But no one knows where."

"Almost no one," Lannae corrected.

A most peculiar feeling came over me. Ever since Captain Dollapan and his crew found me, and treated me with such reverence, ever since I had learned enough of their language to understand that they saw me as a religious figure, and especially since I had understood how important a figure Harbinger was, I resisted the notion that Harbinger might be me. But now, as Lannae Dollapan suggested that very thing, it seemed to fit me. It seemed right.

"Perhaps," I said, "it is time to consider that the initial reaction of the Deloré crew might have been correct."

There was silence.

"We are blessed if we are in the presence of the Harbinger of God," Lannae said. "But in these circumstances...."

"What is it?"

Lannae spoke: "Drumae, I apologize for my rudeness, but would you excuse Alex and myself?"

"Mr. Islak said there would be things I should best not know. I wholeheartedly defer to his wisdom, and to yours, child."

Lannae took me by the hand, encouraging me up. "Come, Mr. Boten. Let us walk."

At the doorway, they helped me with my shoes, and Lannae and

I were off. She held my hand, as much to guide me as for any reason, but I was glad to have her hand in mine. We were still too close to the house to speak with impunity.

"Drumae tells me this is a farm. It sounds quiet."

"There isn't much to do; the drought has been long-running."

"Still, isn't there maintenance to be done?"

"Some," Lannae said. "From what I've observed, she saves up projects to be done, then hires someone to do them all at once. When she can afford it."

"That's a shame. She doesn't have anyone here? A husband? Children?"

Lannae stopped, abruptly. I waited for her to speak.

"I am sorry, Mr. Boten. I thought you knew. I don't know why I thought it. I simply did. I assumed."

"Assumed what?"

She paused again, and I had the feeling she was looking behind us. We resumed walking, away from the house.

"The house where you have been staying, where Mr. Islak and the Temple Judges brought you, is the homestead of Mistress Drumae Degg."

"Degg?" I echoed. "Drumae *Degg*? She's related to Andril?"

"Andril," she said softly, "was the widow Degg's only child."

I stopped, short of breath for the first time since my collapse at the window.

"Does she know what happened?"

"Yes, Mr. Boten, she has long since come to terms with her grief."

"But does she know... how it happened. The circumstances. Do you know?"

"That Andril survived the sinking, that he rescued you and then drowned? That is how you remember it, I can tell. But as Mr. Islak relates it, Andril was still safe after he rescued you. It was his effort to save the third horse that cost him his life." We continued on.

"Even so. My being here must be a constant reminder. I don't know what to say to her."

"Say?" asked Lannae. "Say about what?"

302

"About Andril. Her son is dead. I can't just act like he never existed, or like I don't know he was her son."

"Mr. Boten, her grieving is long ended. It was nearly ended by the time you were brought to her."

"Her grieving... has ended? What are you saying, that I should act like I never knew him?"

We stopped again. She stood squarely in front of me.

"Andril Degg is dead. His mother has grieved for him. She has been comforted by those closest to her—her neighbors, and his traveling companion and shipmate, Mr. Islak. Andril is gone. Had he been buried instead of lost to the waters, would you now dig up his body, to reunite him with his mother? Would you reach into the depths of her loss and grief, to float his memory before her yet again?"

I stood speechless.

"Mr. Boten." Her tone had softened. "My father and Mr. Islak both explained to me that you come from a place of different customs. That your ways are not our ways. Is this matter, your dealing with the dead, one of these ways? Are you from a place where people grieve differently? No, do not answer. I can see that it is. Again I must apologize, but this time not for thoughtless omission. This time for thoughtless arrogance. I know you meant Drumae no harm. You could not have; it is not within your nature."

"Yet hurt her, I would have. Had you not intervened. Our ways are different. Perhaps better, perhaps not. Certainly they are different. But I will be well served if there is someone at my side who will sense that I am treading where a Mirran ought not go, and alert me."

"I hope you can find someone who will perform such a task with greater compassion than I have shown."

"Lannae Dollapan, we have begun badly, not understanding the scope of the differences between us. But if we both understand the lack of ill will in the other's nature, I cannot imagine anyone performing such a task with greater compassion than yourself."

Again, my inability to see her expression hit me hard. I was feeling an attraction to her, and had no clue what her response was, if any.

"We came out here," I said, tentatively resuming our walk, "because there was something you wanted to tell me."

"The word is out," she said gravely. "It was intended to be withheld for now. The Temple Judges did not want it generally known. But the word is spreading across the land: Harbinger and Restoration are one."

"Forgive my ignorance. But how could my being Harbinger be good, yet my being Restoration be bad?"

"Harbinger," she said thoughtfully, "Harbinger... is like a bookmarker. The man of five fingers..." and here I perceived the faintest tightening of her hand on mine—or was it mine upon hers? "...is just a sign that Restoration is about to do his work. Harbinger himself does nothing. He is just a portent. An omen."

"But Restoration actually does... does this thing. Causes this event," I said.

She stopped and turned. I knew she was facing me, looking into my eyes.

"Restoration will do exactly what his name says." Still holding my one hand, she took my free hand in her free hand. "He will restore us to communication with the Almighty God. He will cause us to hear God's voice. Alexander Boten, tell me. Is that why you have come?"

"Lannae, I am sorry. I don't know how to restore you, how to restore your people." I could hear the pattern of her breathing, and I sensed she was crying. I didn't know what to say to make her stop. I just knew I had to say something. "I don't know why God has been silent all these years. I don't know...."

She waited for me. "What?" she finally said.

I turned, as if I were looking around me for something I had dropped.

"The Adjunct," I said. "I have to go to the Adjunct."

"You have been there, and it cost you your sight." Dropping my right hand, she clasped my left in both of hers. "Go again and it might cost you your life."

"No," I said. "No, it won't."

Book III, Chapter 1: Awakening

"How can you know that?" she whispered.

"I don't know," I whispered back. "I can't know that it is safe. But I do know it. I won't die if I go back"

"But what *will* happen if you go back? What good will it do?"

"If I am Harbinger, then I am Restoration, and I am to restore your people to God, and God to you. I don't know how to do that. And I also don't know what happened to me in the Adjunct. But there is... a commonality to these things."

"A *commonality*?" She laughed. "You sound like Judge Raddem."

"The Temple Judge?"

"The Senior Temple Judge. You sound like something out of his book about historical inevitabilities."

I smiled. "Historical inevitability. Yes. That's what I'm beginning to feel like. Does Drumae have horses?"

"Yes she does, but...."

"And can you ride?"

"Yes, but Mr. Boten...."

"My name is Alex. Prepare two horses for us."

"Alex. There are horses. We shall travel to the Temple Adjunct. But there are... considerations."

"Name them," I said, with a playful defiance.

"Your health, for one." She began leading me back to the house. "I will not saddle any horse for you before another quarter passes. You must eat, and rest, and walk some fair amount before I am convinced your body is up to the strain of a long ride."

"I will entertain your consideration, although I reserve judgment on whether a full quarter is required."

"And propriety, for another," she said. "A journey to the Temple Adjunct will last through many watches. You and I, traveling over such distances, unaccompanied...."

"Lannae Dollapan," I said, stopping. I lifted the hand with which she guided me, holding it between us. "Forgive me for not knowing the rules of etiquette and propriety among your people. I should never do anything to compromise either your integrity, or the reputation of your integrity."

"Rest assured, Mr. Boten... Alex Boten... I never considered such a compromise to be your intent. And I think all things shall work together for us. By the time I am confident of your health, Mr. Islak should be with us."

"Anned Islak is coming?" We resumed walking toward the house. "When is he due?"

"No specific time, but he will be on his way. Before reaching the doctor, I sent word to Barnable, advising Mr. Islak of your return to the world of conscious men. I was here on the Degg farm for a time before Mr. Islak left, and from what he said then, I know he will return with great haste, knowing you are back."

Although I did not intend it or even realize it, my pace quickened. Lannae, however, did realize it.

"You miss him, this tinkering thinker," she observed.

"Yes, I guess I do. And I worry about him."

"He has adapted well to his blindness," she assured me.

"Hmm." It would be wrong to tell her of the Lyderis acid that Islak kept, and why. Something—maybe some subtlety of my expression—must have revealed I was holding back:

"Perhaps," she ventured, "he has not adapted as well as I have thought?"

"There are other things, besides his blindness, that weigh upon him." I felt I needed to deflect her line of thinking, lest I betray Islak's confidence. I thought back to his melancholy after the discussion with Mr. Mennetek, after that absurd discussion of the spelling stones.

"Other things?" she said. "Those being...?"

Without naming names, I relayed to her the argument that had been laid before us—how a random drawing of stones would, from time to time, produce a meaningful message. When I had finished, we continued walking in silence.

"This argument," she inquired, "it was raised aboard my father's ship?"

"It was."

She mulled that over. At last she said, with contempt in her voice: "Arken."

"Beg pardon?"

"Arken Mennetek," she explained. "This sounds like a piece of his handiwork. It was him, was it not?"

"How did you recognize it?"

"The argument reflects the man. Clever, while intellectually shallow. And it is a cleverness that masks a certain dishonesty."

"Dishonesty?"

"The argument is a fraud, a transparent fraud. I cannot imagine Anned Islak troubling himself over it."

"I must confess, I was unable to refute it."

"Oh, Alex, surely," she said, without realizing how naturally she had now slid into using my given name. "The whole matter is absurd, on its face."

"The court is prepared to hear your refutation," I told her gravely.

"Refutation. I would offer nothing so formal, as it is not deserving of it. I offer dismissal, which is all it warrants."

"Islak and I were able to do as much. But Islak wanted more. Anything that is false should be refutable."

"An argument such as Mennetek offered could be used to discount any degree of organization and complexity. If there were virtually no randomness about us, if everything were finely detailed structure, his 'argument' could still be applied."

"But you are still in the realm of dismissal, not refutation. You're talking about degrees. The world you describe, brimming with complexity and order, and the world Mennetek describes, where all is chaos except for one tiny corner of apparent order—these worlds are only separated by matters of degree."

"Granted," she said grudgingly, seeing where my observation led.

"So where the real world fits between these two is a matter of opinion. Are we closer to Mennetek's reality, or to yours? How far along this... *continuum*... do we have to go to cross the line into falsehood?"

"Very well," she conceded. "But as you yourself have said, anything that is false can be proven false. If we agree that the argument is false, we must agree that a disproof exists."

"I heard once that, on Earth, a mathematician set out to prove—methodically, mathematically—that one plus one equaled two. He did it."

"And so? What is your point?"

"It required two volumes of text."

Lannae laughed, good-naturedly. "Point taken," she said. "The more foundational the truth, the harder it is to prove. Thank you, Alex Boten. You have given me a challenge to which I might arise. It has been too long since I have had occasion to beat down the annoying Mr. Mennetek."

After a few more steps, she stopped abruptly.

I thought I heard her whisper "Oh, no...." Releasing my hand, she moved on ahead alone. I heard her moving about quickly, then stopping, then rushing on again.

"Lannae," I called, in the loudest whisper I could muster. I had no idea whether her actions should be kept covert. "Lanny...."

After another brief pause, I heard her voice, at a normal level: "I have him." She returned to me. "It's one of Drumae's birds. A catrille, a male catrille."

I could hear it struggling in her grasp. So, among other things, she kept birds. I doubted they were for food. Not directly... but perhaps eggs? The carnivore within me refused to die.

"Why does she raise them?"

"So many things, Alex Boten. So many things you do not know. Do you even know what a male catrille looks like? I am sorry, I do not mean to make sport of you. Their feathers, Alex. They have a glorious plumage. She harvests their feathers."

I cocked my head in recognition. "Glorious... plumage? A tail feather? Does it have a tail feather... that catches the light?"

"You have seen them before, then?"

"Perhaps," I said, thinking back to the injured bird outside of Barnable. "And this one," I speculated, "this one got out?"

"She does not keep them penned. They come to roost, to breed, to feed upon the residue of the crops."

"Why have you captured it?"

Book III, Chapter 1: Awakening

Her answer was slow in coming, quiet, and directed more to the bird than to me:

"His wing. His wing is broken."

Without a flash of emotion, my father's words resounded in the back of my mind: 'Kill it, or care for it.' My own words, walking away from the bird in the wastes outside of Barnable, came to me as well: 'Best of luck to you.' I had to do better than that.

"Hand him to me."

"He'll escape," Lannae protested. I heard the bird rustling in her grasp.

Reaching out, I found her hand atop the bird. I laid my hand on hers, and the catrille stilled. I slipped my other hand beneath the one she held beneath the bird.

"Now," I said softly. She slid her hands out. "Which wing?"

"The right, I think. Yes, the right."

Sliding my hand to the side, along the wing, I gave the catrille its chance. But it did not struggle out. Feeling along the leading edge of the wing, I found it. It was an abrupt change, a sharp change, a change I knew instinctively did not belong. I moved my forefinger underneath, on one side of the break, and my thumb up above, on the other side. To set it properly, the two ends would need to be pulled apart, then slid together. They would need to be splinted, as had been done to a small bird years ago in a veterinary office in Gaton, Nevada. I did none of that. I squeezed the discontinuity, and it was gone.

I didn't dare stop to think about what I had done, and what I was about to do. I knew what would happen if it flew with an unhealed break, even if it were properly set. The two ends would separate in a single moment. If I spent time thinking about that, I could not have done what I did next.

I tossed the bird up, and away from us.

I heard a fluttering of wings, which was inevitable. But I could not hear either its continued flapping, or its coming to ground. Lannae said nothing.

"Tell me, Lannae Dollapan. Should I be embarrassed, or should we both be amazed?"

I heard her moving slightly. When she spoke, I knew from the

309

direction of her voice that she was kneeling beside me:

"Most blessed Harbinger of God, speak to me what is your will for your servant."

Unsure how to take hold of her to raise her up, I knelt with her.

"This one command I give you, and then no other will I give: Do not worship me. I am not God—whatever I am, I am a man."

*　　　*　　　*

In time Islak arrived, in the company of a traveling companion who served as Islak's guide. They arrived sooner than boded well for the health of their horses. Islak explained they had not ridden them straight through, but had exchanged horses at cities and villages along the way—these being the third pair for them. The exchanges had been fairly costly, but Islak considered the money well-spent, and the time well-saved.

Drumae graciously provided accommodations for Islak. His companion, after watering, feeding, and resting his horse, set off again for Barnable—in possession of a letter from Lannae to her father, which would be forwarded from Barnable to Desidomone.

Islak's blindness had progressed, and was now total. I had imagined us comforting each other, but neither of us was inclined to discuss our sight.

Sadly, there was nothing I could tell Islak that was of any news. He had hoped for some insight into my experience inside the Adjunct. But the news he brought to us was of far greater interest. The three of us rode horseback through the fallow fields of the Degg farm, safely distant from any ears, and Islak filled us in.

The Temple Court was closed. Although lesser courts continued to function, resolving such minor disputes as arose from time to time, the Judges of the Temple Court were locked in private consultation over me, over my identity, over whether I was or was not Harbinger, over whether I was or was not Restoration. Islak knew of this debate from the conversation among the Judges between the Temple Adjunct and the Degg farmstead. It was because of this debate that they elected to bring me here, rather than to Shelaemstet. They sensed it best, for the time, to keep my identity, and the events at the Adjunct, hidden.

As Lannae had said, word of Harbinger and Restoration being one man was spreading, along with the news that Harbinger may have revealed himself to the crew of the Ammanon Deloré, who then smuggled him into Shelaemstet. Some were saying Harbinger had demanded an audience before the Judges, at the Adjunct. Rumor had it that the office of Judgeship had been thrown into turmoil over this man, over his promise to restore. Mirran rumor, while having inaccuracies, bore far more proximity to truth than any earthly rumor I had ever encountered.

Of particular interest to me was news from the eastern coast. Ships had been sighted, with the sails of the condemned. They were huge ships, as big as any Mirran vessel.

"I must be truthful with you, Alex. When you told us what you had seen, I doubted your sanity. But the word has come from too many reliable sources. Your thought is that condemned prisoners have survived being set adrift?"

"Yes," I told him. "There is a continent, as large as this one, on the opposite side of your planet, under an endlessly burning sun."

"But does not this *sun* rise and set," Lannae asked, "just like the Crown of God?"

"No," Islak said. "Sadly not. For those poor souls, there is no relief from the burning light. In a sense, the Crown of God rises and sets for them, as well. But they never see it. The light, the *sun*, burns so brightly that the Crown is washed out. It disappears."

"Utterly fantastic," said Lannae. Her tone was one of wonderment, rather than doubt.

"But why do they not contact us?" Islak asked. "Why do they stay in the distance? And what is becoming of our ships?"

"Your ships? What about your ships?" I asked.

"A number of ships have gone missing in the eastern waters."

"Captured," I said. "Or sunk. Islak, I fear the ships your people have seen are ships of *war*."

"Ships... of *war*?" Lannae asked.

"An Earth word with which I fear your people will soon become acquainted. It is… a fight. A brawl. On a huge scale."

"To what end?" Islak asked.

"The ends differ. But the means are fairly constant. Carnage. Death. Have there been any rumors of explosions? Of any… 'cloudless thunder'?"

"Nothing of the kind, not that has reached me."

"Maybe I am wrong. But after we're through at the Adjunct, I want to travel to these eastern coastal cities. I have to learn more. This could be horrendous."

"And when are we to begin this strange, multi-faceted journey?" asked Islak.

"This question we should address to the keeper of my health. Miss Dollapan?"

"I should prefer to leave that assessment to a proper medical authority," Lannae said. "It has been nearly a quarter since the doctor last saw you; he will be returning soon."

"So then," declared Islak. "We shall set forth upon his blessing."

"No," Lannae said, "despite my concern for Alex's health, I suspect we should set forth before then." We did not prod her, but waited for her to find her words. "The local doctor has expressed some fair interest, at times to Alex, at times to Drumae, and at times to me, about just who this stranger Ellig really is. We urged his discretion, saying that the peculiarity of his fifth fingers would lead to rampant speculation about his being Harbinger, that he would be hounded and unable to get the rest he needed. That we needed to keep his presence quiet, until the true Harbinger was revealed."

"This does not sound to me like the brightest of doctors," Islak observed.

"I don't delude myself that we persuaded him," Lannae said. "I think it is his professional duty to his patient's privacy that is holding him back, rather than acceptance of our pitiable deception."

"But you don't think it will hold him indefinitely?"

"If the anxiety currently afoot in the land over Harbinger and Restoration builds, I don't know if I should trust him. Also, Mr. Islak, I fear your arrival has not gone unnoticed."

"There were men—repairing Drumae's well," I said.

"I didn't know anyone was here when I arrived," Islak said.

"Three men," said Lannae. "They may or may not have known who you were. If they did know, they may or may not choose to spread that knowledge."

"But all things considered," I said, "the time for our departure is now." We turned our horses back toward the buildings of the farm. It was time for us to pack our things, and prepare the horses for the journey.

Book III
Chapter 2: Return to the Adjunct

My admiration for Islak expanded again, as I learned what it was to be sightless and to be led at a gallop. Some measure of faith, fearlessness, and foolishness must be configured in anyone willing to attempt such a thing.

As Islak's horse and my own horse were even-tempered and willing to take a lead, we were able to have Lannae take the point. Islak and I each loosely held a light rope tied to the horn of the other's saddle. In time, it became apparent the ropes were more useful for comforting us than they were for ensuring that the horses stayed together. Nonetheless, we maintained our hold on the ropes. For my part, I must concede the rope's impression upon my palm and fingertips was long-lived.

Islak was pleased that I had made even more progress in adapting to the Mirran watch cycle. Every third or fourth sleep session I needed merely an extra hour or so, and this proved workable to us all. I now had a natural inclination toward the shorter sleep period; I had grown accustomed to the softness of the bed Drumae had provided, and the hard ground padded only by a bedroll held little allure. I continued to picture Lannae in the only thing I had ever seen her wearing—the mourning garb she wore during our ride in the funeral coach. Although I was certain she was wearing something more comfortable, whenever I considered the rigors of the journey she was enduring, my mind kept returning to her in the formal dress.

When our course took us near a lake, we stopped a long time, longer than the needs of our horses mandated. All of our expedition had been on seemingly endless plain, and Lannae's assertion that we were now skirting the Adjunct Highlands did nothing to break the tedium for two blind men. And so we relaxed at the water's edge. There was no wind, and hence no waves. Something like frogs made a steady soft call from places here and there along the shore near us.

Eventually Lannae excused herself. I heard her working through the contents of her saddlebags, and then walking off down along the shore. In time, I realized she had gone off to bathe. I found myself wondering how thoroughly Mirran women disrobed for outdoor bathing. I found myself thinking about it, a great deal. The only way to crowd out the thought was to think of Kathy. That was even worse.

"The water," said Islak, standing, "is cool. We should swim."

We shed our clothes, and wandered tentatively into the lake. The bottom was sandy and weedless. The water grew steadily deeper, but not so quickly as to be alarming.

But suddenly, when the water reached my chest, the idea hit me that perhaps I had gotten turned around.

"Anned?" There was the sharpness of panic in my voice; even I could hear it.

"Yes?" he said calmly.

I tried to settle myself. "Which way is the shore?"

"Do you hear the frogs?"

"Yes," I said. "But they're all around."

"The louder ones are on the near shore. The softer ones are on the far shore. I'm going to move suddenly. Don't be alarmed." He made a sudden thrashing, and then stopped. "Listen for the waves on the shore."

I waited. I heard them splash on the sand. Like the louder frogs, they were in the direction I had originally thought the shore to be.

"Listen again, listen more closely, now. For the horses."

I waited. And waited. I heard one draw a deep breath. Same direction.

"Why?" Islak asked. "Which direction did you think the shore was in?"

"You know," I said, with more than just a hint of annoyance in my voice, "that Ig Doel calls you a conjurer."

"I have never quite convinced myself," Islak said, "that he means that in a positive way."

I moved out deeper.

"I tend to consider you," I told Islak as I cautiously immersed myself to the neck, "as one comfortable in a bachelor's life."

"For ninety percent of the time, yes. Quite comfortable."

"And for the other ten percent?"

I heard him draw air and submerge, then rise up again. He was motionless after he came up. The frogs stilled themselves for a moment. In the distance, we could hear Lannae.

"For the other ten percent," Islak advised, "I have chosen to live near a cool lake."

I floated on my back, imagining the Crown of God in the sky above me.

"You, however," said Islak, "have not chosen to live near such a lake."

I stood up, in shoulder deep water. "And by this you mean…?"

"You spoke on occasion, in your delirium, back at the Degg farm. Your wife's name is… *Kathy*?"

"What did I say?" I asked, resuming my swim.

"Nothing to be embarrassed over. That was not why I mentioned it. I have just chosen to make a difficult, yet opportune, observation. You, Alex, are a married man, accustomed to married life. Married life, in a world to which you cannot return."

I did not reply.

"You may rightly think I am stone blind," Islak said. "But do not think I cannot see *anything*."

"One way or another," I said to him, "I perceive I have been embarrassing myself."

"Do not be so certain. I have been… how shall I put it… extraordinarily attuned."

"Yes?" I said. "And why is this?"

"At the behest of Abbik Dollapan, who is most concerned over your attentions toward his daughter."

"Really, Anned. One rather lengthy hearse ride, heavily chaperoned, hardly makes a romance."

"Although I think Captain Dollapan would rather I speak no further, nonetheless I shall. I perceive the Captain to also be concerned over her attentions toward you."

Something different stirred within me, an adolescent thrill.

317

Questions began popping into my mind, each too childish to voice.

"She has," Islak spoke into the silence at last, "been sending her father fairly regular letters. I have not been privy to their contents. But I do know that she sent one on to him before we left. And if I correctly interpret the subtle nuances I have heard since my arrival, I do not think our Captain shall be well pleased when he reads it."

I resumed floating.

"In several different ways," said Islak, "I find myself compelled to inquire how you intend to deal with this situation."

"I'm not sure we have a 'situation' here to deal with."

"Alex. We have indeed a situation. You are a robust young man, unaccustomed to celibacy. Married, yet unalterably separated from your wife, whom I know you love. You are in the presence of a most attractive girl. Do not forget that I was not born blind. Before the Deloré sailed on her fateful voyage my eyes were as good as any man's, and I know how pleasing to the eye Lannae Dollapan is." For a moment, I thought of protesting that my blindness invalidated his observation. But it was Lannae's beauty that had, in truth, initiated my attraction to her. Islak went on: "This girl, we have reason to believe, may well be attracted to you. And you, unless you have the audacity to deny it, are attracted to her. Add to this mix the fact that she, like every woman whom you shall ever again encounter, is not technically of the same species as you, and yes, Alex, we have a situation."

I stood again. "Not the same species?"

"Technically, no. Not the same species. God has commanded every living thing to mate with its own kind, and only with its own kind. Your people, Alex, did not arise from my people. Nor did my people arise from yours. We are each a separate, and distinct, creation. We did not arise from a common seed."

"Our differences are trivial," I protested.

"Let us set aside the question of your fifth fingers. The loss of the Mirran finger was an act of God—separate from creation, after creation. Very well then, we shall ignore that. Still, look at you. Look at the hair that grows from your face. Look at how forward the hairline of your head is. And you yourself have said that eye colors

318

among the Mirrans include colors you have never seen in eyes on your Earth."

"Even on Earth there are whole lines of people who, by ancestral heritage, have no hair on their face. And where my hairline begins is every bit as transient an issue. And as for eyes? On Earth there are many eye colorings, even many skin colorings, which I have not seen here. Yet all of us sprang from a common seed. We intermarry freely, and have children who stand as proof that these are all surface issues only. That within ourselves, we are one people."

"The only way to test that assertion on this planet, Alex," and here he lowered his voice, as he was unsure just how far Lannae had gone, and when she would return, "would be for you to mate with a Mirran woman. To see if you could successfully impregnate her. See if a child so conceived could survive to birth. Is this what you would consider putting her through? Conducting a grand test, to see if what would grow in her would become a living child, rather than some...." He could not find the word. I suspect the word 'monster' had occurred to him, but he was not so cruel as to be able to say it.

"Anned. I am considering nothing. I have no plans for Lannae Dollapan. She is a sweet girl. She is, as I have come to know her, a thoughtful and compassionate lady. And to all my senses, and to all my body's reactions, she is an intensely attractive woman. And I am very attracted to her. Alright, I grant you we have a situation. But not an out-of-control situation."

"Let me inquire further,' said Islak, "to see if I might lend more chaos to our 'situation'. On Earth, is it permitted that a man may be married to but one woman?"

"Almost universally, yes."

"And on Earth, is it difficult to set aside, or end, a marriage?"

A more difficult question. "Among many it is too easy. Easier than God would will it. But what matters is how things are here."

"By the law God has given us, a marriage is dissolved in two ways. If one person dies—or is legally presumed to have died—the other is free to pursue a new spouse."

"Which is clearly not my situation."

"Or if one person, but not the other, is unwilling to abide by the minimum constraints of a marriage: to live with the other under a common roof, to join with the other sexually, to have such union at times that will lead to conception. I know you too well to think you would charge your Kathy with dereliction in these matters."

"These are the only ways a marriage may be dissolved?"

"There are no others."

"No provision for a husband and wife, though living, being indefinitely separated?"

"Might I ask, Alex, except for the situation you now find yourself in, how you think such an indefinite and unalterable separation might have ever arisen before? No law exists here for such a situation."

"Gentlemen!" Lannae's voice came from the shore, where we had entered the lake. "Seeing your clothes piled here, I shall take this opportunity to ride ahead, to check the quality of the road. If I should return in, say, twenty rounds? Could you be ready?"

"Ready we will be," Islak called back to her.

She rode off, and we emerged from the water. We retrieved fresh clothes from our saddlebags.

"All of these things," I said to Islak. "They did not spring from your own mind, did they?"

"Most of these issues," he conceded, "were brought to my attention by the Captain."

"It is a wonder I survived the hearse ride from Desidomone to Barnable."

*   *   *

Lannae advised us when the light of the Adjunct first became visible. When we had closed that distance by half, she advised us of something else. She eased her horse to a stop, and Islak and I drew alongside her.

"Something is different," she said. Something about the lights."

"The light of the Adjunct?" I asked. "Or of the residences of the keepers?"

She hesitated. "Neither..." she said at last. "They are not the lights of the keepers. Near the keepers, on the flat. There are many lights. It's like a crowd has gathered."

"People have come," Islak said, "to watch for Harbinger. Word has it Shelaemstet is swollen as well. We must take precautions."

"What precautions?" I said.

"When did you last shave away your facial hair? Your skin must be smooth. And we must glove your hand."

"No," I said, prodding my horse to slowly walk forward. "No precautions." Neither Islak nor Lannae seemed to be following. I trusted my horse to have the wits to follow the lights.

"You don't know what their reaction will be!" Islak called after me.

"Nor will I ever," I called back, "if I never give them the chance to react!" It occurred to me then, with a frightful suddenness, that since losing my sight I had scarcely ever been alone. And when I had, it had been a most timid aloneness—indoors, always with someone in an adjoining room. Save for the horse, which could scarcely speculate over what might lie ahead, I was now alone. I prodded him to a slow trot.

This was a bold, empowering sensation. I felt a sense of control—control over the horse beneath me, control over whatever lay ahead. I was uncertain, but not fearful.

I heard a horse pulling near on my left. I prayed it was Lannae. I reached out my left hand into the air, hoping she would take it. She did; her slender fingers wrapped around mine. Every confidence I had felt two seconds before collapsed. It had been a sham. I was blind, and terrified, and grateful to have someone at my side who would face it with me. Islak's horse pulled up alongside my right. He was speaking, but I could not make it out. I suspected that was just as well.

Soon voices began to challenge us, to pepper us with questions:

"Who are you?"

"From where do you come?"

"What news have you?"

"Do you bring any word of Harbinger?"

We continued on without reply. The stubble of my beard was

short, and likely went unnoticed. Perhaps it was taken for smudged dirt. With my left hand wrapped within Lannae's, and my right hand wrapped tightly on the reins, my fingers were concealed. Would it be right to make an issue of my fifth fingers, to wave them before the people? That would be, in essence, making a declaration—which I was not prepared to do. Yet was it right to conceal them?

I thought again of the Select Committee. Congressman DeLibri would have a fit over what I was about to do. Lannae and Islak had my horse between theirs. I was going nowhere that they did not direct. I let loose the reins, and laid my hand upon my thigh. Less than a round passed before the reaction hit.

Cries of "Harbinger!" shot up around us. I could hear a bustling ahead; our horses began to slow.

"We must keep moving," I said emphatically to Lannae.

"We have to slow. They're crowding in around us."

"Slow, then," said Islak. "But do not stop."

"Move aside," Lannae called out. "Clear a path to the Adjunct!"

The chatter about us grew steadily. From time to time, someone would manage to get between Islak's horse and mine, and their hands would sweep across my hand as our horses continued forward.

Lannae pulled up short.

"What is it?" I demanded.

"We are here. Almost. Close enough that we should walk. She dismounted, and then helped me down. It was then that a realization hit the crowd; they had taken my forward stare as a kind of aloofness, or perhaps assumed my attention was held somewhere ahead. But my aimless staring as Lannae helped me down drove the point home.

"Blind! He is blind! Harbinger is with us!"

The connection between Harbinger's appearance at the Adjunct and his blindness sealed the issue for most. They began pressing in.

"Stand back," Lannae yelled, with a forcefulness I would not have imagined to be within her. "Stand back and make clear the way! Open a path to the steps of the Adjunct!"

She drew me ahead. We snaked through the swarm of bodies. Some pleaded for me to heal them, some merely that I touch them. Many touched me, especially my free hand. Those who touched my face recoiled, whether in revulsion or surprise I could not say. It must be a shocking thing to touch a stubbly beard for the first time ever in one's life.

Lannae stopped.

"What?" I said, trying to be heard over the crowd. "What now?"

"First step," she said. Her hand pulled downward, and I knew she had taken the first large step. I followed her.

"Islak," I called ahead to Lannae. "Is Islak with us?"

"Just behind," Islak called to me. "Keep moving."

As I cleared the second, shorter step, I realized no one was pressing in around me. I moved my head from side to side, as if looking.

"No one is on the steps," Lannae said. "Everyone is gathered around the top edge."

After descending several cycles of steps, the crowd was far enough behind that we could speak normally.

"Is there no one on the steps but us?" I asked.

"Only us. There are some men at the bottom, around the Adjunct building itself. Four or five. I suspect it may be the Adjunct keepers."

"Certainly," said Islak. "There is no way to maintain any kind of order up above. In the face of such a crowd, it would only make sense for them to retreat to the bottom floor."

"If the people begin filling the steps," Lannae observed, "the keepers will probably retreat to the very door of the Temple Adjunct itself."

"Will they allow me in?" Neither of my companions ventured a guess.

The climb down was horrible. Previously, I had thought ascending and descending the irregular stairs of the Mirran Stone and the Temple Adjunct was difficult, being unable to establish a rhythm. But now, not even able to see them—this was worse. We seemed to be going down, and down, forever. I remembered preparing to launch the escape pod from the Sirocco, thinking of it as a descent into hell. I had been wrong then; I had landed in a paradise—or at least the closest thing to paradise I had ever known. But what about now?

What if this *was* my descent into hell? What was inside that building? What had I seen that had burned the vision out of my eyes? I stopped, letting loose Lannae's hand. I imagined myself growing dizzy, falling headlong down the stone stairs.

"Alex?" Lannae asked.

I moved to the shallower steps, five or six from the last large one, and there I knelt.

Jesus, I prayed silently. *I don't want to go down there.* I was hoping for some burst of insight. Above all, I hoped for a sudden inspiration—of some alternate course of action, some other place to go. Any other place to go. No such inspiration came.

I think I need to go in.

I remembered Islak's map, the impossibly precise alignment of the Mirran continent to the galaxy. *I know you are here. This world is as much your creation as is Earth.*

I remembered the placement of the Adjunct; its positioning, its identification with Earth. *I know there's a reason I'm here.*

And with that, my course of action was clear. Why else had I traveled tens of thousands of light-years? Why else had I been ripped from everything, from everyone, that I knew and loved, why else, if not to enter this one building? In the entire universe, known and unknown, what one place could I be more certain I needed to be?

I stood up. "I'm ready to go down."

"Alex," said Lannae. "We *are* down. We're at the bottom."

I explored with my foot. One step of four or five inches was all that remained.

"The keepers have moved away from us. I think they're afraid. They may have seen your fingers. They probably heard the crowd at the top."

"They remember him," Islak said. "They remember him from before, when the Judges allowed him in."

"Lead me to the doorway."

"I've never been this close to the Temple Adjunct before," Lannae said.

"You'll be closer yet. You need to get me to the doorway."

Lannae's voice dropped to a whisper, but an emphatic whisper:

"This is a *forbidden place*."

I reached out, and laid my hand on her cheek; it was wet with tears. In some places, the tears seemed to have dried. She had not just started crying. She had been crying during the descent. She was terrified. She had hidden it from me completely.

"No harm will come to you. I would not have brought you here if there was danger." I stroked her cheek.

"Whatever is in there," she said, "is so terrifying, it stole your sight. How can you say there is no danger?"

I stood facing her, imagining I was looking into those strange, green eyes—the eyes that fairly glowed, and that had captivated me on the ride from Desidomone.

"I don't know," I conceded. "But I can say it. And I do. Lannae, take me there."

Slowly, she led me by the hand. "There is something here. A pile of something, near the door. A rope?"

"Still where we left it," Islak called from behind us. "Tie it to him."

"No," I said. "I will leave the same way as I enter, under my own power. Move the rope aside."

"Done. Your path is clear. The entrance is six feet straight before you." She leaned in to me, reached up, and kissed me on my cheek. "Do not die, Alex Boten," she whispered, and then she withdrew. I stood alone.

My mind populated the darkness before me with the image, the memory, of the entrance. A short doorway, through which I had nearly needed to duck. Torch-like lamps on both sides, and one straight above the lintel. I moved forward, and found the left edge of the opening. Moving in and to the left, I built an image before me every step of the way. The shorter inner wall on my right, forming the corridor with the outer wall. I came to the corner; I turned right. My mind constructed the image of the corridor extending to the rear corner; feeling along the wall, I made my way there. Suddenly, there was a burst of sound. I stopped, halfway to the corner. Music? Not quite. Birds? Something like birds. I had not heard any living thing here before. Now there was a riotous explosion of sound. It was the calling of baby birds. It was near, on my right. There was a sound of wings, and I ducked; something flew by, very near my head. The birds' calling grew more intense. I followed along the inner wall. The large bird flew away, but the babies kept calling. Creeping ahead, I stood right before them. I cautiously reached up, and felt the nest atop the inner wall. I could feel it jiggling, as the hatchlings moved about. I withdrew my hands.

This had been a lifeless place. I remembered thinking that even the animals had known it was forbidden. I moved forward along the wall, and turned the corner to the right. The inner opening was where I remembered it, and I followed it along until I stood in the corner, the corner that opened into the main chamber. My mind had trouble filling in images. Mostly I remembered the curtains, but I knew they were gone—just a pile of debris. Dropping to my hands and knees, I crawled forward.

Something moved. I stopped. Something small scurried along a far wall, and was gone. Life was beginning to move back into the Adjunct. Something had happened. Something had changed. This was not a forbidden place any longer. I began fighting back tears, tears I did not understand.

Remembering, the doctor had said. *Remembering may come… in pieces*. It seemed natural that life was returning to the Adjunct. I could not remember why. I just knew that it made sense.

"This is not a forbidden place," I said aloud.

Book III
Chapter 3: Remembrance

Crawling forward along the floor, I passed the rods and fragments of curtain. I moved through them much as I had before, for the swirling clouds of dust had been essentially blinding. As before, I came to the wooden platform. I had forgotten it, but remembered it as soon as my hands touched it. Two layers, running opposite directions. There was stone, I remembered, a flat base of stone. Creeping ahead, I searched for it. My hand found a pile of dust, a deep and wide pile of very fine dust. It extended to the left and right as far as I could reach. I dug into it, looking for the stone base. All I found was more dust, deeper dust. It had a strange texture, almost as if it were made of impossibly small ball bearings. As my fingers slid back and forth with the dust in between, they slid almost as if they were pinching liquid.

The stone base was gone, dissolved, into dust—as was whatever had been upon that base. Everything was gone. The only way to know what it was, what it had been, was to remember. I sat in the dust, craning my head about, thinking back.

In my memory, I could see the stone base, as I had reached out and touched it through the swirling dust of disintegrated curtain. It was smooth, like glass—a highly polished stone. I remembered wiping the settling dust off of it. There was something in the center, something formed of stone, rising from the base. Bit by bit, the memory came back to me. I remembered it progressively, in inches, the same way I had seen it as my hands explored it, and as the dust had settled. Sitting in the dust, I relived what had happened.

Out of the smooth surface of the orbid, a shape abruptly arose. It was not smooth like the base, but textured in astounding detail. It was black orbid stone, expertly chiseled to the form of a downward-pointing human foot. It had been carved as if the toes and an inch or two of the foot were submerged in the base, thus providing support for the stone as it continued upward.

I wiped away the dust, and was shocked at what I felt. There was skin texture; the carving had been done to the detail of skin wrinkles, and pores. I felt the bottom of the heel, and found the expected roughness of worn and calloused flesh, but also irregular tearing—what seemed like untreated foot injuries. For a sickening moment I thought I was examining an actual mummified body. But rubbing it, and looking closely, I was sure it was, in fact, orbid. This was a stone carving. My hand slid up, along the calf. The rear of the calf was strangely flattened, even slightly concave. The texture was strange here, as well, as if it had been firmly pressed against something and had, as flesh does, taken a temporary set to the shape that had pushed upon it. But an insight came to me, an understanding that still strikes me as beyond my range. The calf was distorted by something still there, a current presence. But the distorting article was not the object of the sculptor's attention. It was the human form that was his focus. This was the shape of the calf as it was pressed against the unseen surface. The irregularities on the calf's surface were the detailed representation of how the flesh conformed to that surface.

I had an impulse to look up. I resisted it. Looking down instead, I saw a startling feature I had missed before. There was a large hole in the foot.

This was not a hole that had been punched through by something which then been withdrawn; the wound would have re-closed. This was an open hole, with flesh pushed away; the inside edge, while not smooth, was nonetheless too flat, too uniform. Whatever made the hole was still there, just not depicted. The flesh was conformed to it, like the flattened calf.

Deep within me, a realization formed—a realization of what was before me, and above me, should I dare to look. But I pushed the thought down. It had been the first step, I recognized later, in the loss of memory of everything that had followed.

I worked my way up. It was the black stone figure of a man, in incredibly minute detail; obviously a lifetime's work. Forty reversals, the first Harbinger had spent, working on this. Blind from birth, his every chisel's stroke, every detailed scratching, had been directed by the hand of God. Working a lifetime to carve an image he could not have understood even if he had been able to see it. Was that why he was born blind? The first Harbinger had been born into a world unaccustomed to the brutality, the savagery, of Earth. Could anyone so born and bred be able to see—could they survive seeing—such a thing as this? Again I thought of what was awaiting me as I moved up, and again I pushed the thought down.

As I reached the knees, I noticed a peculiarity that had escaped me before. The figure had no hair. Would it have been impossible to sculpt? Perhaps. But another thought occurred to me, brought on by the Mirran recessed hairline, and the efforts I had gone through to keep myself shaved so as not to stand out amongst them. Hair is a transitory thing, ephemeral. It is not living tissue. As the body builds it outward, its appearance changes daily, hourly. We use it to change our looks, like a mask, or a cloak. What lies beneath—the flesh, bone and blood—this is what we truly are, physically.

The legs were horribly wounded, the thighs more so than the lower legs. The stonework caught the terrible details of flesh ripped up. I had read of the ancient Roman traditions—the whips, fitted with bits of bone and stone to improve their flaying effect.

The thoughts I had held down ran free now; there was no holding them in check. This was a stone carving of the earthman Jesus, of the town of Nazareth near Galilee, as he had hung on a cross outside Jerusalem over two thousand years ago.

The figure was naked. Whether Jesus had hung naked or not, clothing was even more transitory than hair. It was not part of the essence; it was not depicted here.

The further up I moved, the more revolting the flesh wounds were.

I came to a wound in the side, different from the feet. This wound, where a spear had been thrust in, had closed itself up. Here, unlike at the feet, the piercing object had been withdrawn.

I remembered looking away, around the inner perimeter of the Adjunct. Then my eyes went to the outstretched arm and hand above me. In the midst of the black orbid was a flash of white chelsit. The roof, showing through. Again, where a spike affixed him to the implied wood cross, no spike had been carved. But the gap in the flesh that the spike had caused—this gap allowed the white chelsit of the roof to show through.

I could stand no more of this, inch by inch. Steeling myself, I looked to the figure's head.

I had seen a thousand depictions of Christ, living and dead. A thousand artists' views, a thousand interpretations. I had never seen one without hair, which was disorienting. And although I had seen a few disturbing depictions that had gone to lengths to depict the battering and whipping wounds, I had never seen one which I implicitly knew to be one hundred percent accurate. This... this was beyond words.

I looked into the horror of the swollen, twisted face, into the incongruity of an Almighty Creator lowered to hideous abuse at the hands of the created. It was too much to look upon. Sitting now amidst the pile of fine dust, thinking back, I remembered hearing screaming, horrible screaming. My own screaming. That face was the last thing I had seen.

I looked down at the fine dust in my hand, pushed it around in my palm with my finger. What did it mean, that the stonework, so solid in my hands before, had been reduced to dust? Rubbing the particles between my fingers, I examined them closely. It took some time for it to dawn on me that I was, in fact, seeing them.

I looked around. The dust pile was, at its center, nearly a foot deep. It had spread out over the platform, spilling onto the Adjunct floor. It had buried the rods and poles. Looking around, I spotted the bird's nest atop the inner wall. The chicks were silent now, but I could see them moving occasionally.

I bowed my head, and thanked God for my sight. Standing up, I spotted a pile of sticks and grass in a corner of the inner wall. Whatever small animal I had heard was building a nest. No point in worrying about having scared him off, I realized. The place would be overrun with animals, unless the Mirrans came in to keep things cleared away. There was no reason not to, now. I had a proclamation to make. Retracing my steps, I made my way to the entrance. There I found waiting a half dozen or so Adjunct keepers, my friend Anned Islak, and Miss Lannae Dollapan.

She had indeed left her formal mourning clothes behind. She was dressed in what struck me as rather tomboyish, though eminently practical, riding clothes. She also wore no hat, so I could see what I had only surmised: Her hairline, like the other Mirran women I had seen, matched the male hairlines—recessed nearly two inches back from what I had always considered normal. I had wondered what I would think upon actually seeing her, with her head uncovered, if her hair were like this. She was beautiful.

My eyes were locked upon her, which she realized almost at once. She spoke, though not loudly enough for me to hear. Watching her lips, I believed she said:

"He can see."

Her words snapped Islak to attention.

I spoke loudly enough to be heard by everyone at the base, around the Adjunct, but not so loudly that my voice would carry to those ringing the top edge of the stadium-like steps: "This Adjunct to the Temple of the Most High God is no longer a forbidden place."

She stepped up to me, leaving Islak and the keepers behind. She kept her eyes locked on mine. When she got to within five feet, she stopped. She opened her mouth to speak, but she could not find her words.

"I need to talk to you," I told her. "To you, and to Islak. I have a great deal to explain to you. About the first Harbinger, about what he did here. And about why I am here."

*   *   *

A great stillness had come over the crowd, ringing the upper edge of the Adjunct steps. The keepers moved to the rear face of the Adjunct, while Lannae, Islak and I sat along the bottom few steps at the front.

But what was I to tell them? Surely more than the technical details of what I had seen. They needed more than that. Context, background.

331

I thought of the aptitude tests for the Hermes flight crews. Fractions of a point, and I had been disqualified. If there were a test for aptitude in explaining religious beliefs, I would not have been merely fractions of a point from the top of the top. I personally knew dozens of people who could do this better. How could I make these people understand? There was so much that *I* did not understand. Christ's death was inexorably linked to man's fall, man's turning away from God. God had gone silent here. Had this world fallen? Something Islak had said to the Captain came to me... was it atop the Mirran Stone? *His silence is not for punishment over any wrong we have done.* Islak had said that was in their scriptures. What did that leave, then? When Earth had fallen away from God, had the effects reached here as if Mirrus had merely been some remote continent tucked away on some corner of Earth? Could they have been affected by man's fall if, as Islak asserted, they were a separate creation—if we had not arisen from a common seed? A phalanx of theologians could spend lifetimes sparring over these questions. Who was I, to step into it?

The realization hit me with almost comedic clarity. I thought the words through, silently: *So, I'm a missionary.*

Lannae and Islak were waiting, patiently, for me to say something. To say anything.

In English I said, more in their direction than actually to them: "*Not part of my plan.*"

They both looked at me, puzzled. But they didn't ask what the words meant. I guess they sensed they weren't supposed to know.

A fraction of a point had kept me off the flight crew. But suddenly I saw that fraction of a point in a whole new way. If I had made the flight crew, I wouldn't have been alone in the Sirocco when everything went wrong. I might not have been there at all when it happened. Maybe there was an aptitude test for explaining the crucifixion to Mirrans. No, not maybe. There *was* an aptitude test. And I had passed it. This was the flight crew I had been chosen for.

I looked at Lannae. Looked through her, actually, and smiled. Too many chances, too many improbabilities. I remembered Islak's map, remembered the Adjunct lining up exactly where Earth stood. I had a ticket for this flight after all. Being here, now, to say whatever I was going to say. This was my ticket. This was my proof that I was supposed to be here.

The God Who Is Silent, they called him. There was a problem on this planet, a problem that was due to end. Restoration was coming to these people. The death of Christ was central. And perhaps, at this particular point, it didn't matter how it was central. Maybe that would become clear later. Maybe I had to start from what I knew, not from what I could theorize. A phrase echoed through my mind, a phrase whose origins I suddenly could not remember: *Matters of fact. Limit the discussions to matters of fact.*

"I should start," I said, "from what I know."

Simple enough. Now all I had to do was to explain the concept of the sacrificial lamb of God—to a people for whom "The Shedding of Blood" was a mystery. I simply had to explain crucifixion to a people who had no capital punishment. But then I realized: No. I did not need to explain these things to a whole people. At least not yet. For now, I just had to explain them to Lannae Dollapan, and to Anned Islak.

I stood up, marshalling my thoughts. Looking down to where they sat, I saw Lannae watching me intently, and Islak turning in my general direction. I knelt down before him. I took his face in my hands.

"Anned," I said. "I have some very, very strange things to relate to you."

"As I have always suspected," Islak said. Then he added comfortingly: "I am prepared to hear you. Whatever you may say."

The words shocked me. They were Abbik Dollapan's words to me, at the bow of the Ammanon Deloré. I wished he were here; I wished I could explain this to him, as well.

"Prepared, are you, my friend? Do not be too certain of that." I let my hands fall away, but stayed kneeling before him. "Since our days on the Deloré, you have had many questions about me, about where I came from. The time has come for me to tell you."

I stood up again, and began to pace.

"There was a time—long, long ago—when God spoke to my

people, as well. But my people turned away from God."

"How did this happen?" Lannae asked.

"For our purpose now," I said, "it doesn't matter. Something happened. And communication between God and man... was damaged."

"Do you mean," Lannae ventured, "that God became silent for your people as well?"

I stopped to work that thought over. The God Who Is Silent, I thought.

"Maybe I do mean that," I said. "Maybe not. I'm not sure what happened here, to your people. In some ways, it sounds similar. My people lost... the companionship of God. Community with God. All I can say for sure is that both of our peoples lost something in our connection to God."

"And what we need," Islak said, "is restoration. Have you come to bring this to us? Alex, tell us. Nothing else matters. Do you bring us restoration?"

I sat next to him, laid my arm around his shoulders.

"Yes, my friend. I am sure that I do. I bring you what you need. But you must understand—the path to restoration is a terrible one." My thoughts flashed back to the statue. "A terrible one...." My words caught in my throat.

"There will be a price," Lannae said, both fear and resignation in her voice.

"Then," said Islak softly, "it is a price we must pay. We must be restored."

I stood again, and faced away from them, faced the entrance to the Adjunct. "It is a price you cannot pay. A price my people could not pay. A price no one could pay. So it has been paid for us." Turning back, I saw the inevitable confusion in their faces. "I'm sorry. I don't mean to speak in riddles." I needed to cover thousands of years of Earth history in just a few rounds. "God gave my people laws, extensive rules, about how to behave. How we should interact with each other, and interact with God. Rules for perfect existence. If we could have followed them, we would have been perfect, and we would have been ready to be in the presence of a perfect God."

"*If* you could have followed them," Lannae said.

"If," I said. "If. We were a corrupted people. Perfection was beyond us."

"Then why these rules?" Islak asked. "Why would God set before you a task you could not meet?"

"Because our corruption," I said, "was deep. It extended to our sense of self."

"You thought you *were* perfect," Islak said.

"Yes. And although we did not understand it at the time, the rules were given to hammer home this point, that we were not perfect, that we could not live up to the standard required. The laws were valid. The rules were true. But they did not have the power to restore us. Only to prove that we needed to be restored."

"Then how were you restored?" Lannae asked, with more patience in her tone than I would have imagined possible.

"You need to know more, first," I said. "The law included provisions concerning violations. When a man committed a crime against his neighbor, there was a punishment for the harm to that neighbor. But there had also been a crime against God, a crime of disobeying his law. So for every violation there was a sacrifice to be made to God." I drew a deep breath, preparing to take them into uncharted waters. How would they react? How *could* they react? "But these were not sacrifices as you know them. Not the grains and fruits you burn in the inner Temple."

Lannae's hand rose to her mouth, and her eyes grew wide.

"What is it?" I asked.

"You do not mean," she said, "that your God required of you... human sacrifices?"

Smiling, I lowered my head. Perhaps I had imagined this would be harder than it really would be. And yet, at the heart of it, she was right. In the end, that was where this was headed. My smile disappeared as I realized: No, where this was headed was ultimately far worse. Then something stuck in my mind. "*Your* God," Lannae had said. Whether consciously or not, she was separating our concepts of God, distancing herself from what I was telling her. But this Adjunct had been built to bring our understandings of God together.

"No," I said to her soberly. "A ritual of human sacrifice was not what God commanded. But what God did command will be difficult for you to understand. At least at first. But as difficult as this may be, in the end I trust you will see that it had to be. God commanded that certain animals be killed, sacrificed, for the laws men had violated."

The look on Lannae's face was not greatly changed.

Islak lowered his face. "Alex," he said to the stone floor. "Forgive me. But I must ask. Are you certain that the God of whom you speak, and the God of whom we speak, are the same?"

"When I have told you all that I must tell you," I said, "then decide."

"But you are saying," Lannae protested, "that an animal, which has committed no offense, should be killed for the offenses of a man."

God bless the opportune objection. "Yes," I declared. "Yes, precisely. And that is key. You must remember that point. That which is sacrificed is innocent, without fault concerning the wrong that was done. When your people bring in their sacrifices, when they burn them in the inner patios of the Temple, do they ever bring in grains that have grown moldy? Or fruits that are bruised, past ripe?"

"Certainly not," Islak said defensively.

"Why?"

"Such a thing," Lannae broke in, "would be unacceptable. It is not fitting to sacrifice such things to God."

"Only perfect sacrifices, then? God commanded the same thing of us. Only animals without blemish, without flaw. Generation after generation passed this way, in endless cycles of sin and sacrifice, with the people never being restored to God."

"But if this was the procedure mandated by God...."

"Like the law itself, the animal sacrifice did not have the power to restore. The animals being sacrificed could not erase the evil men had done; they merely covered it. The animal sacrifices were only a hint, a suggestion, of what was to come." I wrung my hands together. "And that... that brings me to the very threshold of what I need to tell you." I resumed pacing. "What I need to tell you is so horrendous,

336

so incomprehensible... you need to understand one thing more to be able to understand it. You need to understand just what was at stake."

I looked at Islak, sitting patiently, waiting for me to go on. How could I explain this, so he would understand? I remember the bottle of poison he had told me about once, at this very place.

"Consider a fine bottle of Pinoae," I suggested. "Add to it a few drops of some deadly poison." Islak did not seem to react to this image. "You no longer have a bottle of Pinoae," I continued. "You no longer even have a bottle of Pinoae and some poison. What you now have is a bottle of poison."

"The poison spreads through the entire bottle," Islak said. "What is your point?"

"We agree that God is holy, perfect."

"Like the unsullied bottle of Pinoae," Lannae added.

"Exactly."

"And you are saying," Islak ventured, "that any exposure to imperfection... would destroy God?"

"No," I said. "Alright. Forget the Pinoae. Bad example." I took off my riding cloak and tossed it onto the stone floor. "Underneath my cloak, there is darkness. Above it, out here, there is light."

"The light," said Islak, "is God's perfection. The darkness, the evil that men do?"

"The darkness can only exist when there is something to block out the light, to shelter it. And when the shelter is removed...." I plucked up the cloak.

"The darkness is gone," Lannae said.

"Utterly destroyed. It ceases to be. It has to be destroyed. Darkness and light cannot exist together. The darkness can be burned away, or the light can be extinguished. But they cannot exist together. If God were to tolerate imperfection in his presence, he would not *be* holy, would not be perfect. It's not that the imperfection would destroy him. It is that the presence of imperfect, by definition, would mean God was no longer perfect."

"To be holy," Lannae said, her eyes wandering off, "he must be separate from what is imperfect."

"Then we must know," said Islak. "How can the evil deeds of

337

men be eliminated, burned away?"

"We must move from the realm of the physical," I said, "from questions like light and darkness, into the realm of the legal. Justice, punishment. When a man steals from his neighbor, he must pay back what he stole. But what if he cannot pay it back?"

"He must work until it is repaid," Islak said.

"But if it can never be repaid?" I asked. "Remember, this is just an example, to explain the relations of men toward God. If God has been wronged, there is nothing we can do to undo that deed. We are like thieves who cannot repay what we have stolen."

"Then there is no resolution," Islak said.

"But what if," I suggested, "the thief has someone who will intercede. A wealthy friend, who will pay back what was stolen, on the thief's behalf. How would your courts deal with such a thing?"

"I suppose," Islak said, "if the restitution has been made, and has been made willingly... perhaps. Perhaps the Court could accept this."

"But we are moving in circles," said Lannae. "In your example, you have stated that no one could pay back what was stolen. So who is this..." she struggled for a word. An uncomfortable look came over her. She looked at me squarely. "Who is this... restorer?"

I shook my head. "Not me. It is not me who will restore you. I only bring the word of how you will be restored. I bring you the pathway. So here we are. This is what it comes down to. The only penalty for disobedience is death. Just as any trace of shadow must be burned away when exposed to light, likewise any disobedience carries a sentence of death. I am not telling you something new. Your own scripture tells you that to look into the face of God is to die."

"'Ask not to look upon me'," Lannae quoted, "'For to look upon the face of the living God is to wither and perish.'"

"'Like green shoots,'" Islak finished, "'in the smith's fire.'"

"But *this* is new," I said. "The only way to have disobeyed, and yet survive in the presence of God, is to have the punishment of death be paid."

"If not you, then who?" Lannae protested. "Who can pay this punishment?"

"If you have found what I have said thus far difficult," I conceded, "you will find the next impossible. There is nothing I can say that will make it easy. I can only pray to God that you will be able to comprehend it."

Turning from them, I stepped to the front wall of the Adjunct. I slid my hand over the cool, smooth chelsit. Without turning to them, I added:

"Because the truth is, *I* cannot comprehend it. I can accept it, barely, but I cannot comprehend it. Not when I really think about what it means. Especially now. Especially after having looked upon it."

"What was in there, Alex?" Lannae's voice was just above a whisper. "What did you see?"

I could not answer her, could not even turn to face her.

"Alex," Islak said. "We have stayed with you this far. Trust us, that we will be able to accept what you have been able to accept. Test us, in this last way."

I turned to them. "God... a part of God—on my planet Earth long, long ago—gave up his limitless power and was born as a human child." I looked to them, but saw no visible reaction. Perhaps no reaction was possible to such an assertion. "This child was both fully human, and fully God. And for this, I offer you no analogy, no alternate way of thinking of it. This child grew into a man, the only perfect man to walk the earth since the terrible falling away that I mentioned at the outset. He was the only thing adequate, the only thing perfect enough, to be an unblemished sacrifice."

I let that statement hang in the air. Perhaps they needed to digest the thought. Or perhaps I was unable to go on.

"The only thing," Islak said at last, "perfect enough to be a... sacrifice?"

"You are suggesting," said Lannae, "that God, as you claim this man to be, could become a sacrifice? That God... could die?"

"God as you understand him cannot die. God as my people understood him could not die. But this was a new thing. A totally new thing. That part of God that became a man, *that* part of God *could* die. That part of God had to die. That was the reason that he came."

I looked to the keepers, huddled at the rear corners of the Adjunct. Were they trying to hear? What would they think, had they been able to hear? What were Lannae and Anned thinking, being able to hear?

"You are saying, then," said Islak, "that God can die, thus paying the penalty for a man?"

"Not for *a* man. For *all* men. But there is a caveat. In the case of our theft, imagine that the restitution is not simply a matter between the victim and the criminal's wealthy friend. If it were, it would just be a charitable gift from one party to another. Imagine that for the Court to recognize it as repayment for the theft, the thief must acknowledge that it is a repayment."

"But what thief would turn it down?" Islak scoffed.

"Perhaps a proud thief. Perhaps a thief who did not believe the wealthy friend was paying without exacting some other cost. Perhaps a thief who didn't even believe this wealthy benefactor existed. But this is all allegory, all analogy. Here is the basic fact: God became human, and died as payment for our evil. If we acknowledge that, our debt is paid, and we stand before God as if we have never done any evil act."

"This killing," said Lannae, without looking to me. "It was merciful, and quick?"

"It was not," I said harshly, and her eyes shot up to mine. I softened my tone: "The animal deaths were merciful and quick, but they were just an echo of what was to come. The point was that blood had to be shed. And let me assure you, there is more to the Mystery of the Shedding of Blood than you even yet imagine. But the point was that the animals had to die, to be an adequate symbol." Here, I had to look away from her. "But the heart of man could not bear to routinely do to animals the things... the things that would one day be done to the true sacrifice. No, Lannae. It was not merciful. It was not quick."

I turned to her again. "The only recompense I can offer you, for the things I am about to tell you, is that the horror of it testifies to God's love of us, that he would submit to it, for our sake. I always knew the details. All my life, I knew the details of what happened back then. But in the Adjunct, when I entered it for the first time, I saw them. I saw them as if I had been there."

"Is that," asked Islak, "what happened to you? Was that the reason for the madness?"

I nodded.

"If you could not bear it," Lannae said, "then how can you think that I can bear it?"

Looking at her, sitting at the bottom of the Adjunct stairs, I knew she was stronger than she credited herself. But the details I would in time relay to her would tax her limits.

"I can only tell you two things," I said. "First, we don't need to delve into that yet. You have been told much, and you need to come to terms with it. Second, in the end I think you will want to know."

"Do I understand, then," asked Islak, "that your reason for being here is to relate this information to us?"

"I do not know whether your people are fallen from God," I confessed, "truly fallen, in the way that my people are. If you are, I do not know if somehow our falling is what damaged your world, and caused God to be silent."

"Like ripples spreading out on a calm lake," Lannae suggested.

"But I do know, absolutely know, for a fact, that God wants you to know what happened on Earth. And if I am Restoration, I know that the understanding of this sacrifice is the path God has chosen for your restoration. So tell me, Anned Islak. Tell me, Lannae Dollapan. What do you think of what I have told you?"

"You ask for a reaction," Islak protested, "to all of this?" He shook his head. "What can I tell you, Alex? I have questions to ask you. Questions I am too stunned to even begin formulating as yet."

Lannae stood up. "I have many questions as well," she said. "I need to hear more, desperately need to hear more. But I sense already, within me, that what you say is true. It is a terrible, terrible truth. But it is the truth."

I smiled at her. Then a sad realization hit me. What if Islak, rather than asking for more time to think over what I had said, had instead rejected what I said outright? And what if Lannae had joined him? I was not sure I could pursue the matter any further. Everything—my presence here, the construction of the Temple Adjunct, the life's work of the first Harbinger—could have been for nothing. But, I realized, Anned Islak and Lannae Dollapan, being who they were and being the ones with me now, was no happenstance. No more that the work of the first Harbinger was happenstance, or my being here was happenstance.

"This man," said Lannae. "Did he have a name? Was he given a name, by his parents?"

"Yes," I said. "In all ways God, and in all ways man. He was given a name by his parents. A name told to them by a messenger of God." I stopped and thought. What name do I relay? Jesus was the name I had grown up knowing. But that was an anglicized version of the name he was actually given. In Hebrew it was pronounced... I had heard it before... Yeshua. If we were speaking English, 'Jesus' might make more sense. But not here.

"Yeshua" I told her.

"Yeshua," she replied. As she said it, I knew it was right.

There was a disturbance in the crowd ringing the top row of stairs. People were moving away from the edge, and there were agitated voices.

Lannae and I helped Islak to his feet, and we began climbing up.

As we neared the top, it became clear that the crowd had pushed back from the stair face that we were climbing, forming a huge semicircle. At the center of this semicircle, waiting near the top edge, were the six Temple Judges.

Upon recognizing them, Lannae stopped. I left Islak with her, and continued up. The anxious sounds of the crowd, which had no doubt begun with the Judges' arrival, had ended. Achieving the bedrock plain, I stood looking at them, as they stood looking at me. I made a point of making eye contact with each of them; none of them seemed surprised that I could see them. And none of them looked particularly pleased to see me.

Book III
Chapter 4: Inquest

Two of the keepers were summoned up from the Adjunct, to serve as guards around the building where the Judges and I would meet. Initially, Lannae and Islak were made to wait outside. Within, the Judges seated themselves along one side of a long table, facing me. As I stood before them, with them seated left to right by seniority, I realized I was having, in effect, an audience before the Temple Court.

"Mr. Boten," said the senior justice.

"Justice Raddem," I said, nodding my head.

"It is difficult to know where to begin. When rumor of your recovery reached us, we moved with haste to call upon you at Drumae Degg's farmstead, for there were issues of grave importance that we needed to discuss with you. Upon our arrival there, we learned that you had left some several watches earlier. Left, by all accounts, to come here. This leaves us with a separate set of serious issues pressing upon us."

They had no idea what kind of serious issues my being here had raised. But they would soon. And once we moved to a discussion of what had stood inside the Adjunct, all other topics would be forgotten.

"Learned Justices," I said, looking across them all. "I apologize that my presence here has caused, as you describe, serious issues. If there is a question over where to begin, I pray you indulge me by discussing the original matter, the one that drew you to return to the Degg farm. Nonetheless, I submit to your wisdom regarding our agenda."

"By Mr. Boten's kind leave," grumbled Buelle, "let us proceed with our original issue."

Message received. Until I knew what was going on, I would say as little as possible.

Raddem stood up.   Moving around the end of the table, he approached me.

"Mr. Boten.   What we are about to discuss has never been known by anyone, outside the office of Temple Judge, for as long as that office has existed.   Your discretion, your absolute discretion, is assumed."

"Yes sir."

"You profess ignorance of our ways, our traditions."

"Yes, sir."

"I would assume this extends to the workings of this Court."

"I know only what I have seen in operation."

"And you know nothing of how our decisions are reached."

I began forming ideas of where this questioning was leading. Oral tradition versus written law?   Weight of opinion based on seniority?   "That is correct, sir.   I do not know.   I only have my assumptions.   That your decisions are based on the written laws you have been given, interpreted and applied to specific situations with the highest integrity.   But beyond that...."

"Beyond that, Mr. Boten," Judge Poznanek interrupted, "you know nothing.   You know precisely what everyone in the world knows.   Precisely what each new justice, before his appointment, knows.   Nothing."

"Your Honors, forgive me.   I am confused.   Is there something you were expecting me to know?"

"Mr. Boten," Raddem resumed.   "May I call you Alexander?"

"You may indeed, Your Honor.   But I would count it a privilege if you would simply call me Alex."

Raddem smiled, sitting back onto the front edge of the table.

"Alex, then.   Alex, it is we who should ask your forgiveness. Our nerves are frayed.   Our tempers are on edge.   For we are confronted by a most disturbing situation—one for which we have no resolution.   And that is something none of us, in our terms as Judges, has ever had to face."

He stood, and began to pace.

"I will tell you now," he said, "something no one beyond a sitting Judge has ever known.   Something that traces back before our memory, Judge by Judge, back presumably to the time the office of Judgeship was instituted. The basic process for reaching judgment is basically as you outlined. The written law exists. In most cases, its application is so clear, disputes need not come to any court. In some cases a dispute will rise to a lower court. Rarer still is the situation that will pass beyond that, and be presented to us. Once it is so presented, we review it, attempting to apply, as you so generously stated it, the highest integrity of interpretation and application of the law. But as might be expected with cases that have reached us through all the filtering I have described, there often arises a difference in conclusion. For this reason time is taken to discuss and debate amongst ourselves the relative merits of the opposing views."

Here he ceased speaking, but continued to pace.

"Justice Raddem, what you have described thus far seems in no way greatly different from procedures followed on my Earth."

He resumed his pacing. "There are times when one or more Judges cannot come into accord with the others."

"Then," I ventured, "does not the majority rule?"

"Mr. Boten," said Buelle. "The decision rendered in a particular question is either right or wrong. It cannot be five-sixths right."

"To emphasize this," Platius broke in, "God commanded that there be six Judges in the Temple Court."

"An even number," Raddem observed. "Judges empanelled for regional fairs to judge baked goods have odd numbers, so that no tie is possible. But no such 'tie-breaking' will come into play before a court such as this. There must be unanimity."

"Judge Raddem, forgive my temerity. But you yourself just said that there are times when the Judges cannot come to accord. If unanimity is required, what then?"

"It is a rare thing," Raddem said.

"But not so rare," Platius said, "that every Judge now sitting, no matter how junior, has not experienced it at least once."

Usettet spoke: "Since the office of Judgeship was instituted, our people have relied upon God to resolve such impasses. When God decides that the debate has gone on long enough, each Justice is presented with a dream, the same dream, making clear the proper resolution."

"The God Who Is Silent," I said, "speaks to you?"

Raddem sighed. "Since the time God ceased speaking to his people, these dreams have been strictly visual. So in a sense God has been silent to us as well. But in a truer sense, Alex, yes. God has always continued, when necessary, to speak to whatever six Judges are seated."

Usettet and Lode lowered their heads slightly. The other Judges were not looking at me. I waited for one, any one, to look my way, so I could meet his eyes. I realized they were purposely looking away from me.

"God has always spoken to the Temple Judges," Raddem said. "Until now. On the question of whether you should be declared to be Harbinger, we have received no guidance. We cannot achieve resolution."

"Perhaps," I offered gently, "this particular question was not meant to be settled by the office of Judgeship."

Raddem sat again on the edge of the table. "Considering this very proposition, we decided—unanimously—to set aside the question of your identity. To move on to other issues."

Here he stopped. Neither he nor any of the other Judges seemed prepared to speak further. I waited.

"I have said," Raddem finally continued, "that disagreements among the Judges, disagreements we cannot resolve, are rare. Once we set aside the question of your identity, the next case before us was a matter of inheritance, inheritance of a plot of land. Curiously, it was one over which we deadlocked, three by three."

"Curiously?" Poznanek said. "I think not. An even deadlock by providential intent."

"No dreams have come," I said. Raddem resumed his seat. The God Who Is Silent, I realized, had gone silent for everyone. Even for those who, secretly, had maintained a tenuous thread of communication.

"If we are to be," I suggested, "in the business of dismissing curious coincidences, of instead recognizing them as the handiwork of God, there is another coincidence ripe for discarding."

"Yes, Mr. Boten?" Platius said.

"The coincidence of which I speak is this. That the one you suspect of being Harbinger, the one that I hereby declare to you *is* Harbinger, should appear, and should recognize his own identity, just when God has finally and completely gone silent. That Restoration should come to you at the moment you most desperately need him."

Lode said to me: "Do you suggest, Mr. Boten, that you can restore us to communication with God?" There was exhaustion in his voice; not a physical exhaustion, but an exhaustion of the spirit, and the will.

"I cannot wave my hand and restore you. But I know the path that God has chosen to restore your people. Whether there will be any need any longer for Judges to receive some special communication, I cannot say. Once God speaks to everyone, perhaps the need for Judges will disappear altogether."

"This Court remains divided," Raddem said, "over whether you are, in fact Harbinger. And as for whether you are also Restoration, our division is clearly insurmountable. The one thing on which we agree is that we cannot continue in this way. Without guidance from God, the people are without a functioning Court. You claim, even if unable to restore us yourself, to know the path to restoration. We call upon you, then, to reveal it."

I drew a deep breath. What lay before me was formidable. Lannae and Anned Islak had been a receptive audience. But here I knew I had one, and likely more, actively hostile experts in Mirran scripture.

"Learned Judges. The thing you have said that you wanted kept confidential has been spoken. No more about it need be said. I request therefore that my two companions be allowed to join us."

"To what end, Mr. Boten?" Lode asked.

I had to think on that.

"For no practical reason," I conceded. "Because I want them here. Because... because what I am about to say to you has already been said to them. And because if I lose my way in what I am about to say, they may remind me of things I have said to them."

"It is a matter," said Usettet, "of such complexity?"

347

I smiled, unsure of what to say. "It is," I ventured, "a curious thing. Simple enough that a child might avail himself of it. Yet raising issues so complex that wise men on my planet still debate over it."

Buelle leaned forward to speak to Usettet: "If he has already seen fit to tell these people, before even consulting us, what point is there in excluding them? They have already heard what he has to say."

Usettet did a silent canvass of the Judges, who all seemed to be of the same mind.

"Very well, Mr. Boten. Admit them. But this Court would appreciate your consulting with us, in the future, before dispensing such information to the citizenry."

"I understand your concern, Your Honor." I understood it, but I was not certain I would be willing to abide by it, depending on their reaction. My semantic dance did not escape Usettet.

Going to the door, I asked one of the keepers to send in Anned and Lannae. They took chairs and sat behind me and to my left.

With my moral support system in place, I began my explanation. I tried, as best I could, to walk them through what I had said to Anned and Lannae earlier. I skipped those points that seemed least effective, or least material. With some discomfort I realized they were not posing questions, or suggesting concepts, as my friends had. They received my words in a stony silence.

I reached the point I had reached with Anned and Lannae, and I pressed on. *Move on, or they'll never let you finish.* I told them, in the most basic outline fashion, of Christ's birth, a handful of his miracles, and of his teachings. I told of his betrayal, his trial, and his execution. And on this point—his execution—I finally began going into detail. In some aspects, more detail than I had even known before my visit to the Adjunct. Through this, I paced back and forth—partly because it helped me think, partly because it allowed me to catch glimpses of Lannae and Islak. They were both shaken by my words, but Lannae was more so. The Judges registered discomfort as well, but it was different. More of a distaste. *Move on.* I told of his burial, his resurrection, and his ascension to heaven. I wanted to go on—to the Pentecost, and to the believers speaking under the direct power of God. For a people longing to hear God's voice, this could be key. But I had been speaking for hours; my strength was flagging. I paused, looking for any sign they wanted me to continue.

Judge Lode leaned forward over the table, his hands folded before him. "Mr. Boten. This... information you relate to us. What evidence of these things can you present to us?"

"Your Honor. Among my people, those who were there at the time recorded what they saw. To this date, those who do not believe in God dismiss these writings as obviously unreliable, because those writings assert what cannot be. Those who believe that God does exist, or may exist, find great credibility in these accounts."

"Mr. Boten," said Usettet. "I fear you have misunderstood my colleague's question. He is not asking what evidence your people present to each other, or what evidence they have in the past presented to you. He is asking, as am I, what evidence *you* present to *us*."

I was taken aback; at once I understood the ramifications of something that had not previously even occurred to me. These were a people one level removed from any evidence I had thought of giving. No historical record I could cite could be checked or even argued by them.

But if being on Mirrus had lost me one form of evidence, it had gained me another—I myself was an eyewitness. Not to the crucifixion, but to what the first Harbinger had made.

In a way, I was far less like a twenty-first century Christian, and far more like a first century Disciple; I was an eyewitness to events of which I had no physical proof, but which I knew, by my own eyes, had for a fact happened.

"Within the Temple Adjunct, your first Harbinger carved a representation, in exacting detail, of precisely these events."

Poznanek's eyes lit up. "Since it is forbidden that we enter, might you bring this carving out to us, that we might inspect it?"

"The stonework," I said, "is dissolved. It was intact when I first entered, and I believe it was still intact when I first left. But upon my return I found it reduced to dust."

"So the only tangible proof," said Lode, "is destroyed. And we are left with the word of a man, who, after two shortmonths of unconscious delirium, tells us he recalls seeing something in the Temple Adjunct that matches this... this... remarkable story he has told us."

"Your Honors, Judge Lode's comment is well taken. But I should remind you all, that the carving was unlike any representation of Yeshua's death I have ever seen, or ever imagined. It was not a vision born of delirium. If it were, I would have dreamt it as I have always envisioned it."

My palms were sweating, and I rubbed them together as the Judges mulled that observation. I looked down at my hands. I let my left drop away, holding my right before me. I raised it to almost my eye level, and turned my palm to them. I met their eyes, from left to right.

"And," I said, "you have my testimony. A man of five fingers, appearing to you in accordance with signs your own holy writings affirm." I gave them a few seconds to ponder that. "Based on these things, you will believe me, or you will not. You will believe that a planet, circling a star near the edge of the Crown of God, once had born to it a man who was God, who gave his life to draw to God men such as yourself. Men who were identical to yourselves, before God fell silent and marked you with a missing finger. You will believe this, or you will not. You will believe God sent me here to give you this news, or you will not. You will believe that this is the path he has given you to restoration, or you will not."

"And," said Raddem, with pain in his voice, "if we will not?"

"That is in the hands of God. But I suspect that refusing the path of restoration God has set before you, will mean you will not arrive at restoration."

Buelle snapped: "So you threaten us with withholding from the people the promise of restoration?"

"That," I answered calmly, "is not in your power. Each man, each woman, each child, will accept my words or not. Your power extends no further than whether each of you will accept it yourselves. For good or ill, for belief or doubt."

Usettet spoke again: "Are you suggesting you will present this tale to the people, at large, regardless of our command? This is not something the people at large can decide upon."

Lannae stood up. "But the people at large have begun to decide." She moved forward, standing next to me. "I believe what he has said."

"Child," said Usettet. "I know your father. Judge Raddem and I count him among our friends. In his absence, allow me to offer you some paternal advice."

"I..." said Islak. I turned to him. He was still seated. "...would like to hear more, before reaching any firm conclusions. However, based on what I have heard thus far, I am inclined to believe him as well."

The table of Judges ignited with chatter, and I could make out none of it.

Usettet stood. "This is precisely the point. Learned colleagues. A radically new teaching, a radically new understanding of the nature of God, and how God interacts with his people, is being accepted upon the word of a single man, of whose origins we know nothing. We are *told* much, but we *know nothing*."

"Your Honors," I said. "It had not occurred to me that you would have the power to prevent me from speaking. It occurred to me even less that you might want to exercise such a power. If that is your judgment, then understand: I will not obey it."

Raddem joined Usettet in standing. "We have heard all we need to hear."

I stepped forward, to the leading edge of the table. "But you have not seen all you need to see. You know I have been blind for these shortmonths, yet I stand before you now, sighted."

"You were examined by doctors," said Lode. "What were their diagnoses, and their prognoses?"

"Hysterical blindness."

"And their prognoses," Lode insisted pointedly.

"Perhaps indefinite, or perhaps not."

"A blindness with no physical cause, which might end at any time, has ended. What, in this, would you have us find remarkable?"

351

A thought occurred to me—a course of action so outrageous, I was unsure I could follow it. I bowed my head to pray, to ask God if this could possibly be what he would want. I never began that prayer. In that moment, I knew it was right. In that moment, I could not have been more certain. Not even if the voice of the God Who Is Silent had spoken to me audibly.

I turned from them, walking back to Islak's side. He heard my approach, and turned his head as if to ask me what was happening. I turned again to the Judges, looking squarely at them, one by one.

"Anned Islak," I said, still looking at the Judges, "doctors have examined your blindness as well. What were their diagnoses? And their prognoses?"

"Alex," Islak whispered. "What are you doing?"

I continued in full voice: "Anned Islak, I am asking you what your doctors have said. Diagnoses. And prognoses."

"Overexposure to light," Islak said, "resulting in permanent damage to my retinas, and permanent and progressive damage to my corneas."

I turned to face him. "Stand up."

He did, facing the Judges. Again whispering, he said: "Alex, we have tried this. It did not work."

Now I spoke back to him in a whisper. "It was not meant to work, then." In normal voice, I said to him: "Scientist Anned Islak, you have asked me for scientific insights. I have not been free to give them to you. But what I am free to give you, I give you now. In the name of Yeshua, see."

Upon these words, Islak promptly clamped his eyes shut.

"Anned?" I said softly. He did not reply. "Why are your eyes closed?"

"Alex. I am afraid."

I waited for him to explain.

"I… have grown unsure," he said quietly, "whether I can go on like this. Blind. It has been a fascinating experiment in adaptability, but its novelty has long worn off, Alex. It has become more than I can bear. But now, for the first time since the Ammanon Deloré returned from her voyage, hope stirs within me. Not the desperate, wild-eyed hope I had when I asked you to heal me on the ride from Desidomone to Shelaemstet. This is different, Alex. This hope hangs upon something nearly... tangible." His tone remained soft, but his voice lowered: "If I open my eyes, and I do not see... Alex, I can't go on. Having that hope dashed would be like being blinded all over again. I cannot bear it if that happens."

"I understand that you have fears," I said. "I shared them, for a time. But you are a man of science, a man who has explored the order of things because you believe God created order, and because you believe order to be in his nature. Is this not so?"

He thought for a moment, and then nodded.

"How can you believe this," I asked, "if you are not also a man of faith? Trust God. Open your eyes."

Feeling down along my arm, he took my right hand, and looked down to the floor. For a full round, and then two, nothing happened. I felt him squeezing my hand, massaging it, shifting it within his grasp. I realized what he was doing. He was counting my fingers.

He breathed deeply, and let the breath out. With his eyes open, he craned his neck back, so he was staring at the ceiling. Then he craned his neck back down, staring at the floor. A shudder rolled through him.

With his free hand he reached into his breast pocket, and pulled out a bottle made of dark glass. Although I had never seen it, I assumed it was the bottle of Lyderis acid. The bottle Ig Doel had brought to him, half in jest. The bottle he had kept with him, always. He held the label up, and turned the bottle, as if reading it. Then he held it out to me.

"Would you return this to Igren Doel?" he said.

"If you won't be needing it," I said, smiling.

He looked to me with his clear, violet-flecked eyes. "No," he said. "I won't be needing it." Releasing my hand, he stepped forward, halfway to the Judges' table. There he stopped, and, one by one, met each of the Judges' eyes. "Most respected Judges of the Temple Court," he said. "There is still more I wish to hear from the Harbinger Alexander Boten. But it is no longer to establish whether or not I believe him. For even if I hear nothing more from him, that question is settled. I do believe him."

As Islak was speaking, a growing sound came to me. From outside, horse hooves were approaching. It was more than one horse, I was sure, but not many.

I began to speak, as the sound of shouting arose outside: "Your Honors. I will spread the word that I have told to you. I dearly hope it will be with your blessing, your assent, even your assistance." The keepers began knocking. As Platius arose and moved to the door, it seemed no one was listening to me. "But even if you oppose me with every fiber of your beings," I finished defiantly, "I will still spread this word."

Platius returned to his place with an unfolded piece of paper. He did not resume his seat.

"The communications towers which Mr. Islak has engineered have delivered a message from the eastern coast to Shelaemstet. In our absence, the message has been relayed to us here. It has been corrected for some errors, likely due to the urgent nature of the signaling. It reads as follows:

"'Fleet of thirty-five, under sails of condemnation, descended on Mej Moribor. City afire. One third sailing north. One third sailing south. Last third here. Panic. Killing. Bands of....'"

Platius dropped the paper to the table. "That is the extent of the message. The tower in Mej Moribor no longer transmits. Its locator beacon is out." As one, the Judges arose. They filed past us to the door. The last to leave the room was Buelle.

"So, healer," he said. "Will you heal us of this, as well?"

Book III
Chapter 5: To the Highlands

As the carriage bearing the Judges pulled away, Lannae, Anned and I made our way through the crowd to the edge of the Adjunct stairs. Some in the crowd were talking about the fact that I could see. More were talking about the fact that Anned Islak could see. All of this I ignored. Looking down from the top edge, it struck me what a fine amphitheatre it would have made. I could imagine the crowd—those already around us, and more from the nearest towns, perhaps even distant towns, filling the steps as if they were seats. I could see myself, at the bottom. Maybe not the very bottom. Maybe perched upon the peak of the Adjunct roof. From there I could turn in all directions, speaking to everyone. I had never envisioned myself as a preacher. Not until now. Not until the entire prospect crumbled away.

"What will you do?" Islak asked.

"I don't know," I confessed.

"Could this all be true?" Lannae asked. "Could these people be attacking, destroying? Even killing?"

"It could," I said. "It could all be true. Or it could be a horrendous misunderstanding. A misread message along the towers from this city... Mej Moribor, was it? Possible. But I don't think so. In the back of my mind, I have feared this since I first learned what those sails meant, when we were waiting for our first audience before the Court, in Shelaemstet. But I was so distracted, so fixated on the question of Harbinger, of Restoration. I should have raised some sort of warning, then."

"What would we have done?" Islak asked. "Is there some defense against such men?"

I looked at him—looked him squarely in the eye. It felt good to do so. When we had first met, he had already begun losing his sight. We had never, ever, really looked into each other's eyes before.

355

"I do not know," I conceded. "For your people, a people accustomed to living in peace? Maybe there is no defense."

"No defense," said Lannae, "save for one. You have just spoken sight into the eyes of a man forever blinded. You have done this by the power of the living God."

"He has promised," Islak said, "to restore us. To speak again to us. Would you imagine God plans to speak to piles of dead bodies?"

"God means for us to survive," Lannae agreed. "The question is, how?"

I kept looking down, to the Adjunct, and the steps encircling it. I thought of all the people longing for restoration. Waiting, for the message I was poised to give them.

But now, crisis was bearing down on them. I could teach them how to fight. I could introduce weapons that would undoubtedly far surpass anything the invaders might possess. Was this to be my mission? To introduce an idyllic culture to Earth's twenty-first century warfare? I shook the thought off. Two things seemed equally improbable—one, that God would want such a thing, and two, that these people would be capable of receiving it.

I pulled from my pocket the bottle Islak had given me. I held it high overhead.

Whispering, I said: "To life." I threw it down, shattering it across the steps below. I turned to the crowd. "Men and women of Mirrus!" That was quite successful in catching their attention. I doubted anyone had ever addressed them just that way before. "I and my two companions arrived here by horse. These three horses are strong and healthy animals, but are not possessed of the speed that we now need. Do any of you own three swift horses which you might be persuaded to trade?"

"Blessed Harbinger!" a voice broke out at once. "I will not trade with you, but would consider it an honor if you would take my horse as a gift!" Shouted concurrences rolled through the crowd.

"Kind people, hear me! Your generosity is appreciated. However, we will be unable to attend the horses we arrived with. It will be a comfort and aid to us to know that they have good and caring owners. Relent, we ask, and trade."

356

A brief competition ensued over who within the crowd had the horses that were the fastest. But by imploring the crowd over the urgency of our departure, we convinced them to come to agreement. Finding ourselves quickly over-supplied with provisions, we maneuvered our new horses out through the crowd.

"Do we then head," suggested Islak, "for Mej Moribor?"

"No," I said, without even stopping to think. Islak and Lannae looked to me as our horses emerged from edge of the crowd. "No," I repeated, struggling to think why. "No, they would be gone by the time we got there."

Islak stopped his horse, and Lannae did likewise in response. I turned my horse to face them.

"And where are they going?" Islak asked.

I could imagine them, moving across country, and swiftly. Not on foot. On horseback. And I could imagine them driving their horses madly.

"Shelaemstet," I said. "Mej Moribor is only a taste of their anger. Shelaemstet, and the Temple Court. That is their focus."

"The Judges," said Lannae. "The Judges who banished them."

"Who banished their forefathers, more likely," I said. "I doubt there are many, if any at all, who were themselves condemned. This is a hatred that has festered through generations."

"To Shelaemstet, then?" said Islak. "Or to some other place, to intercept them?"

"I think we have no time to intercept. We must race to beat them to the Temple."

"You think they can move so fast as that?" asked Lannae.

"I think they will come on horseback."

"Horseback?" said Islak. "To bring horses by ship is a daunting prospect. We don't even know if they have horses in their land. Surely none was ever sent with a condemned man on his boat."

"I have no argument against your reasoning," I conceded. "But they will come by horse. We must ride swiftly, if we are to arrive before them." Turning my horse, I was off at full gallop. I could hear Islak and Lannae close behind.

It would be much later that we would learn the details of what had happened at Mej Moribor. The invaders, as Islak had asserted, had no horses. In fact, they had almost no knowledge of the beasts. Their ancestors who had known of them were long gone, and the stories they told—of riding the backs of these large creatures—were remembered fancifully. But upon beginning the land attack, the marauders saw some Mirrans fleeing upon these very animals so long dismissed as myth. The power, and speed, and military value of the horses were obvious to them in an instant. As they fanned inland by foot, they came upon farms and ranches with corrals full of horses. Although knowing nothing of horsemanship, the invaders had two things to their advantage. They were quick learners, and they were brutal taskmasters. Where they could not immediately adapt to the horses' ways, the horses were made to adapt to theirs. Those horses that were not compliant were shown the same mercy as was shown the Mirrans. It took a time for the invaders to master riding. But it had also taken a time for the initial message, after arriving in almost real time at Shelaemstet, to reach the Adjunct by horseback. The marauders were sweeping west at full speed at almost the same time we began racing north.

On the southern plain leading to the highlands, I came to appreciate the joy of breakneck speed. This was unlike speeding along in an automobile, or hurtling through the atmosphere on a shuttle. My engine was a living thing, beneath me. Between the Crown, and the ascension of both Dessene and Hon, our path was lit brighter than a full moon night on Earth; I rode faster than I had ever ridden any horse in my youth.

We skipped every other sleep cycle. For Mirrans, accustomed to just two hours of sleep, this is not too difficult in the short term. When we did sleep, we took an extra half watch.

Approaching the Adjunct Highlands, I grew uncertain over how fast I wanted to proceed; Islak shot past me. Lannae and I struggled to keep up with him through the winding passes. In time, we lost him. For a time, we rushed forward, hoping to regain sight of him. But eventually I reined in my horse, and Lannae circled back to rejoin me.

"In time," I offered, "he may notice we are not behind him, and return to us."

"And until then?" she asked.

I prodded my horse forward at a walk. "Until then, I think we should carry forward at a pace more in keeping with these winding paths."

"There!" Lannae cried, pointing ahead and up. Upon a crest, some two hundred yards beyond us, Anned Islak was silhouetted against one of the arms of the Crown. His horse reared, and then settled. Had he issued a peal of maniacal laughter, I would have thought us transported into Washington Irving's 'Sleepy Hollow'.

"Shall we press on?" Lannae asked, clearly ready to drive her horse back to a gallop.

"You may if you wish," I said, dismounting. "But as for me, I'm giving my horse a rest. Walk with me?"

She dismounted as well. "But if he rides on without us?"

I laughed. "Let him. Along with his sight, his very life has been returned to him. Let him expend his exuberance. He'll return." We began walking the path side by side, our horses outboard of us.

"You seem sure of yourself. You think you know him that well?" Her question seemed more playful than a matter of genuine concern.

"Well enough to know he would not abandon us. Anned is a serious man, a sober man. He will not let his emotions carry him away." I smiled. "Not far away. I know him at least that well." We walked on, silently for a time. "But you." I said. "You, I do not know."

"Indeed?" she said, "Am I such a mystery?"

"Thus far, yes you are. You have too much intelligence, too much awareness, to spend your time idly. Am I correct?"

"I have been able to make myself useful. My father has a number of business concerns. Two of these I run for him."

"And yet you left these, to tend to a blind and bedridden man. A man, shall we say, of dubious origins. Not the sort of behavior I would have expected of a woman bearing such responsibilities."

In saying this, I had unknowingly committed a social faux pas, one that Islak had earlier allowed to pass; Lannae Dollapan would not, at least for several quarters, be properly referred to as a woman. A ring on the middle finger of her right hand, now white, would in just over two quarters of a longmonth be replaced by one of deep blue, signifying to those she encountered that she could properly be referred to as a woman. She made no comment of my indiscretion, either out of gracious concern for my feelings over having trampled a tradition, or because she enjoyed being referred to, for the first time in her life, as a woman. In retrospect, I suspect both were in play.

"My father wished to stay ashore for a time," she said. "Being present in Desidomone, he was quite capable, with my mother's assistance, of handling his businesses."

"I am glad," I said pointedly, "that your tending to me at Drumae Degg's farm did not cause him any distress."

She did not respond to this, nor did she look to me. With her gaze fixed ahead, she simply walked on.

"What, exactly," she said finally, "did Mr. Islak tell you?"

"Enough. Enough to know that your father is concerned over my... attentions to you."

"Enough also," she asked, "to know of his concern over my eagerness to attend your convalescence?"

"There was a suggestion of that, as well."

"Alex , I find myself in a most difficult situation. I find myself needing to ask an outrageous question. One which even now I cannot imagine passing my lips."

"I can imagine several questions," I said to her, "now coming to the fore, which would fit that description. Let me say simply that, although you consider your question outrageous, I promise that I will not be outraged by it. Please, speak freely."

"The question itself presupposes much. About where this conversation is headed."

"Ask."

"Alexander Boten," she said. She was steeling herself. "How... human... are you?"

"A fair enough question. And rest assured you are not the first to ponder it. There is only one thing I can say. Apart from our hands," and here I took hers in mine, "your people and mine seem identical in every practical, significant way." I continued holding her hand.

"Alex, if we continue to step around this issue, we shall stumble over each other. I must tell you—the thing my father most dreads seems to be occurring. I believe I am falling in love with you." We stopped, and she held me, burying her face in my chest. "You seem to me to be a man who has had everything he loved torn from him. All his hopes, his dreams, his expectations of what life would bring. I have seen men lose a fraction of that, and immerse themselves in self-pity, or turn their disappointment into bitterness toward the Most High. But through this all, you have continued to serve and to seek almighty God. You are a man of uncommon character." She was crying. "It is wrong for me to express this now, before you have had a chance to meet other women of this world. I am cornering you, leading you to pledge something you ought not yet pledge."

"Do you think," I said, "that if I search through the villages and cities of this land, I would find a woman of more stunning beauty? A woman with courage enough to gallop into the night leading two blind men through a wilderness? A woman with enough compassion to tend to an invalid man with no specific prospect of recovery? Or a woman of your intelligence? Perhaps your world is filled with such women. But even if it is, there is still only one among them with whom I am falling in love."

She held me tighter. "There are other problems to be addressed. Besides... physical compatibility," she said.

"You understand," I said, "that I am married."

She nodded. "It seems unfair. Under the circumstances. The law was never intended to deal with a situation such as this." Then quickly she clarified: "Such as yours."

"But that does not mean the law can be ignored."

"You and my father," she said, "are of one mind."

We resumed walking up the pathway. The incline grew steep.

"I have not abandoned hope within the law," I told her. "The law came from God. When he gave it, he knew all things that were to unfold. If the Temple Court survives what is ahead, and if the Temple Judges survive to take their seats, I will pose the question to them."

The path eased to a gentle climb. We continued for a time without speaking.

"I know you still love her," Lannae said.

At first, I did not respond. "I take it, then," I said, "that Islak was not the only one listening to my ramblings during my convalescence."

"No one meant to intrude upon you," she said. "We were so closely involved in caring for you. And you spoke so clearly. At times, we thought you had come back to consciousness. You mentioned a Kathy, and a Katie."

"One person. My wife. Those are variants on her name. Katherine, officially. No one called her that though."

"There was an Ally, and an Abbey. Variants of someone else?"

"No. Different people, this time. Abbey was my sister. Ally was my daughter... one of them. Ally and Madeleine."

"Daughters. Oh Alex, I didn't know. So much loss."

"And yes," I said. "I do love her, very much. I love them all." Even as I said it, I wondered: What was I really feeling? Was I loving them, or was I grieving for the loss of them?

"You have lost so much, in coming here," Lannae said. "Was there other family, besides your wife, and your daughters? Parents? A mother, a father?"

"Our mother died, many years ago."

"And your father?"

"My father," I said, tossing back my head. We continued up the path. It grew rockier, steeper. "My father. What can I tell you about my father? He was loud, opinionated, belittling of anyone who differed with him. I think our mother would have left him long ago, but it... wasn't in her nature. She was trapped, in a way. I don't know—there was probably more to it than that. I suppose she loved him. I suppose that was part of why she stayed."

"Even so," Lannae said, "it does not sound pleasant."

"No, it wasn't. But the badgering, the derision, that wasn't really the worst of it."

"There was something worse."

"It was something more subtle, more pernicious. You need to

362

understand, Lannae, We grew up in high country, *desert* country. Isolated. There were no other families anywhere near. So we had nothing to compare ourselves to. So we didn't understand. We didn't know… what was missing."

"And what was missing?"

"What he didn't do. We didn't understand, until we were grown up. Till we had moved on with our lives. He wasn't… there. Emotionally. He was always around, physically. But we had no… emotional connection with him."

"Would you have wanted an emotional connection to someone who was so… unpleasant?"

I looked to Lannae, and she to me as we walked on.

"In all the years I've wrestled with this," I told her, "I don't think I've ever thought of it quite that way. But there was one thing I knew. I would never be the kind of father that my father had been." The path grew even steeper. My eyes raised up, beyond the rise ahead, up to the galaxy hanging above us. My eyes sought out the point on the spiral arm that, a lifetime ago, had been home. I thought of my girls. Girls fated to grow up, never knowing their father. Girls with the ultimately isolated father. Every unfolding circumstance of my existence conspired to make me more and more like Jeremy Boten.

"Do you think he disliked you, you and your sister?" Her question brought me back, across thousands of light years of intergalactic space. We reached a leveling in the road, and I paused to catch my breath.

"No," I conceded. "I don't think it was us. It was just him."

"Why do you suppose he was that way?"

I shook my head in silence; I could not voice an answer. I knew fragments, bits and pieces of what Jeremy Boten's childhood had been like. I knew that what little he had given to Abbey and me was more than he himself had been given. But to voice that would be like excusing him. And that was something I was not prepared to do. Lannae's hand tightened around mine. We spoke no more of Earth, and the life I had left behind.

"We are near the crest of the highlands," Lannae said. "I had all but given up hope, yet at this rate... we might reach Shelaemstet by the Crown of God Reversal."

"Reversal. This has to do with the Crown of God passing overhead," I said. "But why is it called 'Reversal'?"

She smiled. "Alex, I must apologize. Despite what you have told us, I still have it in my mind that you are merely from some distant province. I continue to assume that you understand things—things that I must remind myself you have never seen. Reversal is soon upon us. It refers to Dessene and Hon. You see that as they track the sky, they draw nearer to each other. When they are upon each other, they will reverse."

"Reverse? You mean, move backward?"

"No, not a reversal of direction. A reversal of... of roles. Of positions. For now, Hon is the swifter."

"But they will... reverse?" Looking up to the imperceptibly closing gap between them, I said to her in wonderment: "Cassini Dancers. Hon and Dessene—they're Cassini Dancers."

"Cassini...?" she echoed.

"Giovanni Cassini, a man who studied the stars long ago. The effect was named after him." I stopped, and used my toes to draw a circle in the dirt.

"Hon," I said, "travels about your world in a circle. Like this. At a set, very precise, speed. Dessene..." and here I scratched out a barely larger concentric circle, "...is ever so slightly farther out. And because of this, it moves ever so slightly slower. At its own very precise speed."

She nodded her understanding.

"But when they meet. Oh, Lannae, when they meet. They do not pass close enough to touch. But they come close enough to pull at each other. The faster, inner moon pulls the outer one inward, to the faster track."

Her eyes narrowed as she looked at me. "And the outer moon. It pulls the inner one? Pulls it outward?"

"To the slower, outer track. They do not simply reverse roles, reverse speeds. They reverse their places. Inner becomes outer, outer becomes inner. Your moons dance around each other at the time of reversal."

"It sounds," she said, "like a remarkably delicate thing."[4]

"It is," I told her. "Remarkably delicate. And remarkably rare. But Lannae, you called this a 'Crown of God' Reversal?"

"Reversals always occur when the Crown of God is directly overhead of the Mirran Stone. But the reversal itself, the crossing of Hon and Dessene, can occur anywhere along their path. Indeed, half of all reversals occur when the moons are out of our sight. But every twentieth reversal happens when Hon and Dessene are within the center of the Crown. It is a cause of special celebration. Or it would be, if the times were not so dire."

We came upon a tree, long-dead and fallen across the path. Any tree, living or dead, was a rarity in the highlands; little more than knee-high scrub was to be found. It looked to me as if it had died, and perhaps even fallen, long before the drought; rivulets left by the final rains had conformed themselves to the obstruction.

The hoof prints of Islak's horse told a story.

"Crazy old *goat*," I muttered, leading my horse over the obstruction.

"*Goat*?" Lannae echoed.

"He jumped it. At full gallop." I looked ahead. Then I called out, as if he might hear: "You've gained sight, not indestructibility." Turning back, I saw that Lannae and her horse had crossed the tree, but were not proceeding. She stood looking down at the log.

"Lannae?" She did not respond. Then she laughed. I led my horse back to her.

"The humor escapes me."

"Behold," she said, still looking at the tree, "the fall of the mighty Mennetek."

"It's… a tree."

Again she laughed. "Forgive me. There is a story. A riddle. A philosophical discussion. About a tree." Her eyes locked on mine. "You and Islak… on your way to the Adjunct… you passed through the groves of trees along the southern oil marsh, south of Ohlmont."

---

[4] See Appendix C

"Yes."

"It was among the oil workers that the question is said to have arisen. A worker is walking through the groves. A tall tree, weakened by age, collapses. It crashes near him, with a tremendous thundering noise." She paused, looking intently into my eyes.

"Very exciting," I said playfully.

She smiled, and nodded. "The next day, the worker decides not to walk through the grove. Disturbing memories, almost crushed, all that. But at the time he would have passed through, another tree collapses. It slams into the ground. But the man is not there. No one is there. So...." Here she paused again, looking at me askance.

"So... does it make a noise?" I suggested.

"Yes! Exactly! Does it make a noise?"

"*If a tree falls in the forest, and no one's there to hear it, does it make a sound?*" Her confusion over my English didn't dampen the excitement in her eyes. I translated it into Mirran. "It is a common philosophical question on Earth, as well."

Her smile widened. "Behold," she said again. "Mennetek's folly."

"I don't understand."

"Think of Mennetek's proposition," she prodded. "Transpose it. If lettered stones are pulled from a bag, and no intelligent being is there to read them...." She waited for me.

"Do they..." I declared cautiously, "...still spell 'tur'?"

"Precisely! They still are T-U-R, but do they spell 'tur'?"

I turned away from the tree, clearing the image of it, and the entire tree-falling-in-the-woods scenario, from my mind.

"The 'order' that Mennetek demonstrated, arising from the pouch of letters, is an illusion."

"The letters T-U-R," she affirmed, "are every bit as random as the ones that came before or after. They only have meaning if an intelligent being who has been taught their meaning is watching, is reading them. And even then, the meaning only exists inside that being. Not in the letters themselves."

"*Icing on the cake,*" I said. I turned to her. "I didn't even know what the letters meant, until he explained to me what a 'tur' was. If he had pulled..." and here I named off the Mirran letters for a hard 'C', a short 'A', and one of the letters they used for a 'T', "...it would not have meant '*cat*'. Not unless an earthman were there to see it, and interpret it as such.

"The 'order' that Mennetek demonstrated was not in the tiles he drew, but in the minds of himself and Anned Islak. And in your mind, once you were taught what a tur was."

"*Teleonomy*," I said. "*Teleology*. Information theory. Information does not spontaneously generate." I grabbed her by the shoulders and kissed her squarely on the mouth. I released her, instantly wondering how great of a transgression I had committed.

She read my eyes, read my concern over possibly violating a taboo; without allowing a moment to elapse, she said:

"Mr. Islak will now have to subject you to the Ritual of Pain."

For a few seconds, a few very long seconds, I was unsure how to read her.

"When I think of what a Ritual of Pain should entail," she said, "I'll let you know."

I took her hand and headed up the trail.

"Funny," I said. "Very funny. Some day I'll return the favor, trim a few years off of *your* life, as well."

As if she had not heard me, she said: "I look forward with relish to my next meeting with the estimable Mr. Mennetek."

"It sounds as if there is some history here."

"Arken Mennetek is a sort of project of mine," she conceded.

"Indeed?"

"I would not mind him nearly so much, if he really believed the poison he sometimes spews. But he does it as an amusement. He is... a bad influence... on those around him."

I understood her, understood whom she feared Mennetek was influencing. The reticence now creeping into her tone made sense. She would want to discuss it no further. When I had asked Captain Dollapan if there was someone in whom he could confide his doubts, he had told me: *There are two. They have sustained me thus far.* His wife, most likely, was one. But Lannae was certainly the other. She knew everything he was going through. And she knew who was, at least in part, responsible for it. I admired her concern, her protectiveness. More than that, I envied it. No, even more than envied it. I was truly jealous of it. I held tightly to her hand, as if the feelings, the mindset, might somehow spill through from her, into me. What must it be like, to feel for one's father what she felt for Abbik Dollapan?

*　　*　　*

Just past the crest of the pass, we found Islak tending a small fire beside the dwindling remains of a pond. He made no comment over how slowly we had closed the gap to reach him, nor about our hands, which had carelessly remained entwined until he had seen them.

As I lay trying to sleep, Lannae began singing, softly, to herself. The tune was one of the shanties I had heard long ago, on the Ammanon Deloré. I had heard it somewhere else, after the Deloré. Where had it been?

Drumae. Drumae had been singing the same song, when I emerged from my haze. I remembered the instrument I had thought of back then—the instrument that, in a dream, I had seen bent and distorted by the power of the shanty's tune. The instrument whose name I could not remember.

"*A clarinet,*" I declared aloud. Lannae's singing stopped. There was silence for a moment. "Nothing," I said in Mirran, as if in answer to an inquiry I expected would soon follow. "*Nothing,*" I whispered to myself, in forced English. It was hard to recall the word.

Lannae did not resume her song. In the silence, I tried to play out the Mozart clarinet piece in my head. I could not. The Mirran tonal scale had supplanted all traces of European octaves. Mozart, Bach, Vivaldi, they were all gone now, now and forever.

The only thing outside myself, beyond myself, that I had brought with me from Earth, had now been lost, as well. Not suddenly, not in some flash of quantum mechanical magic. No, it had been taken slowly, bit by bit, without my even seeing it slip away. Could I have retained the memory of earthly scales, and thus earthly music, had I focused on it, had I tried? Could I have kept the Sirocco within the golden measure, if I had turned the controls a little this way, or a little that? Could I be at home with Kathy—Ella at her feet, Maddy asleep in my lap—if just one of a hundred little details had played out differently?

"You know now, why you're here," Lannae said softly, perhaps so that Islak would not hear. When I did not reply, she spoke on: "It must have seemed to you that your being here might be an accident, a mistake of some kind. That the events that brought you here might all just be some tragic happenstance."

I digested the words for a while.

"No," I breathed. "I knew it was more than that. From the outset. It was the odds. The odds were just too great. They were... impossible."

Now it was she who took time to digest.

"But still," she ventured. "It must have been difficult, not to know the reason. To believe there was a reason, and not know what it was. Now you know."

Shifting myself, I tried to conform to the ground beneath me. I didn't know as much as she thought. I didn't know how the cross fit into this world—if it applied to Mirrus the way it applied to Earth. But she was right—I knew, at least in part, why I was here. In some way, the message of the cross needed to come to this world. I closed my eyes to the Crown of God above.

"Alex?"

I pretended not to hear. She waited.

"Alex? Have I misunderstood?"

"No. No, you've seen it all. Very clearly." I kept my eyes shut, as if they could hold in the thoughts. Was I the only one who could bring this message? Was there no one else on all the Earth who could? Was there no one, no one single, without children, or the prospect of children?

Lannae's next words took my breath away, and made me wonder if I had been thinking aloud:

"Do you think he was wrong?"

"What?" I said, regaining myself. But I knew what she had

369

meant. With a wisdom that shook me, she showed me gently that she knew I had understood:

"Do you think he was wrong?" Every element of her tone, inflection, and volume had been exactly repeated.

I opened my eyes, letting in the view from overhead but refusing to consider what it was. The enormous spiral was just a pattern of light to me.

"He is God," I said. "How can he be wrong?"

With a patience beyond my understanding, she waited. And, when the time was perfect, she delivered the knockout blow:

"Do you think he was wrong?"

I clenched my muscles, as if to keep myself from being washed away in the flood I felt all about me.

"Why are you doing this to me?" I asked her.

"It seems...." She paused to measure her words. "Something is missing. In your reaction to all of this." She waited, and I did not respond. "I believe you have been hurt, hurt beyond what I can comprehend, by what has happened. By what you have lost."

I lay motionless, staring and unseeing, like the focus of a med school anatomy class. I was being eviscerated.

"You know who he is," I said, as much to myself as to her. "And you know who we are." I drew a breath, and said the words: "There are some things..." I told her, "...that you just... don't... say."

The sky was afire. Dessene burned orange, as Hon burned yellow while closing the gap between them. But brightest of all was the massive Crown of God, filling the sky. I looked up at the display, seeing it, understanding it, until I could bear to see it no longer. Rolling onto my side, and then onto my stomach, I laid my face on the ground. With the smell of Mirran ground filling my senses, I fell asleep.

Book III
Chapter 6: At the Mirran Stone

Leaving the highlands, we followed a new route. Rather than north and east, which would lead us back to Ohlmont and a boat voyage to the Temple, we went north and west, skirting Drumae Degg's village, for a landward approach. With horses such as these, and all of us of sound body, the long route around the western lobe of the Great Lake would be the fastest. And time was imperative.

Along the way we encountered many couriers hastily making for the areas of Mirrus not yet served by Islak's communications towers. Most of these couriers raced past us, carrying their dispatches to certain distant parties. But two among the couriers carried general dispatches. The riders carrying these were obliged to stop, ever so briefly, to relay their news to every passerby. It was clear they had become versed in relaying the messages with speed. They rattled through them about as fast as one could cogently follow. Then, without pause for question or comment, they were off again.

The first dispatch said:
Invaders taken to horseback.
Sweeping west, approaching Eastern Highlands Pass.
Wanton destruction, death.
Towers being silenced.

The second added nothing of comfort:
Invaders descending from Eastern Highlands Pass.
Approaching Great Lake.

By the time we had encountered this latter message, we were only a few watches from Shelaemstet—if our horses would hold out. We were pushing them harder as we went, allowing them, and ourselves, less and less rest time.

371

To ward off a total collapse, we gave our horses one last brief rest before our final push to the Temple. After they drank from a shallow pool beside the road, they lay down at the water's edge. Lannae, Islak and I poured water over their heads—the standard treatment, Islak explained, to avert heat stroke.

"I've been thinking about these messages," I said. "About these dispatches."

"I'm certain none of us has thought of anything else," Islak observed.

"How many do you suppose have died?" I asked him.

"Hard to say," Islak said, wiping the water down his horse's neck. "At least dozens. It could easily be hundreds."

"Have your people ever faced death in such numbers?"

"There have been outbreaks of disease," Lannae suggested. "But nothing like this."

"Not like this," Islak echoed, "either in scope or... intent."

"Strange," I said. "The timing."

Islak sat at the pool's edge, his boots carelessly immersed in the muddy water. "Timing," he repeated.

"You'll have to excuse me," I told him. "As dire as the circumstances appear, I have the sense that we're going to survive this. Despite all the deaths so far, somehow I think we'll survive. And if we do, it leaves your people with... a situation."

"Indeed?"

"Your people have never faced such a willful outrage. They have never been so desperately and so damagingly violated."

"This," said Islak, "I will grant you."

"And this happens just as a message comes to you, whose central point is forgiveness."

I had both their attentions fully, now.

"What are you saying, Alex?" Lannae asked.

"There is so much more I need to explain, about what happened on Earth, and what it means. But one central thing is, that the forgiveness God bestowed upon his people, the forgiveness paid for by his death, demands that God's people forgive each other. That they forgive those who wrong them."

"And you would have us extend this forgiveness," Islak answered, "to these murderous thugs who even now descend upon the Temple?"

"It is not what *I* would have. It is what *God* would have. And yes. It must extend to them."

"So this message of forgiveness... it is the death of justice," Lannae said.

"It may sound that way," I told her, "the way I explained it. But no. My people, the people of Earth, have tended to make two opposite mistakes about this. First, that personal forgiveness can supplant societal justice. But that is the beginning of the death of society."

"And the second mistake?" Lannae asked.

"That society's justice, once enforced, is the greatest end. That it eliminates the need for personal forgiveness. And that is the beginning of the death of the soul."

Lannae sat and stroked her horse's mane.

"The death of the soul," she repeated.

"God himself told my people—he will not forgive us, if we do not forgive those who wrong us."

"But if hundreds have died," she said, "even tens of hundreds, how is that something we can forgive?"

"How is it something we can *not* forgive? If we cling to that anger, it destroys us like a poison." Even as I said it, I thought of my father. And it was then that the strangest sense of release hit me. I realized that I had decided many times, in my mind, that I would not hold him accountable for what he had been... and what he had not been. I had decided it, but I had never spoken it. And it now seemed pitifully obvious why my anger toward him kept resurfacing.

"But how is it possible to forgive," Lannae asked, still working over my last words, "when one is still living in the pain of a parent's murder? Or a spouse's? Or a child's?"

"Pain is a feeling," I told her. "Loss, at its essence, is a feeling. We cannot control feelings. God never told us to feel forgiveness toward someone. Forgiveness isn't a feeling. It is an act. A conscious, voluntary act. A decision," I said, looking away from her, and speaking more to myself, "a decision of the will."

Despite all the horror swirling about us, descending upon us, I was struck by an incongruous sense of peace. Although this was not the time, and was not the place, I knew I would need to speak some words to Jeremy Boten.

Without speaking, I prodded my horse up. The others followed suit, and we began the final leg of our race.

One thing that struck me as odd, at first, was that the cities and villages we passed, which had received these messages, showed no signs of evacuation. But I remembered that these were a people who had never known war. They were staying put. Maybe it was courage, maybe it was ignorance. Whatever you called it, they were ripe for slaughter.

This assault had been a long time in coming. As many times as I ran it over in my mind, I kept coming back to one thing. I hadn't caused it, but I had been dropped down into the middle of it. There had to be a reason. There had to be something I was supposed to do. As our horses thundered past the outer homes and businesses of Shelaemstet, my only thought, my only prayer, was to figure out what that something was.

Although no one was fleeing, the City was different. Many people were milling about. Each flash of news coming in to the tower fanned out by word of mouth. All functions of urban life had ground to a halt, as a kind of paralysis came over the whole of the city.

The crowds grew thicker, forming into knots, as we approached the Temple Complex. Our horses had to move slower and slower as the crowds grew denser. At last we abandoned the horses, along with our provisions, turning them over to the nearest persons at hand, so we could make our way on foot.

The Mirran Stone was awash with people, rising and descending, preparing themselves to visit the Temple. But by now the Temple was overfilled, and those waiting to enter were spilling out around the base of the Mirran Stone.

Near the base, constables and their deputies were trying to dissuade people from the climb, assuring them that the Temple itself was full. But those who doubted them, or who were willing to join

374

the impossibly huge crowd waiting, or who merely wanted to cleanse themselves in preparation for the disaster most believed was coming, pressed on and began their ascent.

With Lannae and Islak in tow, I moved forward. A constable laid his hand on my shoulder.

"The Temple is filled, the porticos are filled. Please, go to your home."

"My friend," I said, holding up my hand before him. "The Temple is not my destination."

The constable's eyes were fixed on my hand.

It then occurred to me to say a curious thing: "Turn no one away. Let everyone who will, come to cleanse themselves." We moved past him, and began to climb. I wondered about what I had said to him. Was I following an unspoken prompt from God? Or was I recklessly playing with these people's lives? A sounder command would have been 'Have everyone flee the city!', or even to have said nothing at all. But I had instructed them to gather at the most likely focus of attack. Even so, I never gave thought to rescinding my instruction.

As we neared the top the crowd grew denser until we were at a stop. I did not identify myself again. We waited until enough people had finished, that we had a chance to approach the pool. Due to the size of the crowd, the tradition of leaving one's shoes and foot wrappings by the twin torches had been abandoned; each kept their footwear beside themselves at the pool's edge.

Sitting at the edge, Lannae and Islak began removing their shoes.

"No," I said to them quietly, so no one else would hear. "Wait for me." Removing my shoes and wraps, I lowered my feet into the pool and washed them. When I had finished, I moved into the pool. The water came up to my knees. My standing in the pool caused a fair sensation—a mixture of shock, disgust, and confusion. An unpleasant murmuring moved through the crowd.

"Lannae. Give me your foot."

Flabbergasted, she complied. I removed her shoe, handing it to Islak. He was without words. I unwrapped her foot, handing him the wrapping as well, and lowered her foot into the water. I ran my hands over her skin, washing it, and then followed with her other foot. I remembered Jesus had washed his disciples' feet. I was sure that was why I was doing this now—either by the leave of God, or because I was clutching at any biblical reference I could spot. Part of me preferred to think it was my own idea rather than God's; as I recalled, Jesus washed the disciples' feet the night he was betrayed—just hours before his execution.

I had Islak hand Lannae her things, and I began washing his feet, as well. I became aware that all ceremonial washing around the pool had ceased. All attention was on us. Everyone was silent. My actions had drawn attention to my hands. Among those seated at the edge of the pool, and among those standing immediately behind them, no one was unaware that it was the man of five fingers kneeling in the pool.

"Alex," Islak said. "I do not understand this. But if it is to be done, shouldn't it be I who washes your feet?"

I smiled, without looking up at him. "Peter, Peter, Peter…" I said.

"What?" Islak said. "*Peter?*"

I laughed, and raised my gaze to meet his. "Nothing, my friend. Just know, that you have a gift for saying precisely the right thing, at precisely the right time."

"I see…" he said, obviously not seeing at all.

I had finished with his feet, and slapped him on the arm. "You remind me. We are all in the hands of God. Whatever will come, what better place to be?"

I waded boldly into the center of the pool—which, fortunately, was of uniform depth.

"Mirrans," I called out. "Blessed are you who come to cleanse yourself in the face of approaching danger. Continue to wash, and to make way for those who follow. Those of you with a destination, proceed there. But those who are here simply to cleanse, I ask you to stay."

With the help of a few dozen conscripts, Islak, Lannae and I managed to arrange the flow of people. After washing themselves, those who had no destination, those willing to stay, we seated on the steps, beginning from the top, and filling downward. On each of the four faces, we had them seat themselves to leave two pathways, one for people arising, and one for people descending. Those descending we directed to fill the space first between the descending and ascending columns, and then to fill the greater space on the other side of the descending column, until they reached the ascending column on the next side. In this way we continued to fill the Mirran Stone, row by row. It filled more slowly as the occupied steps reached lower and lower and the girth expanded, but even so, by the time it was filled halfway to the floor, it seemed clear that not all who wished to come would find a place.

For a time we stopped people at the upper edge, preventing them from moving into the crowd that filled the top square. Once enough people had finished and moved down, so that the perimeter of the pool was still filled, as was one ring of people waiting behind them, we again let people pass. But we only let a person or group enter once the same number exited; in this way we kept most of the top square clear, so we could move about.

The carriage that had borne the Judges away from the Adjunct finally arrived, pulling around the Mirran Stone, and stopping directly before the Temple Court. From atop the Stone I looked down, watching them emerge. They surveyed the situation—the general gathering in the Temple Complex, the filling rows of the Mirran Stone. They seemed to note even the figure atop the Stone looking down at them. I fancied that they guessed it was me. Regardless, they did not ascend, but went directly into the Temple Court building.

Turning, I saw that both Anned Islak and Lannae, on the far side of the top square, had stopped guiding and directing people. They stood hugging two men, while a third man stood by. Incredibly, as we stood here waiting for death to sweep down on us, a wave of jealousy tingled at me. I couldn't remember when I had felt so small, so petty. Moving around the pool, I walked toward them.

Islak leaned back from his embrace, and I could see the man whom he still held by the shoulders. Tall and lanky, with a nose that was unmistakable: Igren Doel. In that moment, I knew whom Lannae was embracing. I prepared myself for whatever manner of encounter I was about to have with Abbik Dollapan.

I approached them, but did not want to disturb them, and so stood silently nearby. As I waited, the third man circled around, and stood by my side.

"It is good to see that you are well," he said.

I turned to him. It was Opper Degg. I opened my mouth to speak to him, but could not find my words.

He raised his hand, as if to halt me from the effort. "Save your breath. There is nothing to be said to me. Prepare your words for the criminals bearing down on us. Have words to stop them."

Lannae turned from her father, looking to us.

Opper went on: "Your being here has come at great price, *Harbinger*." There was accusation in his emphasis. "Make sure that price has not been wasted." With that, Opper turned, descending the Mirran Stone without washing.

"Pray forgive him," said Ig Doel. "He has been distraught since the news of Andril's death. Of the circumstances." Igren's close-set eyes moved over me, as if he were seeing me for the first time, as if he were examining me.

"The circumstances," I repeated.

Captain Dollapan stepped away from his daughter. "Come, Alex Boten. Let us speak." Dollapan walked away, and I followed him— followed him as I had once long ago, aboard the Ammanon Deloré.

At a comfortable distance from our party, and from the lines of people entering and leaving the pool, he spoke: "There are several issues pressing upon my mind."

"If there is an issue you share with Opper Degg, perhaps we could start there."

"Very well then. You could enlighten me as to the circumstances under which Andril Degg was lost."

Puzzled, I proceeded to relate to him the events upon the Great Lake, skimming across aspects that I assumed would be of little interest, and focusing on those elements where Andril and I interacted. When I had finished, the Captain seemed to be still expecting something more.

"That," Dollapan said, after studying me, "is the extent of the events?"

"It is, sir. But it seems clear you were expecting something more."

Dollapan looked out to the south, to the distant Great Lake. "As the story traveled north, as it reached us, it was in a somewhat different form." He waited, as if hoping I would prod him on. I simply waited. "The story," he finally continued, "was that young Andril Degg had managed to reach the safety of his horse, and was headed for shore. But that he was drawn back out by calls of distress." Dollapan turned to me. "By your calls of distress. The story, as it was told to us, was that you claimed to be unable to remain afloat. That to convince Andril Degg to abandon the safety of his horse, you professed to him to be Harbinger. And that, unwilling to let the Harbinger perish, he relinquished his horse to you. That in this way, you reached the shore alive. And that he did not."

At first, I could not speak. "And... have you believed this version?" I asked at last. My tone was even and non-accusing, not so much from diplomacy, but more from shock. As he tried to answer, I could see in his eyes that—to whatever degree he had credited the story—he now no longer could. Not now that he faced me.

He looked down. "Consider my judgment tainted," Dollapan confessed, "by other issues."

"Speak them to me."

"First," the Captain said, regaining his normal forcefulness, "what plan have you in the face of the threat bearing down upon this place? And second, whatever that plan may be, why is my daughter so integral to it that you would have her stay here, at what seems to be the very focus of this invasion?"

"Captain, I speak to you in utter honesty. I have no plan. I long for a plan. I have struggled to formulate a plan. I have prayed fervently for a plan to be revealed to me. But I have none. None but to trust the God who brought me here." Now it was my turn to look out to the distant waters. "And as for your daughter's presence here, I can only say this. In this entire world, no two people wish her away from here, at some place of safety, more than her mother and yourself. But if there is a third who wishes it nearly so strongly, I would claim that person to be me. I would gladly sacrifice my safety

379

to ensure hers." I turned to him. "However, Captain Dollapan, you know your daughter. Do you think there is anything I could say that would persuade her to leave this place?"

Captain Dollapan struggled with his next words, trying twice to begin to speak. The third time he managed to say it: "If you love her, Alexander Boten, you will find the words needed to make her leave."

Apparently, Islak's assessment of Lannae's letters to her father was not far from the mark.

"Forgive me, sir," I said. "But *you* love your daughter."

Dollapan looked to me.

"If I were not in this mix," I said. "If it were just she and you here in this place, in the face of what we fear is coming, and if you refused to leave, would you be able to find the words to make her leave?"

Dollapan snorted, and looked down to the crowds packing tighter around the base of the Mirran Stone.

"You have come to know my daughter well, Alex Boten."

"Yes, to know her very well, sir. To know her, and to love her."

"You will not leave this place?" Dollapan asked.

"That is correct."

"Then," said the Captain, "she will not leave. And therefore, I will not leave."

"You were at my side," I observed, "almost upon my very arrival on this world. It is good to have you here now."

"We have much to discuss," he said, "about my daughter. But know this: If we survive to have that discussion, I may be able to accept whatever conclusion that discussion comes to."

"Indeed," I said, incredulously. "From... things I have heard, I would not have expected that."

"I was against your involvement with Lannae," he admitted. "Bitterly against it, I confess. We corresponded regarding it, and with each letter I grew more set against you. But there was one letter. The last one she sent. The one she sent before you left the Degg farm." Here he reached up and fingered his lapel. I had the feeling it was an involuntary and unconscious gesture. I suspected he carried the letter still—carried it in a breast pocket.

"And something in this letter," I suggested, "swayed you?"

"Swayed me?" he said. "Melted me, Mr. Boten. You may think me a stern father, an overprotective father. But at the heart of all things, I love my daughter. I would not have her stumble into heartache. But neither would I stay her from her true course, and give her heartache by my stubbornness."

"I should like," I said, "to see this letter. If it is not too personal."

"Survive what lies ahead of us," the Captain offered, "and perhaps you shall see it."

I felt something I had not felt in a long time—a relationship with Abbik Dollapan that I had felt blossoming aboard the Ammanon Deloré. It was something I had not felt since I had first met his daughter, and since he had seen me reach out to take her hand in mine.

A voice broke my musings: "Reversal!"

All eyes lifted to the center of the Crown of God, where Hon's pursuit of Dessene had nearly reached its climax. It had begun to eclipse its orange twin.

"A Crown of God reversal," Dollapan said in wonderment, "and we had almost not noticed it."

"These are distracting times," I said, gazing up with him. As Hon crept forward across the face of Dessene, it began to accelerate. It quickly cleared the orange disc, and then paused as if hovering before it, just as Lannae had said it would. And, as it slowed, Dessene itself moved forward faster until it began to eclipse the yellow face of Hon. After finishing its journey across the front of Hon, Dessene continued as the faster moon, while Hon lagged behind it, now as the slower. So the dance continued, as it had for untold generations. As it would for untold generations more. Nothing in the world before, neither life nor death, neither peace nor slaughter, had the power to change it.

I excused myself from the Captain, wandering to an open, private area of the square. There I prayed. I prayed more desperately, more earnestly, than I had ever prayed before. And from this, I came away more alone, more desolate, than I had ever felt. No prayer I could issue, it seemed, would dissuade God of the course he had set before us—a course destined to play itself out as surely as the clockwork heavens moving above us.

As I wandered back to Islak, he came forward to meet me.

"Ig and the Captain," he said, "have been helping us direct the flow. The steps of the Mirran Stone are filled. The people who wish to stay are sitting on the ground now, forming a widening circle around the base. But the flow of people coming up has slowed. Soon everyone who wishes to be cleansed will have done so."

"Then," I said tentatively, "it appears we'll be... ready. For whatever awaits us."

"Some of us are always ready," Islak said. "It's Ig. No bottle of acid this time, but he's come here ready to die. I tell you, Alex, I don't know when I shall die, but when the time comes, I'll wager Igren Doel will be at my side facing it with me."

"I can't tell you," I said, "just what a comfort that is."

"Come, Alex," Islak said, slapping my back. "You yourself have said it. We are in the hands of God."

I made a confession to him. "Perhaps it is wrong of me, but I find myself longing for this to be done. For good or ill, I wish it were done."

"Then," said Islak, looking beyond me, "turn the eyes God has restored to you, out to the Great Lake."

As I looked out across the distant waters, a murmuring arose among those lining the upper steps of the Stone. To the south and east, there were three lights, closely spaced, upon the waters.

Like a wave, word spread downward to those too low on the Stone to yet see the lights.

Lannae stepped beside me, as Islak withdrew. "I have not wished to disturb you," she said.

"Don't think of yourself as a disturbance," I told her. "What is it?"

"I want you to tell me this will work out. That we will survive."

"I believe we will survive."

"God has not spoken to me," she observed, "nor to anyone else of whom I have inquired. Has he spoken to you?"

I did not answer her.

"I know," she said, "that the decision is not yours to make, as to how and when God will speak to his people. So I say this, not in any effort to put pressure upon you...."

"...however..." I filled in for her.

"However, now would be an excellent time for God to speak."

Islak rushed up to us. "The Judges," he said. "They are ascending."

Together, the three of us approached the face of the Stone that adjoined the Temple Court. Near the bottom, moving upward with the rest of the citizenry, was the single-file cluster of six men in judicial robes.

"I should meet them alone," I said. Lannae and Islak moved off, and resumed guiding traffic and aiding people in the washing. It took a long time for the Judges to ascend, affording me much time to decide what to say. I had time to think over my lack of defensive plans, my non-existent evacuation plans for the city, my fantasies of how I would call God down upon these marauders when they landed. I had time to remind myself I had no plans whatsoever—to remind myself, when they asked how I was protecting the people, that I was laying them bare to destruction. Whatever they would say against me, I would have no argument. Any charge they cared to level against me would be true.

As they drew nearer, I saw that they were ascending the Stone in the same way they were always seated—in order of seniority. That meant I would meet Raddem first. *Better than Usettet or Buelle*, I thought to myself.

The three lights upon the Great Lake had resolved into three ships, laboriously rowing towards us. The regular rowers? I wondered. Or had they been slaughtered as well, leaving the attackers to man the oars? And had they brought their horses across? Or would their final triumphant march into the heart of their enemy be done on foot? I looked across all the people milling between the Mirran Stone and the docks. I wanted to order them to clear a path. *Not yet. Not yet.* If anyone asked why, what would I tell them? What could I tell them? What reason could I offer for delaying? *Not yet.*

Raddem reached the top, and I braced myself. He walked past me, as if I weren't there. Buelle and Poznanek followed him. They went to the pool. They had come to wash. Usettet passed me. Not, I thought, as if I weren't there. But rather as if I were a ghost, some presence he could sense, but with which he was fated not to interact. Lode passed, and Platius. I moved to the pool's edge, where Raddem was finishing.

"Don't you have," I asked quietly, "anything to say to me?"

"Do you have," asked Raddem, without looking up, "anything to say to us?"

He stood up and moved to the edge of the top square. One by one, the other Judges came to stand with him. Letting others descend before them, they waited until the last of their group had joined them. Raddem spoke, either to me or to himself, while staring out at the Great Lake: "All the condemned that were set adrift, throughout the years. This... this is the Historical Inevitability I should have foreseen." Then they descended together.

I had thought that Usettet treated me like a ghost. Now it seemed to me that they were the ghosts, men who had already died, merely waiting for circumstances to catch up with them. At the base of the Stone, they had a small knot of citizens shift places. They stationed themselves between the upward pathway and the downward pathway, in a single row facing away from the Stone, facing the docks.

They were the current inheritors of the office of Judgeship, the lawful heirs of those who had condemned the invaders. They stood before the Stone, prepared to die.

The ships had drawn close enough to see some detail. Their brightness was due to fire. Torches, not oil-burning lanterns, were carried by all who crowded the decks. It made sense, I thought. These are people who lived in eternal burning daylight. They would not have put their technical sophistication into developing lanterns. On the rare cases when they needed light, a crude torch would do.

Could that be our answer, I wondered? Might a carelessly tended torch ignite their boats? Destroying them before they reached the shore? I was getting desperate; they had safely made it across the expanse of the Great Lake. And now I was counting on three separate simultaneous accidents? On three separate ships? At least it would have the unmistakable imprint of divine intervention. The boats were approaching the docks.

I turned to see Lannae and Abbik Dollapan behind me. Flanking them were Islak and Ig Doel.

My eyes met the Captain's.

"This is your last chance to flee," I said to him. "For your sake, for Lannae's… take it."

"My daughter," he said, "has explained much to me, about what has happened. Things I knew nothing of. You are the Harbinger of God. I will stand at your side. If that leaves no one to force my daughter away, then so be it. She is nearly an adult. I leave her to make her own decision."

I could not bring myself to look to Lannae; I felt too much guilt over not having forced her to leave earlier, and over not wanting her to leave now.

I looked to Islak.

"Don't ask it of me, Alexander Boten," he said. "I've been along for too much of the ride to jump this ship now. These eyes you've given sight to? They need to see how this ends."

I looked to Ig Doel, who smiled at me wryly. "Don't expect me to go anywhere. I'm just looking for a little excitement. I *came* here expecting to die. It just seems like every time I plan an exit party, God has some other plans."

"No little bottle, this time?" I asked.

His narrow-set eyes shifted away.

"Know about that, do you? No, no little bottles this time." His attention seemed to fix behind me. "No need for one, I should say."

I turned. The ships had docked.

"Our doom should be swift enough," Ig said, "that it need not be prodded."

The exact goings-on at the distant docks were blocked by the surrounding buildings, but an outflow of people leaving the area was clear. The whole dock area grew brighter. Presently we saw why.

The ships were burning. The attacking soldiers had set fire to them. Clearly, they had no intention of retreating, or of even departing. This was to be their capitol, the focal point of their new dynasty.

Flames crept up the unused masts of two of the ships. The third would surely join it soon.

From the steps below me, someone called out. Through the buildings near the docks, a procession could be seen. Carrying torches, they were advancing on us. A few on horses, most on foot, they moved slowly now. This was not the lightning advance of an army slicing across open terrain. This was a victory march. Most of their horses they had abandoned on the far shore, before capturing the barges. Those they brought across, they brought across for show.

As they advanced, the citizens around them shrank away. But the body of attackers was approaching the periphery of those who had gathered at the Mirran Stone. Those people, I surmised, would not move. Or at least, not so quickly. Even at this distance, I could see the flash of broadsword metal reflecting their torches. What would happen soon would be unspeakable. The stories we had heard relayed by the communications towers were about to be played out before us.

My hands shot up into the air. "Mirrans!" I yelled. The murmuring around me ceased, and the silence spread out like a wave. All eyes turned to me. At least I finally had a sense of something to do. "Make a path!" I yelled, moving my arms apart. From the base of the Mirran Stone that faced the docks, and proceeding outward, the Mirrans moved to either side, forming a wide, open pathway. I felt like Moses, parting the Red Sea. It was a comforting image; one, at least, that didn't suggest my impending death. I tried to imagine these invaders proceeding forward, and then the Mirrans crashing in on them like the sea that had swallowed up the Egyptian pharaoh. Ridiculous. These people could not form an attack, no matter how propitious the circumstances. It wasn't a matter of courage. Attack simply was not in their nature.

The invading army had drawn near enough that I could make out some details. They wore armor—what I assumed was metal, but later learned was layer upon layer of tanned leather. They wore headgear. At first it seemed some kind of helmet. But as they drew nearer, I saw that they had fashioned them from huge animal skulls. To the outside of their leather armor, on their legs and arms, they had attached long bones. Perhaps human, perhaps animal. Whether these were meant to afford protection, or to inspire fear, I could not say. I saw no signs of bows, but all carried swords or spears. Many carried both. None of them, I noted, carried a shield. Odd, for people equipped with swords and spears. I later learned they had come equipped with shields. But after their first few encounters with the Mirrans, they decided defenses were not needed. In order to travel more lightly and quickly, they had discarded their shields.

They entered the opening in the crowd. There they paused. Looking around, they seemed uncertain. I knew they were seasoned by battles back in their homeland; it was obvious from everything about them—their dress, their weapons, even how they carried themselves. And it was clear they had never faced an enemy so passive, so submissive. They feared a trap. But the easy slaughters they had enjoyed between the coast and here were persuasive enough. A single horseman proceeded. The other horsemen and foot soldiers fell in around him. The advance continued, with the soldiers brandishing their blades, swinging them threateningly to ensure the Mirrans stayed back.

Not all of them wore headgear. On those without helmets, we could see that they had shaved themselves bald.

Lannae moved up behind me on my left. I felt her right hand taking my left. My fingers closed around hers. So much still unsaid, I thought. I felt Captain Dollapan's hand upon my right shoulder. It had taken a long, long journey to find a father. At least I would enjoy him for a few minutes. Looking up, I saw Dessene leading Hon away from the glowing center of the Crown. At times, I had thought of it as the Crown of God; at times I had thought of it as the galaxy. Now, it was just the Crown of God. I looked to where Earth was. I didn't imagine the Earth, orbiting the sun. I just saw stars. Just more jewels in the Crown.

"Alright," I said aloud, though not intentionally loud enough for those around me to hear. "I'm here. I'm where you want me to be. Speak to your people. Will you speak to your people? Tell us what to do."

Later, much later, in looking back on things, it occurred to me that the word "us" was so very interesting. I was no longer a creature of Earth. I was Mirran.

I heard: "I have planted my people in the shelter of darkness."

A shudder played along my bones, as if moving through my body in waves. I looked around. Behind me, those standing with me were transfixed on the approaching force.

I thought of the voices of each of them, of Abbik, and Anned, even Ig Doel, comparing them to what I had just heard. But what was there to compare to? The modulation, the tone, the accent—they all faded in my memory. I could not remember the sound of what I had heard, only the meaning. *Have planted my people... in shelter of darkness.*

Two logical alternatives presented themselves. One was that I had progressed from hysterical blindness to an advanced dementia. But the other. The other.

My eyes locked on the bright torches the approaching soldiers carried.

"Shelter of darkness..." I said.

Lannae leaned forward. "What?"

"The shelter of darkness," I said, louder. My eyes moved away from the soldiers, across the wary crowd, to the homes and businesses surrounding the Temple Complex. To the lights.

My hand tightened on Lannae's. "There is shelter in darkness." Releasing her hand, I stepped ahead. I stepped to the very edge of the top square.

"Mirrans!" I shouted. Even the invading soldiers stopped. "Put... out... all... lights!"

Everything within the sound of my voice came to a halt. I thought over my diction, my pronunciation. Had I spoken in Mirran, or English? Mirran, I was sure. But the command itself was so bizarre.

"Now!" I screamed. The crowd began to writhe. Those nearest to streetlamps extinguished them. Those outside of buildings went in, and lights began to go out. The invading army stood, looking about themselves as lights went out. They would have suspected a trap, except for the absurdity of it. Their own torches burned far brighter than the extinguishing Mirran lamps. And the star display above was almost as bright as their own torches. The lights now being put out were trivial.

"The basins," said Ig Doel. "The oil basins." He was pointing to the huge twin basins on opposite sides of the pool, burning brightly.

"Can we put them out?" I asked.

"There is no provision for it. They burn always. Keepers replenish the oil, and they never go out."

"They go out now. Think of something." I turned back to the invaders. A new sound was reaching me. I did not recognize it at first. It was laughter. They resumed their march. Looking behind me, I saw my friends and those along the top rows converging on the basins, trying to use their coats to douse or at least disperse the flames. It seemed a losing proposition. The flames rising from the basins resisted them, dancing amidst their flailing cloaks. And dancing in the wind.

My head snapped around, looking out across the city. A wind was growing. I could see it moving in swaths across the Great Lake. The invaders seemed to ignore it. Wind was certainly no new phenomenon to them. But wind, an inland wind, had not been known to the Mirrans since the Great Lake had ceased its churning. Looking again to the waters, I watched the wind buffeting the surface, drawing patterns across its smoothness. The water was not churning. The wind was from elsewhere.

A new sound reached my ears, displacing the invaders' laughter, which now fell away. The new sound was a deep rumbling, like a freight train. Had I been on Earth, I would have suspected a tornado. Then, across the Great Lake, I saw the source of the rumbling rolling in. A blast of wind unlike what was now sweeping us. Unlike, I suspected, anything the Mirrans had experienced. I saw it raise whitecaps on the lake as it powered toward us.

"Hold on! I yelled. I pulled Lannae down to the stone floor. At the docks, the blast hit like a hurricane. Debris flew up in a cloud. The burning ships extinguished like matches being blown out with barely a thought. The leading edge of the gust was bearing down on us. I looked to the north side. A distant roiling cloud of dust greeted me. I looked in all directions. On all sides, powerful winds were simultaneously headed for us. Two words flashed through my mind. *Absolutely impossible.*

"Hold on tightly," I told Lannae.

"What is it?"

"We're going to survive the invasion," I told her confidently.

"How? What's going to happen?"

I laughed. "I haven't a clue."

When the blast hit, it was perhaps easiest on those of us at the top of the Mirran Stone. We were hit from all directions at once, and so we were blown in no direction in particular. The eddies and gusts were sharp, but we stayed put. The twin basins were blown out in a flash. Water and oil were sprayed all about us, but the oil was extinguished almost the moment it hit us. No one was burned. Those seated on the steps of the Stone were hit by the blasts but had nowhere to go; the wind simply pressed them back against the steps. Those on the flat below were almost all knocked over, as were the horsemen and many of the foot soldiers. Most of their torches were extinguished, and although the Crown of God still yielded plenty of light, they desperately passed around the surviving torches to relight those that had gone out.

Pulling myself up to my feet, I watched them nervously working. Their swords were still deadly, but they seemed far less ominous now. I was so fixed on them, that it was up to Islak to point my attention to the sky. The same wind that had swept along the ground was now clearly at work aloft. Low banks of clouds were tumbling in towards us, north, south, east and west. They seemed to be sliding across the top of an inversion layer, like an avalanche sliding down a mountain. But in this case, all mountains converged on one point. I tried to imagine what would happen when it all met. There was no atmospheric standard to compare it to; I had never heard of such a phenomenon. But when two fronts met, collided….

Looking up, I watched the incoming clouds encroach upon the edges of the Crown of God. The main remaining source of light dimmed as the clouds covered more and more of it.

A sheltering darkness began to cover us.

The invaders' nervousness shifted to outright panic as they watched the source of light being swallowed up in clouds. Most had relit their torches by now, but the few who had not began fighting for access to the flames.

The Mirrans around them had gotten back to their feet now, and watched them in wonderment.

The Crown of God still shone through the translucent blanket of clouds, but as the clouds met above the city, it was not hard to imagine what took place above us. The wet air continued to flow in from all directions. With the inversion layer below, there was no place to go, except up. An enormous thunderhead formed. And as it piled both taller and wider, the clouds grew more opaque. Soon even the brilliant center of the Crown was obliterated. No light from above reached us. In all directions, at least as far as my voice had reached, there were now only two sources of light: The invaders' torches, and the first flashes of lightning above us.

I had no way of knowing whether these people had lightning on their lit half of this globe. I deduced they did, for the lightning itself did not seem to frighten them. Not at first. Not until the rain came. It poured abruptly in a deluge, nearly forcing me to my knees. The pool of the Mirran Stone, always kept nearly full, was almost at once overflowing. The water, pouring across the top square, cascaded down the Stone on all four sides. The downpour lasted less than a dozen rounds, and stopped as abruptly as it had begun.

The torches had been extinguished, to the last one. I could see nothing. But from listening to my friends, it was clear that some light was still available to their well-tuned eyes. I had imagined my own eyes to have adapted to the perpetual Mirran night as well as theirs had. I was wrong. Generations of breeding had brought forth sensitivities beyond my capabilities. But my ears functioned as well as theirs. From below, there was a sound of panic.

"They're blinded," the Captain said. "They're helpless!"

A flash of lightning gave me a moment of vision, and then another. In those snatches of sight, I saw the Mirrans moving in amongst their enemies. I badly misperceived what was unfolding. The Mirrans did, in fact, press in upon the invaders. In what I took to be a completion of the Exodus scenario I had toyed with earlier, it seemed the Mirrans were attacking them. I was simultaneously thrilled and repulsed by the idea. It seemed just, it seemed fitting, and, for the Mirrans, it seemed entirely wrong.

Ultimately I confessed to no one other than Lannae that this was what I had thought was happening, for when I learned the truth, it shamed me to realize how badly I had misread the situation. The Mirran citizens of Shelaemstet had fallen in upon their attackers, and seized hold of them, not to destroy them, but to protect them. The Mirrans had wrestled from them the broadswords and spears, for in their panic, the invaders had begun blindly lunging at each other. Eventually the Mirrans dispersed them, holding them as captives in a manner more like accommodating unexpected guests. Each was kept separate from the others, and in the company of at least three or four Mirrans. Lights came on inside homes so the strangers could be calmed. But the outdoor lights were kept unlit, lest any of them be tempted to move about and meet up with their fellows.

Overhead, the clouds stood as silent guards, shielding the greatest light of all, the Crown of God, as we worked to formulate a plan.

The language of the Shah-Tek, as we learned they called themselves, had dialectically diverged from the Mirrans' language, to the point where neither could understand the other. But Islak, Ig Doel, Captain Dollapan and I had had some extensive experience in bridging language gaps. In time we were able to communicate.

The picture that emerged was not a pleasant one. The Shah-Tek had been intimidated by what had happened, but they had in no way been softened by the kindness shown to them. The ruthlessness they had shown on their drive westward was only in part due to an ancestral hatred of the Mirrans for having exiled their forefathers. In larger part, it was simply their way.

In the end, it was negotiated that they would be brought, disarmed, to the coastal towns where they had landed. They agreed that they would, upon arriving there, convince those manning their ships that the invasion had ended, and that they would return to their own hemisphere, unescorted, free, as a gesture of good will.

The Mirrans, some time thereafter, would send a delegation to discuss some form of relations, or at least to try to forge some non-aggression pact.

Whether the Shah-Tek would return all the way home, or turn and attack again, was anyone's guess. What manner of reception a Mirran delegation would receive was even more problematic. But one thing worked for us. The being that the Mirrans called *the God Who Is Silent* had proven himself a staunch defender of his people, stronger than the string of gods the warriors relied upon. That was something to build upon. In the end, I realized, it was the only thing to build upon.

Book III
Chapter 7: Aftermath

In the wake of the invasion, and the Shah-Tek's collapse, the Temple and the Mirran Stone were swarming with visitors giving thanks to God. And so, although the Temple and the Stone both seemed logical places to conduct the business still before me, they were impractical. On horseback I went beyond the bustle of the city, and found a quiet stretch of wilderness. Dismounting, I left the horse unsecured, and walked some distance away. Looking up, I found the place within the Crown that I fancied to be Earth.

"Jeremy Boten," I said aloud, for I knew I had to speak it, not just think it. I imagined what it would be like, to finish the words. To say it at last and be done with it. I wondered what manner of sensation I would feel. That wasn't the reason I was out here, that wasn't the reason I was going to say it. But I couldn't help wondering, nonetheless.

"I'm sorry," I said, "that I never did this when I was with you. When you could hear it. Maybe you wouldn't have been able to receive it. Maybe that's why I'm only saying it now. But I am saying it. Jeremy Boten, I forgive you. For the things you did. For the things you didn't do. For the things that you weren't, when we needed you to be."

I breathed in deeply. I exhaled. I felt not the slightest bit different. And then I laughed, and headed back to my horse. I realized that what I had come here to do, I had already done. Beside that shallow pool outside Shelaemstet, when I was explaining forgiveness to Lannae Dollapan and Anned Islak, at the moment I knew I would forgive my father, that was the moment that I *had* forgiven him. The words spoken here had value, I knew as I approached my horse. But I had already been released, back then. It was finished.

Still a distance from my horse, I spotted something I had missed on my way out—a bird, a dead catrille, laying on the ground.

I knelt to examine it. It bore no evidence of any obvious cause of death. But its wing—its right wing—had been broken.

The chances that this was the same bird I had held at Drumae's farm were minuscule, laughable even. But I found nothing to laugh at as I stroked its still-warm form. A random, chance encounter? A happenstance without meaning? Or some bizarre and indecipherable sign from the hand of God?

Laying the bird down, I stood and shook off the thought. I resumed my walk back to the horse. That I was within God's will had been irrefutably shown atop the Mirran Stone. I would need something far more direct and clear to dissuade me of that.

It was later—far, far later—when the truth of the encounter broke over me. Years ago, I had cursed God, cursed him bitterly, when my effort to save a bird's life had failed. A lifetime later and light-years away, in the empty expanses outside Shelaemstet, I had been given another chance. A chance to repeat my folly, and to rail against God as death's agent. Or to accept the coming of unpleasantness, and to trust that whatever I had lost, or might still lose, God was with me even here.

And, in between the extremes of those reactions, there was the realm of relationship that Jeremy Boten had so thoroughly corrupted. There were lessons to be learned—that a loving father can receive questions, even questions born of pain and doubt. There would still be more for me to learn, and more to forgive Jeremy Boten for than I even understood as of yet.

*　　　*　　　*

As arrangements were being made to march the invading force—disarmed, and in small bands—toward their ships off Mej Moribor, Captain Abbik Dollapan delivered to me the letter of which we had spoken earlier, the letter Lannae had written to him as we had prepared to leave Drumae Degg's farm. He gave it to me, along with the assurance that he had Lannae's blessing to deliver it to me.

Beloved Father, Giver of Life, Protector, Guardian of My

Heart:

I hope that being in the company of one such as Anned Islak has had the effect for which you had hoped. For yes, dear Father, I do perceive this was the reason that you pressed the Shocktele Shipyards to accept Mr. Islak's charter, despite their better judgment concerning all of that charter's curious provisos and secrets. The directorate of Shocktele is satisfied with the charter's results; if the charter achieved for you what you had hoped, then the directorate is well pleased in all regards.

Yet even if Islak's confidence in the workings of God has not taken root with you, I trust that, in time, the hand of God will draw you back to him, if you will but wait for him. Remember always, what was written long ago:

> *If we abandon him, he will abandon us.*
>
> *But if we become faithless, he will remain yet faithful:*
>
> *God cannot reject himself.*

The coming of doubt does not mean you are any less the possession of the living God.

But regardless of your current estate, know that I will follow the God of our ancestors, the God of whom you taught me, with an unwavering steadiness. Yet even as I do this, understand I may not do so in the same way as you. Much has transpired here, and I sense much is yet to unfold, but even as things now stand, know this: I believe this man, Alexander Boten, to be the Harbinger of God, perhaps even, as rumored, Restoration himself. To follow the will of God, the God whom you taught me to believe and follow, is to follow whatever path God sets before us—even if it is a new path, a path hitherto undreamt of. I pray that you will follow me on this path. But even if not, please reconcile yourself that it is a path I must follow, if I am to be true to God.

This brings me to a far harder issue, one treading upon matters not easily discussed.

As I have said, and as you have so eloquently reminded me, I am truly not yet of adult age. But we are both aware that that point is not far off. As you know there is a matter that has for some time, even before the Deloré's last voyage, been troubling me. And as my father, I know it has thus troubled you as well.

Although it is with joy I have taken the reins of your business concerns, nonetheless the very nature of these business endeavors has meant that my range of contacts has been limited. Mostly the contact I have enjoyed with boys and young men has been either with sailors—be they deck hands or officers—or workers of the port. All of these lead transient lives, lives filled with travel— travel which is ill suited for any female, minor or adult.

The prospect has seemed that with whomever I would develop a relationship, I would, at great lengths, be separated from him. This has been a burdensome prospect, lightened only by the thought that it might be a relationship of such devotion, and such passion, as shared by yourself and Mother.

Although these words will be hard to hear, understand that I have felt the stirring of such passion, not for the Harbinger of God, not for Restoration, but for the man Alex Boten. I plead with you to try to come to know him, not only as a figure sent from God, and not as some creature from off the Mirran sphere, but also as I have come to know him—a man of extraordinary courage and resolve, who has faced incredible tragedy and yet remained true to God, perhaps even truer to God, through it.

This is a man who seems fated to travel much, but whose journeys it seems likely I will be able to share.

If it seems to you there is a chance that he and I might share but half the joy that you and Mother have felt, I pray you not dismiss him out of hand. Rather consider him thoughtfully and prayerfully as to whether you deem him worthy of me.

Events are falling upon us with great speed. I should vastly prefer to extend you the right as my father of responding to these pleadings, before taking the matter any further. However, Alex, Anned Islak, and I leave even now for the Temple Adjunct. Whether we shall linger there or move on at once I do not know. If we move on, our next destination is unknown. And the questions within me burn beyond my ability to contain them.

Forgive me, Father, but I must inquire of him whether my sense, and yours, is correct: Whether he feels the same things toward me.

There are issues he and I must confront. Some are known to you, some are not. But if he feels for me what I feel for him, if he is willing to commit to me as I am willing to commit to him, and if you and Mother would be willing to accept him into the House of Dollapan, I am confident they are all issues we can surmount.

I remain, now as always,
Your Lannae

Abbik Dollapan and I shared a private meal after the last of the warriors had been led out of Shelaemstet, for the long journey back to the coast, and their ships. We did not speak of the letter. There was no need. He had made his reaction to it, and to me, clear when we had stood atop the Mirran Stone.

"Tell me, Harbinger of God," the Captain said, "have you come to peace with the course your life has taken?"

"Excuse me?" I said.

"It is something you once said to me. A lifetime ago, halfway around the world. As we leaned upon the forward rail of the Ammanon Deloré, you said that 'the Harbinger of God' was not what you were meant to be. That it was not what you had planned, for your life."

I leaned back from the table, and let my mind drift back, far back.

"I remember that," I said, distantly. Then, popping forward in my seat, I added: "And I would not tell you what I *was* meant to be. What I *had* planned for my life. I was afraid to tell you, then."

"And now?"

I leaned back again. "By now, you know everything. You know where I come from. I was, as the Temple Judges dubbed me, a traveler. A traveler of the empty space between planets. An explorer. At least, that's what I wanted to be."

"Wanted to be?" Dollapan inquired.

I finished the last of the drink in my glass, then refilled both mine and the Captain's. "It was a failed dream. You see, the competition was intense. I never quite made the grade. I didn't qualify."

"I don't understand. You came here."

I smiled. "A mistake, my dear Captain. An outrageous mistake."

Now the Captain leaned back in his chair.

"So," Captain Dollapan said. "If I understand this…. You were not supposed to go anywhere. Yet by this, as you say, outrageous mistake, you have traveled between planets. You have come here—a place none of your people have ever seen, or dreamed of. And now we are planning to set sail to a land, or lands, unknown even to those of us who have lived here all our lives."

I raised my glass to him. "Point conceded," I said. "And dream realized. I am an explorer."

"That you are," Dollapan agreed. "But more importantly, for us at least, you are the Harbinger."

"Which," I added, "interestingly enough, I would not have been—had things gone the way I hoped."

"Alex?"

"If I had scored the extra fraction of a point… if I had made the grade… if I had been chosen for the mission seat… I would not be here. The Hermes project was never meant to be aimed at a place as far from Earth as this."

"Indeed?"

"The hope was that, after years of extending jumps, Hermes might reach the half-dozen stars nearest to Earth. And I would think that if, after maybe a few hundreds of years, we used it to reach systems as far away as this, this would not be the system we would have aimed at."

"Really?" asked the Captain playfully. "Should I be offended? Are we lacking, somehow?"

"You're in the wrong place. Orbiting an isolated star, far beyond the galactic plane. If we even spotted your star, it is not one we would have targeted."

"This 'outrageous mistake', my dear Alex, sounds almost like an act of... providence?"

Providence. The word settled on me like dust.

I had been viewing my life like a pair of scales. On one side, everything I had lost: My wife, my children, my sister, my life as I knew it. Balancing that, the things I had found on Mirrus: Lannae, and her father, possibilities of the new life unfolding before me. Even the office of Harbinger, now that I had come to accept it, hadn't seemed enough to outweigh the losses.

But there was that word. And if it did settle like dust, then it settled far more heavily on the Mirran side. Heavily enough, I realized now, to tip those scales, ever so slightly.

"Providence it is," I conceded. "Providence has defined me. Explorer. Harbinger. Restoration? I guess we'll see on that one." The one title for which the Mirrans had no word was the one I remained the most uncomfortable with: Missionary. "We can try to chart our courses," I observed. "But the wind... the wind blows where it will."

"Both wind and wave," Captain Dollapan added.

"Waves..." I said, as the phrase struck the memory the Captain had intended. "The mind of man is a wave on the waters, changing course...."

"'The mind of man is like a wave upon the waters; / It changes course for reasons it does not understand.' Your memory is sharp, Harbinger."

"Sharp enough," I told him, "to remember the context in which you quoted that to me once before. So tell me, Captain Dollapan. Has your mind changed course?"

A look came over Captain Dollapan's face, a look I had never seen there before. I had seen it often on Ig Doel's face, sometimes on Islak's, but never on the Captain's. It was an expression of whimsy.

"I am," he said, "a foolish man. I seized the opportunity to head Islak's charter because I hoped he might find some evidence, some incontrovertible evidence, of God."

I smiled, thinking of the papers Islak had carried with him during the whole voyage.

"And on that voyage," Dollapan continued, his face more serious now, "I saw the coming of NewStar, and was convinced God had sent it. But in time that proved to be not enough. I came face to face with the Harbinger of God, and fell on my knees before him, fully prepared to worship him. Yet, in time, that proved to be not enough, as well. Later, atop the Mirran Stone, I felt the breath of God extinguish the torches of those who marched against us, saw him cast our enemies into utter darkness and terror. And I tell you truthfully, Harbinger Alexander Boten, the same thing I have confessed before God—even now, those events have proved to be not enough."

"You are what my people would call 'a tough sell', dear Captain." The whimsical look returned to him. I was beginning to like it.

"Signs, wonders, miracles," the Captain said. "Fleeting. All fleeting. But what I always have before me..." and here he held up his hand before him, turning it over, examining it, "...the wonders of my own body, of my own mind. The rivers flowing endlessly from the Great Lake to the sea. All that is around me. If these are not enough, then what can I hope to find elsewhere that will convince me?"

"And are they?" I asked him. "Are they enough?"

He seemed to think over the proposition with care, and then answered: "I believe they are."

"You *believe* they are?" I asked.

He laughed. "You have caught me, Alex Boten, running in circles. Yet I stand by my words. I *believe* they are."

I thought of Congressman DeLibri, thought of the whole Select Committee. I thought of how relieved they would be that Captain Dollapan had resolved his questions for himself, how relieved they would be that my assertions to him had had so little impact. And I thought of how shocked they would be over what I hoped to do next, over how I hoped to spread the message—what I had come to think of as the Message of the Adjunct—to every corner of Mirrus, perhaps even make it an aspect of the delegation that would go to the Shah-Tek. The Committee would be apoplectic. But in the end, I didn't really care.

"These are dangerous times ahead that you chart for yourself,

Harbinger."

"What is that?" I asked, snapped out of my reverie.

"The delegation you plan to head. I can scarcely imagine what will greet you."

"How can you be sure I will head the delegation? Or even count myself among its members, for that matter?"

Dollapan scoffed, finishing his drink. "You're the Harbinger of God. You think to convince me you would not be the first at the rail to travel to their land, to tell them of this 'Yeshua'? I know you better than that."

"But there is much to do here, first. If I am Harbinger, I am also Restoration. Somehow I doubt that the restoration God promised you was only having him speak once to Restoration himself. Something grander is in the works."

"Something grander *is* in the works," Dollapan declared. "I sense that. Everyone senses that. But there is still much time for God's next move to work its way out. This delegation will not leave for some time."

"This delegation," I observed, "has not yet even secured a ship."

The Captain's eyes met mine. He stared me down. I held his gaze.

He burst out laughing. "The Deloré it is, then. And Anned Islak will front the money," he said.

"Of course."

"I'll continue taking charters for him," the Captain said, "until the Ammanon Deloré is destroyed. Mark me on this. It will be an Islak-sponsored voyage, with you on board, that will be the death of us all."

"Igren Doel," I said, "will never forgive us if we do not extend to him an invitation."

403

Coda

The roiling of the Great Lake stopped, for the first time in three longmonths. The mists clinging to the small ship rose.

"It's clearing," Alex called out. There was no response from below decks. Leaning back in his chair, he settled into the fabric straps. The mists hung like a low cloud, perhaps thirty feet overhead, and rising. He closed the logbook that had been lying open in his lap.

It just might clear in time for this pass, he thought. He reached over and dimmed the lamp beside him, staring up into the ascending cloud. He couldn't see anything.

The twin anchor chains, one off the bow extending far ahead, another off the stern extending far behind, began bustling. A residual up current was buffeting the boat. But the anchors, placed on opposite sides of one of the great chasms, held the boat centered.

A high wind began sweeping aside the rising fog and cloud, revealing the Crown of God directly overhead.

"It's clearing away! You're missing it!"

The Crown of God was once again at apogee. Off to the side, still hidden by the mists, Hon was preparing to displace Dessene as the faster twin. But it would be many Reversals before that would again happen directly over the Temple Complex in Shelaemstet.

So much had changed. The acceptance of the Message of the Temple Adjunct had stalled for a time; resistance to so many alien concepts had been strong. And when Alex made it clear that the Message of the Adjunct was for the Shah-Tek as well, preparations for the Deloré's voyage were stalled, politically. For a time, Alex had approached despair.

But none of this was outside the boundaries of divine intent. The few words Alex had once heard atop the Mirran Stone had only been a foretaste. At the proper time, the voice of God had swept out across the populace, and the resistance to the Message had dispersed like the last wisps of fog above him now.

He set the logbook, the Ammanon Deloré's logbook, on the deck beside him. Captain Dollapan had lent it to him, so Alex could compare it with his own notes about the voyage to the Lit Continent. It was important, Alex knew, to get all the details clear, and written, while those who had been aboard her were still alive. Generations from now, people on both sides of the Mirran globe would want to know precisely how things had unfolded—the triumphs, and the tragedies. The Message of the Adjunct had been spread to the Shah-Tek, but at a great price. The back of his hand slid along the cloth bag beneath his chair. *Perhaps too great a price*, he thought. He made certain the bag was still tightly knotted at the top, as Lannae insisted.

Lannae emerged from the cabins below.

"Has it passed?" she asked.

"Not yet," he answered. "Come, watch with me."

"You only bothered to bring one chair," she pointed out.

"One is enough," he said, scanning the skies.

"You'll regret this," she warned.

"I haven't so far," he said. She settled into his lap. Together, they watched the sky in silence.

The Sirocco arose, tracing its path across the heavens, headed for a point near the galactic core. Or, as Alex now always thought of it, the center of the Crown of God. Its orbit had steadily shifted as it moved lower and lower. It was now nearly equatorial. It astounded him that it still endured. He thought it would long ago have decayed its orbit and burned in the atmosphere.

But it had not. It continued on. Perhaps some trace of battery power still sent out the faint impulses of his distress beacon. Sirocco passed the outer tips of one of the spiral arms. Alex cocked his head to orient himself. It looked like it would pass near alignment with Earth. Lannae took advantage of his shifted position to nuzzle in more closely.

With her head low on his chest, his eyes moved over her hair, over the range where the delicate strands feathered out to nothing down her neck. His eyes were drawn, as they always seemed to be, to the star-shaped exit wound near her collarbone. Seeing the wound again returned his mind to the Deloré's mission to the Shah-Tek, bringing them the Message of the Adjunct. Would that mission seem quite so worthwhile to him now, had that one Shah-Tek arrow been a few inches to the left? If it had cost Lannae her life?

As the Crown of God shown brightly down on them, reflecting off of the waves of the Great Lake, its sparkling light accentuated the outlines of their small ship's makeshift figurehead. If Lannae's wound was a reminder of what the mission *might* have cost, that domed carving was a reminder of what it *had* in fact cost. He would mount the figurehead on whatever ship he sailed. He would always remember. The Mirran's would never understand; for them, the dead were to be forgotten. That was their way. But it was not his.

NewStar flared. Its path changed. There was a green flash, and it was gone.

Neither of them breathed.

She wondered what his reaction would be. She felt him breathing again.

"Was that... it?" she asked cautiously. "Is it gone?"

Alex nodded.

"Did you have any idea?" she asked. "That this would be the last crossing?"

"No," he said. "No idea at all. So it's gone. It's over. No more signals. Done."

She looked up across the breadth of the Crown.

"Show me again," she said.

He raised his hand to point out Earth. Almost exactly where Sirocco had flared out, they both realized.

"Do you miss it?" she asked.

"My father," he said, "my birth father, is dead by now. Long dead. And nothing would have changed if I had been there." He looked earthward. *You weren't an evil man, Jeremy Boten. Just twisted, and broken. You were what you were. Can I blame you for that? Everything I've ever done, I've been forgiven for. How can I do less toward you?* He hugged Lannae. "Your father is a good man. I came out better on the deal."

"But you lost..." she struggled to remember how to pronounce the name. "…Kathy, in that deal," she said. After all this time, she still felt guilty over taking Kathy's place.

Alex stroked her cheek. "She's gone, Lan. You've got to let her go. We both have to."

"And your family," she said.

He sighed. Reaching over, he caressed Lannae's growing abdomen.

"I'll always wonder about them, about what they'll be like as they grow. But God has given me a new child. A son."

"It could be a daughter," she reminded him.

He smiled. "There will be daughters. But this one… this one will be a boy."

As for the baby—all of the rancorous debate aside, about whether it was proper for them to marry, and whether it would be possible for them even to conceive, Alex knew one thing. This child would be born with five fingers. As would all of his descendants, as they continued to marry with their four-fingered brethren. Five fingers would be the dominant trait.

Call it a matter of faith.

Postscript

...Almost Forty Days...   Enthusiasts of numerology may have noted that, in the foreword, I stated that annually approximately forty days of darkness precede the rising of the Crown of God. Numerologists, particularly biblical numerologists, recognize forty as the number of testing. Forty days in the ark. Forty days of wandering in the wilderness. Forty days of fasting in the desert.

The celestial mechanics of Mirrus (orbital distances, distance from the galactic core, etc.) were set up in order to achieve certain specific results. Forty days of darkness was not one of these concerns. And yet, there it is.

There are three explanations: A remarkable happenstance, the outgrowth of some phenomenally complex and utterly subconscious calculations, or divine guidance. It must be left to the reader to assess what is most likely. As for my own view, the reader by now suspects my views on happenstance, and, while having a healthy ego, my sense of my own subconscious analytical skills does have its limits.

The Thundering Legion   At the time I wrote of the attack of the Shah-Tek, and of their ignominious defeat, I was (as best I can tell) unaware of the story of the Thundering Legion. The marginal inquiries I have made since into this issue have suggested some debate over its veracity. I make claims neither to the broad outline of events, nor to the interpretation of its meaning, but relay it here merely as an interesting aside. The story, as forwarded to me and as I later found it on the internet, is as follows:

The Thundering Legion was the name given to the Melitene Legion in the days of emperor Marcus Aurelius, a persecutor of the Church. Tertullian says that in AD 176, the army of Aurelius was engaged in a campaign against the Germans. In their march, the Romans found themselves encircled, and tormented by thirst because of drought.

The commander of the Praetorian Guard then informed Aurelius that the Melitene Legion was made up of Christians, who believed in the power of prayer.

"Let them pray, then", said the emperor. The soldiers of the Legion bowed on the ground and earnestly sought God in the name of Christ to deliver the Roman army.

A great thunderstorm arose, accompanied by hail. The storm drove their enemies out of their strongholds. Descending from the mountains, they pled to the Romans for mercy. His army delivered from death by the drought, the emperor decreed that this legion should be thereafter called the Thundering Legion.

It is possible I heard the story long ago, and it percolated up through my subconscious. But I have no evidence whatsoever that this is the case.

The Foremost Edict, So To Speak The edict (or, one might say, directive) of the Select Committee may have some familiarity to fans of Gene Roddenberry's Star Trek™. In my youth, the concept of "The Prime Directive" seemed admirable. As I have aged, I have come to view it as anti-missionary. Perhaps I am merely growing crotchety.

But if I feel there is anything that missionaries can take from Mr. Roddenberry's universe in general, and from The Prime Directive in particular, it would be the value in separating transient cultural values from immutable spiritual truth. As we spread "The Message of the Adjunct", we would be well advised to decouple it from the spreading of our own societal norms.

There is much said in the gospels about morality, which must be proclaimed without hesitation. But there is likewise much that is not said. Burdening the gospel with things that—despite their burning import to us—are irrelevancies to God, is tragic. It is almost as sadly limiting as stripping the gospel of the values that it does proclaim.

To some degree, this is an issue with which all missionaries—accidental and otherwise—are faced. I do not doubt for a moment that they are up to the challenge.

Appendix A : Recommended Reading Continued

This extension of the foreword is recommended for readers seeking a fuller understanding of various aspects of the Mirran world and culture, to more readily understand the book.

Months

Mirrus is orbited by two small but disproportionately bright moons, Hon and Dessene, of nearly the same period; 14.2 and 15.1 Earth days. Much more could be said of these moons, but the story brings forth those aspects. The relevant point here is that the Mirrans have two periods referred to as months; the *shortmonth* and the *longmonth*, each of which is roughly half of an Earth month. The slight difference in the orbital periods results in a cultural idiom. If Mirrans wish to emphasize the shortness of a time period, they declare it in shortmonths; to stress the greatness of a time, longmonths are used.

Rising and setting of the moons are expressed similarly to our "sunrise" and "sunset", with terms like "Honrise" and "Honset".

Language and Distances

Language: Although the Mirrans have their own language, everything in this story is presented in English, and wherever an object or animal has a near-Earth equivalent, the English word is used.

- As an example, a *brigantine* is a sailing vessel with many (but not necessarily all) of the characteristics of a particular Mirran sailing vessel. The Mirran craft is therefore referred to as a brigantine
- References to their own species are translated "man", "woman", or, in some cases, "human".

Distances: Except where noted, Mirran distances are rendered in familiar English units—and when spoken of in round terms, have

411

Alan Havorka

been liberally converted to English units so as to maintain the roundness of the original figure.

The Mirran World

The Mirrans initially refer to both their entire world, and to the prominent continent shown on the following map, interchangeably as "Mirrus". This is because the continent shown and the expanse of vast water about it are all they know of their world. The most common assumption among Mirrans is that the rest of their globe, apart from scattered islands, is water.

Dates and Time

Dates   One last point warranting explanation is the Mirran reckoning of time, manifested in the date notations in most of the clippings. The format of date notations is essentially Shortmonth / Year (referred to as Reversal) / Judgeship. The category of Judgeship is irregular, referring to the appointment of a new Judge to their Temple Court (their highest court for resolving disputes). That aspect of their dates is thus akin to the reckoning by the Dynasties of China or Egypt. As an example, then, "6th Dessene / 7th Reversal / Illaneg" or "6D/7R/Illaneg" refers to the 6th rising of the moon Dessene, during the 7th year after the appointment of Illaneg to the High Court.

Quarters   When something more precise than a 14-Earth-day block of time is needed, a notation of Quarter is added; the path of the shorter-period moon across the sky being divided into four sections. Since four additional quarters exist with that moon being hidden, there are Light Quarters (LQ) and Dark Quarters (DQ).

Time   Regarding shorter spans of time, the approximate time between an average Mirran's heart beats (seven tenths of a second, as is our own) is their shortest measure: the beat. One hundred beats comprise a round (just over a minute). One hundred rounds comprise a watch (almost precisely two hours).

Those who can endure the tedium, and want the fullest background before embarking upon the novel, should continue on to *Appendix B: Assumptions.*

Appendix B: Assumptions (Optional Reading)

The suggestion of a world in perpetual night raises a number of immediate assumptions that may, depending on the reader's disposition, need to be addressed.

If the reader is the sort who, upon reading a declaration that things are a certain way, is inclined to say "Oh, very well then," and move on, then that reader should skip this section.

If, however, the reader is inclined to react to an assertion by saying, "That's not how things would be in this type of world," then that reader should read through the points that follow.

The reader may or may not find these arguments persuasive, but they will clarify the assumptions upon which this novel is based.

Plants: On Earth, the vast majority of plant life derives its primary energy from the sun. This process is known as photosynthesis, and is facilitated by a chemical known as chlorophyll. Owing to chlorophyll's natural color, almost all earthly plants are green.

In a world without sunlight, photosynthesis is not an option. Chlorophyll would be needless, and plants could be of widely varying colors. Without photosynthesis, two things would likely be true.

First, plants would have to draw far more sustenance from the air and ground than earthly plants do. It is entirely possible that some chemical or chemicals, other than chlorophyll, would be a common agent for pulling energy from these sources.

Second, plants would likely be far less robust than on Earth. The sun provides a huge amount of energy, and there would simply be less available energy to draw from ground and air, no matter how efficient of a process a non-Earth plant might employ. Therefore plant life would be less pervasive, and less luxuriant.

Some effects of this reduced plant life might include:

<u>Minimal raising of domesticated animals.</u> Feeding of plants to animals is an inefficient use of resources. On Earth, a huge amount of corn is needed to bring one cow to maturity. On Mirrus, vegetarianism would likely be common.

Heavy emphasis on agriculture. Passive gathering of plants would be ineffective due to the plants' reduced numbers. The societal division of labor would be far different; clustering of food-growing onto large farms run by a few people, thus freeing the majority for availability in industrial development, would either not occur, or would take far longer to achieve.

Trees: Although plant life would be on a smaller scale, there could be exceptions. In areas where a plentiful source of ground-based nutrition could be had, plants as large as tress could be common.

Colors and Vision: Although Mirrus is described as being in perpetual night, that does not mean perpetual night is the normal state for creatures living there. On Earth, with the advent of candles, oil lamps, and later, electricity, nighttime does not equate to darkness. From the days of candles forward, man has illuminated the nighttime (at least indoors) to the level of dusk or dawn, or even more. From the days of oil lamps forward, at least in those areas where oil was plentiful and cheap, indoor nighttime is barely distinguishable from indoor daytime.

This having been said, beings starting off as essentially human, and having a generous supply of oil to rely upon, would likely retain a visual capacity and color perception similar to ours.

Appendix C: Cassini Dancer Moons

These drawings, not done to scale, demonstrate the Cassini Dancer process. This was suspected, and eventually confirmed in 1980 during the Voyager I mission, in the Saturnian moons Janus and Epimetheus.

The phrase Cassini Dancer is not official. Technically, such a situation is referred to as co-orbital moons. How artless.

Some day we will elect to bestow such a wondrously delicate configuration with a more fitting moniker. For what it is worth, Cassini Dancer is my suggestion.

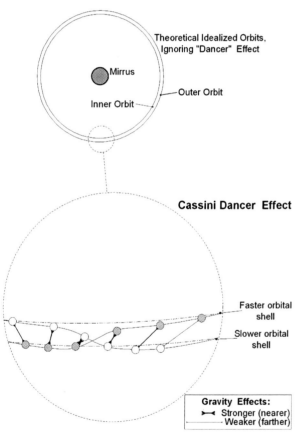

Theoretical Idealized Orbits, Ignoring "Dancer" Effect

Mirrus

Outer Orbit

Inner Orbit

Cassini Dancer Effect

Faster orbital shell

Slower orbital shell

Gravity Effects:
Stronger (nearer)
Weaker (farther)

About the Author

Alan Havorka began his college career at the University of Minnesota as a Math major with a Physics minor, making the Dean's List early on. During his time at the U of M, he won 3rd place in a Science Fiction writing contest; his short story was published in the Minnesota Technolog—the periodical of the University's Institute of Technology.

During Havorka's time at the U of M, the seeds of *Within a Sheltering Darkness* were planted by an astronomy professor. In time, this vision merged with an unpublished short story, and was formulated in a unique storytelling style. But as a novel, it never materialized; the few scraps of handwritten notes were lost over time.

After the University, Havorka eventually settled into the family business for a number of years. During this time the company computerized, and Havorka developed a database to mimic an elaborate paper tracking system. Ultimately, he left the family business and became an Application Developer, which he likes to describe as "a computer programmer with an attitude".

After spending ten years as a professional Application Developer, Havorka was laid off and took the opportunity to create the book that had all along been percolating in his mind. In late 2003 and early 2004, *Within a Sheltering Darkness* came forth with surprising speed.

Havorka lives in Minnesota with his wife and teenage son. He is working again as an Application Developer, and Database Architect. He still maintains "an attitude".

Printed in the United States
87284LV00006B/1/A

9 780979 484902